The Reaction

The Reaction

Helena Coggan

CANDLEWICK PRESS

First U.S. edition 2017

Library of Congress Catalog Card Number pending
ISBN 978-0-7636-8973-5

17 18 19 20 21 22 BVG 10 9 8 7 6 5 4 3 2 1

Printed in Berryville, VA, U.S.A.

This book was typeset in Minion Pro.

Candlewick Press
99 Dover Street
Somerville, Massachusetts 02144

visit us at www.candlewick.com

This book is for Dad.

*Trying to come up with a joke for this has made
me very aware that you could have done it in about a
second and a half, with effortless intelligence and wit,
and with exceptional comic timing to boot.*

*I then would have made fun of it anyway, because
that's just how the system works.*

I know, it's unfair. Sorry.

Gifted (adj.)

Anyone with magic — this will be apparent from their green eyes. As an employee of the Department, this will include you. Subcategories include:

Angel (n.)

Our now-and-forever government. Angels are more powerful than you could dream of. As an average Gifted, your magic is nothing compared to theirs. There are six hundred of them crammed into the Houses of Parliament, and if even one of them wanted to kill you, they could do it effortlessly. You will never be asked to swear an oath of allegiance to them; your absolute obedience is assumed.

Pretender (n., inf.)

Slang pejorative for a person with weak magical Gifts. Their eyes tend to be a slightly lighter green than other Gifted, and infinitely less so than that of an Angel. (*NB: Offensive language is sternly forbidden in the Department offices.*)

Leeched (adj.)

Ex-Gifted who failed their Tests as adolescents and have had their Gifts forcibly removed. In part because of resentment at this, they tend to be more likely to engage in criminal activity than the Gifted population in general.

Ashkind (n.)

Non-magicals, distinguishable by their gray irises. Ashkind make up roughly half of the global population, and roughly sixty percent of all criminals. This is not, incidentally, grounds for arrest without adequate evidence. Ashkind, criminal or otherwise, hold citizenship just as any Gifted does. The Department do not condone Gifted-on-Ashkind violence, especially by its own troops.

Demon (n.)

A subset of Ashkind, with very dark gray/black eyes. They are invariably dangerous criminals, and must be captured and contained wherever they are found. Unfortunately, as these individuals are generally unwilling to give themselves up, in the vast majority of cases they must be hunted down.

Hybrid (n.)

If you even manage to detect one of them, congratulations — you're one up on the rest of us. But if you do: Don't think. Don't even shoot. Just run.

(Extract from *Guide to the Identification of Criminals* by Major David Elmsworth of the Department for the Maintenance of Public Order and the Protection of Justice, distributed to all Department employees from the Seventh to the Eighteenth Year of Angels.)

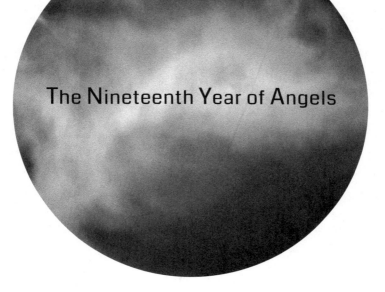

The Nineteenth Year of Angels

– Chapter 1 –

The knock on the door came at half past five in the morning. Rose, who had long since trained herself to be ultra-sensitive to any kind of suspicious noise, woke immediately. She stared for a few long moments at the glowing clock on her radio, then turned on the light.

Angels knew she didn't need this now.

She sighed, wrapped herself in a bathrobe and got up. Her coordination was not at its best this early, but she tried to keep her footsteps light as she passed Tabitha's bedroom. The girl got precious little sleep as it was.

Loren was waiting at the bottom of the stairs, messy-haired and disgruntled, his yellow-green eyes bleary with sleep.

"If it's journalists again," he whispered, "do I have your permission to kill them?"

"Do you need it?"

"No, but it would be nice to know you wouldn't hold it against me."

"I wouldn't do anything of the sort. I'd help."

"It might be messy."

The knock came again. Loren considered, and nodded.

"It will be messy," he said, and went to the door. Rose made to follow him, but he put up a hand to stop her. She ducked behind the door frame of the living room.

"Who is it?" she heard Loren call hoarsely.

"It's me," came a familiar, muffled voice. Rose froze. There was a noticeable pause before Loren pulled the door open. His voice was abruptly curt.

"I don't know what you think you're doing here," he said, "but I'm going to give you one chance to leave."

A hesitation. "I need to talk to Rose."

"No, you don't."

"She needs to explain —"

"Like hell she needs to explain anything to you, you traitor."

"Please, Loren. You don't understand —"

Rose stepped out from behind the door frame and waited as his voice trailed off. James Andreas stood in the doorway, dressed in khaki, pale and shivering. There was snow and streetlight glow in his red hair. He stared at her. Loren looked between them and sighed.

"Come in," he told James. "But one wrong word . . ."

"I understand," said James immediately. "I won't . . . I'll behave myself."

"And if you say —"

"I *understand*," said James vehemently, almost angrily, and

4

Loren stopped. James glanced at him, and stepped over the threshold.

"Why are you here?" asked Rose in a low voice. "It's been —"

"Six months," he said. "I know." He looked at Loren. "Any chance of a coffee?"

"No," said Loren, and walked past him. James sighed, and gestured to the living room. Rose nodded, and sat down on her armchair. He took the opposite sofa. He'd been working in the army, apparently, over the past half-year, as a strategist. He was up for promotion. A fitting step for the man who had revealed her father's secret to the world. That was a big break for a seventeen-year-old.

Of course it must have been embarrassing, working with David Elmsworth and his daughter for eighteen months and not suspecting a thing, but then Elmsworth had taken everyone in. And true, the story almost certainly would have broken without James. But it had been he who had filed the report, he who informed the authorities, he whose career had benefited the most from her father's downfall.

Rose watched him settle himself uncomfortably on the sofa. He looked up at her.

"I need to talk to you," he said, somewhat lamely.

"Clearly," replied Rose. From the kitchen, she heard Loren chuckle.

James bit his lip.

"They say your father's not cooperating with his lawyer," he said, softly enough that Loren would not be able to hear him. "They say he's refusing to confirm his name and address."

"Is that why you're here, James?"

He hesitated.

"No."

"Then get to the point," she said. "What do you want?"

He paused again. "I needed to ask you some questions."

"Then ask them."

"Why didn't you tell anyone what he was?"

"Because I love him," she said. "Next question."

He persisted. "But *why?* Surely it would have been better —"

"To hand him over," she said. "To tell people what he was."

"Yes."

She leaned back into the armchair, studying him, trying to keep her voice flat. "James, you think he murdered those people, don't you? Rayna Arkwood and Thomas Argent and God knows how many others?"

All sound of movement from the kitchen stopped abruptly at the mention of Loren's sister's name.

"That's not what I'm here about."

"Oh, yes it is. You think he's evil, and you want to get me to admit it."

He lowered his voice. "Rose, he's a monster. You don't know what he's capable of."

Something inside her burned and broke. She got to her feet.

"I do," she said. "I know exactly what he's capable of. James, you worked with him. You *trusted* him. You don't really think he's evil. The man you knew was not a monster, not in any voluntary sense."

"I didn't know . . . I wasn't paying attention. He could have . . ."

At her look, he faltered; she was glaring at him with such utter contempt that anger flashed across his face for a moment.

"Get out," she said. "You don't deserve answers."

"Rose, I need to know."

"No, you don't," she said. "You haven't come here for information. You've come here to try and convince me that he's a killer. And that's not going to happen."

"No! Rose, I just . . . I want to know. Do you care more about justice, about what's right, than you do about him?"

"Of course not, you bastard. He's my *father*."

"I know it looks like that to you, but . . . the circumstances in which he found you — the fact that your birth parents never came forward — it looks suspicious. You must see that —"

He stopped. Loren was standing in the kitchen doorway, watching him in the half-curious way a hunter might watch a deer he had just shot. After a second's hesitation, James burst out, "He's brainwashed you, Rose, can't you *see* that?"

"Get out," said Loren quietly, "or I swear to God I will kill you."

James got up, angry now, pulling on his coat. "Rose, please see sense. I'm trying to help you."

"Get out of my house," said Loren again, quite calmly. "Now."

James edged his way out of the living room, backing toward the door. "Rose, we used to be friends."

Loren pulled out his gun and cocked it. Rose glanced at him, worried. He was stone-faced.

"Out," he said.

James's eyes narrowed. "You wouldn't shoot me. I'm a soldier."

"And I'm the acting Head of the Department," said Loren. "You of all people should know the order in which we shoot and ask questions."

James glared at him and pulled open the door. They watched him. His expression softened as he looked at Rose. He was close to pleading. "Rose, I want to trust you."

"Oh, good," she said flatly.

7

"Rose . . ." Something strange passed over his face, a pained contortion. Then, with obvious effort, he said, "I am . . . sorry . . . that he is suffering."

"I will forgive you the day he is exonerated," said Rose. "That good enough for you?"

"Rose —"

She glanced at Loren and stepped forward toward the door, toward James; he almost stepped back, but stopped himself just in time. "James," she said. "I love him, and that's never going to change, so you may as well accept that now and work from there, all right?"

He looked at her for a long moment, muttered something under his breath, and then left, striding down the garden path and slamming the gate behind him.

Rose looked back at Loren, who still had his gun in the air and was staring after James, his eyebrows knit together.

She closed the door carefully. "Did you hear what he said?"

Loren put the gun down and sat on the stairs, still staring after James.

"I think it was 'Give it time,'" he said.

Her father had been arrested six months ago.

He had simply walked into the office, calm and composed, exactly three weeks after the Department had found out that he had faked his own death. He had been dressed in his best suit; it had been a particularly wet June, hot and thick with damp clouds, so it must have taken effort to get there on the Tube. Rose had found out only afterward. He must have known they'd put it on the news.

The footage was blurry but coherent. Rose watched him,

8

over and over again, opening the door, not flinching at the blaze of gunfire that slammed into the doorway over his head, holding out his hands to the squad team that surrounded and handcuffed him.

Terrian was there, reading out his arrest warrant, and James, in the background, watching him with his arms folded and on his face a look of the most concentrated hatred that Rose had ever seen. Rose had looked at her father's wry smile on fuzzy CCTV, played over and over again by somber newscasters, and understood.

He had always known this was how it would end.

Fifteen years working for the Department, nearly sixteen raising her — eighteen, even, from the beginning of the War — and he had always known that this was coming.

In all likelihood so had she, but she hadn't wanted to think about it.

Later, visiting him in his cell, she'd brought him fragments of news like crumbs: that Loren was acting Head of the Department in his absence. That Rose was living with Loren and Tabitha, his eight-year-old niece, in their spare bedroom. That the Department had banned the use of all magic, everywhere — on the streets and in homes — to try and claw back what remained of law and order. That the press had found their house, and that, shortly afterward, so had the general public, smashing their windows and spray-painting graffiti on the walls. She didn't tell him what they had written, and he didn't ask.

She brought him the trial dates. Rose had notebooks full of scribbled speculation as to how the prosecution might make their case, every possible charge worked through in careful detail.

In the end, though, there was only one charge, and it was as good as a death sentence.

Loren and Tabitha had been taken into Department custody a year ago. The reasons for their arrest were never made public, but the struggle during their arrest had claimed the life of Loren's sister, Tabitha's mother. Consequently, he became the first person ever to escape a Department prison — and a member of the squad team that had killed his sister died in mysterious, very violent circumstances shortly afterward.

David, as the leader of the Department, had been in charge of hunting Loren down.

He hadn't succeeded, as, unbeknownst to him, Loren had blackmailed Rose into helping him.

It had taken a long time for David to forgive Rose for that. She still wasn't sure if he had.

After his arrest warrant had been issued, the newspapers had been quick to associate David with the deaths of Loren's sister and the squad member; but he had had nothing *at all* to do with them, no one cared about burden of proof anymore, it wasn't —

At this point Rose would realize she was about to think "fair," and stop herself.

The day he had been arrested, the story had spread across the headlines slowly, fragmenting and blossoming in the way of all scandals. For this *was* a scandal, she had realized with some astonishment: it was the biggest power scandal in post-War history. The police and the army, after all, took orders and advice from the Department — the home of elite soldiers, the law-enforcement center of the country. And the Department took its orders from its brilliant young leader, David Elmsworth.

For fifteen years he had worked for them, and no one had suspected a thing.

Concealment of illegal powers, the charge read. It sounded so innocent.

Most people called them "Hybrids"; David called it a "condition." It was an illness, a disease; during the War, its victims had haunted the nightmares of ordinary soldiers. In peacetime it had sunk below the radar somewhat. But with David's arrest it had surfaced again, and with it rising paranoia: How many of these creatures still lived unnoticed? Did all of them occupy positions of power as high up as David had? Whom could the people trust?

People like David were hard to spot because, for forty-one days out of every six weeks, they looked human. For the remainder they were . . . nothing. Not human, at any rate. Not sane, either. Their normal selves, their human selves, had no control over their actions. They were creatures of pure magic, and unfortunately for their victims, they were programmed to kill.

They were, in short, monsters.

And they were very hard to spot, people like David.

People like David and Rose.

Since the case had received so much publicity, David had been the subject of several dozen psychological assessments. He'd relate their questions back to Rose through the bars of his cell, smiling wryly, his hands shaking. How do you feel, Mr. Elmsworth? Do you understand the charges put to you? Do you understand what's going to happen to you? What do you think about your current situation? Do you remember much of the War? Why did you hide your condition? What do you see when you close your eyes?

How do you feel about your daughter?

It deeply annoyed David that they kept asking him about Rose, because they thought she was his pressure point, and he hated them for being right.

Is she like you? Does she share your condition?

To which he would always reply, disgustedly, *Of course not.*

If they found out what Rose was, they would assume David had turned her into one of his kind, and then he was dead without doubt. And so, probably, was she.

Of course not.

Apart from David, Loren and Tabitha were the only people in the world who knew Rose was a Hybrid.

Nearly every day for the past six months she had sat with David, separated only by the bars, as they exchanged flat bits of news during their ten minutes' visiting time; and every time, when they came to escort her out, he would tell her he loved her, and that everything was going to be fine, in a way that suggested determined conviction for the one and halfhearted hope for the other. As they both knew perfectly well, it was not going to be all right.

But that didn't mean it was going to be all wrong.

– Chapter 2 –

David's lawyer was a quiet woman of about thirty called Madeleine Ryan. She had a quick smile and pale gray Ashkind eyes; non-magicals with high IQs often went into the legal profession. By all accounts she was extremely intelligent, although Rose had yet to see her in action in the courtroom. She had a fiancé working as a schoolteacher in Croydon, and they were expecting their first child in May. All of this was background Loren had managed to get from the Department files.

The reason they had chosen her was because, of all the barristers — and admittedly there weren't many queuing up to defend David Elmsworth, but still — she had shown not the slightest sign of fear upon meeting him. Rose liked her for that.

She was not sure David did.

The day after James's visit, Rose and Madeleine went to see David in his cell. Madeleine did not shout. She spoke in a very low, controlled voice when angry. Rose stood at the other end of the corridor for a moment, listening.

"I don't understand, David. What possible purpose do you think this could serve?"

"I'm doing what I need to do."

"I need you to elaborate on that. Why would denying your name and address help your case? All you're going to do is disrupt the legal process and put the judge against you."

"That's not all I'm doing."

Rose watched him. He seemed strained, but calm.

"You know," he said to her. "You know why I'm doing it."

"No, I don't," said Rose, pressing her fingers to her sinuses.

"Yes, you do," he said. "Because it's true."

Madeleine stared between the two of them. "What do you mean, it's true?"

Rose sighed. "Denying your address won't do anything. They can prove that."

Madeleine's composure broke. "Rose, please. Explain."

"His real name isn't David Elmsworth," said Rose. "He changed it during the War. But then —"

"So did everyone," finished Madeleine, staring at him. "David, pointing out that the name they're charging you under isn't the one on your birth certificate won't stop them charging you."

"It doesn't have to."

Rose exploded. "Dad! Please, tell us what you're doing! You can't *do* this on your own — you have to tell us. We're trying to save you here!"

He smiled. It was a very eerie smile.

"No one can save me," he said.

Rose turned away from him. "Don't say that. Don't *say* that."

"She's right," said Madeleine gently. "We have to stay positive."

"I am trying to. You have to trust me."

Rose sighed. "Of course we trust you." At a dark look from Madeleine, she amended it hastily. "Of course I trust you."

"That's good," he murmured, and sat back down on his prison bed.

Madeleine sighed, and changed the subject. "Have you thought any more about the witnesses we want to call?"

"Not many people are willing to speak up for me these days," said David quietly. "I'm not hugely popular."

No one answered that.

"Has anyone from the Department spoken to you about this?" he asked Rose, after a moment.

Rose glanced at him. "James."

"When?"

"Last night."

"Ah." David leaned back. "I take it he was less than sympathetic to our cause."

"He wanted me to switch sides."

A brief, ghostly smile. "Oh, there are sides now, are there?"

"There were always sides," said Rose, quietly. "Those with you, and those against. But I will never side with him as long as he counts himself against you."

There was a slight pause.

"Can one of you explain something to me?" asked Madeleine.

David inclined his head. "Of course."

"The Department are a part of the Government, are they not?"

"We are, yes."

Rose winced slightly at his use of the first-person plural; his eyes flickered to her, and she tried to look unconcerned.

"Then why have they turned on you like this? Why are they treating the Department now as if they were . . . renegades, rather than a part of their own organization? Surely you were following their orders?"

"They never gave us orders," said David calmly, leaning back against the brick wall of his cell. "They gave us troops and weapons and told us to do whatever we saw fit in the name of law and order. They closed their eyes and put their fingers in their ears so that if it all came out they could pretend they weren't responsible. And I was in the unlucky position of being the perfect scapegoat when it did."

"And how are they treating the Department now?"

David gestured to Rose. "She can tell you that."

Rose glanced at him uneasily before addressing Madeleine. "I think the Government are trying to pretend the Department don't exist. They won't do anything to help them, but they won't stop them, either. They need the Department — they hate that they do, but they still need them. The city is unstable enough as it is. If the Government tried to get rid of the Department, everything would collapse."

It might collapse anyway, she thought, but she didn't say it. Madeleine had gone slightly pale at her words.

"So if it — if it came to war —"

"It won't," said David sharply.

"But if it did," pressed Madeleine, "what would the Government do?"

"They'd probably complain about everything the Department did," said Rose with a slight smile, "but they'd let them do it anyway."

Footsteps in the corridor; all three of them rose. Two soldiers rounded the corner; at the sight of their guns, Madeleine's hand went to her stomach.

"Time's up," one of them said.

Rose glanced at her father. "Stay safe, okay?"

He nodded. "I'll keep out of trouble. And, Rose?"

"Yeah?"

He gave her a gentle salute. "Fight the good fight."

"I always do."

The first time she had gone back to the Department after her father's arrest had been in August, just after Loren had been appointed acting Head.

His promotion had been quiet, almost unnoticed under the shock wave that followed David's arrest. Loren was only getting the job, he knew, because there was no one else left who could do it.

Well, that wasn't quite true. There was Connor Terrian, who had been filling the position in recent weeks, but no one at the Department really trusted Terrian anymore. He had been responsible for too many screwups in the past few months. He had also spent nearly fifteen years working with or for David, all without suspecting a thing; and it didn't help that his son Nate was widely known to be close friends with Rose. It was a matter of public incredulity that Terrian was still working for the Department at all.

But for whatever reason, he was still there, and his hate-filled glare was the first thing Rose had to contend with upon walking into the office.

The whole room went suddenly very still and silent. Everyone stared at her. Rose met their gazes with the closest thing she had to calm. These were people she had known for years, David's colleagues, his — well, not quite friends, but acquaintances: people who, at any rate, should not be looking at her as if she had just stepped out of a spaceship.

Terrian stepped forward.

"You're back," he said quietly.

Rose said nothing.

Terrian took another step forward.

"You've got some nerve," he said. "Coming back here after what your father did."

"He did nothing," said Rose, too quickly, too loudly; any heads that had not already been turned toward them snapped around so fast she could hear necks cricking. *David Elmsworth did nothing*. What a ridiculous idea.

She took a deep breath, and could almost taste the skepticism and mistrust in the air.

"Whatever you think of my father," she said, "I am not responsible for anything he might have done."

This was as close as she was ever going to come to an admission.

"You knew," snarled Terrian. "All those years you were here, working with us, you *knew* he was a monster."

"I didn't betray my own father. You hold that against me?"

"Yes. Absolutely I do. You could have said —"

"Connor," said Loren, quietly. Terrian rounded on him.

"Don't you dare. You're as close to her as anyone. You're letting her stay in your *house*."

"She's a child," said Loren. "Think what you like, but she's still fifteen, Connor, and her father is in prison. She has no other home. You would have her sleep on the streets?"

Terrian spluttered, but before he could say anything, another woman spoke, her eyes on Rose. Rose didn't recognize her. Her gaze was unsympathetic and unblinking.

"Leave, girl," she said, and there was a murmur of assent from the watching Department workers. "Your father may have wanted to let you stay here, but we never did. You have no place here. Go."

Her tone was firm, but not, Rose thought, unkind.

Nonetheless, with all their eyes upon her, she felt her heart begin to break. How could this woman say she had no place here? She *belonged* here. This had been her home for almost her entire —

Her home.

She stared at Loren, whose gaze was just as unyielding as the rest, if less hostile.

She has no other home.

He knew she could not stay here. His colleagues hated her. And as long as she remained within these walls, they would not forget that he was linked to her; he would have no authority.

No one wanted her here.

She swallowed. Then, slowly, her face pale and her eyes dry, she pulled on her coat and left the Department.

The months since Rose's banishment had been long and empty. She felt her absence from the Department keenly, like cold on her skin, like a bruise. Since she no longer attended school, the pillars that had held up her life — her home, her education, the Department offices — seemed to collapse, leaving her to spend

19

her days outside the bars of her father's cell, or sitting with Madeleine trying to work out ways to defend him against the indefensible charge of his monstrosity.

That wasn't to say she was completely cut off from news of the Department. She was updated on events every few days by her old school friends, Nate and Maria, who spent what little time they could spare away from their medical training in the Department offices. As Terrian's son, Nate had spent almost as much time there as Rose had growing up. Maria had very little experience in the Department, but she had a gift for going unnoticed, and — though she would never have admitted it — Rose suspected she was drawn there partly from the same morbid curiosity that had, a year ago, compelled her Ashkind sister Amelia to join the rebel army Regency. Though Maria would never admit it, they had, Rose suspected, the same hunger for adrenaline.

Rose's greatest source of information, however, was Loren himself, who would often come home in the evenings looking tired and frustrated.

"Bloody Terrian," he would mutter furiously. Almost every senior member of the Department had drawn his ire over the past few months, but it was Terrian that he focused on most often; Terrian, after all, had never trusted him, and was the most hostile to and resentful of Loren's leadership. "He's refusing to put out a manhunt for Stephen Greenlow . . . won't use Department squad teams . . ."

This particular complaint was made on the night after James's visit. Loren collapsed onto the sofa, looking exhausted, hands over his face. Rose sat down on the other sofa.

"Why not?"

"Thinks it will cause a panic. Doesn't want to make the situation worse."

Rose gave a hollow laugh. Stephen Greenlow was the leader of the Gospel, the smaller but far better organized of the two rebel militias the Department currently had to deal with. The Gospel was made up of Gifted and some Leeched who thought the Angelic government had been far too kind to the Ashkind after the War. They were responsible for the random killings of Ashkind that had broken out throughout London over the past few months; they had even carried out a mass Leeching, destroying the magical abilities of every Angel in Parliament, on the night David's monstrosity had been discovered. Leaving Stephen Greenlow at large would worsen the situation far more than any manhunt could.

"What about Regency?" Rose asked.

Loren did not take his hands away from his face. "What *about* Regency?"

"Have you found any of its leaders? Slythe? Vinyara?"

"Nothing doing. Regency aren't like the Gospel. They don't have discipline — or not anymore. They seem to have just . . . dissolved. Terrian reckons it's because you and David killed Felix Callaway. You know what he was to them. No figurehead or leader could replace him — Anthony Slythe and Isabel Vinyara are nothing in comparison. Terrian thinks they broke up when Felix died."

Rose heard something hard in his tone. "And you don't."

Loren twisted his fingers around the back of his neck and looked up at her. He took a hissing breath through his teeth. "No."

"You think they disappeared deliberately. You think they're hiding. That they're waiting for something."

Loren nodded. Rose leaned back into the sofa. "Interesting theory."

"You agree?"

"I don't know," she said, slowly. "I can't believe they've gone entirely."

"Neither can I."

They glanced at each other, and an unspoken mutual understanding passed between them. They had both known firsthand the power of Regency, and of Felix Callaway. Last year, Rose had been sent to infiltrate the organization, disguised as Ashkind, and Loren had previously worked for them for ten years after the Veilbreak, before being driven out by Felix's paranoia. He had been one of only two Gifted ever to have allied themselves with Regency, an Ashkind militia otherwise hell-bent on destroying all Gifted. He had done so only because his sister, Rayna, had been Ashkind, and his services to Regency had been the price for her safety.

The only other Gifted soldier in Regency, of course, had been David.

But that had been a long time ago, during the War.

So it didn't count.

Rose cut herself off, disgusted by the childishness of her own thoughts. But before she could say anything, Loren spoke, perhaps eager to break the silence.

"They're also working on a way to contain Hybrids."

Rose stared at him. It was a moment before she could speak. "The Department?"

"Yes."

Rose gave a shaky laugh. *Contain Hybrids.* They had a way to contain Hybrids. It was underneath her father's house. Two thick steel cells, soundproof, scratches etched in fire on the walls. She had had four transformations during her father's imprisonment. As the police knew about the cells, she could hardly use them anymore, so she had been forced to travel out into the countryside, to deserted fields, and hope for the best.

No one had been hurt, yet.

That was down to luck, though, and God knew she could not rely on luck.

She glanced at Loren. "Whose idea was that? Terrian's?"

"Mine."

She stared at him.

"I thought it might increase your father's chances in court," he said levelly, but she could tell her stare was starting to make him nervous. "They'd be more likely to let him walk free if they knew he would be safe when he transformed, wouldn't they?"

"And what word did you use when you pitched this to Terrian and the rest of the Department? *Contain*?"

"Yes."

Another brutal laugh. "Loren, trust me, they didn't hear that as *stop*. They heard it as *kill*. If there was ever a chance of them showing clemency to Hybrids, it vanished with Dad. To them, the only good Hybrid is a dead Hybrid."

She didn't attempt to hide the bitterness in her voice. Loren said nothing for a moment.

"I'll clarify, then."

"Why? You won't change their attitudes toward monsters. They're the Department. They exist to fight evildoers."

"You're not evil, Rose."

She smiled tightly. "I know that. But they won't change their opinions. There are ways to slow Hybrids down, and they already know them. If you shoot it, or blind it, or make a really high-pitched noise around it, it might confuse it for a moment, but that's not going to make any difference. You'd still die. Nothing works, Loren. Nothing can stop a Hybrid when it's transformed. They know that. They won't show one any mercy, not in human form. This is just a way to disguise that. They just want to *look* merciful."

Loren was still watching her.

"What?" she said, annoyed.

He said nothing. Then: "You know he's not going to be acquitted, Rose. They can prove he's a Hybrid. They already have."

She looked at him bleakly. "If we can prove it's not his fault —"

"That's not the point. It doesn't matter whether or not it's his fault he's a Hybrid. The point is whether he is one, and he *is,* Rose, that's beyond a doubt now."

"So you're telling me to give up on him?"

He looked at her for a moment, and then sank back into the position he had taken when he had first sat down, half-collapsed with his head in his hands.

"No, Rose," he said, wearily. "I'd never do that."

- Chapter 3 -

Five years earlier (age 30)
January 16, 11:02 a.m.

He doesn't show them that he's awake until he can hear Rose's
voice again.

"Dad?"

She's beside his bed, and there are other voices, too — male
voices, one deeper than the other. Terrian and the boy. They fall
quiet when she speaks.

"Dad?"

He gathers she has been standing there for a while. When she
does speak, her voice is hoarse, and breaks.

She says nothing after that.

He is quiet. He lies there in the hospital bed, gathering his
thoughts. He can feel the marks the flames left on his skin.

They've healed him well enough, but he can still *feel* the fire on him, red-raw and stiff and sore. He imagines he still smells of smoke.

He keeps himself still. What are they saying? Did they think he would die? He suppresses a smile at the thought of how Terrian would have reacted if the flames had killed him. He probably already has the obituary locked away in a drawer somewhere. *David Elmsworth. Died aged thirty, tragically young. Valued colleague.* And then Terrian would take over the leadership of the Department. He has always resented that David got it when Malia died. He thinks that, as her husband, he should have been her successor.

Be quiet. Lie still. Don't let them know you're awake. You don't want to face Terrian. Not now, not like this. You only want to speak to Rose. It will be easier to try out your explanations on her first, not them. Ten-year-olds are easier to fool than hostile and suspicious War veterans — even ten-year-olds as clever as Rose.

Terrian and the boy are saying things to her, in gentle voices, and he listens intently because no one has told him anything and they have him so thoroughly anesthetized that it's a miracle he can think, let alone feel. They say things like "third-degree burns" and "sixty percent coverage" and "two Gifted medics had to drain themselves of magic . . ." He stops listening after that. Now that he is faced with the reality of it, he doesn't really want to know.

Two Gifted medics . . .

He can't make himself forget that, now that he knows.

Rose is going to ask how he sustained those burns, and he really doesn't know what to tell her. Not the truth, obviously. It's plausible that there might have been someone in Warsaw with a grudge against him, someone whose brother-in-law's best friend's nephew he killed. He might use that.

She's also going to ask why he was gone for eight weeks, and he can't use the truth for that, either. The first part of the truth, the part he can use, is that the Department sent him to kill the Demon ringleaders of a rebellion in Poland, and it took the lives of the rest of his team to do it, but the criminals are dead. He advised the Polish government before the attack to be more efficient in their monitoring of the Demons. They took two dozen into custody in the days after he left.

After that he wandered around Warsaw for a few weeks — knowing full well that he took a bullet within view of a camera, and that that bullet might plausibly have killed him had he not been a Gifted and able to heal himself; knowing also that, as he had taken great care not to appear on Polish CCTV since then, the Warsaw and London Departments might well think he was dead. He relished the freedom of it, for a while.

It wasn't, he knows, cowardice, or the need for solitude. It was procrastination.

There was something he needed to do in London, and it is done now. But it was a long time before he could do it, before he could find the courage or the energy. He didn't want to go there again. He didn't want to see it.

He didn't want to see it burn.

He stayed in Warsaw until he was brave enough to go back and do it. Perhaps it *was* cowardice, then.

"Dad?"

Rose's voice is astonished, broken, joyful, and it lifts him momentarily. When she touches his skin he feels it, a sudden stab of raw pain, and it is only when he realizes that the steadying, high-pitched rhythm he can hear in the background is his heart-beat that he opens his eyes.

<<< >>>

"I'll answer it."

"Is that safe?"

Loren hesitated. He glared at the door. "If it's the press again, they deserve whatever I do to them."

"So not safe, then."

Rose went to the window and tried to spot the person who had knocked, without luck. Tabitha was on the stairs.

"Dad?" she asked uncertainly.

"Stay in your room," said Loren sharply. Tabitha nodded and hurried back up. The knock came again. "We have a goddamn *doorbell*," he muttered irritably, and strode forward to wrench the door open.

Their visitor was a young man. He had thin brown hair and a sharp, birdlike face. He was not, to Rose's great relief, anyone from the Department; but he had the bad judgment to begin with the words "I'm from the BBC," and Loren immediately slammed the door in his face.

"Please!" they heard him shout through the door. "I need to speak to Miss Elmsworth!"

Loren, with one hand on the banister, shouted at him to do something unspeakable. The instructions were detailed and complex, and had to be conveyed through ten feet and a brick wall, but the reporter got the gist.

There was a slight pause.

Loren and Rose waited, watching each other, to hear the

sound of his footsteps back up the road; but instead they heard the crunch of gravel, and Rose saw that he was standing outside the window.

She jumped back in alarm. The man was carrying a microphone and a handheld camera, and had an expression of almost overly innocent friendliness on his face. He looked, in short, like a poorly disguised and unusually paranoid psychopath. Loren went to the drawer to get his gun.

The reporter guessed his intention. "Wait!" he called. His accent was distinctly American, even through reinforced glass. "This is of the utmost importance!" He fixed Rose with an unblinking stare. The friendly smile was still there. "It concerns your father's safety!"

Rose, still disconcerted, glared at him. Loren now had his revolver out and was pointing it directly between the reporter's eyes. Rose knew the man's chances were decent — not least because the two layers of glass would deflect the path of the bullet, but mostly because Loren had not bothered to turn off the safety — but the reporter had no such weapons expertise, and held up his hands to shoulder height, white-faced. Rose saw that he had another microphone attached to his wrist.

"Should we hear him out?" Rose murmured to him.

"God, no."

"But he said it was about Dad's safety."

"He's lying."

"I know. But just in case . . ."

Loren glanced at her. "I hate you."

"I know."

He gave her a dirty look and went to the door, gun still out. Rose followed. She glanced again at Loren's expression and stood back to avoid ricochets.

29

With his left hand, Loren opened the door. The reporter was already there.

"Put down every single piece of recording equipment you have on you," said Loren, "or I shoot."

The reporter laid the microphone and the camera on the ground. Loren, grudgingly, moved to let him in, but Rose put a hand on his shoulder to stop him. She was still watching the American. Slowly, and with a look of the utmost reluctance, he removed the microphone from his wrist.

"Good," said Loren. "Now come in slowly."

The reporter had barely crossed the threshold before Loren stopped him again. "Hands to shoulder height."

The American glanced at him incredulously. "Why?"

"It just looks funny."

The reporter, now clearly convinced he was dealing with a madman, stepped forward very slowly, staring at every tile he put his weight on as if checking for land mines. Rose rolled her eyes and went into the living room.

Loren and the American sat down on the sofa. Loren put the gun down on a cushion, so it was still clearly visible. The reporter glanced at it nervously.

"Miss Elmsworth," he began, and swallowed. He looked at the revolver again, and then up at Loren, who gave the man his best shark-like grin. "Miss Elmsworth. I have come to offer you a great opportunity."

Rose did her best to look skeptical. "Hit me."

"I want to give you the chance to prove your father's innocence to the public."

"I thought that was what criminal courts were for."

He narrowed his eyes. "I expected you to be more welcoming. This could save your father's life and reputation."

"Forgive me for not trusting the press wholeheartedly. You've devoted most of the last six months to ruining mine and my father's lives."

Loren interrupted before it could come to blows. "Who are you, anyway?"

The American looked disbelievingly at him. "Oliver."

"Oliver who?"

The reporter glanced again at the gun, but seemed to be regaining his confidence now that he was fairly certain he wouldn't actually be shot. "Cromwell," he said, sarcastically. "No, you thug, I'm Oliver Keen. Don't you ever watch the TV? I'm the BBC's security correspondent. I'm the *face* of this trial."

"I think you'll find," said Rose, somewhat testily, "that the defendant occupies that position at the moment."

Keen turned to her. "Every report I do has millions of views. A single word in one of my reports can sway the public for or against your father."

"Are you asking me to bribe you to tell the viewing public he's innocent?"

Keen sat forward. "No. No one's going to believe that — there's no possible way he could be acquitted, not after he's been filmed . . . transforming." A look of revulsion crossed his face. Rose went very still. "No, his guilt is beyond doubt, but still, this story is gold. We're going to ask for the rights to make a documentary about this, and I want you to help me. You and me together? We could make a stunning exposé. An in-depth study of his past, his thinking, his motivations . . ."

"Motivations for what?"

Keen blinked at her, and then adopted a very pitying, gentle expression, as one might wear when having to explain the concept of death to a small child. "Well . . . he's a monster, isn't he?"

"Get out," said Loren, suddenly, without moving.

Keen ignored him. "I could tell the viewers your version of the truth about David Elmsworth. A psychopath badly damaged in childhood, forced to carry out terrible acts by forces he couldn't control—"

Rose told him to do something that made even Loren raise his eyebrows.

Keen's eyes went cold. "I won't be this kind again, Rosalyn. You don't know what you're saying."

"Yes, I do. You are asking me to be complicit in lying to the public about my own father, and I am telling you to go to hell."

Loren had his gun in his hand again. "You want me to do it, Rose?"

She considered. Keen, seeing her expression, stood hastily.

"No," he said quickly, "I'll go. But you'll regret this."

"What, not killing you? No, I don't doubt it."

He glared at her and rushed out the door, grabbing his equipment as he left.

When he was gone, Loren looked at her.

"He's going to make the documentary anyway," he said.

"I know."

"And he's going to be ruthless about it."

"I know."

"So what purpose did that serve, exactly?"

Rose went to the cupboard and took out a glass. She held it in her hand for a moment, and imagined what it would feel like to make it shatter. She hadn't done magic in six months. It was killing her.

Then she put the glass back and went to the wall. She kicked it viciously.

"Did that help?' Loren asked, mildly.

<<< >>>

Five years earlier (age 30)
January 4, 8:08 p.m.

It is accomplished very quickly, and as if in accordance with some fated credit system, it goes wrong just as fast.

He does not remember opening the door, or coming up the stairs. He expected a flood of memories here, of all places, but his mind has stayed strangely silent on this one. Perhaps, after a decade and a half, his mental walls are doing their job.

He doubts it, though.

It has been twelve years since he performed the last cremation. He has been fool enough to think that perhaps all remnants of him burned with the school, but he has, of course, been wrong. Wrong enough to put himself and the girl in danger.

She still doesn't know. And for a while he has tried to believe her ignorance is enough, but it isn't.

She has no reason to suspect. It would be entirely down to him if she *did* suspect.

But the rest of the world is a lot more cynical than she is, and it is closing in on him again.

The room is painted blue and thick with dust. He remembers it, but only vaguely: the residual recollections of something forcibly forgotten. It seems to have shrunk, if only slightly, in the years since he was here. The books are undisturbed, the bed perfectly made and untouched.

Of course, if the laws of statistics held any sway where he was concerned, this would have been one of the places torched by the rioters in the six years — six years!— of the War, and he wouldn't have to do this.

But it wasn't, and he does.

He takes out the old cigarette lighter from his pocket, and suddenly he is fourteen again and smoking on a street corner with Michael, and his lungs are burning with the tar but he holds it in. His hands are shaking. It takes two attempts for the flame to catch, and he presses it to the blanket until the corner of it curls into blue flame.

He is thirty years old and he has a child, and yet he stands and watches helplessly until the bed is burning, and smoke is scalding his mouth again and the flames are caressing his heels.

For the longest time he cannot move.

– Chapter 4 –

"Loren?"

He started. It was the boy, Nathaniel. Terrian's son. He was standing over Loren's desk with a strained expression.

"Can I have a word?"

"Of course."

Loren stood up and walked with Nate to a quiet corner of the office — if indeed such a place existed in the Department; noise, of shouting and swearing and the whirring of computers, seemed to press against the walls like expanding air. Loren glanced at the boy. He had turned sixteen a few weeks ago, Loren remembered, an adult now by post-Veilbreak law, and he looked as exhausted as anyone else there.

Nate sat down in an empty chair and placed the sheets of paper he was holding on the desk in front of him. He spoke in a low, intent voice to Loren, who had sat down next to him.

"Regency are kidnapping Demon kids."

"*What?*"

Nate pushed his hair out of his eyes. "Look." He pushed the papers toward Loren, who stared at them. It was the list of those declared missing in the past few weeks. "Look at them. Stan Roald, eight, status: Demon, reported missing on the second. Sophia Afolayan, eleven, status: Demon, missing on the fifth. Halim Samara, *three*, status: Demon, missing on the seventh. There are thirteen of them in the past fortnight. Think about it, Loren. Demons are a tiny fraction of the population, aren't they? The number of Demon kids must be even smaller. This isn't a coincidence."

Loren pulled the papers closer and stared at them. "You're sure they're not just the Ashkind the Gospel are killing? Part of Greenlow's massacres?"

"I'm sure. They're not dead. I mean, they could be, but the bodies haven't been found. The Gospel never clean up after themselves that thoroughly. They're being taken. By Regency."

Loren looked at him intently. "What makes you think so?"

Nate scratched the back of his neck. "I'm not sure. Instinct. I can't understand why the Gospel would do it — they'd have no reason not to just kill them. And it's . . . stealthy. Stealthier than it needs to be. No one cares about Demons, and Regency would go for kids because they're easier targets. And I know Regency haven't disappeared entirely." He glanced nervously around the office. "I know Dad thinks so, but I don't."

Loren said nothing, still staring at the list.

"But, Loren," said Nate suddenly, "your niece is a Demon, isn't sh —?"

They heard it before they saw it. It was a hard *crack*, followed by irregular snapping noises, and it came from their left. The whole office went quiet. Loren turned and saw a bullet lodged in the reinforced glass of the window, surrounded by a multiplying white web of fractures.

"Get down!" he yelled.

The entire office — oh, Angels bless their emergency training — threw themselves under their desks. Those who had guns reached for them. Into each of the three remaining glass walls a single bullet cracked, and the breaks in the glass raced toward each other like drops of ice until the window was nearly opaque with fractures.

Nate was on the floor beside Loren. "Exactly how reinforced is that glass?" Loren asked him quietly.

"There's another layer of it between us and the bullets."

"How long will that last?"

"I don't know, you think we do this routinely?"

There was a walkie-talkie lying under a desk just out of reach of Loren's arm. Nate saw what he was looking at, and shuffled over toward it. He pushed the walkie-talkie toward Loren, muttering, "I was meant to be a bloody *doctor*," under his breath.

Loren caught it and pressed down the button.

"Ground floor, we're under attack."

"We know," came the grim reply. "It's the Gospel."

Loren swore viciously, and then collected himself. "Do you need medical attention?"

"No, not yet. They're just shooting at your floor."

Loren pressed his head to the carpet for a moment. "How many troops do we have in the building?"

"Ready to fight? Twenty-four, sir."

"Send eighteen up here. I'm sending the other six our non-combatants. Tell them to get to the ninth floor."

"Understood."

Loren disconnected and rolled over so he was on his back. He raised himself up on one elbow. "Anyone who isn't trained to fight," he shouted, "go *now*. Get up as high as you can."

There were maybe sixty people in that office, of whom twenty ran for the door. Fifty-eight fighters then, in total. Not enough. Not nearly enough.

The eighteen soldiers came into the room, crouched low, guns pointing at the windows. They looked around in bemusement at the half-shattered glass.

"Well, what was the point of that?" one asked, and then the bombardment began.

When the knock came at the door, for the third time in as many days, Rose knew better than to answer it.

She suspected, of course, that it was James or Oliver Keen returned, but even if it wasn't, by this point answering it again would be nothing less than stupid. She wasn't going to make that mistake again.

The visitor knocked twice: three hard raps, regular and strong. Rose ignored it.

Tabitha got up from where she sat playing with her toy farmhouse — a birthday present from Loren — and sat down in front of Rose. She said nothing, but her message was perfectly clear.

"No," Rose told her. "I'm not doing this."

The girl sat at Rose's feet, patient and implacable.

Another knock. "Please!" came a voice, through the door. It was female, and shot through with true, or at least very well-feigned, desperation. "Please! Let me in!"

Tabitha's black eyes were fixed on Rose.

"No," said Rose, again, almost pleadingly.

"Please!" shouted the woman. "It's my mother! Please — I think she's dying!"

Tabitha's eyes widened.

"She's lying," Rose said.

Tabitha got up and went to the window. Rose, in resigned despair, went with her. The visitor had the grass-green eyes of a weakly Gifted. She was pale and gaunt, with thick dark hair and lips white with fear. In her arms, half-collapsing, was a silver-haired Ashkind woman of about seventy. She wore every year of her life in the lines on her face and her failing body, but her expression was utterly serene.

"Dammit," said Rose, and opened the door. The younger woman breathed her thanks and pulled her mother into the hallway. Tabitha shut the door behind them. There was a look on the girl's face of terrible understanding.

The elderly woman lay prostrate on the cold tiles. Rose doubted she could move. She and the daughter knelt down beside her, trying to find a pulse.

"What can I do?" asked Rose. "What do you need?" She rounded on the younger woman. "Why didn't you call an ambulance?"

"She wanted to see you," said the younger woman. Her face was losing color every second, her anguished expression deepening with the realization of the true danger her mother was in. "'Take me to the Elmsworth girl.' That's exactly what she said."

From her tone, it was clear she understood the reason for her mother's instruction no more than Rose did.

"Should I get water?" asked Tabitha, with trembling quiet. The daughter seemed to notice her for the first time. At the sight of Tabitha's black eyes, the daughter shrieked involuntarily and recoiled.

"You deal with her or I throw you out on the street," said Rose, without taking her eyes off the mother. "Tabitha, do you remember where the first-aid kit is?"

Tabitha nodded and rushed into the kitchen. Rose knew she would be hurt and shaken, but this was by no means the first such reaction she had received. Even those Gifted who could tolerate the society of Ashkind — and there were comparatively few of those around — reacted with disgust at the sight of Demons. Many of the Ashkind disliked them, too.

Rose found the woman's pulse. As she had expected, it was irregular and slowing.

"Defibrillator?" she asked of the daughter, who shook her head.

The mother still seemed absolutely calm. She reached out a hand toward Rose, who tried not to flinch when it touched her face.

"You're . . . his," said the mother. Her voice, like her breathing, was hoarse and rasping.

Rose had no doubt as to what she meant. "Yes."

The pulse flickered. It occurred to Rose that the ban on using magic probably did not extend to saving lives. She searched desperately for something to heal, but even if she could — and that was certainly not a guarantee, she had always been a terrible healer — she doubted that magic could cure old age.

Tabitha came back with the first-aid kit. "Here."

Rose looked at it. Her mind had gone abruptly blank.

"Call an ambulance," she told Tabitha. "Please."

Tabitha nodded, looking terrified, and ran to get the phone.

"He's . . ." whispered the mother, and her voice failed for a moment, descended into coughing. The daughter looked terrified. They waited.

"He's not innocent," said the mother, finally.

Rose tried to quell her growing anger. "Listen, please, just stay with me, we're trying —"

"He is still . . . lying to you. He still has not . . . his true . . . what he has done . . ." She swallowed. "When I saw him . . . I recognized . . . I knew . . ."

She was losing coherence. Rose could hear Tabitha talking to the emergency-services operator.

The daughter leaned forward. "Mum. Please. Don't go. I'm here, you understand?" She shook her mother's shoulders, tried to get her eyes focused. "It's me. Tara. I'm here." She spoke with the utmost tenderness, and Rose knew that she, like Tabitha, understood what this was. Grief already hung in her eyes. "I am *here*."

She sounded desperately angry.

Tabitha came through again. "They're on their way."

The mother had not taken her eyes off Rose, their fading gray almost the same hue as her hair. "Tell him," she whispered, "tell him he is not free . . . I found him again . . . I know . . ."

The daughter, Tara, watched speechless; she was crying very quietly.

The woman's last words were very simple. She took her hand away from Rose's face and touched her daughter's, and for a moment the world vanished into the two of them, and the mother said, "Thank you. I love you," and she died, the light vanishing from her eyes; the arm fell to the floor, and she was gone.

There was a soft hissing sound from the next room. Tara knelt over the corpse of her mother, blank-faced. Tabitha backed away, tearing her eyes from the body, and into the living room.

The world around Rose seemed oddly still and quiet. She tried to get up and leave Tara to grieve, but the floor lurched.

"It's an emergency broadcast," said Tabitha, from the living room, in an empty whisper. And then, more strongly: "Rose. *Rose.* That's the Department."

It was obvious enough from the start. The machine-gun fire was relentless, pounding bullet after bullet into the glass. The first half-shattered layer collapsed almost instantly. The second took longer — thirty seconds at least — and then the walls collapsed, and the occupants of the fifth floor were separated only by fifty feet of empty air from the ground. The wind could be felt almost instantly, and the light was hard and unyielding.

"Remind me," Loren hissed to Nate, who knelt hard-faced on the floor beside him, gun pointed out into the sky, "what was that meant to withstand, again?"

He didn't have time to reply before one of the soldiers, shuffling on his knees across the carpet, approached Loren. "Orders, sir?"

Before Loren could answer, a horrible, smooth, assured voice boomed artificially loud over the Department building. It was the voice, terribly familiar, of Stephen Greenlow, the leader of the Gospel.

"We believe you are guilty of protecting non-magicals and the supporters of non-magicals," said the voice. Loren saw Nate's knuckles whiten with the force of his grip on his gun. "You will face the justice of the people of London. You have one chance to surrender yourselves."

Loren raised himself on his elbows and glanced around at the office to check that the Department fighters shared his general sentiment. Then he shouted down to Greenlow and the assembled Gospel soldiers where exactly he could shove his justice.

"Very well," came Greenlow's voice smoothly, and there came the screech of feedback as his loudspeaker was turned off.

The Department waited, tense.

A wave of heat swept over the office. Several Department members cried out.

"What are they doing?" asked Nate. There was no fear in his voice, only cold anger. Loren looked at him with new respect.

"Magic," he said. "They're doing magic."

"In public? That's against the law."

"Doing it *anywhere* has been against the law for six months n — Why on earth was *that* your question?"

Something cold touched Loren's hand. He looked up, and saw the soldier trying to give him a small black box.

"Is that a bomb?"

Loren said nothing. He merely clicked his fingers and pressed the spark to the long piece of string attached to the box. Nate looked at his fingers and said, deadpan, "That's illegal, you know."

"Extenuating circumstances," he answered.

The heat wave intensified. Muttering rose from the back of the office, loud enough to be audible. "What are they *doing*?"

Loren was about to offer reassuring platitudes, anything to stop them panicking, when he saw — out in the open, rising just above the level of the floor — the tops of heads.

43

"Flying," he said, almost impressed. "They're flying."

Though his words carried across the office with unusual clarity, most did not understand what he said, and these were the ones who died first. The tactic the Gospel was using was not new, however, and those who remembered it from the War realized what was happening and started firing immediately.

The Gospel soldiers rose slowly, hovering like ghosts against the gray sky, energy pulsing almost palpably from them. Under any other circumstances, it would have been a breathtaking sight, but these were not any other circumstances. The flying soldiers were already shooting at the Department, and the bullets ripped through desks and carpet and flesh indiscriminately. The Department fired back, of course, and Gospel soldiers were hit and fell screaming from the air. But each fallen soldier was replaced by another — eerily smiling, green eyes bright, white uniform gleaming in the half-light of the sun.

Nate's aim was assured next to Loren, the muscles in his face taut, his grip on the gun unwavering, putting bullet after bullet into the shoulders of the Gospel troops — enough to knock them out of the sky, but not to kill them. And still the Gospel kept coming, soldier after soldier.

Where were they finding all of these Gifted, Loren wondered absentmindedly as he reloaded, all powerful enough to fly? Flying was a skill, and a rare one at that: half the Department office wouldn't be able to do it. And yet these flying soldiers kept coming, weightless and merciless, cold-eyed and savage; and Loren glimpsed in that moment what an undignified death this was going to be.

And then.

Something beside him began to beep. It was by his elbow, and slowly getting hotter, almost painfully so. The bomb. The bomb was ready to detonate.

Oh, for Ichor's sake.

He grabbed it with his left hand and threw it with a roar of desperation off the edge of the office. It bounced off a Gospel soldier, but didn't adhere; it fell to the earth beneath, and such was the screaming and the breaking of glass and bone that Loren didn't hear the impact with the earth. For a second all the natural fears flitted through his mind: Had he not prepared it right? Had it not worked? Would he —?

BOOM.

It was a thundering shatter, more sensation than sound, and it ripped through the Gospel masses below. The flying soldiers looked disoriented, terrified. They did not stop firing, but when the Department bullets hit them and they fell, no one replaced them now, and very soon they were gone, plunging to earth again like young birds.

There was a long quiet. The wounded were groaning and the dead were very, very silent.

"Casualties?" Loren called.

A moment before the reply: "Eleven wounded." Pause. "Five dead."

Loren rolled over and closed his eyes.

He got up after a few seconds and surveyed the destroyed office. "Call a medic," he said sharply to one soldier, who stumbled away, eyes on the bodies. Then Loren walked to the edge of the office and looked down at the bomb-broken mass of flesh and blood that lay beneath. He fired a couple of shots down at the surviving Gospel, now fleeing with their wounded, scanning them for Stephen Greenlow, but he wasn't there. Perhaps he had never

45

been there. Perhaps it had merely been a recording. He wouldn't have needed to be there in person; he could hardly have expected the Department to accept his ultimatum, after all.

He closed his eyes, swaying slightly in the soft breeze over the yawning drop beneath.

It had all been going so *well*.

– Chapter 5 –

The ambulance staff were not pleased at being asked to treat a dead woman. It must have been an extremely bizarre scene, all told: Tara crying over her mother's body in the hall, Rose sitting staring bemusedly between her and the television, and Tabitha frantic at the images being broadcast live on-screen. The Department office was all but destroyed, and Loren stood looking exhausted on the edge of the precipice. His left arm hung dead at his side, blood trickling from the elbow; he did not seem to have noticed.

So when the ambulance staff arrived — trying to break down the door first, before Rose hastily opened it — they did not quite know what to make of what they saw. It was only due to Rose's semi-aggressive persuasion tactics, and the obvious distress of the eight-year-old girl, that they agreed to do anything at all; and even then, it was on the condition that all three of them submit themselves to a basic checkup by a psychologist to alleviate whatever damage they had suffered. Rose was on the point of arguing over this, as well, but a quick glance at the television showed her that ambulances were drawing up outside the Department building — presumably also on their way to Chelsea and Westminster — and she acquiesced.

And so it was that Rose came to be riding in an ambulance with Tabitha, a stranger, and a corpse. When they finally arrived at the hospital, as the doctors glanced at their eyes and tried to filter Tabitha and the dead woman in one direction and Rose and Tara in the other, she ended up — for the first time in her life — having an argument with a doctor who wasn't Terrian.

"I don't care if she's a Demon. There's a man in there — a Pretender. She needs to see him; he's her uncle —"

"Now, young lady, there's no need for that kind of language."

Rose pressed her fingertips to her sinuses. "Pretender" was, indeed, a pejorative term for someone with weak magical Gifts and the light-green eyes that went with them, but since Loren cheerfully used it to describe himself, she had almost unconsciously fallen into doing the same.

"At least let the Gifted woman go with her mother. Please."

Tara was not paying any attention to this; she was gripping her mother's stretcher as the medical staff tried to carry her away, still crying. The doctor Rose was speaking to glanced at her, and nodded curtly. The Ashkind doctors reluctantly let Tara stumble toward the non-magical ward. Rose silently gave thanks that Loren was Gifted. His chances of being able to use his arm again were much higher on the magical ward, with doctors who could themselves use magic to heal him, than on the Ashkind ward, where the death toll was much higher.

David had always hated that sort of thing.

Rose cut off this train of thought and spoke to the doctor again, forcing herself to return her attention to the matter at hand.

"Now, the girl . . ."

"She's a Demon," said the Gifted doctor, his lip curling slightly as he looked at Tabitha. *He* was not a Pretender by any means. He was at least as powerful as Rose, his irises a deep green. Gospel-supporter material, she thought. "She cannot possibly enter a magical ward."

Rose glanced back at Tabitha, because she knew what the girl was on the point of saying — white-faced and anxious and angry as she was — and it must not be said. Tabitha, though she was a Demon, *did* have magic, and powerful magic, too — as powerful as any emerald-eyed Angel, fifty times stronger than Rose and a hundred times stronger than Loren. This, of course, was meant to be impossible. It was a fact of life that Ashkind, those with gray or black eyes, did not have magic. Finding one that did was like finding someone to whom the laws of gravity didn't apply. But there she was; and given that this information had gotten her and her uncle arrested and her mother killed, it would do no good to mention it now.

"Do you even know who we're talking about here? Her uncle — the man in that ward — is Loren Arkwood. He's the acting Head of the Department."

"Of course," said the doctor, testily. Rose knew he must be aware that the ambulance parking lots were filled with vehicles carrying injured Department fighters. "And it carries no weight with me. She is a Demon. The rules apply."

Rose and Tabitha looked at each other. Hospitals were the one place exempted from the new laws on magic — the one place where using it was not yet illegal — and she could feel it surging from the Gifted doctors' fingertips in the ward ahead. It made them both almost furious with envy.

"All right," said Rose finally. "Tabitha has to go for psychological testing, right?"

The doctor shot a nasty look at the retreating backs of the ambulance staff, but said, "A quick checkup, yes."

"Then can you at least make sure it happens in a room where she can see her uncle when they roll his stretcher down the corridor?"

The doctor hesitated. Rose knew he was trying to find some kind of objection, but eventually he relented. "That can be arranged."

Tabitha gave the doctor her most brilliant smile and let a nurse guide her toward the Ashkind ward. The doctor turned again to Rose.

"Now, young lady, I believe you too have to be checked over."

"Oh, no," said Rose quickly. "I'm fine."

"That's your opinion, but it has been recommended —"

"I understand that, sir, but I really need to go."

"And what exactly is more pressing than your health at this moment?"

Rose sighed. "I need," she said earnestly, "to go to prison."

* * *

David was silent for a while after Rose told him what had happened. He sat down on his bed and put his head between his forearms. His cell was fairly large, all things considered — eight feet by ten — but such was his reputation that it was at the end of a long brick corridor, utterly deserted and silent, with the only view the metal door at the other end. Rose had visited him almost every day for six months, but she had never been allowed inside. The bars always separated them.

"This was planned?" he asked finally.

"Sorry?"

"It was planned out. Organized. It wasn't just a random overspill of mob violence."

"Definitely not. Stephen Greenlow himself was there."

She told him about the tactics the Gospel had used — first making the windows opaque, then destroying them and bombarding the Department with fire from all sides with the flying soldiers.

"Was Aaron there?"

Aaron was Stephen Greenlow's son; he and Rose had history. Rose knew what her father was getting at, and tried to feign nonchalance. "Yes. I saw him. He was on the ground."

"And did he . . .?"

"No. He got out of the way before the bomb went off."

His voice was gentle. "Rose, surely you don't still have feelings for that boy."

"Only murderous ones," Rose said tersely, "and I would appreciate it if you would drop that. It was a long time ago."

"Half a year."

"He wasn't killing random Ashkind, then."

"Not to your knowledge."

Rose was about to snap when she saw that he was smiling at her. "Oh, for the love of the Angels," she growled, but laughed nevertheless.

"What, am I not allowed to tease you now?"

Rose waited for a moment until his smile faded. "So what do you think?"

"About what?"

"What do you think Greenlow's plans are, now that he didn't take the Department?"

"You think he was trying to take it?"

Rose glanced up. "You don't?"

"What would he stand to gain? That building wouldn't be easy to defend — not with the computer programs we'd still have control of, and the weapons systems . . . No. By the time they tried to make sense of it all, the Department squad teams would have rallied round and taken back the building. I don't think he was trying to conquer anything — he was just trying to damage us. Destroy us, maybe, but I doubt he seriously thought himself capable of that. But what he's done is enough. We won't be back on our feet for days at least, and we'll have to find a new base for a while."

"So we didn't win?"

He smiled his ghostly smile. "Oh, no, Rose. He knew what he was dealing with. He planned on losing men. Not as many as they clearly did, but some. And they can take it. There are enough of them. The Department will take longer to recover."

Rose bit her lip. "Loren's arm was damaged."

"Irreparably?" His tone betrayed no concern whatsoever for Loren's well-being.

"I don't know. Probably not."

"Did the Terrians make it?"

"Yes. I saw them. Shaken, but okay."

David was quiet for a moment. Rose sat back and rubbed her face. "I don't understand," she said, finally. "What do they want?"

"What do you mean?"

"The Gospel. Greenlow. What is he aiming for? What's his end result? What does he think he's doing?"

"Well, he wants to rule the world," he said. "And take out everyone he doesn't like — the Government, the Department, Ashkind, Hybrids . . . He wants to eliminate all his inconveniences. And sometimes, Rose, sometimes you can see where he's coming from, can't you?"

She stared at him, and was about to reply, but the guards started walking down the corridor toward her and she knew her time was up. "Have you and Madeleine prepared for the arraignment tomorrow?"

"Yes, of course."

"You'll be all right?"

He reached through the bars and touched her hand. "Of course I will, Rose. Have a little faith."

She smiled. "I love you, Dad."

The guards were almost within earshot now, so he didn't reply.

They returned Loren home late that night. Because of his status as acting Head of the Department, the Gifted doctors had turned their attention to him first, and consequently his arm was now in a sling, but still recognizably an arm. The bullet had gone very deep and could not be removed, but the wound it had created and the nerves it had damaged had been repaired.

He came in late at night, drawing Tabitha in his wake, and sent her to bed immediately. Rose's fitful sleep was instantly broken by the sound of her footsteps on the stairs, and she got up immediately — she was still sleeping fully clothed — and went into the corridor. Tabitha hung in her bedroom doorway uncertainly. She looked pale and drawn. Rose drew her close and kissed her on the forehead, moved by pity. These were bad times to try and live out your childhood.

"How is he?" she mouthed.

Tabitha shook her head.

Rose put her to bed and made sure she was settled, if not asleep, before going downstairs. Loren had collapsed onto the sofa and now seemed to be deeply asleep, but she knew him too well to be fooled. He looked exhausted and cold; his clothing was torn and stained with blood. Rose closed the curtains, sat down on the sofa, and waited.

After a moment, Loren spoke.

"I hate the bastards," he said without opening his eyes. "I hate them all."

Rose said nothing.

"I am going to hunt them down," he continued, head still resting upturned on the sofa cushion, "and find them, and then I'm going to kill them, and their families, and their friends, and their colleagues, and maybe their pets, and I'm going to burn their houses and scrawl my name on the ruins of the walls, and I'm going to make sure no one ever tries anything like that again."

Rose nodded slowly, taking this in. "And Greenlow?"

"Greenlow?" Loren gave a hollow laugh. "That's *nothing* to what I'll do to Stephen Greenlow. He'll *wish* I'd done that to him."

"How many of them did you kill?"

"Me personally, or all of us?"

"Either. Both."

"I don't know how many I killed. Half a dozen, maybe."

"Pathetic."

"I know. All in all, the Gospel lost maybe . . . I don't know, ninety men?"

Rose sucked in a breath through her teeth.

"They wouldn't have risked that many if they weren't prepared to lose them," said Loren. "That tells us a lot about their numbers. A thousand, at least. Maybe two. And that's only active fighters. Their suppliers, their donors —"

"Yeah," Rose said quickly. She didn't particularly want to hear again how strong the Gospel were, not at the moment. "How long is your arm out?"

He opened his eyes at last, and glanced with disgust at the dirty-white fabric of the sling. "A few days, maybe."

"At least you're right-handed."

"Yep." He closed his eyes again, then said, almost nonchalantly: "Tabitha said someone died here this afternoon?"

"Yes," Rose said slowly, and told him about Tara and her mother, and what the dying woman had said about David. "I managed to get some information out of the daughter in the ambulance. Her mother's name was Clare Matheson, she was seventy-two, and she lived in Oxford after the Veilbreak."

"He's not innocent?"

"That's what she said, yes."

"Anything else?"

"The only other coherent things were 'He's been lying to you,' and 'He is not free.'"

"The opinions of the general public, I'm afraid."

55

She glared at him, but his eyes were still closed. "She came to see me. Not him. *Me.* When she was dying. She knew what she was talking about, Loren."

"And you told David about this, I assume?"

Rose hesitated. Loren's eyes snapped open.

"Interesting," he said.

"I just . . . I just don't see how it would help. Not with the arraignment tomorrow."

He nodded slowly, but she could tell he did not believe her in the slightest. "A mature decision."

He heaved himself up from the sofa and started to make his way toward the stairs, but she stopped him.

"Loren."

He turned.

"The way you acted today—" She hesitated. "Please don't do anything stupid, if something like this happens again. Don't risk yourself. You're not a soldier anymore, however they might act in the Department. They need you alive, you understand?"

He gave her the briefest of bleak glances, and went upstairs, toward Tabitha and sleep, without a backward look.

– Chapter 6 –

The Devil incarnate went by the name of Adrian Teller.

He was a small man, to contain such concentrated evil. He was balding, but what little hair he had was a graying black, and his skin tone alternated between flushed and ghostly pale. He was a Pretender, as Loren would say — his eyes were a very light green, the color of rot. His voice was slightly nasal, but he spoke even one-to-one as if to an audience, and he had the distinct air of someone who was used to holding the attention of a room, even if that air did not match up with actual circumstances. He was, in short, the object of Rose's most potent and subjective hatred; and, incidentally, he also happened to be David's prosecuting attorney.

Rose, Loren and Tabitha were admitted into the courtroom, where they sat in the gallery, side by side with the press, including the BBC correspondent Oliver Keen. Teller was already there, with his notes and his script ready in front of him. His expression was one of the utmost serenity. Madeleine looked considerably tenser.

From her vantage point, Rose could also see her father, sitting alone in the dock, wearing his gray prison uniform and his handcuffs, his face drained of color.

The bailiff shouted his usual commands, and Rose stood up without thinking. Justice Malvern entered, along with the jury. The jury sat. Judge Malvern sat. After a pause, so did everyone else. Rose was now finding it hard to breathe.

Silence while Malvern gathered her papers. Teller was smiling. Madeleine's expression was unreadable. Then, finally, with jarring abruptness, which almost pushed Rose over into panic: "If the prosecuting attorney could read out the indictment to the court . . ."

Teller stood. He faced the judge at all times, but Rose could still see his face, and trace the movement of his lips.

"We, the prosecution, on behalf of the state, believe that the accused is guilty of concealing illegal powers from the authorities, namely, the ability to transform, once every forty-two days or thereabouts, into a monster fueled by magic and with both inclination and capability to murder."

At this, David probably should have looked cowed, or at least defiant; instead, the color had been returning slowly to his face with each word Teller spoke, and now his expression was one of an utter lack of concern. Rose could tell he was fighting the urge to put his feet up on the stand.

After Teller finished, a silence fell. Madeleine, too, looked calmer; now, at least, she knew what she was fighting. Rose could feel it spreading over the court, that half-excited readiness that

58

sweeps over a performer who has taken their place on the stage: *It begins.*

There was only one thing to do now, and that was what they had prepared.

Malvern was slow to react; she watched Teller sit down, and allowed quiet to fall for a minute. She, too, was watching their expressions.

"Will the defendant please rise," she said.

David stood. He seemed perfectly at ease in his prison slacks; he wore them as he might a suit. The only sign of strain was in his hands, which he kept out of view of the judge and jury, between the hard, dark wood of the dock and his body. Rose could see them. The thumbs of each hand were holding down the middle fingers, whilst the others stretched out and upward, pointing toward the ceiling. Rose had seen the gesture a hundred times while he paced the Department floor, trying to pinpoint the location or identity of some murderer.

"To the charge of the continuing offense of the concealment of illegal powers," she asked him, "how do you plead?"

David exchanged a glance with Madeleine. It was deafening, the conversation in their gaze: rapid-fire bursts of intent that were no less clear and audible for being entirely unspoken. In that moment, David held the room more tightly under his control than Teller ever had.

"Not guilty," he said.

They came home quietly.

They did not say a word to each other on the journey back to the house, and when they walked through the door, Loren went straight upstairs to his study. Tabitha went to her room, to do homework and to sleep. So it was only Rose who went into the living room and saw the dead woman's daughter lying on their sofa. The tear tracks had washed themselves from her face overnight. Now she was hard and clear and determined.

"How did you get in?" asked Rose quietly.

"Sheer force of will," said Tara, "and a lock pick. I'm here to help you, if it matters."

Rose sat down on a chair slowly. She did not take her eyes from the intruder. For a second they sat in silence.

"I don't think we've been formally introduced," said the woman, staring at the wall. "I know who you are, of course. My name's Tara Priestley. I am a criminal."

Rose hesitated. "High level?"

"Thief, mostly. Hired help on some occasions. There aren't many Gifted criminals outside of the Gospel, so my magic sells pretty well. No murders as yet. I'm not someone your Department would have bothered with."

"Good for us."

"Very good for you. Now, listen very carefully. My mother was dying, and she used her last moments to find you. Her last words were about your father. I don't understand why, and I want to. And to do that, I need to keep David Elmsworth alive."

"And this, then," said Rose warily, "is where our ambitions coincide."

"They do, indeed. Now I think I know how I can save his life. Possibly even prove his innocence. But to do that, I need you to tell me the truth."

"Anything."

"Are you a Hybrid?"

"No."

Tara rolled over on the sofa and stared very hard at Rose. "I'll ask again. Are you a Hybrid?"

"No."

She was angry now, and she stood up. "Listen to me. I'm not going to rat you out. I don't care — I've dealt with worse, believe me, and if you've managed to go through all these years without killing anyone, then you have my respect, but that doesn't matter to me. If we're going to save your father's life together, then there must be an understanding between us. I will ask you one more time, and if you say no again I will walk out this door and I will take his life with me. I'm asking you, Rosalyn: Are you a Hybrid?"

Rose paused. Then she put her face in her hands. Tara growled in anger and began to walk away, and just as she reached the doorway, Rose said, "Yes."

Tara sighed, and put down her bag. "Thank you."

"How did you know?"

"Logic. The ability to believe the worst in people. Finding your medical records on the hospital database yesterday. Your father never let you take a blood test and your immune system weakens considerably at six-week intervals. It's hard to spot the patterns if you're not looking for them, but luckily for you, I was."

Rose stood up. "So what do you want?"

"I know a woman who might be able to save your father."

"Where is she?"

"In hospital. And she's not allowed visitors."

Rose stopped. A slight shiver passed over her. "Ah. So that means . . ."

"Yes," said Tara calmly, "I'm afraid you're going to have to be injured."

61

<<< >>>

Six years earlier (age 30)
March 6, 5:29 p.m.

The newsagent gives him a disapproving look. "Those things will kill you, you know," she says.

He ignores her and puts the money on the counter. She pauses for a second and then takes it.

"One pack?"

"Just the one."

She gives him Marlboros, perhaps knowing he doesn't care. He takes them and leaves. Ten seconds later he is back again.

"Lighter, please," he says.

This time there is a definite hesitation. "Don't throw your life away, dear," she says reproachfully. "It's not worth it."

He says nothing, but holds out a two-pound coin. She sighs, and gives him the lighter.

"Try to quit, at least, dear."

He looks back at her. "I haven't started yet," he says.

She stares at him as he leaves.

He walks across the road and leans against the wall of the hospital. The day is hot and cloudy, heavy with the prospect of rain. Even the sky is trying to dissuade him. He takes a cigarette from the pack with old dexterity and clicks the lighter into flame.

He draws on the end, trying to make it like breathing. He holds the smoke inside him for a long time, finding the long, deep, low thrum of nicotine beneath the rough tar.

"I didn't know you smoked."

62

He blows the smoke from between his lips in a gray stream, like silent whistling, and doesn't answer.

"She's breathing."

"Well, yes."

"It was a deep wound."

"It was in her *arm*. It was never dangerous."

Terrian comes to stand beside him. "I'll have you know I used to be a doctor."

"Good for you. Now you kill people for a living."

"I'd advise you not to destroy your lungs, but I don't think you'll live long enough."

"Good," says David. "Someone gets it."

He draws on the cigarette again.

"Does Rose know about this?"

"No."

"How long has this been going on?"

David looks at him. "This is my first smoke in twelve years."

"Why did you quit?"

He doesn't answer.

"She wants to see you."

"She's awake?"

"It hit an artery, David."

"I know. I was there."

"My son is saying he did it," says Terrian, with unexpected anger. "He's saying he fired his gun by accident in a lesson you were giving him. But I know for a fact neither you nor Rose were in the Department building when you called the ambulance."

David says nothing.

"Does Nathaniel know something I don't?"

"I'm sure he knows many things."

"David." Terrian stands directly in front of him, so David has to resist the urge to blow smoke into his face. "Where and how did Rose get shot?"

David lets the cigarette drop and grinds it into paper and ash before taking another one from the pack. "I didn't do it, if that's what you're asking."

"I'm not —" Terrian stops. "Why don't you *care*?"

"If you think you can read my emotions from my face, you flatter yourself. Let me be the detective, Connor."

Terrian hits him across the face. David moves with the blow and stands there for a moment, pressed against the wall. After a few seconds he takes out his lighter again and touches the flame to the end of his second cigarette.

"You're forgetting your Hippocratic oath," is all he says, before drawing on the smoke again.

"You're a terrible father."

"Ah, yes, but I never promised I wouldn't be."

He glances up at the No Smoking sign over the hospital entrance. He considers for a moment, and then blows smoke at it.

"Where is she?"

Terrian seems uncertain whether he should answer.

"Ward nineteen," he says at last.

"ICU?"

"Of course."

He drops the cigarette into the dust again, and lets its fire fade to a soft glow.

"I hope you get addicted," says Terrian, viciously, "and I hope you get lung cancer and stop breathing slowly, and I hope you die screaming her name in agony."

"I'll make sure you're there to get me on tape."

He opens the hospital door. He pauses, and takes the pack of cigarettes out of his pocket. He throws it to Terrian, who catches it involuntarily.

"Burn them," he tells Terrian, and then he winks. "In whatever way you see fit."

Terrian is openmouthed. David grins, and goes in to the hospital to find Rose.

– Chapter 7 –

The prosecution's first witness stood on the stand and tried to stop fidgeting.

"Your name?" Malvern asked him.

"Colonel Connor Nathan Terrian of the Department for the Maintenance of Public —"

"Thank you," said Malvern firmly, and Terrian fell silent. "I see no reason to overexert the court scribes so early in the morning."

A quiet laugh from the journalists. They were the only ones who could laugh, these days; to everyone else, the somber atmosphere of the court was crushing. Terrian looked like he felt it. He was sweating already, but he held a quiet, unbroken dignity about him that not even the gazes of the jurors could penetrate. His eyes kept flickering up toward Nate, his son, who sat beside

Rose in the gallery. Rose felt a pang of something unidentifiably bitter. David never looked at her. He wasn't looking now. His eyes were on Terrian — which, she supposed, was entirely reasonable.

Still.

"Do you promise to tell the truth, the whole truth, and nothing but the truth?"

"I do," said Terrian calmly. Rose pressed her forehead to the wooden bench in front of her. This was going to be painful.

Teller rose. He was smiling again.

"So, Colonel," he said. "How long have you known the defendant?"

"Fifteen years," said Terrian, "since he joined the Department. I started working there during the War, but I knew him before then, through my wife."

"Your wife was Malia Peterson, the defendant's predecessor as leader of the Department."

"Yes."

"And did you, through that time, suspect anything . . . untoward about him?"

Terrian was silent for a moment. "I knew something wasn't right," he said, after a while, "but I never thought anything of it. Your Honor"—here addressing Malvern—"you know what we do at the Department. I won't deny that . . . the defendant . . . was a good leader, but he was never a good man. In our environment, amorality can be useful."

Rose relaxed slowly, despite herself. Nothing too damning so far.

"And as to the charge against him," said Teller, "do you believe it to be true?"

"Yes," said Terrian. "Yes, I absolutely do."

67

Rose ground her teeth.

"And why is that?"

"Because I know him to be capable of killing. Because I know that he would have valued his own safety over that of others. Because he was a monster. Because I knew him to take pleasure in murder. Because he could hide it. Because he could fool us. Because he could."

David's hands slid over his head, so that the chain of the handcuffs tightened around his neck. He was bent low, his head in his arms. Rose could not see his face. She did not want to.

"Did you get on well, in your time working together?" asked Teller. He was smiling slightly now. Rose had never hated anyone so much in her life.

"No," said Terrian. "And when we didn't, when he was angry, I could see that he was . . . violent . . ." He swallowed. "It disgusts me. He disgusts me, now, Your Honor, and he frightens me. That kind of monster — near my wife, near my son, all those years. And the girl . . ."

The eyes of the journalists were on Rose now. She leaned back in her chair, and ignored them. She had suspected she might come up.

"The girl of his . . . I was there the first day he came in. My wife had recruited him. He had developed something of a reputation for what he had done in the War, and the Department was only a few months old then — we needed all the psychopaths we could get. He came in — maybe twenty years old, he looked like a boy — and he was carrying this cradle. And in it was this baby. He'd put her on his desk when he was working, so he could see her. And as she grew older, she was always quiet. She'd always watch him, more than any of us, watch him when he spoke. I

68

never knew why . . . but of course she knew, she'd always known, what he was. I don't understand why she never spoke . . . the terrible things he must have done to that girl to make her keep quiet, Your Honor, I shudder to imagine —"

"And the requisitions?" cut in Teller, intently. Rose was shaking with anger. She was clenching her fists so hard, she could feel her nails break the skin of her palms, the stickiness of blood.

Terrian hesitated.

"Were there any incidents," asked Teller, his voice so soft it was almost menacing, "involving David Elmsworth's daughter and the requisitions?"

The scar in the crook of Rose's elbow seemed to have gone suddenly cold. In the dock, the color had drained from David's face again, and Madeleine was staring at him with such intensity, it seemed she was trying to read his mind. The court was utterly silent.

Terrian swallowed.

"Once," he said, "when they were nine years old, I think he tried to take them — my son and his daughter, I mean — on a requisition."

"Explain the concept of a requisition to the court, please, Colonel Terrian," said Teller, still in that soft, dangerous voice.

"It's when we send troops to take a criminal in, or — or to kill them." Terrian wasn't meeting the jurors' eyes anymore. "There was one, to collect a gang of smugglers — Nate was with him, and the girl. He said he was giving them a weapons lesson, teaching them how to shoot, but I think he took them to the operation, to show them what it was like. They had guns. There was a shoot-out. The girl was injured. My son — Nate — he said he'd done it by accident, during the *weapons lesson*." Terrian's voice

69

closed up, tense with disgust. "I think he tried to shoot one of the smugglers, and shot her. That's what he does, Justice Malvern. Elmsworth. He takes children and makes them into weapons. My own child —"

"Objection," said Madeleine loudly, standing up. David had gone statue-still again, and the scribbling of the court artists and the sound of furious typing was almost too loud to hear Terrian speak. Rose had closed her eyes. "Does the witness have any proof of what he is alleging?"

"The girl *was* injured," said Teller quickly.

"But can you prove these circumstances? Can you prove that David Elmsworth was in any way responsible for her injury?"

Teller hesitated. Madeleine gave a slight smile, and addressed the judge.

"This isn't evidence, Your Honor. This is speculation."

Malvern considered for a moment. "Sustained," she said.

Teller looked disgruntled, but knew to quit when he was ahead; what Terrian had said had caused immense disquiet within the court, and it would make up the bulk of the articles written about the case tonight. Certainly the jurors looked shocked. "No further questions," he said, and sat down.

Terrian turned to Madeleine, looking apprehensive. Her eyes were coldly angry, but her voice was perfectly calm.

"Let us return," she said, "for a moment, to the realm of fact, and to the charge at hand. Colonel Terrian, did you ever for a moment suspect specifically that your colleague was a Hybrid? Did the thought, the *word*, ever cross your mind? You work in the business of detection, after all. So did you ever guess what he was?"

Terrian hesitated. "I always knew that something wasn't —"

"I don't want your *something*, Colonel Terrian, I want you to answer the question truthfully. I will remind you that you are under oath. So again — did the phrase *David Elmsworth is a Hybrid* ever cross your mind in fifteen years?"

A long silence.

"No."

"Thank you," said Madeleine. "So you were never harmed or affected in any way by what you now know about him. He never hurt you, nor did he do anything to make you suspect he might be afflicted by a condition that would make him want to hurt you."

"No."

"All right. Now we're getting somewhere."

Teller was standing now. "Objection, Your Honor. Just because the witness did not think the defendant responsible at the time does not prove the defendant's innocence."

"No," said Madeleine, before Malvern could respond, "but you are trying to use the witness's suspicion as evidence for the defendant's guilt. I am trying to establish whether Colonel Terrian, working very closely with the defendant for many years, ever encountered so much as a shred of evidence — after-the-fact speculation aside — that the defendant was ever guilty of this charge. Is this reasonable, Your Honor?"

Malvern considered for a long moment. "Yes," she said. "Carry on, Ms. Ryan."

Madeleine nodded. "Colonel Terrian, in your opinion, is the defendant evil?"

"I'm sorry?"

"I will rephrase, then. You have tracked down countless killers, rapists, thieves, thugs, treason-plotters, and Demons. You have seen firsthand the worst of humanity. So I will ask again, in all the years you have known him, do you think that he is evil?"

Terrian paused. "I . . . don't know," he said, slowly. "*Evil*, well — I wouldn't —" He paused, and then seemed to collect himself. "Yes," he said, firmly. "Yes, I would."

Madeleine closed her eyes for a moment, and turned to the court.

"Ladies and gentlemen of the jury," she said, "I will admit to you an ulterior motive. I have not been attempting to prove my client's innocence these past few minutes so much as dissuade Mr. Teller from proceeding on his current path. He knows, and I know, that this is not a normal trial. The question is not really whether or not David Elmsworth has the condition of which he is accused — in other words, whether he is innocent or guilty — but whether or not he deserves criminal punishment for this. Mr. Teller's strategy, it would seem, is to prove that he does by bringing out a stream of disgruntled acquaintances to tell the court their opinion of him. I want to make this very clear now: Speculation is not admissible in court, not even from those who knew the defendant well. Anyone, no matter how closely connected to the case or the defendant, would be forgiven for thinking ill of David Elmsworth, given the huge amount of negative publicity"— a glare at the journalists in the gallery —"circulating around this case. No matter how evil he is *thought* to be, proving his unpopularity is not grounds for sentencing.

"I would like you, Your Honor, Mr. Teller, honorable jury, to pretend that you have never heard of the defendant. I would like you to pretend that this is just another court case — as if my client has no previous reputation, as if you have never heard anything about him, as if at first glance he might be thought an unremarkable civilian. And then I would like you to bring before me your evidence of his guilt — firm, corporeal, undeniable evidence — and convince me that he is evil, that he is a heinous criminal, that his condition poses a *direct threat* to innocent people. Then, and only then, will I admit defeat. Until then, Mr. Teller, no more witnesses from the defendant's past claiming that they knew something was wrong all along, no more outraged ex-colleagues or betrayed acquaintances. Until such time as you prove to me otherwise, Mr. Elmsworth is just like any other defendant, and will be tried in the manner that we always try suspects: with *evidence*, Mr. Teller, with *evidence*."

Outside the court, Rose hugged Madeleine. She was wrapped in a woolen coat that just about concealed the swell of her belly; she looked suddenly frail and exhausted after her fire in the courtroom.

"Thank you," said Rose fervently. "That was a wonderful speech."

Madeleine nodded absentmindedly. They stood together against the white-stone walls, watching the buses roll past them.

"It's not going to be enough, is it?" said Rose quietly.

"No," said Madeleine. "Not remotely."

– Chapter 8 –

"How do you do it?"

Loren was sitting at his desk, feet up beside his computer screen, trying to grab a few minutes' worth of sleep while no one needed him. His judgment of this was, clearly, faulty.

"I want to know how you train yourself," said the girl. He kept his eyes closed, working out the voice. It was the medical student. Rose's friend. Maria Rodriguez. Oh, dear God. "How you kill."

He didn't answer, but blinked and looked up at her.

Maria regarded him for a moment, arms folded. "You were a part of Regency, yes? During the War."

"And after it."

"How old were you?"

"I started when I was sixteen."

"And when they drove you out?"

He hesitated. "Older."

She waited. He sighed. "Twenty-four."

"That's a long time."

"Did you come here to do anything constructive?" he asked, tersely. "Because, if not, I have better things to be getting on with. Those kidnapped Demon kids, for instance. We still can't find them."

Maria Rodriguez paused, looking down at him.

"I told you," she said. "I want to know how you train yourself to kill."

He rubbed his face and sighed.

"It's not a matter of training," he said, finally. "It's not a matter of preparation, or readiness. No one starts out with the intention to become a killer. You kill once — not accidentally, not quite, but in self-defense, or in battle. It's what we call a hot-blooded kill. You kill someone without quite meaning to do it, or if you do, your objective is something else, like a military victory or your friend's life, not a dead body . . . And then, after that, once you've killed, it only gets easier."

"Is that what happened to you, in Regency?"

"Yes."

"Then what was your hot-blooded kill?"

He thought for a moment; it had been so long that he almost didn't remember. "A couple of weeks after the Veilbreak. My sister and I were hiding out in an empty flat in Acton. A group of Gifted thugs went for our supplies. They thought they could take us. One of them saw my sister's eyes, knew she didn't have magic. Went for her with his knife. So I went at him with mine. He bled out and died in the flat. That night I didn't sleep, but I did every night after."

75

Maria's face was closed. He knew that expression, and appreciated it — it had been a long time since anyone had had the tact to conceal their revulsion. "So that was it? After that, you were . . . gone?"

"What do you mean?"

"Your conscience, it didn't bother you?"

Loren smiled at her bleakly. "Your conscience never *goes*, Maria; don't worry about that. It's just anesthetized. You pretend your cold-blooded kills are right, for a good cause, and that little uneasy voice shuts right up."

"And what was your cause? What could possibly be enough to justify something like that?"

He closed his eyes again, was silent for a moment. "Well, of course, for Regency it was the War. Still is, of course — they won't believe the War is over until they've won it. They want to — how did Rose say David put it?—*destroy their inconveniences.* They want to slaughter everyone whose existence they dislike. They want to kill the Gifted, and the Angels, and the Leeched, and everyone else whom magic ever touched. And perhaps then they will be happy, but I doubt it."

"But you *are* Gifted."

"Correct."

"So how could you possibly have fought for them?"

He kept his eyes closed and said nothing.

"Loren," said Maria, softly, "please. You know why I'm asking this."

He sighed. "You won't understand Rose by trying to understand me."

"I don't want to understand *her.* I want to understand what she wants."

"She wants David's safety. She wants our trust. She doesn't want her father and the Department to be at odds. She wants everything to be the way it was a year ago and nothing to have changed. And she knows she won't get any of it."

Maria was quiet for a moment. "*I* trust her."

"If you did, we wouldn't be having this conversation."

The girl was silent again, for so long this time that Loren opened his eyes.

"I didn't know what she was like," she said. "I've known her for, what, twelve years, and it was obvious that she was different, but I didn't know quite how, or why. And then I met you and David."

Loren sat forward. "You think she's like us?"

"More each day."

He watched her for a moment. "You disapprove of us, don't you?"

"Of who?"

"Me. The Department. This whole arena of violence for a cause."

"I worry she's turning into David," said Maria suddenly, looking back at him. He raised his eyebrows. "The more of him they show in court, the more of him I can see in her. She doesn't fear anything, not really. She just hardens, under pressure. She drains of emotion. He does that. You've seen it in court. You've seen it in both of them."

Her face had closed again. He was careful not to break her composure. "And how do you think that will end, for her?"

"She won't end up like him. She still believes in doing the right thing. I think he gave up on that years ago."

He had no reply to that, and after a while Maria got up and started walking out of the office. He stopped her.

"Maria?"

She turned.

"If you're right, there won't be anything you can do. You can't change people."

The girl looked at him for a moment. "Maybe not," she said. "But I can heal them."

<<< >>>

Seven years earlier (age 29)
April 3, 3:36 p.m.

"What would you do if you had to keep a secret from me?"

They sit on the beach underneath Blackpool Pier, throwing rocks at the sea.

He shrugs. "It depends."

"On what?"

"Whether it were for your safety."

"Let's say it wasn't."

He looks at her. She is staring at the sea, wet-haired and slimy with seawater, wrapped in a sandy towel. She is nine years of cold and fire and silence and anger. She is beautiful.

"Let's say it was for yours."

"Were."

"What?"

"Let's say it *were* for my safety. You're describing a hypothetical situation, you need a subjunctive. Carry on."

She glares at him. The clouds are coming in.

"If you had to lie to me to protect yourself, would you?"

"Yes."

"Good," she says, relieved. "I was worried."

"About what?"

She takes a moment. She digs a smooth, gray rock from the sand and brushes it off. Then she hurls it into the rushing water. It lands short, but the sea rushes up to claim it, and when the wave retreats, the stone is buried, or gone.

"Don't do stupid things for me," she says. "Please."

<<< >>>

Rose was waiting outside the hospital when he approached her. She was nervous — that, she thought, was the best way to describe it. He saw her hands shaking.

The young man was holding a knife. She couldn't stop staring at it, but she didn't move.

"Tara Priestley wants me to hurt you," he said.

"Yep." She didn't take her eyes off the knife.

He stared at her. "And you're not going to . . ."

"Run? No. Do your worst."

He looked at her for a moment, puzzled, and then he shrugged and the knife flashed silver and she cried out as a line opened up along her collarbone, seeping red, and she stumbled back against the wall, hissing with the shock and the pain of it.

By the time she looked up, furious at her own coward-ice, blood spreading slowly through her shirt like infection, he was gone.

Through dimming eyes, she saw the hospital staff converging on her.

She had to see the woman. She had to see the woman who Tara said could save her father.

She had to do this. She didn't have a choice.

Not anymore.

She closed her eyes and passed out as they approached her.

– Chapter 9 –

Nine years earlier (age 27)
May 15, 9:01 p.m.

Terrian is crying. His tears are thick and gray, like rainwater.

"No," he keeps saying. "No. No."

David does not have the heart to say "Yes"— to try and tell him what no one else is going to: that she is gone, and dead, and not coming back. He simply sits there and watches.

The boy does not understand either, not yet. He is only Rose's age, and innocent by the standards of Department children. He sits on the hospital chair, staring at his father in incomprehension.

By now, he has stopped asking where his mother is.

"No," says Terrian. He leans back into his chair, and stares up at the hospital ceiling, his breaths breaking, fingers twitching. Grief pours from him like smoke. "No, no, God no, no. Please, no."

David considers what to say. He will not insult Terrian with platitudes. Instead he says, with all the gentleness he possesses, "She loved you. Unconditionally."

Terrian is not listening, cannot hear him. David knows he is thinking only of Malia — her voice, her smile, the shape of her eyes; the way she moved toward him without thinking, a constant second gravity; how she would have looked on their wedding day; every word she ever said now suddenly finite, a treasure.

He won't remember her weak and injured, in the wheelchair. He won't remember her like that, ever again.

David gets up.

"David?" asks the boy. He has eyes of a brighter green than Malia, but the shape of his face is hers, and the color of his skin — the deep mahogany of forest shadows — is hers, undoubtedly his mother's. To David's surprise, the sight of this hurts.

"Tell me the truth," says the boy fiercely.

"I can't," David tells him, sadly. "It's not my truth to tell."

In the hospital administration room, he sits talking to the secretary.

"He can't know," he says. "I'm sorry — I am — but if he ever finds out who did this, he will go after them. And he won't be able to kill them, and when he tries they will destroy him, and his son. He has to think she died of some kind of natural cause."

The secretary eyes him suspiciously. "I'm sorry, Mr. . . ."

"Elmsworth."

"I'm sorry, Mr. Elmsworth, but that's against the —"

She trails off abruptly, staring at him. He watches her ruefully as it sinks in.

"Yes," he says, before she can ask. "*That* Elmsworth."

He shows her his license, in case there is any remaining doubt.

"Acting Head of the Department now, I should think," he says, "and I'm afraid I have to inform you that Malia Terrian, née Peterson, died of undiscovered inoperable cancer, and absolutely not sudden massive heart failure resulting from gunshot wounds."

He stands.

"But why?" asks the secretary, almost in a whisper.

David sighs and holds up the note before leaving — not long enough for her to read anything, but he still shows it to her, and that is something. It still has Malia's blood on it; it was shoved into her hand before she died. In scrawled, terribly familiar handwriting, it reads: *Behold the Interregnum.*

<<< >>>

She woke up in the hospital with a healing scar on her collarbone, sore but mending. The Gifted doctors had left her to sleep. She was going to be kept in hospital overnight; with the aid of magic, she should be more or less all right by morning.

Rose lay there, waiting, absorbed in her own thoughts. The morphine drip in her arm kept her wavering on the edge of sleep.

At nine o'clock Loren came to drop off her clothes, and stared blankly at her. He looked very tired.

"How the hell did you let this happen?" he asked. "Why didn't you fight back?"

She was saved from explaining to him about Tara, which she wasn't sure how to do anyway, by passing out again.

The next time she awoke, it was dark. Someone had left a comms tablet beside her bed. She picked it up and stared at it. Tara had sent her three words:

To your left.

Rose put the comms tablet down and rolled over so she was staring into the blackness of the beds beside her.

"Hello," she whispered.

Pause. Then, a reply, from six feet away, the bed next to her: "Hello."

"Are you all right?"

This was, in retrospect, the most pointless question ever asked in a hospital. The voice did not answer. Rose lay there silently in the dark.

"I know you," said the voice after a while.

"I'm sure you do."

"You're the Hybrid's daughter," she said, with mild astonishment. "Rosalyn Elmsworth."

Rose said nothing.

"Tara Priestley told me you would be here," said the voice. "What do you have to do with her?"

Rose struggled for a moment for the words. The anesthetic thickened and slowed her thoughts. "We're working together."

"Why?"

"Her mother died."

"And?"

"She knew something about my father. She tried to tell me as she was dying. Tara wants to know what it was. So do I."

"Ah," said the voice. "So what do you want me for?"

Rose paused, and turned on the lamp beside her bed.

She and the woman looked at each other for a moment in silence. The room was cold and bleak, full of empty beds, and the faint gray light of the lamp deepened the shadows that clustered at the edges of the trolleys and in the corners. A shaft of street-light lay warm on the floor, trailing from the window: a yellow-ish, sickly light, too bright for stars.

The woman in the bed opposite Rose's had the look of ill-gotten age, of years worn into her by exhaustion, or fear. It gave her a kind of agelessness. She had thin, straggly blond hair, and bright gray eyes: no magic, then.

"Tara didn't tell me your name," said Rose, quietly.

"Why do you want it?"

"You know mine. It's only fair."

Humor edged her voice, but clearly the woman didn't hear it.

"Fairness doesn't come into this."

Rose gave her a grim smile. "I know."

"You want to save him," said the woman. It sounded like a statement, but the upward inflection in her voice hinted at doubt. "That's why you're here."

"Yes."

"He will never be acquitted," said the woman. "They can prove he is a Hybrid. You do accept that."

Rose was silent, watching her.

"You don't," said the woman, slowly.

"Does this matter?"

"More than anything. If you've come to me, that means you think *I* could be of some use in saving him, that I have some information to give, and if I'm going to do that, I want to know what *saving him* would mean. What would you want? His life? His freedom?"

Rose said nothing. Then, after a long silence, the woman said, "My name is Cassandra Mayhew. Did Tara tell you I would be willing to help?"

"She said you could."

"Did she say why?"

Again Rose kept her silence. The woman's gaze intensified.

"I don't believe your father is a good man," she said, after a moment.

"You don't have to believe it. You just have to say it."

"In court? In front of a judge and jury? Under oath?"

Rose did not reply.

"I don't understand," said the woman, quietly. "They said he raised you in the Department of the Maintenance of Public Order and the Protection of Justice. I thought you would care about what was right. I thought you would be troubled by innocence and guilt."

"Not his," said Rose.

The woman seemed to have no reply to this. She simply watched Rose with unsettling concentration, but Rose had gone beyond being unsettled.

"Listen," she said sharply, "will you help or not?"

A silence.

"Why should I?" asked Cassandra Mayhew, her voice firmer now. "Why should I risk myself for him?"

Rose's voice was hard. "I don't know," she said. "I was hoping you would do it out of the goodness of your heart."

– Chapter 10 –

Nine years earlier (age 27)
May 5, 10:09 a.m.

On Malia's first day back in the office, she sits in a wheelchair facing the computers. Her husband, Connor, is beside her at all times, helping her when she isn't strong enough to push the wheels. Her eyes still don't focus properly. The concussion she sustained was serious, but they hope the damage won't be permanent. Rose has been trying to cheer her up all day, telling her amusing stories and long-lost anecdotes of missions that went wrong and so forth, but Malia doesn't seem to see the girl, and she certainly doesn't laugh.

"Oh, thank God," says Laura, closing the office door behind her. "Report's back on that squad team we sent to arrest the weapons smuggler. He had all kinds of stuff in his place. Tried to fight them off with machine guns."

"Christ," says Connor, alarmed. "Are they alive?"

"Yes, thank the Angels. One of them has a bullet graze, but she can walk. They got pictures of his accomplices, though."

She brings them up on the screen. They are vague, blurred photographs, not clear enough to determine even whether the subjects are Gifted, Ashkind, or Leeched.

"Can we track them?" asks Connor.

"Not with so little information, no." David sits down in his chair. "We just have to hope they pop up again. Weapons smugglers are a restless lot. I doubt we'll have to wait long."

A soft noise comes from the corner. They look over, and Malia is sitting in her wheelchair, eyes fixed on the screen. Tears roll down her face slowly, as if she were not aware of them. She doesn't speak. She looks pitiful, sitting there crying. No one, not even her husband, can do anything but watch.

There is a long, long silence.

<<< >>>

In the morning, the woman had been taken away, and Nate and Maria sat at the end of Rose's bed.

"Can we just have one day," said Maria exasperatedly, "*one day*, when no one gets hurt?"

Rose's wounds were sufficiently healed for her to shrug.

"You can come home," said Nate. "Or . . ."

"I'm going to the trial."

"That's a bad idea."

"I'm fine, Nate."

He and Maria glanced at each other.

"What?" asked Rose angrily, and Nate, after a slight hesitation, pulled down the television over her bed so that she could see it, and pressed play.

"The trial of David Elmsworth reached new dramatic heights yesterday as his closest friend delivered a scathing testimony against him."

It was Oliver Keen. He stood outside the courthouse, looking somber. Rose stared at Nate blankly.

"His 'closest friend'?"

"He means my father," said Nate, heavily.

"What?"

"Along with statements to the court that David Elmsworth had always displayed psychopathic tendencies, Colonel Connor Terrian shed new light on Elmsworth's troubled and possibly abusive relationship with his adopted daughter."

Rose was by now utterly unable to speak. This seemed to unsettle Nate and Maria more than shock or fury would have done. They glanced at each other. Oliver Keen kept talking.

"Colonel Terrian told the judge that Elmsworth's maltreatment of his daughter started at a very young age, possibly from infancy, as he brainwashed her into keeping his terrible secrets even from those she most trusted, including —"

"Here I come," said Nate, grimly.

"— the Colonel's young son, who lost his mother, Malia, in suspicious circumstances nine years ago — circumstances that allowed David Elmsworth to rise to power within the Department, which he held, by all accounts, with an iron fist. What other horrifying secrets we will see emerge from this trial, no one knows. But for Rosalyn Elmsworth, now just days away from adulthood, his conviction might just be a rescue."

The report ended. Rose lay silent for a very long time. Nate and Maria watched her apprehensively. Then she grasped the IV stand and tried to heave herself out of bed. They scrambled forward and pushed her back down immediately.

"Do *not* try to stop me," she growled at them, still struggling to get out of the bed.

"Rose," said Maria quietly, "you can't make everyone believe your version of the truth."

"It's not *my version* of the truth! It's *the* truth, Maria. It's what actually happened, and he's just — lying! He said . . ." She couldn't bring herself to repeat any of it. "How can anyone believe these, these stupid, horrible, moronic bloody *lies*?"

"Because they could be true," said Nate. "The public don't know your father. They don't love him like you do. To them, Rose, this is just a juicy scandal."

"I don't —"

"I know you don't understand. You couldn't understand, because you're at the center of this. But, Rose, believe me, to the rest of the world, Oliver Keen looks far more credible than you or your father. Even if you tried to tell them the truth, they wouldn't believe you."

"I don't care if they believe me. I just want him to *shut up*."

"If you really didn't care, you wouldn't mind if he shut up or not. Rose, listen to me. You're just going to have to get used to this."

"How can you *say* that? How can you even imagine I could *possibly* get used to this?"

Nate finally snapped. "Don't act like you're the only one hurt by this. Weren't you listening, Rose? That report was about my father's testimony. Keen just called him the closest friend of the most hated man in the country. He implied that your dad benefited, somehow, from Mum dying. Next report he'll probably be telling the world your father killed my mother."

"But it isn't tr —"

"Don't insult my intelligence. Of course I know it isn't true. My point is that my family is just as caught up in this as yours. Maria has a sister in Regency." Rose saw Maria stiffen out of the corner of her eye. "A journalist from the *Letter* has been sitting outside James's parents' house. *Everyone* is being hurt by this case, Rose, not just you, and you don't see us threatening to kill the people doing it. Act like an adult for once and take it on the chin."

Rose stared at Nate in astonishment. He glared down at her, and then turned on his heel and left. Maria kissed Rose on the cheek and sat down beside her.

"It will be okay," she said gently. "These things don't last forever."

Then she left.

The ward was silent. Rose looked bleakly over at the empty bed where Cassandra Mayhew had lain last night. She was looking increasingly like David's last hope.

Rose couldn't bear that thought. She closed her eyes.

<<< >>>

Nine years earlier (age 27)
April 17, 6:33 p.m.

The office empties slowly. It has been an uneventful week; their days have been mostly taken up with chasing down old criminals and narrowing down the Wanted lists, with little success. David is exhausted. He has his feet up on his desk and his eyes closed when Rose comes up to him.

"Can we go home, Dad?"

It is the night of their transformation, but they still have a few hours to go. She is pale and terrified and trembling, small and silent, full of dread. He has no energy to console her, and nothing reassuring to say. Clearly, "it'll be all right" does not hold any weight.

"Give me a few minutes. Wait for me in the lobby."

She nods and leaves. He tries to go to sleep again.

The shot goes over his head and he nearly falls off his seat. The second bullet comes much closer, and he scrambles to the floor, reaches for his gun. He knows with absolute certainty that Malia is shooting at him. Of course it would be Malia; no one else is in the office, and at any rate he has always approved of Malia's way of doing things. Kill them first. Don't keep them alive to tell them your cunning plan.

Of course, he never imagined her methods would ever be directed against him.

He goes for his own gun, scrabbling in the drawer, and the third bullet hits his hand. He cries out in shock and pain and falls to the floor. Malia is standing over him, gun pointed at his head.

"Am I allowed last words?" he asks, lying there, letting the blood soak into his shirt. The agony is a physical thing, constricting his throat.

"No," she says.

She fires again, but she misses because her hands are shaking. Anger, he suspects, rather than any kind of nerves, or reluctance to kill him.

"Damn you to hell," she says. "I should have done this years ago. It was a mistake to even hire you."

"You know, then?"

"Of course I know."

Another wobbly shot. He tries to focus so that the handle of her gun goes white-hot, but she is Gifted, too. She narrows her eyes and his bullet wound starts to burn. The pain is intolerable. He screams.

"You bastard," she says. "You think I don't watch you? The way you act? I followed you into your house, I saw you preparing for tonight. You — how dare you — you've been near my *son*!"

"I was never going to harm him, Malia."

"I don't care whether or not you *wanted* to. You are a monster."

He kicks at her ankles and she stumbles back, trying to fire again. He swallows.

"You're going to kill Rose, too?" he asks, with a slight tense smile.

She doesn't answer. He's trying to find his gun on the floor, and then his good hand closes around it. He raises it but doesn't fire.

"Drop the gun, Malia."

She drops it after a moment, her eyes dark with fury. That's when he knows he's won. She doesn't really want to kill him if she doesn't have to.

He gets to his feet slowly, trailing black stains along the carpet.

"I don't want to hurt anyone," he says hoarsely.

"Yes you do — you bastard, you psychopath. You pathetic self-centered monster."

He pauses, and tries not to kill her. "Are we going to be able to talk this over?"

"I'm going to kill you."

"My daughter is downstairs. You are very, *very* lucky if no one heard those shots, but if she finds me dead, and you standing over me with my blood on your hands, you will die. No one wants that. I admit, it's particularly bad for me as a premise, and if you kill me I won't be much predisposed to care about your well-being, but I don't want Rose to have to kill someone. She's only seven years old. And she'll do it. Believe me. It might take her years, but she'll do it. She'll hunt down whoever kills me."

Malia is breathing very fast. She's looking around for ways to kill him. She doesn't care about what he's saying.

"Look at it this way," he tells her, with bite in his tone. "You know what I am, yes? That I'm not quite human? That — in your words — I'm a monster?"

That makes her look at him. It is always strange to them when they hear him say it, so calmly, as if it doesn't matter.

He's waiting for an answer.

"Yes," says Malia.

"So is Rose," he says.

It takes her a second to process this, and her mouth falls open. He follows her thoughts, tracing the pictures of the screaming, smoke-skinned, white-eyed, clawed, brutal monster; compressing it; trying to find a way of visualizing it bursting out of the small girl, changing her body and her mind. Seeing it hiding *inside* her, somewhere deep in the corners of the child. She can't imagine it.

He drops the gun at last and sits down at his desk. With his good hand he opens the drawer and takes out a pair of tweezers and some antiseptic. He pauses for a second and then rips off a strip of fabric from his shirt, folds it and bites down on it. He clenches his injured hand so that he can see the gray-blue gleam of the bullet, wipes the tweezers with antiseptic, and slowly, slowly, begins to draw it out.

It is, unsurprisingly, excruciating.

"Her, too?" asks Malia softly, incredulous. "She's a monster like you?"

He nods.

"How long . . . ?"

The bullet clatters onto the wooden desk, and he puts the bloody tweezers down before taking the cloth out of his mouth.

"Since I found her."

Malia is silent for a moment. "That's why you adopted her."

"It's all making sense now, isn't it?"

She is silent. "I can't believe I trusted you."

He blocks her out, summons his concentration and begins to heal himself. Luckily for him, the wound carved in him by the bullet is extraordinarily clean. When it seals up, the flesh almost melts together, leaving a thin white scar tracing the impact. He passes his other hand over the scar and that too is gone.

"To be honest," he says, "neither can I."

He moves very quickly, and in three blows — leg, ankle, side of the neck — she has fallen. She was off-guard, and he is two inches taller than her, not to mention twenty kilos heavier. He is vicious. He uses all the power he has left in him.

She falls onto the desk and her head smashes into the wood. She lies there silent, twitching.

He kneels beside her.

"Malia," he says, softly. "Listen to me. Whatever you might think of us, we haven't changed. We were always like this."

She looks horrified. No, worse than that, she is breathless with fear, her eyes unfocused and flickering.

He sighs, and gets up to go to his drawer again. The memory serum is there, ready for almost precisely this occasion. He knew that one day he would have to use it.

He did not suspect how soon, or on whom.

He bends low and slides the needle into Malia's vein. Her breaths become short, hoarse and rapid as she watches the clear white liquid slide into her blood. As her eyes flutter and close, he bends over her. Now is the time to tell her the truth.

"We are not monsters," he tells her, and then she goes to sleep.

He walks over to the intercom and tries to make his voice low and panicked.

"Excuse me? Yes. We need help, here. There's been an accident . . ."

– Chapter 11 –

Witness number two for the prosecution was Lieutenant James Andreas.

Rose's conversation with Maria and Loren about going to see him had been very short.

"I'm going."

"No, you're not."

"I'm going."

"No, you're not."

In the end they had relented. The mark from the man's knife was almost gone now.

James shifted on the witness stand.

"I swear —"

Rose blocked her ears before she could hear him promise to tell the truth. It was too painful to hear the oath taken so soon before it would be broken.

If Terrian could butcher the facts in front of a jury, James most definitely could.

Teller stood up. He was not smiling this time.

"What were your first impressions of David Elmsworth?"

"The first time I met him," said James, "he was deciding whether or not my life was worth saving."

"When was this?"

"I was kidnapped by a Demon. A spy for the Department gone rogue. This was . . . oh, just under two years ago. I was a trainee soldier."

"And what did you think of Elmsworth then?"

"Well," said James with a wry smile, "I liked him, at first, since he decided to keep my heart beating."

"And after that?"

"He was a good leader—a good Department head. He had a lot of kindness in him, and a lot of violence, but he only took out the violence on the people he hunted down."

Teller's tone hardened, perhaps annoyed that James wasn't being vicious enough. "When he spoke of the Department Wanted lists—those whom he was trying to capture—did he ever mention the possibility of killing them?"

James nodded. "That was always a possibility if they resisted."

"Did he go into any detail?"

"He would talk about how it would be done. He liked the idea of bleeding them."

An appalled silence. David leaned back in his chair, his eyes closed. He did not react.

"And do you now," said Teller, "have any other evidence to give, Lieutenant Andreas?"

"Yes," said James, "I do."

He took a USB from his pocket and gave it to Teller, who plugged it into the laptop in front of him. The projector above them lit up. Slowly, the beginnings of a picture began to form on the opposite wall. Rose stared at it blankly.

"If you will, Lieutenant Andreas," said Teller softly.

James folded his hands behind his head and looked up at Rose in the gallery. She looked back at him impassively. He sighed.

"Unlock," he said loudly. "Play."

The laptop beeped, and the video started. On the wall, running through the Department, was David. He was younger — perhaps thirty — and there was no gray in his hair or lines on his face. The camera was positioned just above the lobby. It showed him pushing his way through the gathered office workers, toward the glass doors. Someone put out a hand to stop him and he turned, hands clenched as if about to attack. There was something visibly wild in his eyes.

"David, stop."

His refusal did not need words. His colleague sighed, and handed him a gun. David turned away without thanks.

A whispered conversation at the edge of the frame.

"I don't —"

"No."

"I can handle myself perfectly."

"No, you can't. Let your father do this on his own."

Max — a now-retired subordinate of her father's — and a young, fierce Rose, ten or eleven, arguing with him. She wanted to go out and help him. She would have thought herself capable of beating a grown man in a fight. Of course, she would have been wrong. The painful obviousness of this fact weighed heavily on the Rose sitting in the gallery.

Nate, beside her, leaned over. "Do you remember this?"

Rose said nothing. She had a terrible feeling that she might.

David—the younger David—pushed through the doors, and now the angle had changed; another camera watched him from above. It must have been positioned on the outside wall of the building, because they could see the gray pavement laid out beneath David's feet like some twisted, cracked field, and the faint roars of Westminster cars in the distance.

Three angry, gray-eyed, gray-faced men stood before him. They had knives and guns, but they did not use them. They watched David warily.

"This is who they send out?" asked their leader. He had a rough voice, a rough face. "The intern?"

"Guess again."

"You're the one who makes the tea."

David was silent. Incredulous anger flickered briefly across his face. His hands opened and closed again. The court watched him on the video, tense.

Rose leaned over to Nate in the pause and said quietly, with heavy apprehension, "I think this is the Reynolds incident."

Nate's eyes widened.

After a long time, the video-David said quietly, "Why do you hate us?"

"You're tyrants."

"Only to those on whom we have to exercise our power."

"We will not be moved on this."

"I didn't think you would. And now you're going to kill me, correct?"

"Oh, yes."

"That's going to hurt."

"Yes, it will." An evil grin. "You'll scream."

David sighed. He turned around, perfectly at ease, so that the camera could see the gun on his waist.

"Open the doors," he said.

They slid aside, so the attackers could see the office workers gathered there. There were perhaps forty of them: all strong, lithe, Gifted and armed. David turned back to the Ashkind criminals.

"So why," he said, "with all of them on my side, have I come out here alone?"

The Ashkind attacked. Despite herself, Rose couldn't help watching the footage analytically. One at a time: first mistake. Using knives: second mistake. Triangular formation, two of them trying to flank him: third mistake. The first one was put down with a gunshot to the stomach — lots of blood and screaming. The second went for David's stomach with the knife and this one did hit, went deep, and David moved before the pain could stop him. Sweep to the legs, hard. The whole force of his fists on his attacker's chin. The man stumbled. David moved forward. The blood was soaking his shirt now. David's hands went hot with magic, and he grabbed the man's neck and kept squeezing as his attacker began to scream. Began, and did not stop.

"David —"

Max came out of the glass doors. The third attacker had dropped his knife and was running.

"David, you can't —"

A low hissing sound: burning flesh.

"David, let him go!"

It took a long time for David to hear him. His shirt was soaked crimson from the wound in his stomach now, and the man had long stopped screaming by the time David dropped him. He hit the floor and stayed there. There was no possibility of him still being alive.

David fell to his knees at last, his bloodstained hands pressed to the stab wound in his stomach. Max looked aghast.

"David . . ."

The image froze on Max and her father and the dead man, and it became clear that the video had ended there. Rose jumped to her feet, outraged. The court could not just see Reynolds's death. They had to see David checking his pulse. They had to see the ambulance come, and David in hospital with that stomach wound, and his brief appearance at Reynolds's funeral. They had to see all of what she remembered. But as Teller turned back to James, it became clear they were not going to.

Rose sat down slowly. She was shaking again.

"Lieutenant Andreas, do you believe that man had to die?"

"No."

"Do you believe that anyone apart from David Elmsworth caused his death?"

"No."

"Do you believe that his actions were deserving of the painful death he clearly met?"

"No."

"Do you believe that David Elmsworth suffered mentally because he killed this man?"

James glanced at David, who had not opened his eyes since the start of the video, apparently oblivious to all that was going on around him. "No."

"Do you believe that he would hesitate to kill someone he wanted dead or who he believed should die?"

"No."

"And do you believe," he said softly, "that this act was evil?"

James glanced briefly up at Rose. In the instant their eyes met, she was frozen to the spot, because she knew what he was going to say, and she could not believe it.

"Yes," he said.

Teller looked around at the court. The looks of horror had not left their faces.

"No further questions," he said softly.

"I tried. I tried."

Madeleine stood outside the court, muttering half to herself.

"I tried to get him to retract it."

"I know," said Rose quietly.

"I tried to take it apart —"

"I know."

"But against that sort of character evidence . . ."

Rose stood against the wall and tried to get herself to think.

"No more character testimony," said Madeleine. "That's it. They think they have his conviction. And now they want his death."

"He'll never come out of there, will he?" said Rose quietly. It was the first time she had thought it, let alone said it. "Not alive."

Madeleine looked at her.

"There is always hope," she said, but her voice felt heavy on the cold winter air.

– Chapter 12 –

Fourteen years earlier (age 22)
May 3, 4:54 p.m.

"Are you ready?"

The target is a house. He didn't expect this. In his mind the militia was based in a huge office block, or an impenetrable ware-house. Not . . . this.

He glances at Malia. "You expect me to back out?"

She shrugs. "I don't know. Did you do a lot of this sort of thing, in your day?"

The War is ending: they have known this for many months now. The Angels and their Gifted compatriots — the Department's employers — are winning, and sooner or later some kind of truce will have to be reached. Once there is any peace to keep, any remaining fighters will officially become terrorists, and the Department will be able to go after them with impunity.

For now, however, they can't hunt down whole armies: they just don't have the supplies or troops to be able to provoke the entire London branch of Regency. They have to destroy the neutral criminals, those few bands of drug smugglers or traffickers who don't care about the outcome of the War so long as they profit.

God, he can't wait until the War is over.

"My day was two years ago, as you never cease to remind me."

"Yes, well." Malia leans back into her seat. They have ridden here in a police car, alone. Two squad teams — bands of well-trained ex-soldiers, heavily armed — are in vans around the corner. "You seem unsettled."

"I was expecting something less . . . innocent."

"Appearances can be deceptive."

"Yes, thank you, I was aware. Look up and to your left."

She does. "What?"

"Window. You see?"

Someone inside has noticed the police car. A burly Ashkind man is standing in the window, gun pointed at the car door. Their windows are tinted, so he won't be able to see who is inside.

"Do not," he tells her, "get out of the car."

She rolls her eyes. "How much magic can you do?"

"At the moment? Enough."

"Can you make that window explode in his face?"

"I thought we wanted to take them alive."

"He'll live."

"Says the doctor's wife. Those glass shards will explode into his face, Malia, from two inches away. If they don't get his brain, and they will, he'll lose his eyes and a lot of blood. He might live, but he'll be a vegetable. We certainly wouldn't be able to try him."

"Then what do *you* suggest we do?"

He thinks for a minute, and pushes himself against his seat. She sits forward, alarmed. "David. What are you going to do?"

"Get in the back of the car."

"What? David, you can't."

"Get in the back. I'm going to open the door and he can't see you or he'll shoot."

"David Elmsworth, don't you dare. That's an order. From the Head of the Department."

"Oh, good try."

"You insolent bastard. If you get yourself killed, what will Rose do?"

That thought stops him for a moment. His daughter is nearly two and a half, and, the abomination that she is, would kill anyone non-monstrous who tried to raise her. How would she grow up, without him? Violent and true to her inner demons? Angry, suicidal, full of self-loathing? Would she remember him?

"She would survive," he says, and this is certainly true. "Get in the back of the car, Malia."

"You're insane."

"You want this cartel destroyed, or not? We deal with them now or they attack the Department base. They'll know we're on to them now that we've come here."

She pauses, and then climbs into the back of the car, muttering.

"You know what? I don't care if you die."

"Just you keep telling yourself that."

He opens the door and steps out of the car, shutting the door quickly so the marksman does not catch sight of Malia. The sniper in the window does not fire. David meets his eyes, straightening his jacket. The Ashkind man's eyes widen.

David walks up to the door. It is opened before he gets there by an astonished-looking gray-eyed woman, staring up at him. She too has a gun in her hand.

"Get out of the way," he tells her, very gently.

She is openmouthed with fear. He raises his hand, and the handle of the gun turns white-hot. She screams and drops it, and then she runs into the house. He steps inside and closes the door behind him.

"It's all right," he calls to them. "I don't mean you harm."

Panicked muttering from up the stairs. They're frightened, of course, because Regency's Angels of Death, David Elmsworth and Loren Arkwood, are the nightmare of every soldier — especially Elmsworth, the quiet one, the one who made the weapons that killed them in their hundreds, the one around whom the more terrible rumors circulate. Never mind that he left Regency years ago. Never mind that he hasn't played this part in just as long.

This is amusing. This is really very amusing.

He comes up onto the landing. They are gathered to meet him — five Ashkind men of varying sizes and the woman. Three of them have guns. Clearly, they are hesitant about firing at him. Perhaps they think he can stop bullets. A laughable idea, but Ashkind rarely know much about magic, except that they hate it.

For effect, he looks up at the lightbulbs, makes them flicker ominously.

"Come on," he says, smiling. "Don't be afraid."

He holds out his hands, sending heat coursing over his palms. One of the men comes forward, uncertain, and takes his hand. His fingers are shaking; he seems not to be able to control himself. The moment he touches David's hand, his skin starts to sizzle. He shrieks in pain, but David grips his hand tightly, his grip merciless, until the flesh starts to melt. He keeps walking forward, letting the man drop gracelessly to the floor, whimpering.

"What are you?" asks the woman in a whisper.

He doesn't answer, but gets out his gun from his back pocket. He holds it out in front of him, other hand raised to shoulder height, as if about to drop it. Then he fires four shots into their ankles. They scream and fall. He bends down and takes their weapons from their flailing hands.

He goes to the window of the house and opens it, ignoring the cries behind him.

"You can get out now," he calls down to her. Malia climbs slowly out of the car. Her gaze is perfectly steady and does not leave his face, but he cannot read her expression, and this troubles him.

"You're alive," she says.

"Surprised?"

She looks up at him, at his jacket and his gun, and considers. "No," she says. "Disappointed."

<<< >>>

A knock on the door. Loren opened it with his gun in his hand.

"Who the hell are you?" she heard him ask wearily. His right arm, she knew, was still in a sling.

Rose lurked behind him, watching. She edged warily into view, and saw Tara Priestley standing in the doorway, looking exhausted and angry. Her eyes were on Loren's weapon.

"Loren. It's fine. I know her."

"She's not a journalist?"

"She's not a journalist."

Loren scrutinized her, eyes narrowed. "You trust her?"

Rose nodded and, after a short pause, Loren walked away toward the kitchen. Rose came outside to stand beside Tara and shut the door.

"Do you want to walk?"

They wandered for a while down the streets and alleyways in silence, away from the low, constant hum of the roads.

"Your trust is easily gained," said Tara, after a few minutes.

"Is Mayhew talking?"

"She is. She's not convinced."

"But if *she* doesn't give evidence —"

"Then your father will be convicted and sentenced to death."

Rose rounded on her. "Don't say that."

"You don't like the truth?"

"It isn't the truth yet," said Rose. She was burning with anger again; the familiarity of the feeling was beginning to weary her.

Tara said nothing for a moment. Then:

"You don't want Loren Arkwood to know about this yet. About Cassandra Mayhew."

It was not a question, so Rose did not answer it.

"Why not? Don't you trust him?"

"I did," said Rose slowly. Tara looked at her sharply.

"And then what happened?"

"It's not just that he doesn't think Dad will survive this," said

Rose. "It's that I don't think he wants him to. I think Loren wants Dad to be found guilty and sentenced to death. And I . . ." She scratched the back of her neck. "I had to choose between them once before," she said eventually. "I chose against my father. I won't again, not ever. Not even if it means endangering Loren. Or abandoning him."

Tara was still staring at her.

"Do you think it will come to that?"

"I gave up making predictions a long time ago," said Rose grimly.

Another silence.

"What will you do, when this is over?"

Rose twisted her fingers around the back of her neck. "I don't know," she said. "I don't know how it will turn out."

"Everyone else thinks they do."

"Everyone else," said Rose tightly, "is wrong."

"The words of a crazy person."

Rose tilted her head back, and stared bleakly up at the sky.

"Don't do anything stupid to try to save him."

"Does this not count as stupid? Asking Cassandra Mayhew to testify?"

Tara considered. "It's unlikely it will work," she said, "but that doesn't mean that it's stupid to try."

"If he dies," said Rose — she had never said the words aloud before, and they hurt just as much as she had thought they would — "if they kill him, do you think I should leave?"

"What do you mean? Leave London?"

Rose said nothing.

"You're talking about leaving your life," said Tara. "Leaving your name, your identity. Starting a new life somewhere else and not being Rose Elmsworth."

"He's my only family."

"He's not the only person who loves you, surely."

"I used to think that, too," said Rose. "But they'll find out what I am, one day, all of them. It's only really a matter of time. And they won't love me then. It will change who they think I am. I won't *be* Rose Elmsworth anymore. I'll just be a monster, and a monster's daughter."

Tara looked at her for a moment.

"You think too little of them," she said, after a moment.

"If they hate Dad, they can hate me."

"You are not your father."

Rose looked at her sharply. They stood for a moment in silence in the grip of the winter cold.

<<< >>>

Fifteen years earlier (age 21)
June 4, 11:18 a.m.

They are on a beach, he and the girl. The sand is glittering in the sunshine, and she steps onto it tentatively, as if worried it might swallow her whole. She has not, he thinks, seen sand before: when it absorbs her foot, she shrieks and tries to step back, only to slip and fall into it. She screams, and then, when it doesn't suck her down into its depths, stops, astonished. She lifts a handful of sand up, watches it twirl in streams through her small fingers, and then she smiles — wide and white-toothed and delighted. He steps forward and lifts her up from the sand, balances her on his arm so she is tucked away from gravity, head beside the curve of his neck and his shoulder like Laura taught him. She is very light.

"You like it?"

She nods, suddenly shy. He looks around and sees that there are other families on the beach, hundreds upon hundreds of them, some of them with children her age. She is eighteen months old now; she treats it like some kind of achievement, and he does not tell her otherwise. This is War, after all.

"You can play with them if you want," he says, "but you mustn't use magic, or tell them anything about yourself except your name. All right? And if anyone offers you anything, or tries to take you anywhere, you come back to me."

She nods. "Love you, Dad," she says unexpectedly, and he knows it is the closest she will come to saying that she is afraid. He kisses her on the cheek.

"The children won't hurt you," he says. "It's the grown-ups you need to keep an eye on."

He puts her down onto the sand and she walks unsteadily away. She is not confident, but neither does she look back at him.

She is small and jewel-bright and beautiful — or that is how he sees her, anyway. Her name is Rosalyn; she started speaking eight months ago, but she cannot quite pronounce it, so she calls herself "Rose." He is trying to train that out of her.

She knows what she is, of course, and what it means, and though she hates it she is curious, as all children are. But he has not told her as much as he would like to, not yet. She is far too young to know everything. He will hide her from the whole truth for as long as he can.

Her magic bubbles up from her unbidden sometimes: sudden

fires when she is upset, or objects knocked over in tantrums. He has taught her to use and control it as best he can, but there is only so much he can teach her, given her age. He brings her into the office; he has seen her wandering around, watching silently as he and his colleagues try to impose law on a war zone. She knows that they live in a War, but does not really know what that means.

She does not know about the Angels, either, though he knows they have been paying attention to her. They are cooped up in the Houses of Parliament, all the army leaders, and David's small bureaucratic unit is the way they watch the civilian population, to keep as many people as safe as possible. They have begun to watch the rising stars — David, Malia, and Laura. All three of them have small children, and Malia's and Laura's husbands are both on the front line. Connor is a medic, and David can see from Malia's growing distress that it is beginning to break him. If the Angels ever want to get to her, they have ready-made leverage — Connor and Nathaniel.

If they ever want to get to David . . .

Rosalyn has befriended a little blond Pretender girl, and together they are watching the sea in fascination. Rosalyn has never seen it before. This is her first holiday: they are up north, on the eastern coast, where he used to come with his parents as a child. Since the power came back on, city families have been slowly trickling northward, into the open spaces and the country-side, where the guerrillas don't come. He cannot leave London for any great length of time, of course, not with the Department so low on troops, but it is at least refreshing to see that there are parts of the world the War cannot touch.

Rosalyn and the girl move cautiously toward the sea. When the wave comes back toward them, the girl screams and runs;

Rosalyn gasps softly as the cold water rushes over her feet, but she does not move. She crouches slowly as the wave moves out again, digging her fingers into the sand so that the water streams through them in thick silver ropes. She watches in fascination as the wave rears, and crests, and surges toward her, and she kneels in preparation, and she waits.

– Chapter 13 –

A camera flashed in her face and Rose stopped.

She had been on her way to the prison and, knowing there was a risk they would be waiting for her there, had taken precautions: big jacket, scarf around her face, head down. Not enough. Never enough.

Oliver Keen stood on the edge of the street, watching her intently.

Do not respond. Keep walking.

"What do you want?" she asked, as calmly as she could.

He walked over to her, and she had to quell the urge to run away. She had nothing to fear from this man. He was a journalist, not a fighter.

"I don't want anything," he said. "I give the story to the public, nothing more."

"You've been lying to them."

"I can only do my best with the facts I am given, Rosalyn," he said. "Perhaps, if you would be willing to clarify things for me . . ."

"No. Never in a million years would I tell you anything."

He regarded her sternly. "You're very small-minded for someone so young."

"How dare you. The things you've said about me, about my father —"

"Absolute proven fact."

Magic. Guns. Her own fists. She could hurt him with all of these, but that would only fuel the flames this man had lit. "You are ignorant and stupid and cruel."

He paused. "Have you ever heard the saying, Rosalyn, that the job of a journalist is to speak truth to power?"

"Of course I have."

"You forget, young woman," he said tersely, "that in this situation you have the power."

She stood there speechless for a long time. He smiled at the look on her face, and walked off, swinging his microphone from his wrist like a pistol.

Teller looked exhausted. When he stood, he seemed to stumble slightly.

"The prosecution calls its next witness," he said.

The witness was Evelyn Wood of the Anti-Corruption Commission. The job of the ACC, as Rose had learned all too well last year, was to make sure the Government's record and reputation were as clean as possible. They had had regular contact with David throughout his career; the Elmsworth scandal, as it was now known, was the biggest failure in their history.

The ACC and the Department had always been enemies, and Rose counted the fact that David's discovery had damaged them as one of the very few upsides to this situation; but nonetheless, there was no denying the fact that when Evelyn looked at David — still, to the untrained eye, maintaining the appearance of uninterested calm — there was deep and very personal hatred in her eyes.

"Ms. Wood," asked Teller, "do you believe that the defendant is a Hybrid?"

"Yes, I do. The evidence leaves no doubt."

Rose glanced across at Madeleine. She seemed very tense. Rose knew she was waiting for the witness to say something objectionable. But Evelyn Wood was no ordinary witness: she was from the ACC, and she would know how to navigate a court case. Rose realized with a sinking heart that Madeleine had very few options here; Wood was unlikely to retract anything under cross-examination.

"And do you believe, Ms. Wood, that the defendant is an evil man?"

"I do."

Teller leaned forward conspiratorially — as if he and Wood were alone together, and not in a vast, echoing, cold courtroom, with David and Madeleine and Rose and Nate and Ichor knew how many court journalists and artists watching them.

"And in your respected opinion," he said, "what punishment should be inflicted on this man?"

Evelyn looked at David coldly. He had his eyes fixed on the ceiling and appeared not to be listening.

"He has betrayed his Government," she said calmly. "He has betrayed all those he promised to protect. He has lied at every turn, in order to keep himself safe. The man is, in every sense of the word, a monster. He is far too dangerous to be allowed to live. He is far too evil to be allowed even to *think*. There is no question about it. He must die."

<<< >>>

Sixteen years earlier (age 19)
January 21, 9:34 p.m.

They click off their safeties instantly, but they don't shoot. He stands in front of them, pale, shivering in the rain, wearing his full Regency uniform for the first time in months, the child cradled in his arms. He is still terrified of dropping it.

The guards stare at him.

"Elmsworth?" one of them asks, uncertainly.

He nods. He has brought no weapons; appearing unthreatening is key to the plan, but he suddenly feels very vulnerable. "Please," he says. "She'll get pneumonia."

He nods, a jerky sort of movement, at the baby. The guards follow his gaze, and their mouths fall open. The child is staring up at him with its intent olive-green eyes, raindrops condensing like beads of crystal on its face; it takes no notice of the guns. It does not even know what a firearm is. He envies it.

"Elmsworth," says the guard weakly, "what the hell are you playing at?"

"Please, let me in." He does not look behind them at the Regency base, looming dark and threatening above him; he knows it will do little for his nerves. "I need to speak to Felix."

At the familiarity the guards' grips tighten on their guns. "The Commander has given orders relating to you."

"Do they involve my execution?"

A pause. "No."

"My arrest? My imprisonment?"

Another pause. "If you appear, you are to be escorted under armed guard to the Commander."

So Felix wants to kill him in person.

"Then our aims are similar. By all means escort me to him, with whatever arms you please. I really don't care. I just need to talk to him."

They glance at each other. After two days' unauthorized absence, after Felix's first attempt on his life, High Command probably doubted he would ever return to Regency, unless it were to mount an attack; had David left it another forty-eight hours, the guards most likely would have received orders to shoot him on sight, instead of leading him directly to Felix. If he did appear, they would have expected him confident, cocky, holding all the aces. Not like . . . this.

They most certainly will not have expected the child.

"All right, then," says the guard, warily, and with a jab of his gun, three of his fellows dart around to press guns into David's back. The other two point at his chest. The guard hesitates, and then holds out his arms for the child.

"Give it to me."

"No."

"Elmsworth . . ."

"You will not win this argument, Lieutenant."

The guard looks at him, at the fire in his eyes, at the way he clutches the child — this monster child, who transformed last night and nearly killed him, and whom, therefore, being of his kind, he cannot now abandon — and sighs.

"You aren't doing much to make us trust you, Elmsworth."

"I don't need your trust."

The guard's eyes narrow, and he turns around and walks inside without another word. No sooner has David set foot in the lobby than Felix himself appears, looking furious, flanked by Arkwood. The guards stand to attention immediately, and David, despite himself, relaxes slightly as he feels the pressure of the guns against his back disappear.

"Ah," says Felix, quietly enough to make David very, very tense.

"Commander . . . he just showed up . . ."

"Leave us," says Arkwood. Like Felix, his gaze is fixed on David's face.

"But, sir."

"Do not question me," says Arkwood, in that same soft voice, and the guards, looking very disgruntled, salute again, and march back outside. David has no doubt they will stand as close as they can to the entrance, trying desperately to overhear the conversation.

There is a long pause.

"Why have you come back?" asks Felix.

The child in David's arms makes a small sort of mewling noise, still staring unblinkingly up at him, and Felix's eyes snap down to its face. He takes a step backward — an actual, physical step backward — and stares, eyes wide, at the baby.

"What the *hell* is that?" he asks, with something approaching horror.

Arkwood's reaction does not betray the same shock as Felix's. He pales slightly at the sight of the child, but says nothing.

"Felix," says David quietly, "you don't have to kill me. I'll leave. I'm leaving and I'm not coming back. Are you going to try to stop me?"

Felix looks up at David again instantly. There is a long moment where the two men stare at each other, and neither blinks. Then Felix says, levelly, "I can't let you leave Regency, David."

He could have just run. He could have left. After Felix tried to kill him, that is what they probably expected. But then they would have sent people after him, and he can't allow that.

But Felix can't let him leave here alive, either, knowing as much as he does.

So here they stand.

"He's come prepared," says Arkwood quietly, his eyes on David. "He's been preparing this for a long time. He knew he would have to leave."

Felix doesn't look at Arkwood. "Is he right, David?" he asks quietly.

David takes a small black remote out of his pocket, shifting his grip carefully so that the child is not disturbed; he does not want it to start crying. Felix's hand twitches toward his gun, but he does not draw it; he knows that neither he nor Arkwood can kill David in the time it will take him to press the button on the remote.

"If I press this," he says, "your power generators shut down instantly and permanently. I set up the electricity here, Felix. If I destroy it, no one here will be able to restore it again. And without electricity, you'll lose the War."

Felix does not seem to be able to speak for a moment. Then he says, "Arkwood helped you to build the power systems. Arkwood and his sister."

"He did most of it," says Arkwood, glancing at Felix. "I don't think we could rebuild it if he wrecked it."

"There are no loopholes," says David. "If you try to kill me, I press the button. If you try to stop me leaving, I press the button. If you try to hurt her"—he nods down to the child, without breaking Felix's gaze—"I press the button. I'll keep this with me for the rest of my life, and if I ever think you're coming for me, Felix, if you ever approach me again, if I *ever* think Regency pose a threat to me or to my . . . my daughter, I will press the button. Do you understand me?"

Felix seems struck dumb. Silently, he mouths the word "daughter." David himself has never used it to describe the child before, not even within the confines of his own thoughts, but he supposes it is true now. David takes a step backward as something heavy settles upon his heart, and for a moment he meets Arkwood's narrow, steady gaze. Arkwood himself does not seem at all surprised by any of this.

"That applies to you, too," he says. He doesn't trust Arkwood any more than Felix.

"I know."

Slowly, he turns his back on them, his heart pounding, and walks out of the compound into the rain. With every step he can feel the chains on him slipping away. The guards stare after him; he doesn't look at them.

Just before he slips out of earshot, he hears Felix say in a rough, hoarse voice to Arkwood: "We should never have trusted him."

Arkwood seems surprised, his voice faint with distance. "I never thought we did."

On the corner of the alleyway, out of sight of the guards, he takes the remote out of his pocket and smashes it against a wall. Through the crack in the black plastic covering, the blank circuit board glints at him in the rain.

He leaves it there in the puddle and walks off with the monster child into the darkness.

– Chapter 14 –

There were two wake-up calls.

The first was immediate and direct. It came in the form of a note left on the desk in her bedroom in Loren's house. She found it in the evening, on torn paper, in scrawled handwriting she did not recognize. Most likely she would not have found it at all, if whoever had put it there had not left the window open.

It said: *Behold the Interregnum.*

She slept fully clothed again that night with all the doors and windows locked, and it still didn't do any good.

The second wake-up call was very quiet: low, dark stirrings through the floor beneath her. She awoke with the very first, hesitant scrabblings, and lay there, tense and open-eyed. She had lived here long enough to know Loren's and Tabitha's footsteps. This was not either of them.

The calmer, saner part of her told her this was nothing to worry about; her fear and her instincts and her thundering heart disagreed. She checked that her gun was in her nightstand drawer and that her magic was at full strength. Screw the ban: if this was Oliver Keen again, she would use whatever force she wanted, magical or otherwise, to get him out.

She did not consider that it might not be Oliver Keen.

She got up, pulling on her jacket. Even fully clothed, she shivered in the cold January night. She went to the window and looked out over the street.

There were people standing silent in the road, clustered together like clumps of shadow. They kept their heads down so their skin would not catch the light. Their uniforms were black. Rose stared out at them for a long time before she understood.

Regency.

Slowly, she closed the curtains and backed away from the windows.

Why were they here? Had they come to kill her?

No. The obvious answer came to her immediately, sped by adrenaline. No. They must have come for Loren.

Of course. In their younger, more violent days, David and Loren and his Ashkind sister, Rayna, had worked for Regency, during the War. Regency bore very deep grudges against them for leaving. The principal holder of those grudges had been Regency's psychopathic Hybrid leader, Felix Callaway. When Rose, fifteen years after her father had left, had infiltrated Regency to spy for the Department, Felix had recognized her as a fellow Hybrid. He had used the monster inside her to do terrible things. People were dead because of what he had made her do.

And in return, Rose had worked with David to kill him.

125

Rose stared through the gap in the curtains at the gathered soldiers on the street.

But now that Felix was dead, no one in Regency knew her secret.

So they couldn't be here for her. Then *why*, why had they chosen now of all times to make an attempt on Loren's life? Why had they come for him?

It took her a long time to realize that they hadn't.

The noise on the stairs sounded again, and Rose grabbed her gun and threw herself through the door of her bedroom and onto the landing. And because she was so, so *stupid*, she was too late. She stood hesitant, irresolute, trying to get her eyes to focus in the sudden light, and saw Amelia Rodriguez — Maria's Ashkind sister — hauling a sleeping Tabitha down the stairs.

Rose raised her gun, backing away so Amelia did not see her face. She did not devote any thought whatsoever to trying to save Tabitha. Amelia held the girl in front of her, blocking the rest of her body. Human shield: kidnapping tactic number one. Amelia was moving very quickly, and if Rose took the shot, she would probably kill Loren's niece. She did not even consider taking the shot.

"*Loren!*"

He was in the bedroom across from Tabitha's, on the landing. He would have no better chance of hitting Amelia than Rose did. Nevertheless she woke him, screaming, if only to try and make Amelia panic and falter. Amelia did not.

"Don't you dare!" shouted Rose, from the shadows. Her gun was up, pointing as close as she could to Amelia's head. "Don't you dare even think about taking *one more step*!"

Amelia ignored her and kept moving. The front door was

wide open, and she had protection outside, from the other Regency soldiers. She knew that in six seconds' time Rose would pose absolutely no threat.

Loren came out onto the landing, unarmed, wrapped in a bathrobe, looking for the source of the confusion. He found it very quickly. The expression on his face was one of inexpressible fear and pain. His scream was torn from him.

"TABITHA!"

He would have taken the shot in an instant — he wouldn't have thought it through, wouldn't have realized how Amelia was shielding herself, would have taken out all the lethal force of his anger on the person threatening Tabitha without a moment's hesitation.

But he didn't, because he didn't have his gun on him.

He still had magic, however: on the last step, Amelia's hair sizzled and caught alight, which might have been a problem for her if she had been farther from safety. But she wasn't, and Loren's weak, grass-eyed magic was spent, and that was it, that was their window of opportunity wasted and Amelia dragged Tabitha out into the open night air.

"*TABITHA!*"

Loren ran down the stairs toward the closing door. Rose, with the utmost reluctance, raised her hand, and as soon as Amelia slammed the door, there was a hissing sound as the lock and the hinges melted. In another moment they had solidified again. Loren slammed his full weight against the door.

"Wh — Tabitha! *Tabitha!*"

He was panicked, terrified, and he wasn't thinking clearly. Rose was shaking. She walked down the stairs, went into the kitchen, took down the first-aid kit from the shelf where Tabitha

127

herself had placed it only days before, when Tara and her dying mother had appeared suddenly on their doorstep.

There was a syringe full of sedative encased within the box. Rose took it out and readied it.

She felt a tug on the back of her jacket. Loren pulled her roughly around to face him. He stood in front of her, white with fear, his eyes glinting madly, towering over her. He looked truly insane.

"You did this! Open the door! *Open it!*"

Rose fought to stay calm. "Loren, there are hundreds of Regency soldiers out there. They'll kill you."

He wasn't listening. *"Open it!"*

"There's nothing you can do for her now. There're too many of them. I can't let you die, not if you don't have to."

His eyes were wild; he was more animal than her. *"OPEN IT!"*

Rose said nothing. She would not fight him, not physically. She waited until he looked frantically back toward the door and stabbed his wrist with the syringe and pushed down the plunger.

He cried out with the sudden pain, and looked down at her. He didn't understand for a moment, and then he did, and she had to dart out of the way as fast as she could because now he really *was* going to hurt her. He lunged toward her, vicious intent in his eyes, but the sedative was fast-acting and his coordination was already going. He stumbled and fell into the table.

"You — Let me — *Open the door!*"

"It won't do any good, Loren. She's gone."

"How dare . . . How . . . You traitorous . . . You *monster* . . ."

She flinched at the insult: the words cut deeply. She pressed herself against the wall and watched him struggle toward her.

He sank to the floor, screaming obscenities, and then finally collapsed in a crumpled, broken heap.

Rose stood there for a long time, breathing hard, pressing herself into the silence. Then, slowly, she edged past him, limp on the kitchen floor, and went into the living room.

The curtains were closed. She turned off the lights so they would not be able to see her inside the house, and knelt beside the window. Tentatively, she pulled the curtain aside slightly so she could see Regency. They were gathered around the body of the sleeping Demon girl — they must have drugged her, too — and were muttering to one another. Then they pulled apart. Slowly, they retreated into the side streets and the impenetrable dark, dragging Tabitha Arkwood with them.

Rose closed her eyes and pressed her forehead against the glass.

The first time Rose had spoken to Tabitha had been when she was risking her life to rescue her from the Government's clutches, back when the Department and Loren had been enemies and Rose had been betraying them by helping him.

During that first conversation, Rose had explained to the little girl what a Hybrid was, and that she was one; and Tabitha had only smiled, with quiet sympathy.

Tabitha, of course, was a magical Demon: an impossible thing.

Rose was a Hybrid: an evil, destructive, *monstrous* thing.

That had been something, at least, for Rose — finding someone even slightly like her.

Rose closed her eyes. She hadn't saved Loren's niece. That would weigh on her conscience for a long time yet.

All right. Plan, now. What are you going to do?

She did not know how long Loren would stay sedated. Her options were few. She closed the curtain again, made sure the windows were locked. Then she turned on the television. She prayed that Loren had set up the emergency video-link. She had told him to do it months ago.

Traitorous . . .

There was only one number left to call, and at too indecent an hour to guarantee an answer. She pressed the name, closed her eyes and counted the rings. One. Two. Three. Please pick up.

You — how dare you. Open the door . . .

After seven rings, just when Rose thought it would go to voice mail, the call went through. She could see the wall of his study on the screen, but not him.

A gruff voice. "For Ichor's sake. What is it now, Arkwood?"

Rose said nothing, let him come toward the camera.

"If you think I'm going to come running to your bloody office at this hour of the —"

"Connor," said Rose quietly. Abruptly, all movement stopped. There was silence. Slowly, Terrian walked forward into the view of the camera.

"You," he growled, very softly.

"If you hang up now," said Rose quietly, keeping her fear and her desperation pressed tight beneath her voice, "Loren Arkwood will die. Do you care about that, Dr. Terrian?"

"What in the bloody — What are you trying to —?"

"This isn't about my father," she said. "This isn't about the trial. Whatever you think of me, you must help me now. It's Regency. They're back. They've taken Loren's niece."

130

<<< >>>

Sixteen years earlier (age 19)
January 19, 6:41 p.m.

That night's attack is the culmination of months of planning. Felix and Arkwood have been huddled together in the office for weeks, working out the exact details of the operation, making sure there is no chance at all of the Angels surviving until the morning. David himself knows very little about the plan, of course. High Command, as they are known, stopped trusting him a long time ago.

The troops are very nervous. They have never participated in such a large-scale attack before, and there will be substantial fatalities. It doesn't matter to Felix. Nothing matters to him now except the Angels, and the imminence of their destruction, and how bloodily they will die. Nevertheless, the army's morale may well be key to their success, so he and Arkwood hold an assembly that afternoon in the Command Hall, in the War Rooms deep beneath London. It is almost too packed to move. David knows this because he is standing with his staff, in their ranks now — not up on the stage like in the glory days.

He does not regret it.

Felix makes a long speech about the importance of this attack and the evil and depravity of the Angels. Then he brings five soldiers up onto the platform — would-be traitors, the army are told — and he and Arkwood turn their backs to the audience and in five clear, ringing shots, they kill the defectors.

The corpses slump like broken, bloody marionettes against the wall.

Afterward, Felix looks at Arkwood, expecting a speech, but Arkwood appears in no condition to make one. He has not been the same since Ariadne died, but today his grief has manifested itself almost as an illness. He is deathly pale. His eyes are bloodshot. He has the look of a man who knows he is only halfway through a long, long run of sleepless nights, and when Felix looks at him, he makes an almost imperceptible shake of his head. Today he is not an orator.

The army is dismissed. David looks for Rayna among the crowd and sees her hunched beside the door. As usual, her health surges and falters with her brother's; she looks almost as sick as Loren. With a concerted effort, she avoids David's eye.

No one is allowed to talk to him anymore.

In the evening he and his seventeen coworkers stay in the labs. They too have their part to play in this attack. It is a vital one, and they must dedicate themselves completely to it. The bombs and gas canisters are set and readied in two hours flat. Five of David's staff will deploy them, when the plan demands it; he is trusted to design the weapons, but not to use them.

By ten o'clock that night, the work is done. All but the designated five are gathering their coats to leave — they have barracks to go to, families — but David, seeing them, taps the barrel of his gun sharply against a countertop to get their attention. They look around at him in surprise.

"Stay," he says. "We haven't finished."

A couple of them — the slower ones — open their mouths to protest, but the others shush them. They have worked with

132

him long enough to know the meaning of the dark, steely glint in David's eyes, and the unflinching surety it conveys; they know to trust him when he looks like that, even when they don't understand why. They nod. They sit down at their desks again and try to look busy.

Not ten minutes later the knock comes at the door. A few move to answer it, but he shakes his head and they back away. He pulls on his bomber jacket and opens the door.

It takes effort to keep his face clear of emotion. Of course he knew this was coming — he would be a fool not to — but nevertheless the sight of so many soldiers, lethally armed as they are, standing outside his door, cannot be taken easily.

"Yes?" he says, trying to sound mildly surprised. "I was just leaving."

He opens the door as wide as it will go, making sure the soldiers can see how many people are still in the room, making sure they know that if they want to end him, it will not be accomplished merely with a single bullet to his brain, but with the uncompromising slaughter of the entire weapons department. Felix's orders will not have sanctioned that.

He meets their gazes. He stares them down.

"Gentlemen," he says softly, and then he walks away, directly through his assassins and down through the complex. And such is his air of confidence that no one shoots; no one even tries.

The fact that they gave him a flat was not a compliment.

They no longer wanted him in the complex. He was considered too dangerous. So now he lives in exile, in this studio apartment on the fifth floor of an abandoned council estate on this half-destroyed street.

He'd had his pick, and yet . . .

He likes it. It is his home.

It's raining tonight. His bomber jacket offers little protection. It is mid-January, bitterly cold, and yet he stands in the rain and holds out his arms like an invitation to martyrdom.

Despair comes over him very quickly, and once it has him, it will not let him go.

He has lost everyone.

Over the course of three years, everyone he ever loved and trusted has betrayed him, or slipped away, or grown to fear him, or died, and he — against all the odds, almost against his wishes — *he*, of all people, is still alive.

He closes his eyes. Milan. Vancouver. The Docklands. Aleppo. So many hundreds dead because of his weapons, his ingenuity, and yet he can stand on this deserted street and somehow hell does not break through the earth to claim him early.

Don't give up hope yet, he reminds himself. There are people seeking to remedy that now.

His options are few. He cannot reenter the complex now, not unless he is seeking a particularly messy suicide. Felix intends this attack on the Angels to be the last great battle of the War, and now that David has played his part in it, the Commander has decided that his life is more dangerous than his death would be inconvenient.

So he should run.

Yes, that's the best option: run, far away from here, where no one will know his name — if such a place exists anymore — and spend the rest of his life running too, from Felix Callaway and his men. So many ghosts to hide from . . .

Suicide, then.

The only question that remains is how.

He wants it to be inventive, surely. A gunshot to the head is too conventional and, frankly, more painless than he deserves; he has no clear route to the top of a high building; fire is messy and self-preservation might take over before the deed is done. Poison, though. That has its merits.

Ah, the burden of the atheist: creating their own hell to consume them when the conscience fails.

Or maybe —

He freezes, aware of a soft, dark rustling beside him in the shadows.

Maybe it won't be left up to him.

Through the rain, he can hear something: if not human breath, then certainly human presence.

He turns slowly toward the house beside him, and sees it.

A box.

A shoe box.

A shoe box covered in cloth.

His gun is out before he can consciously reprimand himself. Shooting a bomb from ten feet away will do nothing to save his own life.

Does he want to save it?

Yes. Oh, yes. His death will be soon, but it will be on his own terms, not Felix Callaway's.

He walks slowly forward, listening for beeps or ticking noises, but he can hear nothing. He has never defused a bomb before, but his hands don't tend to shake, and if this is a bomb, it will most likely be of his own design.

He walks forward softly. His hands are steady but the rest of him is trembling violently.

And then the wind catches the cloth and sweeps it across the concrete, and in the faint starlight he sees the contents of the box, and his heart goes cold.

It is not a bomb.

It is a child.

It is a human child.

– Chapter 15 –

"You have no idea what you're dealing with."

The cold blue light of police cars slashed across the windows of the house. Terrian, Nate and Maria waded through the splintered remains of the front door to stand over Loren's unconscious body in the kitchen, and survey the damage. There was a Department squad team outside too. They were too late, of course, but the old instincts in Rose told her to be reassured.

"The last time she was taken from him," she said, pushing her hair wearily out of her eyes, "he broke out of a Department cell, killed two squad members and forced me to help him. And that was when he knew she was still alive."

"He knew then, didn't he?" asked Nate quietly. "About your father — he knew what David was. He threatened to tell us. That's how he blackmailed you."

"Does this matter?"

Nate looked at her. "Yes," he said, as though it were obvious.

Rose rubbed her face. "He won't rest until he finds her. He'll do anything. We can't trust him anymore. We have to lock him up. Wipe his security clearance off the database. He cannot be allowed to even leave the Department base until we know he's not going to immediately run out into gunfire to get her back."

"And who exactly will verify that?" asked Terrian. "You?"

"Unless you think you know him better," said Rose mildly. "Me, and two clinical psychologists. And I'm not saying that's perfect. He might still lie to us. He loves her more than anything."

"They've been kidnapping Demon kids for a while," said Nate hoarsely. "I was tracking it . . . but I never really thought they would come for her. It would be so dangerous."

"I don't think that's why they did it," said Maria. "I think they did it to weaken us. As long as they have Tabitha, Loren can't be the Department's leader. He'll be too easily controlled."

The squad team medics came in carrying a stretcher, and dragged Loren's body onto it. Terrian followed them out. Nate and Maria stayed, watching Rose.

"Who kidnapped her?" asked Maria.

Rose was silent. She knew Maria could guess. After the silence was long enough to spell out the name, Maria swore, and stomped away.

Nate watched her go. "You're not safe here," he said. "Not alone."

"I am fine."

"Rose," he said, with sudden anger, "one more lie and I swear to God I will walk out of here and not come back ever again."

She stared at him. He closed his eyes.

"Please," he said. "Rose, please. Just — Stop lying to us. Tell us the truth, now. You've got nothing to lose now, have you?"

He gave a weak smile. She felt the words build and thicken in her throat.

I am a Hybrid. It would be so easy to say.

And then impossible to take back.

They looked at each other. Rose's hand went to the scar in the crook of her elbow where he had once accidentally shot her. This was *Nate*, after all. They'd been like siblings once. Perhaps . . .

Nate turned on his heel, and left.

It was not a cell. They told her that repeatedly. Nevertheless, Rose could not help observing how cell-like it looked: gray-walled, white-ceilinged, a single bed. This was where the squad team members slept when they were on night shift. The new Department base was underground; there was no natural light or Internet connection. Rose had a single bag with clothes and her belongings in it, including her gun. The rest would be fetched tomorrow. Provided nothing else happened tonight.

Six and a half hours to daylight. Not that daylight counted for anything down here.

She lay down on the bed and tried to sleep. Then:

"Rose."

She jerked up, scrambling off the bed.

"Rose. Is that you?"

She stopped herself, her hand halfway to her gun. She was not going to shoot Loren.

Why in the *hell* had they put him in the room next to hers?

Well, of course they would.

They were not above a little light punishment.

139

"Rose, where am I?"

Too many answers and he would hate all of them. Let him use his wits.

"Why — Rose, why did you stop me going after her?"

If he did not understand now, he never would.

"Rose, where is she? Is she okay? Is she alive?"

His voice was breaking. She crawled onto the bed and tried to block her ears.

"Rose?"

Don't listen to him.

"Rose?"

Daybreak came. She knew it by her watch.

At two minutes past sunrise, she was in the lift going up toward the Department offices. They were closer to fresh air than the cells.

It did not occur to her until the lift opened that the very fact she was here meant they had left her door unlocked.

The entrance to this office was not reinforced, but neither was that grounds to assume she would be allowed in unverified. She knocked and waited. When no one came, she threw caution to the winds and opened the door.

It opened cleanly. She stood there in the entrance, waiting as the heads turned, until there was silence and she had the attention of the office.

Worn paper maps covered the entirety of the back wall. Red pins and markers jabbed into it indicated the places where the Department thought the kidnapped Demon children might be being held. Huddles of people stood around the maps, looking anxious and muttering to one another. As a toddler, Rose had spent much of her time staring at the mysterious, elegant shifts and swirls of the movements of the Department staff, much as another child might have watched the colors in a kaleidoscope, unknown and unknowable.

Terrian, Nate and Maria were at the other end of the room. They stared at her.

"I know you don't like me," she said, "but I'm here if you need me. And you do need me."

No answer but quiet. She turned, and left.

<<< >>>

Seventeen years earlier (age 19)
April 13, 11:10 p.m.

The school building is deserted and cold. Some combination of magic and explosives took out the back wall in the first year of the War, and he does not know if it took any students with it, but either way the children left fairly quickly after that. Their paintings and essays are nailed to the wall, gathering dust. He remembers it — of course he remembers it — but it has been a very long time, and several classrooms seem to have shrunk. Memories rear up in front of him at familiar smells and shadows, and he shakes them off irritably. Never mind that. There are more important things to focus on.

It is a small school, no larger than a house, so there can only be one place where what he wants can be found, and luckily for him it is the one room for which he has no memories at all. The staff room ceiling is higher than that of most of the classrooms, but he still has to duck through the doorway. The teachers must have been remarkably short. He wouldn't know, of course; he must have been, what, ten, eleven when he left here? Very young.

Of course, by most standards he is very young now. He should be sitting in his room broodily, being rude to his parents and refusing to get a job.

He allows this thought to run its course, testing whether the twist in his gut he gets when he thinks of his parents has gone yet. It has not.

He remembers how, after his mother died, he used to wander into the headmistress's office unbidden, and touch the seat opposite the desk, because on parent-teacher evenings it was where she used to sit. It was a long time before the headmistress understood, but he didn't care. Everything that might carry a trace of his mother's ghost was a jewel, and every memory of her must be chronicled, and saved forever from the carelessness of the human mind.

She was never in the staff room, though, to his knowledge, so he can bear the atmosphere here without impediment. It is pitch-dark, and his residual mental map — which has until now allowed him to navigate this place instinctively, as if the previous eight years had never passed, and he was still shackled to this building — runs out within this room. He was not one of the children who routinely got called in here to talk to teachers.

He pulls out his torch. The power is slowly coming back on, starting in the big cities and spreading outward, but no one will waste it on a disused primary school with fewer than the requisite number of walls left standing. One of the many privileges of being someone Felix actually needs — a rarity, in many people's eyes — is that he has a guaranteed battery supply. The flat and the employees are other perks, but he prizes the batteries above all

142

else, because there is no possible way Felix can know when he is using them.

The torch flickers on. The room is empty, damp seeping through the white-painted walls, and three-year-old tea sits in mugs around the room. The table is still loaded with paperwork, but for the sake of his sanity, he has to assume it has nothing to do with him. Far more likely is the filing cabinet in the corner. He stays by the door and shines the torchlight over the locks.

They explode in a twist and screech of metal, and he smiles despite himself.

He works his way around the table and the dust, and opens the top drawer of the filing cabinet. Student records. Fantastic. This school has been running since the sixties, so he aims for the front of the drawer, where the paper seems whitest. He searches for his year. The class photos, which are the first things he comes across, bother him. He can see himself smiling there: four years old in the first, so young! Such ridiculous hair!

In the Year Six one, of course, he is not smiling. He did not smile for a very long time that year.

He takes his cigarette lighter out of his pocket and sets fire to the corner of the photographs. No need to waste magic on that. He drops it to the carpet, and waits until the blaze is bright enough that the torch becomes redundant. Then he stamps it into ash.

He clicks the lighter into life again, hesitates, and drops it into the filing cabinet.

The papers catch one by one, slowly curling into blackness inside the bright gold of the flame. He watches, fascinated, until the old pyromania starts to unfurl inside him again, and then he slams the drawer shut, trapping the flame inside the box. He pushes magic into the tips of his fingers, presses them to the cabinet, and the metal smears like paint across the seam, congealing as soon as he is out of contact. In this way he seals it shut. Then he realizes — idiot — that the fire will burn itself out within seconds without oxygen. He considers using his gun to punch holes in it, but the risk of ricochets is too great, so he uses magic, and the metal yields in small fire-bright holes.

Everything, now, is burning. Good. There will be no record of his past, of his childhood. He will be a new man for this new world. It will be as if he stepped fully formed from the ether, an adult; as if he had never been a child at all.

He picks up his torch again; at some point he seems to have dropped it. He leaves the room swiftly, and the memories as he retreats — down the stairs, through darkened classrooms, toward the door — suddenly become too loud. They swarm like insects, building into a clamor in his head, but he doesn't listen, putting up walls against them in his mind, killing any tempted thought. He doesn't need that kind of relapse.

He almost does not notice when he is out the door; he has been running on autopilot since the English classroom, and only the sudden, cool clarity of the air jerks him back into receptiveness. He backs away from the building. Something in him wants to attack the windows, the doors, burn the building and raze any trace of it to the ground, but those days are gone.

He looks up without thinking, and the memories push their way in; he is eight years old, and sitting on a windowsill, watching other children in the playground. Clutched in his hand is a small blue pen. He is drawing his mother.

That was before he knew.

He looks up at the window, and sees flames curl around the

wood. As he watches, they intensify, and with a sudden jerk he realizes what he is doing. He doesn't stop. He pushes, pressing the flames into the floor, the walls, until the room is burning, white-hot and irrevocable, wiping any trace of his past from the earth forever.

Then it is over.

Chapter 16

"Are you all right?"

Rose sat up very quickly, breathing hard, wrenched from sleep. Maria stood in the doorway, surprised.

"I'm sorry. I didn't mean to —"

"It's fine," said Rose, angry with herself. She rubbed her eyes. The last traces of her nightmare came away and faded. "What did you need?"

Maria looked at her, her expression unreadable. "I want to help you, Rose," she said. "Please let me."

"There's nothing wrong with me."

Something convulsive flickered through Maria's face; Rose instantly misidentified it as pity, and sprang to her feet. "There is absolutely *nothing* wrong, Maria, and if there were, I wouldn't be asking you to sort it out at any r —"

"No, don't worry," said Maria quietly, "that wasn't what I meant," and left, closing the door behind her. It was only in the minutes afterward, staring blankly at the space where she had stood, that Rose realized what she had gotten wrong. That look had not been pity, not at all; it had been surrender. Maria had given up.

Rose sat down on the bed in her cell and rubbed her face.

Well, about bloody time.

Nate went into the courtroom before her. He came out very quickly, standing in front of the stairs with his arms spread as if attempting to block her path.

"You can't come in," he said, low and urgent. "You can't. Not today."

Rose was too tired for this. "You can't stop me."

"Yes, I can."

She stared at him in amused astonishment. "Nate, are you seriously going to fight me?"

He did not answer. Behind him, she saw Oliver Keen hurrying up the stairs to the courtroom, looking gleeful. She tried to push past Nate, but he stopped her.

"You shouldn't."

"Just tell me what's going on."

He rubbed his eyes. "Rose," he said, with pained gentleness, "they're going to prove he's a Hybrid."

She waited for a moment until he had grown slightly less wary and his grip on her arms had slackened. Then she darted past him and up the stairs, ignoring his cries for her to stop. She worked her way past the spectators —*spectators*, how dare they, how insolent they were to think they had any interest in this, any knowledge of her father — and into the gallery. Nate followed her, muttering angrily as he took his seat.

"Why won't you *listen* to me?"

She ignored him, and waited until his mutters faded with Malvern's call for silence.

"Mr. Teller," she said, "your evidence, please."

Teller got up. He was pale-faced and his eyes kept flickering to David.

"Play video footage," he said.

The projector flickered on. Slowly, a picture came into view: a hard, cold metal room. Video footage dated three weeks ago: their last transformation. So they had taken him back to the house to do it. She had run — taken the Overground as far out of the city as she could, and walked away from civilization, to a deserted field. By four o'clock she had been kneeling in the grass, waiting for the monster to take her. No one had died.

And he had been in the house, like in the old days.

Except this time there had been people there. Filming him.

She did not want to see this.

She could not *not* see this.

Her hand was clutching the bench in front of her so hard it hurt. Nate prized it off gently.

"You can leave," he whispered. "You don't have to stay."

On-screen, David walked slowly into view. It struck Rose — of all the things to strike her then — that he looked very old. He was only thirty-five, but already he seemed ancient, and his eyes did not smile anymore. The lines in his face had been worn by days, not years, though they stood stark in his skin, like old scars; and yet only months ago he had been a young man, with light and magic in his eyes. Not now. Now he looked like a murderer on

148

that screen; and sitting there, in the courtroom, with his back to her, he seemed aged beyond redemption.

Had she done that?

He did not go gently. They had to shove him into that room, and bar the door, leaving him alone with the claw marks that terrible hands had carved into the metal. And still he beat at the door; still he screamed at his captors. The video was silent, but that did not stop Rose hearing every word. She knew him. She knew how to read his lips.

David, in the dock, had bent down with his head almost between his knees and his hands entwined behind his neck. He had all the look of a man unseeing. That was what gave Rose the first true warning sign.

On-screen, he beat at the door, still silently screaming. Then, after a long time, when it became clear it was not going to open, he sank slowly to a crouch. He folded, crumpled, on the metal floor.

The metal room around him seemed to shrink. He looked around at it, bleak-eyed. Then, suddenly: defiance.

Too late. His time was up. She saw it alight in his eyes, and then all the muscles in his body seemed to compress, to seize up, twisting. He leaned forward, his teeth gritted and his face tight with pain, and yet still he looked as though he was resisting it, trying to fight it off.

He bent double, crouched low, one arm wrapped around his torso, the fingertips of the other pressed against the metal floor to hold himself steady. The veins of his hand stood out blue, the muscles of his arm tense with agony.

Then all movement within him seemed to stop, as suddenly as the settling of death upon his shoulders.

And then he looked up sharply into the camera in the corner, stared at them all through that screen, and his eyes were white.

Rose cried out. The sight drew a horrified gasp from the watching crowd, even from Justice Malvern, who usually sat so implacably in her position above the onlookers. Even Madeleine stiffened and paled. David looked — there was no other word for it — *animal.* Everything, pupil and iris and threads of capillary, had vanished from his eyes, leaving them white and apparently blind.

Rose knew better. Rose knew he could see.

He started to shake violently, collapsing into himself, all his grace and agility falling away like water. His hands opened and closed reflexively, the muscles spasming and skin darkening. He bowed his head. She could see his body tightening, the bulges of vertebrae showing through his shirt, his hair seeming to melt and harden to the skull. His fingernails were lengthening, sharpening, yellowing to talons. His skin seemed to age, blackening and rotting, and suddenly it split along the lines of his veins, and smoke seeped like blood into the air. His shirt tore, and he stood, taller and more terrible than any man, and he looked up again, and now those white eyes did not seem so jarring, because he no longer wore a human face.

Rose saw her father close and vanish; saw him fade to nothing as the monster roared, showing its white teeth; and she too started to tremble, started to shake uncontrollably, and she slid slowly onto the floor, dry sobs catching in her throat, fighting to keep herself silent, and the grief and shock and fear and pain and *recognition*, the terrible familiarity like the memory of a nightmare, retreated inside her, sinking its blades into her mind and heart.

150

She could feel Nate's hand on her shoulder, could hear Maria's voice low and anxious, but she shook them off, the weight of the secret heavier than ever on her shoulders; for if they truly knew, after all these years, *why* the sight of it was destroying her like this, they would not try to comfort her.

And when a sob did finally escape her, it was not on their account, nor on her father's — her true, human father who sat there unseeing and unresponsive in the dock. It was for Tabitha, who could not help her now, who might not even be alive, but would, if Regency had not taken her, have understood what Rose was feeling perfectly.

According to Nate, after Rose had left the courtroom, this had been the conversation.

TELLER: Why are there two rooms like that in your
    house, Mr. Elmsworth?
DAVID: To protect my daughter. She is locked in there
    when I . . . transform.
(David's words in Nate's voice sounded very strange.)
TELLER: Why are there claw marks in the second room?
DAVID: We swap sometimes.
TELLER: Why?
DAVID: You can hear the street above us, sometimes, on
    a good day, from the second room.
(This was true.)
TELLER: So in your mind your daughter has never been
    endangered.
DAVID: I would die rather than risk hurting her.
TELLER: Why do you love her?

(Silence here. Rose could understand.)

TELLER AGAIN: Why do you love her, Mr. Elmsworth?

DAVID: She is my daughter. She is my child. I am her
father. How many ways do you need it expressed?

TELLER: She is not your daughter.

(Cold silence.)

DAVID: A matter of opinion.

TELLER: She is not yours, biologically. Why do you
consider her family?

DAVID: Mr. Teller, I wasn't under the impression you
needed the concept of adoption explained to you.

(Anger in the court here, although Rose laughed when
Nate told her.)

MALVERN: Mr. Elmsworth, you will respect the court
and its servants or I will find you in contempt.

TELLER: Why did you adopt her?

DAVID: I . . .

TELLER: You did not love her then, surely.

DAVID: I found her alone. In the rain, in winter. There
was no one else. I came to love her after that.

TELLER: Mr. Elmsworth, who is the mother of your
child?

DAVID: You don't believe me.

TELLER: If I am being honest, I have just seen you at
your darkest, Mr. Elmsworth. I don't think there is
a person in this court who will ever believe you in
anything ever again.

DAVID: (angry now) She looks nothing like me. You've
seen her. You wouldn't believe me her father if you
hadn't seen the documents.

TELLER: I would put nothing beyond you, Mr.
    Elmsworth.
DAVID: No kind of magic can change blood. She is not
    mine. I *found* her.
TELLER: And how do you know she wasn't your child,
    left there by the mother for you to raise?
DAVID: I —
(Silence.)
DAVID: You know, don't you?
TELLER: What do you think I know, Mr. Elmsworth?
    What have you not told the court?
DAVID: You — you son of a *bitch*! How could you — how
    dare you — how on earth have you possibly —
MALVERN: (furious) Mr. Elmsworth, you will mind
    your language and your address.
DAVID: I will not. How dare you? How do you *know*?
    How dare you possibly *know*?
He had been shouting by then, and that was when the
    guards had dragged him out.

They came apart when she walked among them.

That was the first thing she noticed. Her very presence in the office caused them to split and fracture. They muttered and argued with flickering glances toward her; she destroyed their quiet. The thought made her smile. She unsettled them. How fitting.

The maps of the kidnapped Demon children's possible locations were now spread over desks, and most of the Department were gathered around them, looking worried and exhausted. Rose detected panic. Tabitha's kidnapping had made this a high priority. Good.

After five minutes sitting at the desk that, by its position in the office, would have been David's, Terrian strode angrily over. He looked very tired. Nate and Maria followed him uneasily.

"What makes you think you have any right to be here?"

"I was a member of the Department just as much as you were."

"You *were*, once. That was before you betrayed us."

"No, actually," said Rose. "That was after I betrayed you for Loren. It was *before* you realized I had been betraying you for my father. And I question your definition of betrayal in that instance."

Terrian's face darkened. "How dare you. You have lied to us, so many times —"

"No, I did not. I would have been *lying* if you had asked me specifically whether Dad was a Hybrid and I had said no. But you never asked me that question, so I never lied."

"Don't try to weasel your way out of this, girl."

"I'm not weaseling my way out of anything. I am proving you wrong."

"Rose," said Maria, warningly.

Rose leaned forward. "Let me illustrate the problem," she said softly. "What I did was not *betrayal*. It was the protection of someone I loved. I can think of better examples of betrayal, though, off the top of my head. For instance, hypothetically, if I were to betray you, I might stand across from you in the witness box when you were fighting for your life and testify to a court of law that you were a monster."

Terrian bared his teeth at her. "I swore to tell the truth."

"Then it was you who lied. My father is nothing like what you said and he has done *nothing*" — her hand slammed into the desk — "to me."

Terrian glared at her. "You know nothing."

"On the contrary, I know everything about this case. And you told those lies about him and me in front of national media and a *jury*."

Nate put a hand on Terrian's shoulder before he could reply. His father looked back at him, fury still glowing in his eyes, and swallowed, and stopped.

"Listen," said Rose. "You now have two angry ex-Heads of this Department locked up within the city you are supposed to be guarding. You also have two rival militias who are waiting for you to collapse and my father to die to start their war. I have never seen you weaker, and I have been watching for a really long time. You cannot afford to reject me again, Connor. You need everyone you can get. Dislike me if you will, but you will fail without me."

– Chapter 17 –

Eighteen years earlier (age 18)
March 16, 12:19 a.m.

Michael sits in his chains. There is no resistance in his limbs, and all the color in his skin is gone. His shirt is black with blood. There is a small, red hole in his brown hair, and his head lolls forward so that darkness sheathes his face. He doesn't move when David screams.

<<< >>>

By all appearances, Loren was asleep, but Rose knew better than to trust all appearances.

"Is there anyone on the other side of that?"

"If I told you," said Rose, "it would defeat the purpose of a one-way mirror."

He sat up on the cell bed, opened his eyes and stared at her.

"Tell me you're looking for her."

"Of course we are."

This was a lie. She had no idea if the Department were looking for Tabitha. But this was an easy untruth; it slipped from her lips without pain.

Loren looked at her very hard.

"So you're one of them," he said finally. "One of Terrian's lot."

"Not of Terrian's. But I was always one of the Department."

"Not always."

"And what an experience that has been. But now things are back the way they used to be. You, here, in a cell; me, bringing you as little information as I think you need. The proper order of things."

"Why are you trying to make me angry?" he asked.

"I want to know if you're going to hurt me."

"Why would I hurt you?"

"Do not insult my intelligence. I know you, Loren Arkwood, and I know how far you would go to get her back. You would kill me and everyone behind that mirror and everyone in this *city* just to have a shred of a chance of seeing her again. My safety is nothing to hers, in your heart."

He was silent for a while.

"You've locked me up."

"Loren, please let me trust you. If you just give your word that you won't run off to Regency, or try to communicate with them to get Tabitha back —"

"I can't do that," he said, bitterly. "You know I can't. I know

157

you want to be wrong, but you're not. I'd do anything to get her back. I'd do anything to know if she's safe. Even —" He glanced up at her. "Even betray the Department, if I had to."

There was a silence.

"Do you blame me for that, Rose?"

"No," she said heavily. "No, I can't."

He looked up at the ceiling. "Well," he said at last, "I do."

They met outside the entrance to the underground Department base. Tara's sweater was too thin for the January cold. She was very pale.

"I talked to Cassandra Mayhew again today," she said.

"Have we persuaded her to testify yet?"

"I think we might be close."

Rose balled her fists in her pocket. "I won't take anything short of a *yes, absolutely*."

"Then you won't take anything. If she does agree to do it, she'll be very reluctant. This is a dangerous thing we're asking of her, Rose, especially after what they showed today."

"I know."

They darted away from an icy puddle thrown up in their faces by a passing car.

"What is changing her mind?"

"The Keen reports."

Rose said nothing.

"You haven't seen them?"

"Who would it help?"

"She doesn't like Keen himself," said Tara, "but it's mostly his portrayal of your father that gets to her. She thinks there must be more to him than a monster."

Rose rubbed her face. "If only everyone were that insightful."

"He will never get out of that prison," Tara said. "You know that."

Rose said nothing.

"He will never be acquitted. That footage, today . . . that was traumatic."

"I know it was."

"What did Teller mean?" Tara asked. "Why did your father get so angry when he talked about your parentage?"

Rose looked up into the gray sky and took off her gloves to feel the air between her fingers.

"I don't know," she said, "but I have a terrible feeling that it's a long story."

She had asked Loren about it, before she left the cell, and his response had . . . bothered her.

"Loren"—as he stared at the mirror, and she kept her voice casual—"when you knew my father, when he was a teenager, when he worked for Regency, did you ever see . . . did he ever . . . have someone? Was there anyone he might . . . he might have loved?"

And he had looked at her, and a sudden, terrible pallor had fallen over his face, and his expression had closed so much as to be unreadable.

"Don't ask that, Rose," he said. "You don't want to know that."

"All I want to know," said Rose, calmly, "is how it ended."

Loren had swallowed, and he had glanced again at the one-way mirror, and something seemed to fall from him, leaving him hollow and deadened. Rose knew that this was something else, something old, a long-buried emotion dragged up through the sediment of years.

"Badly," he said, quietly.

<<< >>>

Eighteen years before (age 18)
March 16, 12:08 a.m.

They push him roughly into the cell. He stumbles into the wall and falls gracelessly to his knees. Through the darkness — thick and oily and complete — he hears the door slam shut.

The room is dank. He can taste damp on the air.

He slams his handcuffs against the wall in frustration, swearing viciously at the accompanying rush of pain. He is far too exhausted and drained for magic. Even if he did manage to melt the cuffs, he'd burn his own wrists off. There is nothing, nothing, *nothing* he can do.

As he kneels there, overcome with the shock of his sudden powerlessness, he hears hoarse, shallow breathing through the darkness, rapid, like an injured animal's.

He stops, listens, and throws caution to the wind.

"Michael?" he whispers through the darkness.

The breathing cuts off suddenly. Then:

"I hate you."

David stops. Something in his heart seems to be collapsing, rotting through, like wood in rain.

"You could have escaped," whispers Michael, with hoarse fury, and despite himself — despite everything — David nearly laughs in relief.

160

"You — could — have —*escaped*. You could have got away."

"Not when they had you," says David. "I would have gone back even if I had been able to make it. But I didn't. I was caught."

"Who by?"

"Arkwood."

Michael leans backward to slam the back of his head into the wall in frustration. Arkwood, Arkwood: the destroyer of all their plans, second only in that respect to Felix himself. A shaft of light falls across Michael's face as he moves, and David sees the blooming darkness over his cheekbones, sees one eye swollen shut, and Arkwood — whom David has, stupidly, thought of until now only with deep annoyance, as an obstacle, a problem to be solved — suddenly becomes the devil, an evil spirit. Hatred for the man who has hurt Michael like this explodes in him with the power of a bomb. He wants to say, "I'll kill him," but that would betray desperation he cannot allow Michael to know he feels; so instead he keeps his voice low and steady, and says, "Caitlin and Jackson, they got away. It wasn't for nothing. They made it."

Michael nods slowly. The news that his sister and her boyfriend have escaped — to stay with her twin, Eleanor, in Oxford, where he and David should have been by now if all had gone to plan — seems of no more import to him than a weather forecast.

He says, quietly, "And Ariadne?"

"She escaped, too."

"Good."

They look at each other. So everyone got away but them; everyone will find safety but them. David doesn't care. He hates that Michael did not make it, but if Michael had to be captured, then David is glad that he was taken with him. At least now they are not separated. At least now David knows for certain where Michael is, what's happening to him. At least they are together.

Footsteps down the corridor. David and Michael move apart to sit against opposite walls before the door opens. David's eyes shut against the flood of stinging light. He hears Michael say quietly, "You," without inflection.

There is a horrible crunch and a hiss that masks a cry of pain. David's eyes snap open. He sees Arkwood kick Michael again, in the chest, and hears another rib break. Blood is spreading through Michael's shirt. There is no color in his face and his eyes are bulging with pain, but he does not cry out.

David lunges at Arkwood, screaming with fury, but the two guards flanking him step forward and seize him, holding him back, keeping Arkwood's blood beneath his skin, keeping his bones unbroken, keeping his heart beating. For this he will kill them, too.

"STOP IT! DON'T HURT HIM! DON'T YOU DARE HURT HIM!"

"Then tell me," says Arkwood, without even looking up at David, "where Ariadne Stronach is."

"I DON'T KNOW!"

Arkwood kicks Michael again, almost casually. Michael's face is gray now, and his shirt is dark with blood, soaked with it. David screams anguished obscenities at Arkwood, but Arkwood cuts him off.

"All right," he says, calmly, "let's try this. When she came to you, and asked to hijack your escape plan, which one of you did she speak to? Who did she approach?"

"Me!" shouts David frantically. "She came to me. Hurt me, don't hurt —"

In a swift, practiced movement, Arkwood takes out his gun, clicks off the safety, and presses it to Michael's head. David stops suddenly. Everything in the world is still, even Michael's eyes, which stare into David's, taking no notice of Arkwood. They are no longer filled with tears of pain; they are clear and bright.

"Don't tell him anything, David," Michael says, evenly.

"Where did she go?" asks Arkwood, with equal calm. "Where did she say she was going, David?"

"I didn't — she didn't say —"

"Five," says Arkwood, quietly.

Panic floods him. He cannot think. He cannot breathe. All of his intelligence has vanished; all he can see are Michael's eyes, and all he can say is, "I didn't know, she didn't tell me —"

"Four."

"I don't know! *I don't know!*"

"Three."

"I don't know, I don't know, Loren, *please* —"

"Two."

"PLEASE! PLEASE DON'T HURT HIM! I DON'T KNOW WHERE SHE IS! I DON'T —"

"One."

"PLEASE! MICHAEL! PLEASE!"

Bang.

– Chapter 18 –

Teller's final witness was a pale-eyed Ashkind woman of about forty. There were streaks of gray in her blond hair, which she wore plaited harshly back out of her eyes. She had the walk of an old soldier — Rose knew the gait well — but even when she stated her name, Rose had no idea why she was there.

"I, Caitlin Daisy Redmond, swear to tell the truth, the whole truth and nothing but the truth."

Teller stood.

So used was Rose by now to David's courtroom apathy that she did not at first notice his behavior. He sat in the dock and stared at Caitlin Redmond — this in itself was unusual — but only when Rose watched him for long seconds, only when she saw that his chest was still and his eyes unblinking and the muscles in his hands tight and statue-still, did she realize how afraid this woman made him.

Why?

"Ms. Redmond, when did you first meet the defendant?"

"A long time ago," she said. Her voice was crystalline: hard and clear and fragile. "I was, oh, sixteen. He was younger. A child."

David made an indistinct noise in his throat. The court looked around at him. Caitlin Redmond ignored him.

"What was he like, then?"

"I didn't know him very well. I only really began to spend time with him once the War began. He had joined Regency by then. He was . . . effective."

A muttering had erupted around the courtroom, so loud and excited that Malvern had to call for silence. It took Rose a moment to realize why, and then she understood with a shuddering heart: the jury had not known that he had fought for Regency as a young man. This would be a new class of revelation.

Teller pressed. "He fought for the terrorists? The Ashkind militia?"

"So did I," said Caitlin, looking around angrily. "They weren't terrorists then — they were an army just as valid as yours." There was hostility in her voice now. Teller gave her a warning look, and she swallowed.

"They employed him as a killer. That was it. They didn't even call him a soldier. They gave him some rooms, and some workers of his own, and they told him to invent things that would kill enemy soldiers. Gifted soldiers."

"And did he?"

"He did," said Caitlin. "We feared him. Not just because he was so brutal, and so clever, but because he had magic, so we

165

didn't know why he was with us. Most of us had no idea what he was fighting for, where his loyalties lay. There were only two Gifted in Regency, and they were so high up that we couldn't possibly trust them. David Elmsworth and Loren Arkwood. We called them the Angels of Death."

"The Angels of Death," repeated Teller softly. The words ran around the room like a shiver. "And what was your personal opinion of him?"

Caitlin shrugged. "I knew he would save my life," she said, flatly, "if it needed to be saved."

"And why was that?"

"For my brother's sake," she said, and suddenly, just before she said it, it clicked into place in Rose's head. "They were in love, at the time."

This time the muttering was so loud that Malvern had to shout before it stopped. The concept of David Elmsworth in love — in thrall to someone else, under another's power — was not one that came easily to anyone present; Michael Redmond's sister had just written their headlines for them.

David had his head in his hands.

"He was in love with your brother," said Teller quietly, and Rose's loathing for him burned more strongly than ever before, for knowing this piece of her father's heart before she had, and for using it against him.

"Yes," said Caitlin Redmond. "They'd known each other for years; they'd been friends, Michael said . . . I don't know when it began for Michael. I knew David had always loved him, almost since they'd met. You could see it in his face, so easily, in his voice, how much it hurt not to say. Michael couldn't see it. He didn't know."

There was a slight break in her voice.

"They were separated for a year, when the War started. Then, when I saw him again, I —" Her voice shook; she swallowed, and Rose realized suddenly that her hesitation was borne not of anger or fear, but guilt. "I told David where Michael was. David brought my brother into Regency, where he could keep him safe, or so he said. I think it was an excuse. I think he just wanted Michael with him. The first time I saw Michael after that, I knew there were no more secrets. It was —" She swallowed again. "It was beautiful."

David's head snapped up, and for a moment he met Caitlin's eyes. Madeleine was staring between them, stricken: clearly she had not known about this, either. Then Caitlin turned away and continued.

"David was an Angel of Death, by then. He had his reputation. Michael didn't like it. He hated what David was doing, hated how many people he was killing, but it didn't make him love David any less. If he had . . . I don't know what would have happened. But eventually it became too much. Michael threatened to run. He said he was escaping Regency, with or without David, that he would break his own heart rather than stay here. I think it was his way of saving David.

"I decided to go with him. We would leave the city and join our sister in Oxford. For a long time David refused to go — he said he had duties here, that Regency would be helpless without him."

"And was he right?"

"Oh, yes," said Caitlin, "eventually. I like to think that without Michael's intervention, Regency might have won the War. It took weeks of pleading, persuasion, but finally David agreed to leave with us. He would abandon Regency."

"Did he keep his word?"

"Yes," said David, savagely, from the dock. This was the first time he had spoken of his own accord during the trial, Rose thought; his voice was tight, hoarse. The courtroom swiveled to look at him. He was glaring fiercely at Caitlin Redmond. "Yes, I did."

Caitlin took no notice of him, but continued.

"We ran," she said. "The plan was to go in two groups. David and Michael went together, and then me and my boyfriend Jackson. We escaped Regency's territory. We were meant to meet up with Michael and David on the outskirts of the city. They weren't there." Her voice broke. "We waited for three days, but they didn't come. Eventually Jackson persuaded me to leave. He said they might be in Oxford when we got there."

"And were they?"

"No," said Caitlin. "I never saw my brother again. When the War ended, and we all thought Regency had come to nothing, I went back to London. Michael would have been twenty-two by then, and I thought he might be with them, that he might have been captured and held."

Teller was somber. "Did you find him?"

"I found his grave," said Caitlin, quietly, and David twisted his fingers around the back of his neck and pulled his knees up to his face, began to rock back and forth. "I found where he was buried. He had died on the night of our escape attempt. I asked around. It was a legend, apparently." She stopped and swallowed again. "He and David Elmsworth had been locked together in a cell, and when the door was opened, only David was alive."

"*No!*" roared David, leaping to his feet. His guards tried to pull him down again, but to no avail. He leaned over the dock, the chain of his handcuffs pulled around his neck as if he had put himself in a stranglehold. "No! I did everything! How *dare* you! I did — I tried to save him! *Caitlin!*"

Slowly, dispassionately, she turned to look at him. No one tried to stop David speaking; even Malvern was transfixed. Perhaps they thought it would be more effective just to let him run himself into the ground.

"*I did not kill him!*" shouted David. Rose had never seen him so broken. "I would never have hurt him, Caitlin, never! I would have given my life, a hundred times over — I would have taken a *thousand* bullets rather than see him harmed!"

"Then why didn't you?" asked Caitlin, and David stopped, stared at her, breathing hard. His mouth opened in the sudden silence.

"I tried," he said, hollowly. "I tried."

Caitlin looked at him for a moment, and when she spoke, she managed to compress fathomless contempt into her words.

"Not hard enough," she said.

David's face was expressionless; all of his anguish had vanished. He looked dead.

Caitlin looked down at him for a moment. Then, after a long time, she turned and looked up directly into the gallery.

"Who is the girl he calls his daughter?"

Rose hesitated before she stood up. She looked down at the sister of David's soul mate and tried to judge her. There was no cruelty in the woman's eyes.

"I don't know what you've been through," said Caitlin. "For all I know, you might be completely innocent. At any rate, I doubt he told you anything about my brother. I don't know. But listen to me." She glanced back at David, still watching aghast from the dock.

"If I were you," said Caitlin Redmond, "I would be very careful of what he calls love."

<<< >>>

Eighteen years earlier (age 18)
March 15, 10:43 p.m.

Running. Running. Running.

Electrified fence. De-electrified, thanks to yet another completely innocent fluctuation in the power supply. He jumps, manages to get fingerholds in the wire mesh. His body slams against the fence. He takes a second to breathe. Caitlin has made it over. He can see her silhouette in the distance. He starts climbing.

The fence is sharp, and it draws blood from his hands. At the top, he touches the barbed wire. It is very thin. He summons his strength, and electrocutes the wire with as much magic as he has in him. It turns to dust. He throws himself over, and slams against the other side of the fence again. He cannot see Michael. It is very dark.

He climbs down slowly, dropping the last three feet.

Running. Running. Running.

Land mines in the field. He planted them there himself, of course, to fend off approaching enemies, so he knows the layout. Michael, Caitlin, and her boyfriend Jackson all have maps. He does not think about how dark it is.

He starts running, placing his footsteps away from the grenades.

Running. Running. Running.

Shouts in the distance, gunshots, and then suddenly an explosion. Apparently the soldiers following them do not have maps. He does not think about the alternative.

Running. Running. Run —

In the blackness beside him, another set of footsteps. Known steps. Him.

He says nothing, because he is not sure, he cannot be sure.

He trips, slams into something hard — wall — and stumbles with the impact, sinking to his knees. Someone says, haltingly, "David?" and there are hands on his: known hands, known breaths. Michael pulls him to his feet.

"You all right?"

"Yes, yes."

"Where was the explosion? Did anyone . . . ?"

"I don't know."

"It can't have been Caitlin," says Michael. David looks up, can just about make out his expression through the darkness. He is staring out over the minefield, though it is far too far away to make anything out. "It must have been the soldiers."

"Yes," says David, still breathing hard. He has no reason to think it was not Caitlin, but at the slightest possibility that his sister is injured, Michael will start running back toward the camp; and it is imperative that Michael keep running this way, with him. "It can't have been Caitlin."

Michael wrenches his eyes from the landscape. "You ready?"

"Of course."

Running. Running. Running.

Then, suddenly, to his left: *BOOM!*

He cries out without realizing, throwing himself clear of the rubble, hitting the wet earth and trying to stumble back onto his feet again, but the pull of gravity is shifting skyward. He cannot keep his footing, and he falls. He screams, "Michael!" and then the second explosion goes off, to his right this time, and he is curled up into a ball, terrified, his senses obliterated by light and noise. They are between two buildings, but neither of them falls on him.

Inexplicably, neither of them falls on him.

"Well, look who it is."

A very close voice. His left ear has been wiped out, clearly, so he puts his hand to the injury before realizing that he has no energy left to heal it. He used that up destroying the wire. He can only hear the voice, then, through his right ear, and it is not Michael speaking.

The voice is casual, easy. "Nice night for it," it says, "you treacherous little bastard."

A hand on his shoulder. It throws him effortlessly onto his back. The sky lurches again, and he stares up into the eyes of his captor, hands still over his ears.

"Good-bye, David," says Arkwood, and hits him, very hard.

– Chapter 19 –

"Now here's a mystery."

One in the morning. Rose had not slept. Closing Loren's cell door behind her, she ignored the hand he threw over his eyes at the sudden light she snapped into being on her palm.

"Have you found her?" he asked, instantly.

"No," said Rose. "They've made arrests, though. They're trying."

Loren blinked slowly. He looked exhausted; fear and anxiety for his niece had worn him out. His eyes flickered to the closed door. Rose locked it.

There had indeed been three militia members arrested today — two from Regency, and one from the Gospel — but none of them had anything to do with Tabitha. The Department knew that trying to find an eight-year-old Demon girl in a city long since predisposed to look away from them, if indeed she *was* still in the city, was close to impossible.

Rose sat down.

"You have plans to *escape*?"

Too terse for innocence. He stared down at her.

"What do you know?"

"This isn't about what I know," she said, though of course that was a lie. "Who killed Michael Redmond, Loren?"

"What happened in court today?"

"Give me an answer."

"Not until I know what you're asking."

"Nothing more than the question," said Rose. She tried to sound nonchalant, but her voice was shaking with anger. "You had captured David Elmsworth and his partner. They'd tried to defect. They were treasonous. You've told me Felix said you had to keep Dad alive, but you were a fanatic then, weren't you, and he would have had to be punished for what he had done. So who killed Michael Redmond, Loren?"

He fell back onto the bed and swore. There was a silence.

"It was the right thing to do," he said eventually.

A while passed before Rose could laugh at that. It came out bitter, trembling with fury. "All right. Let's see you try to back that up."

"I was eighteen."

"So was he."

"I was young. Foolish."

"Not an excuse. I'm two years younger than you were then. If I had killed Rayna, would that mean I was innocent?"

"I'm not saying I'm innocent."

"You're not saying you're guilty."

He flared to anger. "What do you want me to do, Rose? Bring him back to life? Because if I could, I would."

"That's not enough," she said, quietly. "It will never be enough."

"Have you spoken to him about this?"

Rose said nothing. Loren looked at her.

"Here is the difference between you and your father," he said. "You can admit to yourself that you don't care about right and wrong. He cannot."

"How dare you," said Rose, evenly.

"You misunderstand me. It's not an insult. You've told me yourself: you care about his safety, first and foremost, far more than you care about morality. If someone hurt him, you'd track them down and hurt them a hundred times more in return. But he's not like that. He doesn't think he holds grudges. If someone hurt you, he'd still track them down, but because they'd committed a crime, not because you were their victim. And of course he'd be far more vicious with them than he would be with an ordinary criminal. But he doesn't let himself admit that. He thinks he's objective, he thinks he's moral, but he's not."

"Stop talking," said Rose, quietly.

"Let me tell you something. The day the Department came for me, last year — when they took me and Tabitha, and killed Rayna — they knocked me out and took me to the experimental wards and strapped me to a slab, and David came in. I hadn't seen him for fifteen years, but of course I knew who he was. And he stood over me as I was strapped down, and he said, "Michael would want me to forgive you. So I do." And then he put the needle in my arm and walked out and let me be tortured. Because he thought I was a war criminal." Loren gave a bitter laugh. "Hypocrite. He was an Angel of Death just as much as I was. He just got out earlier. But you understand, Rose, he never forgave me, and he never will. He just gave himself another reason to hate me."

"He never looked like he hated you," said Rose. "When you were working together, he didn't hate you."

"Oh yes he did. But he covered it up, even from himself, because there was a bigger enemy. Then it was Felix; now it's Stephen Greenlow and his prosecutors. When they're all dealt with, he'll come for me. He's efficient, Rose. It's perhaps his only good quality."

They sat in silence. Rose looked up at him.

"You broke my father's heart," she said, quietly, "and you deprived me of a second parent."

"I . . . regret it," he said, levelly.

She resisted the urge to hit him and stood up, walked to the door. Then, suddenly, she turned back.

"Loren — How can you expect me to trust you now? How can you expect me to care what happens to you?"

"Because I trust," he said quietly, "that you are a better person than him. That you can forgive me, even if he can't."

She turned away in disgust.

"Rose?"

She did not look back at him.

"Please find Tabitha, Rose. Please find her. Don't let bad things happen to her just because I killed Michael Redmond. Please."

She left.

<<< >>>

Eighteen years earlier (age 18)
March 13, 9:42 p.m.

That night the power levels fluctuate, entirely at random, in David's labs. It's terrible, really, though admittedly the generator is built out of scrap metal and hope and, given the inexperience of its constructors, is expected to fail every now and then. One unfortunate side effect of its temporary malfunction is that the cameras and microphones in David's labs all go completely dead.

The pressing business of getting the generator back up again keeps David and Michael there long after the guards' shift ends, and so Caitlin and her boyfriend Jackson join them, weaving their way through the benches like sappers through a minefield. Which, he reflects, to a certain extent they are.

"Did you avoid the cameras?"

"As much as we could. I think Arkwood has his eye on me." At Jackson's look, she adds, "Not like that. He just suspects."

"He has nothing to suspect," says Michael firmly. "You haven't done anything."

"Not yet."

"That's ridiculous."

"Then by all means ridicule it. It's not my logic."

"All right," says Jackson. He looks nervous. "David, you said you had some kind of plan?"

"Yes."

They look at him.

"As you know," he says, "I have a . . . condition."

"Disease," says Michael quietly, and David glares at him.

"I am . . . I'm a monster. I'm a certifiable, diagnosable monster. Felix knows I'm Gifted. If he finds out what I am —"

"*Who* you are."

"Can you just shut up?" snaps David, more sharply than he intended, but Michael does shut up — partly because of David's tone, but also partly, he thinks, because they both know that the answer to that question is another manner of secret altogether.

"He'll kill you because of your *condition*," Caitlin finishes helpfully, ignoring the way Michael looks at her. "And he'll get Arkwood to do it."

"Unless he thinks he can use you," says Michael. "Unless he thinks you're more valuable alive than dead."

"He won't," says Jackson. "You're one of the few people in this army who isn't under his thumb." He pauses. "Kudos for that, by the way."

David nods. There is no other response.

"So after he goes for David," says Michael, "he'll come for me, and then for my immediate family, which means you, Caitlin, and he might actually stop there and leave you" — a nod to Jackson — "alone, but no offense, that won't be much consolation to the rest of us."

"None taken."

"So we run," says Caitlin.

"That's the face of it, yeah. You have family, Jackson?"

Jackson shakes his head. "None in London. My brother was at uni in Edinburgh when the power failed; he's stayed there since. All the War trouble seems to come back to the big cities."

"I managed to get in contact with Eleanor," says Caitlin. "Word of mouth from Oxford." She shifts her weight uncomfortably. "She's, well, she's . . . she's Gifted now, but she says she can accommodate the four of us for a while, blame the noise on the baby. We can go our separate ways from there."

Michael's and Caitlin's gazes meet for a moment. The bonds that connected him and his twin sisters frayed when their parents died; David knows that they would all prefer not to have to share each other's ghosts. They are still close enough to save one another's lives, though.

"Sounds like a plan," says Jackson briskly, rubbing his hands together. "How soon do we leave?"

"As soon as I can sort out my projects," says David. Caitlin raises her eyebrows. "I make weapons for a living. If they can't be under my control here, they're certainly not ending up in Felix's."

"So you have an ETA?" prompts Jackson.

"Two days, maximum."

Jackson nods. "The day after tomorrow, then. We'll be ready." He looks at David and Michael. "You two can look after yourselves in a gunfight, if it comes to that?"

Michael and David look at each other.

"If they want to take us down," says David grimly, "they'll need a lot more than guns."

Caitlin and Jackson nod and leave. Outside the glass door they kiss, holding on to each other as if they were drowning. Michael and David watch them.

"Do you remember the last time you promised me one of your ideas wouldn't go wrong?" says Michael unexpectedly, from the other side of the lab.

"No, I'm afraid I've forgotten," says David, with as much dry humor as he can manage.

Michael says nothing.

"I didn't mean that. Do you trust me?"

"Implicitly," says Michael. "But this isn't down to you. It's down to luck."

"My luck has got to improve at some point."

"There's no imperative. It could just have flatlined."

"Thank you for that."

"I speak only the truth, David."

"And a lot of nonsense otherwise."

They look at each other. Caitlin and Jackson are gone from the other side of the door.

"Let's assume Arkwood isn't watching us," says Michael.

"Never assume that."

"Oh, come on. If he knows everything we've just said, we're dead already, so we may as well be hung for a gunpowder keg as a sparkler. Assuming our benevolent Big Brother is blind and deaf for the moment, seeing as you've so kindly disabled his eyes and ears"—a nod to the silent cameras —"is there anything we want to say now?"

"What do you mean?"

Michael rolls his eyes. "If we don't get another chance . . ."

"You are the most pessimistic man I've ever met."

"Yes, I see it now. *You're* the voice of optimism for both of us."

David puts his feet up on his wooden desk in front of him. "Your point?"

"If this were our last good-bye, is there anything you'd want to say?"

"Nothing that you don't already know."

"My eloquent monster," says Michael, sighing. He is watching to see if David's face goes still at the word, and when it does, he says, "It's your term."

"It's one thing to hear it inside my head. It's another for you to say it."

"You would prefer 'invalid'?"

180

"I would prefer 'civilian.'"

"As would we all. You know, don't you think you should come clean with some of your secrets? It must be hard working out which lies to tell."

"Easier than having the truth kill me."

Michael shrugs. "Or I could take them. If you could somehow transfer some of your secrets to me, we could both have tolerable burdens. We could be monsters together."

"I wouldn't want you to be a monster for me."

Michael stands. "Now *that* you haven't said before."

"What about you? Where's your eloquent good-bye?"

Michael pauses, and it is dark enough that David can't see his face. He does not speak for a long time, and when he does, he is suddenly angry. "You know, sometimes I don't know why I put up with you."

He leaves. David, alone in the powerless room, listens to his footsteps down the corridor. It is accompanied by something else, which he thinks is the sound of Michael laughing.

– Chapter 20 –

The first lucky break Rose had had in what seemed like years came at five o'clock that morning, when Maria, looking exhausted, knocked on her bedroom-cell door.

"I have good news and bad news," she said.

The bad news was that since Loren could no longer be trusted, Connor Terrian was now acting Head of the Department. The good news was that he had reluctantly agreed to allow Rose back into the offices on a temporary basis. Rose was on the verge of hugging Maria when she held up a finger.

"There's a catch."

"What?"

Hesitantly, Maria opened the door, so Rose could see James Andreas standing warily behind her. Rose stiffened.

"You work with him," said Maria, "or you're out."

Rose and James watched each other in silence.

"Look," he said, apprehensively, "I know we've had our differen —"

"I will work next to him," said Rose to Maria, cutting him off. He sighed in exasperation. "I will work in proximity to him. I will not work *with* him."

"Rose, he's joined the Department again. He turned down an army promotion for this."

"Why should I care? He put my father in prison."

"It wasn't his fault what your father did."

"My father did nothing but conceal something that would harm him if it was discovered." Rose looked at James. "And it *was* discovered."

"I did the right thing," he said, angrily.

You don't know what you're say — If you knew about me, would you have sai — What would you th —

"I don't believe you."

You would be afraid of me, wouldn't you?

"He's a monster," said James angrily.

Rose flinched away from him.

"We've found some of the Demon kids," said Maria desperately. From the next cell there came a roar of *"WHAT?"*

James peered through the translucent glass window of Loren's cell. "The kidnappings of Demon kids have been going on for months now. Nate picked up on them a while back. About forty kids gone, we think. We've been looking for where they're held, because their parents and siblings have obviously been kicking up a fuss, and now we reckon we have a location on them."

Loren's response was slightly muffled, but there was no doubt of its meaning.

"We're not *waiting* for anything," said James. "The problem is there are two bases — two warehouses where we think they're being stored. One of them is held by Regency."

"And?"

James and Maria looked at each other.

"And one of them is held by the Gospel," he said, heavily.

"*What?*"

James sighed.

"This is going to take a while," he said.

<<< >>>

The first one came, and nobody paid much attention.

He was a small man, this one, dark-skinned and emerald-eyed. He made his excuses as he worked his way out of the Tube carriage, and went to sit down on the platform bench. Now, that should have been a warning sign. This was the southwestern end of the Piccadilly line. The man's train had come from deeper into the city. North. The train was going toward the airport. No other trains came here; there were no other directions. No reason to wait.

He waited.

After a while, another man, slim, shaven-headed, came and sat down beside the first. They murmured to each other. A few of their words — "godforsaken," "hellhole" — drifted gently over the commuters. Heads turned.

Not for long.

The next train pulled up beside the platform. London music: *ba-dum ba-dum, ba-dum ba-dum, ba-dum ba-dum, dum.* Count the beats as they slowed. It was the click of the tracks, really, some

184

kind of grinding machinery buried deep inside the engine of the carriage, but to the jaded human ear it turned feral, a twisted drumbeat. It shuffled messily to a halt and the doors opened.

Three, this time: two men and a woman. Green-eyed again. They sat beside their friends on the bench.

Eyes drifted toward them, and stayed there.

The next train brought with it another three: a man and two boys on the cusp of adulthood. The man was dark-haired and clear-eyed. Briskly, as the train pulled away, he pulled a gun from his pocket and fired two shots down the empty tunnel behind him.

The Gospel soldiers amassed there jumped to their feet at the noise and the screams. Stephen Greenlow stepped forward and assumed his position at their head. His sons, Aaron and Tristan, flanked him wordlessly. All of them were armed.

"This station is mine now," said Greenlow. "Hands up if you disagree."

No one moved.

Stephen nudged Aaron forward. "Go. Find them."

Aaron looked bleakly at his father. "I don't . . ."

"Can't you tell your own kind?"

Deep distaste soured in his voice. Aaron flinched. The green film of light that covered his eyes flickered for a moment, revealing the true black beneath.

Stephen Greenlow did not like Ashkind, so he did not like his son. He despised Demons, so he despised his son. He also feared impossible things. He did not quite *fear* his son, not yet, though Demons with magic were indeed impossible things, unaccounted for by the laws of magic, and Stephen Greenlow was very afraid of impossible things.

Aaron began stiffly to move among the passengers. After a

moment he stopped and said, "You." Black eyes stared up at him, wide with fear. He moved on before he could pity them. "You." Another Demon. "You."

Three of them, altogether, on that platform. A high tally. Two of them were children. Aaron took their hands and led them back to his father.

"Are we sure?" he asked softly. "Are we sure this is a good idea?"

Stephen Greenlow smiled. It was not a pleasant smile. "Oh yes," he said. "My source is not prone to uncertainty."

"Hounslow Central. Hounslow East. Osterley." Nate circled the stations on the Tube map. "All taken and captured in the past few days by the Gospel. Greenlow was present at all the attacks. They stopped before they got too close to Heathrow Airport, because good luck taking that, but it's an inconvenience all the same. Only Gifted are allowed through the barriers. Any Ashkind who try are rejected, if they're lucky."

"And if not?"

Loren sat handcuffed and flanked by two guards at the table. He looked very tired and strained. Nate glanced up at him. Rose kept her eyes on the map. *You can forgive me, even if he can't . . .*

Of course she couldn't forgive him. Not for something like this.

But was she really going to abandon her last true ally for the murder, nearly twenty years ago, of a man she had never met?

But Loren *was* the reason she had never met him . . .

"Two deaths so far," Nate said, pulling Rose back to earth. "It's not strategic gold, but that area of London is effectively theirs.

186

We think they'll go farther east next, toward the city: Boston Manor and Northfields and the rest of that branch of the line. The two warehouses where we think the Demon children are being kept are here"— he circled one right next to Hounslow East station —"and here"— near Boston Manor.

"But they're miles apart."

"Exactly," he said. "And Boston Manor station is just outside of Gospel territory. I think we've been wrong about who's been kidnapping the Demon kids. I think Regency and the Gospel are *both* doing it."

"Why?"

"Well," said Nate, rubbing his eyes, "they can't be working together, because they hate each other even more than they hate the Government, so I suppose the kids must be useful to both of them, in some way."

Loren winced at the word "useful."

"What could they both be working toward? What's their goal?"

This from Terrian. Nate looked up at his father in surprise.

"I don't know," he said. "I have no idea."

"So what are we waiting for?" asked Loren tensely. "Why are we sitting here discussing?"

"We are not going to storm those bases," said Rose, sharply. He barely glanced at her. "We wouldn't take either of them. Listen to what you're saying. That's Gospel territory, and Hounslow is a mostly Gifted area. We don't know how many of them there might be guarding the place."

"We can use the army," Loren said, his eyes still on Terrian, for all the world as if Rose's words were coming from him.

"The Government would never approve the attack. Remember who they are, now. Six hundred traumatized ex-Angels and some civil servants."

"We have superior weapons."

"And what do you suggest we do with them? Bomb the storage facilities full of children?"

Loren's wrists strained against the handcuffs.

"That's your sister," he said eventually. He threw the words viciously at Maria, who stepped back. "She came into my house and took my child. Can't you do anything?"

Maria stared at him, stricken. Nate was on his feet, but she spoke before he could.

"I haven't talked to Amelia in six months," she said, curtly. "Regency haven't allowed outside communications since Felix Callaway died."

Loren opened his mouth to retort, but Rose glared at him. He stared back at her. For a moment, it was as if they were looking at each other through quite different circumstances; as if it were still the two of them against the world, running from the Department. . . .

But those had been easier days, and both of them had done things since then that they could not forget.

Forgive me . . .

She couldn't.

But she had to. She had to forgive him; after all they'd been through, he deserved that. They both did. She would give him one last chance. Needless enmity was a luxury she could no longer afford.

They looked at each other.

Then, slowly, he closed his eyes.

"All right, then," he said, though his voice was shaking. "We wait."

<<< >>>

Eighteen years earlier (age 18)
March 7, 6:56 p.m.

"I need you to forgive me," Rayna says.

He looks at her. She is gaunt, and pale, and thin, and exhausted. Her dark hair, now cut short to her chin, looks almost gray. He cannot get angry at her under these circumstances, so he settles for wariness.

"What are you going to do?" he asks.

Rayna steps forward into the labs. She is shivering. Her uniform seems too big for her. She has to swallow several times before speaking.

"I know what you're going to do."

He keeps his face empty. It is possible — fantastically unlikely, but possible — that she does not have absolute proof and is bluffing, or even that she is talking about something else. Then she blows that hope out of the water by saying, "You're going to run for it, aren't you?"

He does not bother to insult her by lying. "Yes."

"Does it have anything to do with your sneaking away every six weeks?"

He blinks. The shock of discovery thunders through him, adrenaline slinking into his blood like poison. Briefly, he calculates how much energy it would take to overpower Rayna, but nothing short of killing her will keep her silent after that, and he draws a line at taking her life.

"You've been following me."

"Yes."

"Loren's orders, or your own initiative?"

She flinches at the disgust in his voice. "My own."

He turns away from her and starts cleaning up his equipment.

"David." He ignores her. "David, it was because I wanted to keep you safe." He doesn't fall for it. "You and me and Loren, we've known each other since before Regency. Haven't we? We trusted each other. David, please, I wanted to . . . You're my friend. We came here together, the three of us. I know things have changed, but . . ."

He does not dignify that with a response.

"You're an Angel of Death. God knows how many people want to kill you. I wanted to make sure no one did, and I thought — when you kept leaving, every six weeks, on the dot . . ." She pauses. "Well, you couldn't be defecting, because you're not exactly unknown, and it couldn't be a girl, because . . ." Another pause. "Well."

He slams the drawer shut with unnecessary force. "What do you want, Rayna?"

"I want you not to go."

"Which is not going to happen."

"I'll tell Loren."

"By all means. You can have a front-row seat at my execution."

She flinches again. "Who are you taking with you?"

He stares at her. It seems impossible that she could know

190

about the escape, and not know that. "How did you even find out?"

"I heard Caitlin talking to her boyfriend. Jackson."

"Then you know, don't you?"

She pauses, sits down on a chair. "You're taking Michael?"

He looks at her. "Yes."

"Why?"

He pauses, and she says it anyway. "You love him."

He lets it sit there; he has never heard anyone else say it before. "If I go and leave him here, your brother will kill him."

Another flinch, but no attempt to deny it. "I will stop you."

"It would kill me."

"Unless."

He folds his arms.

"I will stop you," says Rayna, in a low, intent and utterly serious voice, "unless you take someone else with you."

"Who?"

She is looking at someone behind him, and he turns. Ariadne Stronach, third-in-command of Regency and Felix Callaway's girlfriend, is watching him gravely.

"Surprise," she says, without mirth.

<<< >>>

Rose awoke at five o'clock in the morning in her not-cell and stared at the ceiling. A dead sort of weight had settled in her stomach overnight. It was, unmistakably, disappointment.

She didn't know quite why she would be disappointed, until she remembered the Demon kids. They'd found them. Oh yes. At long, long last, they'd found them, and it still wasn't simple enough, still not enough simply to *rescue* them. There were always complications. . . .

And she was going to forgive Loren. To give him another chance.

Was she wrong to?

She didn't know why she trusted him. She didn't know *if* she trusted him, even: certainly she had before, in those days last year when they had been running for their lives together, but now was different. Now her father was fighting for his life, and she wasn't sure Loren wanted him to win. Now she knew why her father hated him, and she could understand it.

She lay back and stared at the ceiling.

What would he do in this situation?

She knew exactly what he would do: he would give up on Loren, abandon him, because David, whatever he said, never trusted anyone if he could help it. Trust was a weakness to him, and always had been.

You're a better person than him . . .

Was she? Did trust make you a good person? Did it help you survive?

Trust in the abstract might not. But loyalty to Loren might just save her life, as loyalty to her had saved his.

Trust and pragmatism weren't always mutually exclusive, whatever David thought.

She sighed and got up, and, after a moment, went into the lift and pressed the button for the Department offices.

That was a mistake.

She stopped dead in the doorway. Policemen, uniformed policemen, stood beside Terrian, muttering to him: she heard her own name spoken. Her instincts pulled at her to run, but something stronger, cleverer, told her to stay where she was, to act like an innocent.

The policemen looked around and stared at her.

James saw her and lunged past them, grabbed her wrists. "Rose, you have to go, they say you're wanted for qu —"

But the policemen were faster: they shoved him away roughly and surrounded her. James backed away, looking anguished and helpless.

Rose, for her part, kept her expression flat and calm and composed. She knew what she had to do. She had seen this coming a long time ago.

She did not resist when they put the handcuffs on her.

She did not resist when they dragged her down the stairs and through the lobby and past the staring receptionist.

She did not resist when they put her in the van.

In fact, the only time she reacted to anything was at the entrance to the police station, where she saw the journalists gathered outside. Word spread fast, it seemed. They led her roughly through the crowd, pushing her head down when she tried to look up. No photographs. She followed them numbly until she felt a hand on her wrist.

"Rosalyn . . ."

She looked up. Oliver Keen's fingers brushed her palm. They came away bloody: the cuffs had broken her skin, and the blood had pooled in her half-open hand. His eyes widened.

"Get away from me," she hissed, hot with sudden, hate-fueled anger, and wrenched out of her captor's grip so that she and Keen stood face-to-face in the crowd. Microphones clustered around them. "Get away from me and never come near me again."

The policemen were coming closer. She was going to have to

make this quick. Camera flashes and the scream of feedback were crushing her. Perhaps this was a bad idea. Was this a bad idea?

No. Speak.

"I stand by my father," she said. "And he's going to be all right, and I'm not going to let him die, and I don't know whether you even really care, but I know that it would be a good story, if he died, wouldn't it? There's good money in his death for you."

They were shouting questions at her. The policemen pushed their way toward her. Speak now. No more anger.

"Listen," she said. "He will not die, not when I am alive, not as long as I have breath and blood and heart to save him. I stand between you and your story." She paused. "Do with that information what you will."

And then their hands were on her and the policemen dragged her back into the station.

Chapter 21

They threw her into the cell and she counted the hours. One. Two. Four. Eight. Sixteen.

That was as long as she could hold out. She fell asleep.

When she woke, there was a television in front of her: the old kind, the kind that you had to press to turn off, though, predictably, the off button had been ripped out. It was tuned into BBC News. Rose's strength was returning to her, and while she waited for her wits to follow, she let the reporter's voice wash over her. Confident. Assured. Male. American.

Oh, Angels.

"*Yesterday,*" said Keen, "*saw one of the most dramatic events of this trial to date. David Elmsworth's adopted daughter, Rosalyn, was taken in for questioning about her father's alleged crimes.*"

Rose stared at the screen.

"She is now in custody, and police say they are considering —"

The report vanished. The director had cut back to the news desk. The anchor looked down at her script blankly. Then she looked up at the camera.

"This is breaking," she said. *"Aaron Greenlow, son of the leader of the Gospel, has carried out an attack on —"*

Abruptly the screen went black. Whoever had put in the television to torment her had apparently decided that there was such a thing as too much information. Rose watched the dark screen for a long time.

What was happening at the trial?

What had Aaron done?

What the hell was going on?

<<< >>>

Eighteen years earlier (age 18)
February 11, 4:18 a.m.

"I will not do it."

He says it calmly. Felix stares at him. David thanks God his thoughts are silent.

"Yes you will." Arkwood's voice is almost a snarl. "It's strategically watertight, David. We could get thousands of the bastards —"

"Yes, we could."

None of them, not even Ariadne, who is watching him from behind Felix with concern in her eyes, has the slightest knowledge of how to operate the trap without him. They cannot steer the MoD drone, drop the bombs onto the street, let alone keep it hovering invisibly for half an hour, and then circle back to drop the second load of bombs on the loved ones who have come out to grieve; and then, most importantly, no one else can steer it back through the darkness, find the landing ground, set it back down on the grass unscathed.

His veto destroys the whole operation.

Felix tries the soft approach first. He is more astonished than angry; he is not used to backbone in this quiet, obedient teenager who kills his enemies for him and who rebuilt the power in the Regency complex — including that used for the camera system — with little aid and no thanks. "David," he says, tensely, "this is a prime opportunity. The concentration of Gifted here is unseen. If we wiped them out, it would be a huge blow to the Angels' morale."

"It would," says David, feeling as though his own anger is somehow inadequate in the face of that of his commanders, "but it wouldn't be worth it. They're human beings, Felix. I don't care about whether they've got magic or not. These are *children* we're talking about."

Silence. Regency soldiers are not generally parents.

"And more to the point," David says, voice stronger, "*we're* not killing them. *I* am killing them. You don't have to pilot the drone. You don't press the button. You don't —"

"Enough," says Felix softly, and, to his eternal shame, David shuts up.

Arkwood looks suddenly furious as he watches David, who doesn't meet his eyes.

He never imagined that not killing would be so difficult.

197

"Do it," says Arkwood. Ariadne says nothing; David can tell that she is watching him, and does not look at her.

"No."

The word feels like a gunshot.

Felix leans in very close, and says quietly, "It is their lives, or Michael's."

David freezes. Everything inside him seems to have failed; all his courage is gone.

How on earth can Felix know about him and Michael? He cannot know. Nobody knows.

It doesn't matter. He does know.

And that, he supposes, is the end of all his defiance.

The light is very bright; his pulse is thundering. He looks at them. He thinks of Michael.

Something inside him snaps, quick as shattering.

He presses the button.

<<< >>>

Rose had to concede this to Loren: one-way mirrors were extremely irritating.

"Can you explain your father's actions, Rosalyn?"

The police officer in front of her was not an easy target. He was about sixty, with eyes of cold ash gray, and did not smile easily. In Rose's limited experience of him, he did not smile at all. He had a list of questions on the sheet in front of him that he was going to read out to her if it killed him, and she would answer them and thereby put her evidence on tape, and then he'd lead her back to her cell and that would be the end of the encounter.

Rose loved other people and their other plans.

"He has yet to be convicted of any actions that would be of interest to the police," she said, very clearly. For the tape.

"For the purposes of this interrogation —"

"I will not incriminate him, Sergeant, for *any* purposes."

He looked exasperated.

"You are a very suspicious young woman, aren't you, Ms. Elmsworth?"

"Only to those I believe untrustworthy."

"Well." The officer looked sternly over the top of his glasses. "That makes us rather disinclined to trust *you*, Rosalyn."

"I wasn't aware I still had your trust to lose."

"You make a good point there," he murmured, and shuffled the papers again. Rose watched him.

Behind her, the door opened and Madeleine Ryan walked in.

She sat down calmly next to Rose, nodded politely at the policeman, and, when she saw how they were both staring at her, said, "My apologies for interrupting. Carry on."

The policeman looked aghast.

"I'm sorry — who are you? How did you get in here?"

Madeleine looked surprised. "I'm Rose's lawyer," she said, as though this were obvious. "A suspect — if indeed my client is a suspect, as you have not specified any alleged crimes yet — is still allowed a legal representative under interrogation, are they not? Your colleagues let me in. *They*, at least, know the law."

It seemed to take the policeman a little while to realize he had been insulted. He glowered at Madeleine, swallowed, and then, when he apparently could think of no excuse to eject her, turned with considerable effort back to Rose. Rose, for her part, was doing her best to act as if this were all part of some great plan to which she was privy. She had not expected Madeleine here at all — she was, after all, David's lawyer, not Rose's. But her arrival at least meant the policeman was outnumbered. Clearly, this thought had crossed his mind as well.

"We have new information," he said to Rose, though his eyes kept flickering back to Madeleine, "about the suspected crimes of David Elmsworth."

"Crime," said Madeleine, calmly.

The policeman glared at her again. "I'm sorry?"

"Crime, singular. David Elmsworth has only been charged with one crime — that of concealment of illegal powers. Continue."

The policeman appeared to be on the verge of cutting off the interrogation merely to spite her, but then he glanced down again at his sheet of questions and seemed to calm down slightly. He looked again at Rose. "We believe that you may have more information about the methods he used in order to conceal his . . . condition."

"No, you don't," said Madeleine, derisively.

The policeman turned fully to her in exasperated fury. "Please, Ms. —"

"Ryan," said Madeleine, glancing at the tape. "Madeleine Ryan."

"You must allow me to *question* your client if you hope to contribute anything meaningful."

"An ambition, I'm afraid," said Madeleine, leaning back in her chair, "of which you yourself fall far short. You have no new information on the alleged crimes of David Elmsworth, and certainly none you could reasonably question his daughter about. You have searched his house and his offices multiple times over several months. There is nothing new you could possibly have found."

Now the policeman was truly angry. "It is not for you to make assertions about the workings of the police force, Ms. Ryan."

"You expect your activities to go entirely unquestioned? By bringing my client here, your hope was nothing more than to throw her father into further disrepute, and — if I am correct — to force her out of the Department offices."

"Why would they want me out of the offices?" asked Rose, her eyes on the policeman.

"They don't trust you," said Madeleine. "They don't want you in the midst of a crucial fight. They think you're a liability."

"Do they," said Rose levelly, without breaking the policeman's gaze. He was starting to sweat. This interrogation was clearly not going as he had planned. Wild, panicked thoughts about what might be happening right now to Nate and Maria and James and Loren flickered through her mind, but she kept her voice quiet and steady. "Who are they fighting, Madeleine? Have they been attacked? What's going on?"

"The Gospel have —"

But before she could say anything further, a high-pitched, wailing shriek split their eardrums. Rose, clapping her hands over her ears, recognized it as the standard government attack alarm. The policeman leaped to his feet, cursing, and ran out of the room, leaving Madeleine and Rose alone in the interrogation room, trying to shield themselves from the noise. Rose had gotten to her feet and was looking around guardedly for the attackers. Her heart was beating very fast.

A masked man walked calmly in through the door the policeman had left open, looking up at the ceiling in mild interest.

"Ah," he said, over the din. "It worked, then."

The alarm cut off. Rose lowered her hands slowly, staring

from Madeleine to the masked man. "You're working with the Gospel?" she asked Madeleine, aghast.

"No, of course I'm not," she said tersely. "The Gospel aren't attacking *this* building. That was Plan B, in case I couldn't talk you out of here in time. This is Robert Carlisle, my . . ." She hesitated, and glanced at him. "My associate."

The masked man appeared to raise his eyebrows. "Lest you forget," he said, dryly, "you *have* also agreed to marry me."

Madeleine inclined her head.

"And, unless I am *very* much mistaken, you're carrying my child."

"Yes, yes, all right."

Rose gave her a weary look. "This is the teacher from Croydon, then."

"I am indeed," said Robert Carlisle, "but I have not forgotten everything I learned during the War."

"You learned to set off alarms?"

"I learned to make them."

"We don't have time for this," said Madeleine. "Rose, we need to get you out of here as quickly as possible. The Department need you. Rob will take you up to street level; you'll have to go on your own from there. And Tara Priestley's been in contact to tell me about Cassandra Mayhew. She says she's almost there with getting her to agree to testify."

"You think it's a good idea?"

Madeleine shrugged. "I don't think it's a terrible one, and we don't exactly have much to lose."

"Where are we going? What are the Gospel doing?"

"Rob will explain. I'll have to find another way there. We can't all leave together. Rob —" She gave him a quick kiss against his mask. "Take care of her."

"I don't know," said Robert Carlisle. "From what I've heard, I'm better off under *her* protection."

Madeleine hurried out. Robert Carlisle held the door open and, with a glance at him, Rose went through it. They began to walk quickly up the corridor.

After a few moments of silence, Robert said, "You can ask, you know."

"About what?" said Rose, slightly awkwardly.

Robert Carlisle sighed and took off his mask.

Words died in her throat.

A long, purple scar slashed his face in two: it started at his right temple and ran, ugly and puckering, down his cheek, just missing his eye, nicking the edge of his mouth, and finally ending with a flourish at his chin.

Rose looked away. At last, she said, "You're the reason Madeleine is defending my father."

"Why would you think that?"

She paused before she said it, and the words did not come easily. "Hybrid scars don't heal. Not even with magic."

"Indeed, they do not."

He sensed her question and looked back at her. The corridors were silent, and no one had stopped them: so far, so good. "I was fourteen," he said. "It was a few months after the Veilbreak. At that time, yes, there were relatively few Hybrids in the city. Felix Callaway was the only known one, and now we know your father was another. Of course, I never knew who had attacked me. As you know, Hybrids are not recognizable when they are transformed."

Rose glanced at him sharply, and then, just as quickly, she looked away. "It took a long time for me to realize how much restraint they had showed. My wounds were not severe enough to kill me, but neither did the venom get into my bloodstream, so I did not become one of my attackers. In many ways I was extremely fortunate."

"Do you think it was my father who . . . ?"

He looked away from her. "Until six months ago, I had no idea that he was even a possibility. I had never believed it was Felix Callaway, though. I could not look at that man and believe he would leave any of his victims alive. I was very glad when your father killed him. But when I found out the truth, when everyone did . . . I thought I knew. It was groundless — without evidential basis, as Madeleine would say — but I believed more and more strongly with every news report that I was looking into the face of my attacker."

Rose swallowed. "So why didn't you want him dead?"

He glanced at her, and took a moment to reply. "I did," he said. "I wanted your father dead more than anything in the world. And I cannot have that on my conscience, Rosalyn; I cannot have that hatred stain my soul. This may sound strange to you, Rose, but the War made me a pacifist. It was the only way I survived it. I never took a life, and I never harmed anyone if I could help it."

He rubbed his face. "I could not go back to the kind of hatred I had known in the War. I needed to forgive him. No, I could not just *forgive* him; I needed to actually put in *effort* to make sure he lived. Madeleine wanted the case anyway — it's quite a career boost, this — and I encouraged her to do it. If I forgave him, even helped to save his life, I suppose in some, moral way, I would have . . . won."

He paused, a slight smile on his lips, as if amused by his own logic.

"It has been nearly twenty years since I was attacked. It has left me with too many visible scars without letting it affect my soul as well."

Rose was silent. In the distance, footsteps murmured softly, pattering like rain.

"No wonder Madeleine loves you," she said.

Robert smiled. "Ah, well, this is where we differ, Rose. That particular fact is a source of constant wonder to me."

"You're very lucky."

"I am indeed."

They came to a door. Robert tested it. It was unlocked.

"At which point," he said, "I should leave you. I'm sure you can handle things from here. Anyway, my presence cannot easily be explained away." He rubbed his face again, ruefully. "I am . . . easy to remember."

"Are you sure?"

"Of course I'm sure."

Rose turned to him. "Thank you," she said. She thought she should feel a sense of guilt. After all, here was a man scarred for life by a Hybrid, walking calmly beside her without knowing she herself was one of them. But that part of her had long since died.

He smiled, the scar creasing with the movement of his face. He walked away, and with his hand on the door he turned.

"Oh, yes," he said, "and you were wrong about the Gospel. The whole Department were. They're nowhere near Boston Manor station. That was never their target. They've gone the other way. They're heading for Heathrow Airport."

He left her alone in the corridor, her mouth open.

Chapter 22

"Loren. Loren, wake up. Now."

His eyes opened immediately, and he lay there for a moment on his cot bed in his cell beneath the Department. She crouched beside him, watching the light form and coalesce in his eyes. Then he turned to her.

"Have you found her?"

He meant Tabitha, of course. She shook her head. She saw a flicker of anguish pass across his face, but he did not say anything. He could read her expression well enough. This was not the time.

"What's happened?"

"The Gospel are attacking Heathrow Airport. I reckon the Department need us both. Will you help?"

He sat up on one elbow. "Is it Greenlow?"

"I would imagine so. It's full-scale — they'll have been preparing for this for a long time. This is it, Loren. Our chance to defeat the Gospel. And when they're gone, it'll be that much easier to defeat Regency, and then we can rescue —"

She didn't need to finish her sentence; the merest glimpse of Tabitha's freedom was enough to get him up on his feet, swinging his coat over his shoulder.

"Does Terrian know you're freeing me?"

Rose hesitated. "Desperate times," she said, eventually.

Loren turned and raised his eyebrows. She held his gaze.

"I'm bringing the others, as well. Even —" She hesitated. "Even Tara Priestley. We need everyone we can, and Terrian doesn't need to know if he's just going to fight it."

He shrugged and turned toward the door.

"Loren?"

He looked back at her. "Yes?"

She paused, considered, and then punched him hard in the face.

He stumbled backward into the door. The coat slipped from his grip. He pulled himself up to his full height again, put a hand to his face, and checked it for blood.

"You're fine," said Rose. "I wasn't trying to break your cheekbone. If I had, believe me, it'd be broken. And probably so would the rest of you."

He winced. "I believe you. I suppose that was for Michael Redmond, was it?"

She watched him appraisingly. "This doesn't mean it's over, you know."

"I know."

"But you're right," she said. He glanced at her in surprise. "I'm not my father."

"Thank Ichor," he muttered. He picked up his coat again and opened the door.

"Do you promise you won't be a liability to us?" said Rose, after a moment. "We can trust you?"

He looked at her for a long moment. He gave a brief, thin smile.

"I still have a conscience, don't I?"

<<< >>>

Eighteen years earlier (age 17)
January 29, 7:17 p.m.

Loren is standing at the podium. His yellow-green eyes, so alien and anathema to the Ashkind troops, are glittering; his pale skin shimmers slickly in the artificial light, and his blond hair is on end, twisting with the change in the air currents. It doesn't matter; he is on fire. His voice is hypnotic, shot through with savage triumph. He has the army bound to him, and he knows it. He is electric.

"They tried to betray us," he says. David stands behind him onstage, with Felix and Ariadne, and tries to truly appreciate the fact that the man now speaking is his superior. This capture has bought Loren Arkwood his promotion: he is second-in-command of Regency now, and the guardian of every single one of its members. And very good for them that he is, too, or the captives tied to the bottom of the stage right now might well be spilling Regency secrets to the Angels.

"They tried to bring us to our knees," says Loren, "and take us down — pathetic, arrogant, traitorous scum that they are. But we are cleverer. We are stronger. We are braver."

Felix, sensing a break in the speech, steps forward and places a hand on Loren's shoulder: brotherhood, solidarity. The crowd switches their attention to him, their glorious, brilliant leader, and now he holds the power in his voice, and with it he asks one question:

"Do you understand?"

The response is slow. The question, David notes wearily, is deliberately ambiguous, so that every member of the assembled crowd can interpret it differently, but there is no doubt of what answer they will find. Do you understand what these people have done? Do you understand why they have to die? Do you understand what we're going to have to do, to bring our victory that much closer? Do you understand what each of you, every single one of you, will have to become, to save your world?

Each soldier finds a question to which the answer is "yes," and they nod slowly, or murmur, the noise growing through the crowd until the affirmation is unmistakable. The captives, of course, interpret this as their death warrant being signed, and struggle all the harder. One of them screams.

Felix nods gravely, and four of his guards step forward from the front row, take a prisoner, and start dragging them up onto the stage. It is difficult, and remarkably undignified. The traitors — three women and a man, all middle-aged — are tied to stakes. In the meeting, when the Regency leaders got together and decided how they were to die, Loren suggested burning them. David and Ariadne vetoed him immediately.

The prisoners are shoved up against the wall. David only

knows they are shoved because he is so close; from farther away he imagines it looks very gentle. These executions have been carefully planned, because they must set a precedent. Every death of a Regency soldier, no matter what they have done, is a terrible thing; therefore their killings must be agonizing for the leaders, heartbreaking, and — crucially —*for the good of the cause.* Nothing else would be worth their sacrifice. This is very much Loren and Felix's philosophy.

The prisoners stare out at the crowd, terrified, bleeding from various wounds, and the four Regency leaders turn their backs to the audience and line up. David gets out his gun. It is a good one. He had it made especially for him.

He raises the weapon so that the barrel exactly obscures the woman's face, and then he looks down the row at the others. They all fire together. David makes sure he closes his eyes for the recoil, so that he doesn't see the face until the job is done. When he lowers the gun, the woman is still. Her head droops onto her chest so her position is exactly symmetrical. If you ignore the blood, that is. Blood defies geometric order.

Now that the prisoners are dead, Loren steps back up to the podium. The electricity is in his eyes again. The crowd is utterly silent.

"These are the first," he says. "They will not be the last. And I speak to you now, if your loyalty is in any way compromised, if you have ever, for a second, thought of defecting, if you have considered cowardice, I speak to you. Look at me." His teeth are bared. "If you try, or look like you might try, or talk about trying, then make no mistake. We will find you. I will find you. We will know who you are, and you will die *exactly* like this."

This is off-script. Felix and Ariadne look at each other. Then, slowly, they start clapping. The rest of the army follow, building soldier by soldier to a wall of applause. David joins in, of course, but he's searching the audience. Michael is watching David silently. He is perhaps the last to put his hands together.

When it is over David goes back to his empty labs. He waits. He hears Michael's footsteps from yards away, but Michael still hesitates before coming in.

David sits in his chair, watching Michael carefully as he stands in the doorway. Michael makes a small gesture toward the corner of the room, and David shakes his head. "Cameras are off. I made sure."

Michael sighs. David half expects him to walk over, but he stays exactly where he is. "How did it feel? To kill her?"

David doesn't answer.

"Don't get desensitized on me."

"I won't."

"Oh yeah? You sit here in your control room making weapons and you press big red buttons and people die and you never even see —"

"Michael," David says, though his voice shakes, "I know exactly what I'm doing."

"No you don't. No you don't." Michael puts his hand against the wall and tries to calm down. "David, I can't just stand there and watch you kill. You look . . ." He pauses, wordless. "You look *inhuman*."

David can't speak for a moment. He turns on his chair. "Are you leaving me?"

"No."

A deeper thrum of panic. "Are you going to try to run?"

Michael says nothing, and David is immediately on his feet. "No. *No.* Michael, you can't do that. They'll kill you." His pulse is fracturing at the thought. "They'll make *me* kill you."

"Come with me," says Michael softly.

"I can't."

Michael sighs, and comes forward. The silence thickens the closer they get to each other, and David, who has sat down again, trembling, stares at him, stricken. Michael kneels down in front of him, and they stay like that for a moment, holding the electricity between them, and then Michael kisses him. David's mind shorts out, and he finds Michael's hands, grips them, skin on skin, with all his strength. For a moment he wonders how he manages to live when Michael is not this close.

Michael pulls back. All David can see are his eyes.

"Come with me," murmurs Michael. David gets the impression he can't think very clearly either.

"I can't. They need me."

"Screw them. Who needs you? Callaway and Stronach have each other. Arkwood lives off watching the rest of us. He doesn't even care about his own sister. Run, David. Please."

"I . . ." He shakes his head. "The War."

"You're Gifted," says Michael. "You don't belong here. Let the War end. Let it all crumble."

David stands, breaking away. "I can't. I need the facilities. If I transform outside, I don't know how many I'll kill."

"You're killing *here*," says Michael. "Maybe you're not holding the gun, maybe you're sane and thinking straight, maybe you don't look them in the eye when you do it, but people have died because you're here. Hundreds. Maybe even thousands. It might be traumatic to kill as a monster, David, and I'm sorry for that, but it's better than becoming one when you're human."

David looks at him. "No," he says. "I'll change things. I'll make them change. I —" He sees Michael's skeptical expression and suddenly he is angry. "I can do this, Michael. I'll do things differently. I promise you."

"You can't make them change. They're stronger than you."

"No," says David firmly. "I won't kill anymore. I'll change them. I will."

– Chapter 23 –

They amassed inside the tunnel with smiles on their faces.

It was a long, thin tunnel, just inside the walls of the airport. On one side, the entrance: the model plane and the big WELCOME TO HEATHROW sign that all the cars drove past. On the other side, the terminals and the planes and the security. This tunnel, therefore, was the aorta of the airport. To take this would be to grab it by the throat.

The Gospel soldiers stood along the walls of the tunnel in neat rows, doing their best to look like security guards. None of the cars stopped.

After a long time, after a break appeared and lengthened in the traffic, one of the younger Gospel members — a green-eyed girl of about fifteen — hopped down into the road. She stood there calmly as the cars approached. Bemusedly, they slowed. Horns honked.

Another child, a boy this time, came to join her. The queue of cars in front of them grew steadily. The noise of mechanized outrage was deafening.

A young man came to stand with the children. His gun was displayed quite clearly on his waist.

The horns began to quieten.

Slowly, the Gospel soldiers stood in a long line in front of the cars, daring the drivers to mow them down. No one did. Then, when the tunnel was well and truly blocked, Aaron Greenlow stepped forward.

"Hello," he said.

Absolute silence fell.

"So, we have two options."

They sat around a table in a café in the airport. They looked very tense. There were six of them: Terrian, Nate, Maria, James, Rose, and, to everyone's intense resentment, Evelyn Wood of the Anti-Corruption Commission, one of the witnesses who had testified against David. She was apparently there to make sure the notoriously improvisational Department did nothing seriously inadvisable. Rose could have pointed out to her that that ship had sailed a very long time ago, but for the moment she kept quiet: she was very glad of the presence within their group of someone more disliked by the Department than she herself.

Rose had explained to Nate and Maria about being released from questioning without mentioning Robert Carlisle. The way she told it, she and Madeleine had simply talked their way out of custody. None of the rest of the unit questioned her story, and though her presence in the group had not been acknowledged, neither had it been actively prevented. Perhaps Terrian had finally realized how badly the Department needed her; or perhaps he simply did not have the energy to throw her out. Evelyn Wood, on the other hand, kept throwing suspicious glares at Rose, who personally thought this very unprofessional. She had more than enough reason to hate Wood — it had been her idea to send Rose into Regency as a spy, after all — and *she* wasn't letting it affect her behavior like that.

They were all in plainclothes, doing their very best to look like tourists. James had a map of the airport in front of him and was laying out the plan, and Rose was trying not to look like she was listening to him.

"We can follow protocol," he said, "and issue a mass evacuation order. Everybody out. No planes leave the ground. That way, if the Gospel do manage to get here, no one will be hurt. Of course —"

"That will cause chaos," finished Maria quietly, "which is exactly what Greenlow wants."

Evelyn Wood sat forward, already hostile. "But we can't *not* do it. There are thousands here. We can't let them be present at an open conflict. That would be insanely dangerous."

James sighed, and continued as if he had not heard her. "The second option is not to tell anyone. The Gospel have got the tunnel, so nobody goes in or out, but their soldiers aren't actually in the terminals. At least, not yet. We can frame the tunnel blockage as building work if anyone finds out. We try to defeat them with minimal disruption."

Terrian looked exhausted. "But their lives will be at risk. We'll have to *hope* that no one finds out or tries to investigate. It would be far safer just to evacuate."

"Would it, though?" asked Nate. His father glanced at him in surprise. "Emptying the entire contents of Heathrow at two o'clock on a Monday afternoon onto the M4? That's a pileup waiting to happen."

"But we can *control* that. You don't know how good we have it now, Nathaniel. We have the might of the Government on our side. If we try to keep this insurrection a secret, we won't be able to tell Heathrow's security. We will be operating without Government authority." Terrian looked pained. "We'll be *vigilantes*."

James raised his eyebrows at Rose. "Anything to add?"

She glared at him. He put his head in his hands.

"Rose, please," he said, his voice muffled. "What happened to professional detachment?"

Rose closed her eyes.

"Don't tell them," she said, after a moment. "It'll cause a panic. We don't make this public until it's too late."

"Oh, come on," said Evelyn Wood, with tense anger. "Who on earth are you to take these people's lives into your hands? How do you see yourselves?"

"We're professionals," said Nate quietly.

"Are you? Really? I look around you and I see a bureaucrat, a conscript, two medical students and a girl who thinks she's David Elmsworth."

There was a long, dark silence. Rose glanced at James and saw his fists were clenched. She looked away again quickly before she could get angry along with him.

"Think of us what you will, Ms. Wood," said Terrian, in a strained voice, "but you will need to at least feign respect for us and our institution if you want to work with us."

217

"I *don't* want to work with you."

"Then leave," said Rose tersely. "Leave, and tell your loved ones that you weren't there to save your city when it needed you."

For a moment she thought Wood was going to hit her. She got up.

"I'm going to use the bathroom," she said.

She walked away before they could call her back, if indeed anyone was going to, slipping easily into the swirl of passengers. Outside the glass walls, the airplanes loomed huge over the runways. Rose walked through duty-free into the women's toilets. She found the disabled cubicle and knocked.

"Who is it?"

"Who *knocks* on a toilet door if they don't already know who's in there, Tara?"

There was a rattling and the door opened. Loren leaned against the far wall of the toilet cubicle, bandages wrapped inelegantly around his wrists. Robert and Madeleine sat in a corner together. His hand was on her stomach, her head on his shoulder, her hair covering his scar.

"News?" asked Loren. Rose, looking at him, felt a slight squirm of discomfort: she had failed to mention to Terrian and Wood that any of them were here, and though she felt no obligation to be fully honest with either of them, lying so blatantly to the Department still did not come easily.

"They're keeping it quiet."

A mutual sigh of relief, like a quiet breeze. "Thank the Angels," said Madeleine. "It would have been hell."

"Evelyn Wood isn't that impressed with us."

"Well, no," said Tara. "You're not very impressive. What's the plan?"

"I don't know that we have one."

"And there is my evidence."

Rose rubbed her face. "Does anyone have anything useful to add?"

"Yes," said Tara. "Cassandra Mayhew's just sent me a message. She's agreed to testify for us."

Madeleine sat up straight. Normally Rose, too, would have been overjoyed at this news, but right now she was too tense to feel anything like joy. "That's wonderful, Tara, but I mean about the Gospel. Where will they aim for?"

"Air Traffic Control," said Loren immediately. Tara nodded. "You can't take off without permission from the tower. Pilots won't do it. The airport will be paralyzed. If they get ATC, you've lost before you've begun."

Rose nodded. "Anything else?"

"You need to get the tunnel back," said Tara. "If the Gospel have it for long enough, it will filter out eventually that something's wrong. You can't pass it off as construction work forever."

"And how do you suggest we do that?"

Silence.

"I have an idea," said Loren, slowly.

The teenagers walked past the PRIVATE: NO ENTRY sign without a glance at the door. They closed it behind them, leaning against each other, giggling. They were young — sixteen, maybe seventeen — but there was something to their bearing that suggested a weight on their shoulders. The girl was pretty and blond and laughed easily. The boy was dark-skinned and somber, green-eyed, low-voiced. Strain showed in his eyes.

The guard stepped forward as they kissed, the girl pushing the boy up against the wall.

"I'm sorry," he said awkwardly, "but this is a prohibited area."

The girl shrieked and leaped away from her boyfriend, staring at where the guard's voice had come from. It took her a long time to find him. The corridor was not well lit.

The guard sighed, and said it again. "I'm afraid you're going to have to leave."

The girl giggled, clutching at the boy. "Oh, Angels! We'll have to be more careful, Nate." She took a hesitant step toward the guard. "Is this, like, secret or something?"

"Not secret. Just . . . special."

"Really? Is this where you keep all the planes?"

The guard stared at her. She took another step forward. The boy moved with her.

"No," he said. "This is where we direct the planes from. We call it Air Traffic Control."

She giggled again. "That's such a cool name."

"I'm glad you think so, but I'm afraid you're still going to have to —"

"Can we see it?" She took a step forward so she was only a few feet away from him. "Is it — can we see the secret planes? Because, you know, that would be *amazing*. Like, totally."

He smiled uneasily. "That's not going to be possible."

She looked disappointed. "Oh, that's so sad."

Her boyfriend raised his arm. "Remember, side of the wrist, not the flat of the forearm."

"Yeah," said Maria, "I remember," and hit the guard very hard in the neck. He dropped. She stared down at him in astonishment.

"Jugular vein?"

"I really hope so. It's that or you've broken his neck."

"It's fine. We would have heard something."

Nate glanced at her.

They stepped over the body of the guard and opened the door of the ATC. The place was so full of voices and the click of mouses that no one noticed them, at first. Then, of course, they did. Heads turned slowly.

"Hello," said Nate, before anyone could do anything stupid. "My name is Nathaniel Terrian, and this is Maria Rodriguez. Despite what it looks like, we're from the Department. We're here to give you some bad news. You're in terrible danger."

Absolute silence. Then, slowly, the controllers took off their earpieces. They turned around in their chairs so that Nate and Maria could see the winged-door Gospel insignias sewn into their uniforms. Then, from the chair at the far end of the room, Tristan Greenlow stood up.

"You know, Nate," he said, "I don't think we are."

– Chapter 24 –

They drove in silence. Up ahead of them the Gospel-held tunnel loomed darkly. Rose kept her eyes on the gloom within.

"I am trying to forgive you," he said.

Her voice was tight with anger. "Don't bother."

James sighed. For a moment Rose thought he was going to bash his head against the steering wheel.

"We can't work like this."

"I don't care. I cannot talk to you as if you were my friend. You are not my friend. You betrayed my father."

A flash of darkness across his eyes: "He betrayed *me*."

"Oh, don't you dare. Don't you dare flatter yourself like that. He didn't betray anyone. He didn't care about what you thought. He just didn't tell anyone, to protect himself. And nobody was ever hurt by their not knowing. It wasn't *betrayal* — it was self-preservation."

"And how many people died so that he could be *preserved*? He is a monster, Rose."

The words climbed up into her heart and lodged themselves there. The words had claws. They ripped and tore at her. They destroyed her peace. They made her want to cry. They made her want to hurt him. They made her want to get out of this car and leave herself to the mercy of the racing asphalt beneath.

She pressed her hands to her face. "I hate you."

He flinched. She felt a quiet, savage pleasure.

They said nothing after that.

After a few minutes, the tunnel reared up before them. Its blackness was all-consuming. They stopped at the edge of the pileup of deserted cars and got out. She caught him looking at her waist, to check that her gun was there.

Of course it was.

They walked together toward the thin gray light of the tunnel. No one stopped them. Rose's heart was beating far too fast.

"This is a trap," James said aloud.

"Well, yes."

"How is it a trap?"

"I don't know. Any competent trap-setter would have sprung it by now." Rose turned in a slow circle, pointing her gun up at the walls. "You hear that, Aaron? You're bloody terrible at this."

Silence. Then, after a long time, the emergency exit doors opened. Gospel soldiers lined up along the walls of the tunnel, weapons pointed at Rose's and James's heads. Aaron Greenlow stood in front of them. He stepped down from the wall.

"What exactly," he said, "did you think you were going to achieve with this?"

Rose said nothing. She pointed her gun into his face. James was looking between them and the Gospel soldiers; panic showed in his expression.

"You're outnumbered and outgunned," said Aaron, swagger in his voice. "Put it down, Rose."

She tightened the aim, focused it between his eyes. "You have no right to use my name."

"I can do whatever I like to you."

She would have fired just for that, but then their next moves would have been obvious. Bullet in her head. Bullet in James's. End of scenario. Certainly, she would have deprived Stephen Greenlow of a son, but then she would also be depriving David Elmsworth of a daughter. And . . . whatever James's parents were called, of their eldest child. It occurred to her that she had never thought to ask about his family.

What a stupid thought to be focusing on right now. What a stupid, stupid thought.

"Put the gun down," said Aaron easily, "or I will kill him."

The only point of having a gun out was to fire it. Firing it would cost Rose her life. She dropped the gun.

"And you, ginger."

James glared, but put the weapon down anyway. Three soldiers immediately descended and began searching him.

"So, psycho girl," said Aaron, circling her, "you haven't answered my question. What exactly were you hoping to achieve?"

She shrugged, not breaking his gaze. "We had the element of surprise."

"They say that's half the battle."

"We were working the other half out as we went along."

224

"This seems like a terrible plan."

Rose focused by imagining his blood painted against the back wall. "Seemed like a good idea at the time."

He smiled widely. Too close to her. "Heat of the moment, was it?"

"Sir," said one of the soldiers who had been searching James, sharply. "He's got something on him."

Aaron switched his attention immediately to James. "What is it?"

The soldier withdrew his hand from James's pocket. It was a large, black sphere, covered in blinking red lights. Under the circumstances it could have been either a disco ball or a bomb. The Gospel soldiers jumped to conclusions.

The soldier carrying it shrieked in alarm and dropped it. The ball rolled slowly underneath a car. The soldiers shoved Rose and James roughly back against the wall.

Aaron was frantic. "What is it? What does it do?" He rounded on Rose. "Tell me!"

She said nothing, but smiled. He snarled at her, fake-green eyes wide, so wide she imagined she saw the black beneath them. At times, she had almost felt sorry for Aaron: the Demon son of a man who hated Demons more than anyone else in the world. This was not one of those times.

"*Tell me!*" he roared.

"I don't give information to your kind," she said softly, and even though she knew it was wrong to say it, even though the insult carried no weight, even though she knew that by speaking ill of Demons she spoke ill of Tabitha and all the other kidnapped children in those warehouses, it hurt him, and he flinched.

She smiled again. His anger was savage now.

"Tell me, psycho girl," he said, softly, "or I will put you in so much pain you will wish you'd never been born."

James's hand groped along the wall. He kept his eyes on Aaron, his breathing hard.

"Tell —"

"It's not a bomb," she said tiredly.

He stared at her. "What?"

"It's not a bomb. It doesn't do anything. It'll lie there flashing its lights to kingdom come."

His eyes widened still further. "Then what . . ."

"We don't want to kill you," said James, though the look in his eyes betrayed him there. "We just want to do this."

And his hand found the light switch on the wall and pressed it.

The darkness was instant and complete. The Gospel soldiers cried out in panic. Shots were fired. Rose pressed herself against the wall and slid down until she was a tiny ball, an impossible — or at least very difficult — target in the crumbling dark. James was beside her. She could hear his breathing. She folded in on herself and closed her eyes to cover the open, wide blackness with the inside of her eyelids, and she waited and listened to the Gospel panic.

"What's going on?"

"Turn the bloody lights back on!"

"Where are they? Should we fire on them?"

"Where's the light switch?"

Rose's stomach lurched and she folded in on herself even more tightly. Probability could not stop bullets, but it might dissuade them.

"I can't —"

226

"Sir, what should we —"

"Stop," said a familiar voice, and silence fell starkly over the Gospel. Even their breathing seemed to stop. There was a *click* and the lights came back on. The soldiers stood very still. Each had been forced into a half nelson by the Department soldier who stood over them, guns pressed to their temples.

Rose and James got to their feet slowly. As they watched, Terrian forced Aaron's second-in-command to his knees with brutal proficiency. Evelyn Wood dealt with Aaron. He dropped without needing to be forced.

"Do you have something you say?" she asked Terrian curtly, as Aaron began to hyperventilate at her feet. "Do you tend to read people their rights?"

Terrian shrugged. "Not really. We don't usually leave people alive."

"Ah," said Wood, and swung her gun into the side of Aaron's head. He slumped, unconscious. Rose and James looked at each other.

Terrian nodded slowly. "Yes, that works, too."

They called the police after that. Police sirens were not particularly well designed for stealth or discretion, so they came in quiet, unmarked lorries, and took the Gospel soldiers away in the back. It had been James's idea to keep Aaron with them. As he said, as the vans drove away, Stephen Greenlow's son was not a bad bargaining tool.

Then he hit Aaron again, to make sure he was out. He nodded, satisfied.

He and Evelyn Wood, both still giving each other suspicious looks, went back up to the airport to find somewhere to hide

Aaron's unconscious body. Terrian and Rose went up to Air Traffic Control, to check that Nate and Maria had been successful. She did not make eye contact, or say anything. She did not want to talk to him.

He did it anyway.

"That was a good idea of yours," he said, gruffly. Rose glanced at him to check how sincere the bitterness in his voice was. By the looks of it: very.

She thought of Loren. "Can't take all the credit."

He said nothing, and the conversation ended there, much to her relief.

They opened the PRIVATE: NO ENTRY door to ATC. Terrian looked official enough that no one had looked twice at them. It was so dark in there that they had to peer down the corridor for a long time before they saw the unconscious guard crumpled beside the door.

"That's not right."

Terrian moved before she understood what was happening, sprinting down the corridor. It took her a moment to see the blood leaking around the door to the control room. She followed him, jumping over the guard as he opened the door. The room was empty, the computers dark and deserted. Nate and Maria lay unconscious in the middle of the room. Nate's nose was crushed, his blood pooling on the floor.

Terrian didn't speak. He knelt down beside his son and turned him over, checking for any other injuries. He did all of this with the steady surety of instinct. The fact that, before the War, he had been a doctor came slowly back to Rose. She was staring down at Nate and Maria. Her thoughts were sluggish, stunned.

Terrian, apparently satisfied that Nate's broken nose was the

228

only significant injury to him, was rubbing his hands together, readying his magic. He spoke to Rose without looking at her. "Check Maria."

Nate must have told his father by now that he and Maria were dating. Odd. Rose wouldn't expect Terrian to take something like that very well.

Think, think, what are you doing?

She crouched down beside Maria. Airway, breathing, circulation: those were the steps, weren't they? Were they? She must be stupid. She tilted Maria's head back gently, held her hand over Maria's mouth to feel her breathing, found her pulse in her neck. She looked up at Terrian. "She's okay."

Rose could feel the heat from Terrian's hand as Nate's nose began to slowly reshape, the broken bone and cartilage fusing together. "What have they done to the computers?" he asked her curtly.

She turned, examined the screens behind her. No noise, no light, no heat. She knelt down, saw the bullets that had smashed the hard drives of the computers. "Nothing intelligent. Vandalism."

A groaning noise from behind her. Maria was waking up. Rose rushed to her, grasped her hand.

"Are you all right?"

Maria made an incoherent noise. Rose cursed herself. "It's okay, you don't have to speak."

"Tristan," muttered Maria. Rose went cold. So Stephen Greenlow's younger son had been here as well. "Tristan was here, he . . ."

"What did he do to Nathaniel?" asked Terrian stiffly.

"Knocked him out. Stomped on his face."

229

Terrian went very still for a moment. Rose could see fury pulse through him. It was the kind of truly frightening, bloodlust-fueled rage that Rose had not seen in him in nine years, not since his wife had died.

Maria tried to get up, but Rose pushed her down again. "Don't. You've been hurt. Stay there."

Maria acquiesced reluctantly, and was quiet for a few seconds. Her voice, when she spoke, was hoarse. "They were . . . We were too late, they'd already . . ."

"I know, I know. It wasn't your fault."

Footsteps and shouting grew slowly from the other end of the corridor. Rose got up immediately and went to the door. She stopped dead as soon as she recognized the voices.

She turned to Terrian and opened her mouth, then thought better of it. He looked up. Nate's nose was almost healed now. "Who is it?"

Rose was saved from having to answer by James and Evelyn Wood, who burst through the door, dragging Tara and Loren in their wake. Loren had been forced into handcuffs again. He glowered furiously at Wood as she shoved him against the wall. James was slightly gentler with Tara, though the look she gave him was equally murderous.

"I found them in the toilets," said Wood angrily. Behind her, Rose could see Robert and Madeleine standing together, having apparently escaped being handcuffed.

Terrian rounded on Rose. "You did this, didn't you? You brought them here!"

Rose and Loren exchanged a look. It took her a moment to answer.

"I know nothing about this," she said.

Terrian glared at her, clearly incredulous. Beneath him, his son stirred. Terrian glanced down at him. "Why is *she* here?" he asked, furiously.

"I have a name outside of gender pronouns," said Madeleine, coldly. Terrian glared at her.

"I know full well who you are."

Rose knew he was thinking of his cross-examination, Madeleine looking down at him from her place as defense attorney on the benches.

"I'm sure your professionalism extends so far, Colonel Terrian," said Madeleine, "as not to taint our encounters outside court with the hostility you showed me within it."

He glared at her. "So this was your idea, was it?"

Madeleine did not look at Rose. "Indeed it was."

Rose blinked.

"And what on earth made you think you could take an unpredictable and possibly dangerous individual"— Terrian gestured at Loren, who rolled his eyes —"out of my protective custody and into a conflict zone in which he has no place?"

Loren began to reply heatedly to this, but Tara placed a hand on his arm, watching Madeleine.

"First of all," Madeleine said coldly, "the Department is not *yours*. Secondly, I have seen your judgment in action, Colonel Terrian, and I deemed it best to override it. And a good job I did, too, or Heathrow might now be in even worse shape than it currently is. Thirdly, Mr. Arkwood has not been registered as detained, nor has he been formally charged, so I believe I was the one on the right side of the law in this case by removing him. And fourthly, what you describe as a *conflict zone* is one of the busiest airports in the world. Given that you have not seen fit to evacuate the building, Mr. Arkwood has as much right to be here as any other citizen."

"And how can you be sure he won't sabotage this operation the moment he has the chance? How do you know he won't steal our equipment and run off to Regency to get himself killed over that kid of his as soon as we give him the slightest *shred* of an opportunity?"

"He has given his word," said Madeleine calmly.

Terrian stared at her until his attention was distracted by Nate moaning loudly. He knelt to examine his son again.

Tara glared again at James, who sighed, and began to unlock her handcuffs.

"Colonel Terrian," said Robert calmly, "you have enough sets of enemies as it is, without making others out of those who would rather be helping you."

Terrian did not look up from Nate. "And who the hell are you?"

"Robert Carlisle. Ms. Ryan here, of whom you seem to think so ill, is my fiancée."

There was heat in his voice now. Madeleine nudged him, murmuring, "Don't," as Terrian looked up, taking in Robert's face, his scar. Robert's gaze was implacable. After a second Terrian returned his attention to Nate. He asked no questions.

"Are you seriously implying," said Evelyn Wood with icy rage, "that you intend to let them *stay*?"

Terrian said nothing. James took this for the response it was, and went to Loren.

"Hold out your hands," he said, with weary resignation.

<<< >>>

Nineteen years earlier (age 17)
April 12, 3:01 p.m.

"Can you help him?"

He says it straight, so they do not mistake him: he is asking them to break Regency law. They stare at him, and then at each other.

"How . . . how serious a help would this be?" asks Ariadne uncertainly. She turned twenty-four earlier this week. Felix threw an entire day of festivities for the whole army on account of it. Even the branch in Seattle knew about it.

Ari hates parties. David saw her standing awkwardly in a corner, drinking vodka from a pint glass.

"Just to survive the Darkroom. Just . . . food and water. And sanity."

Rayna and Ari glance at each other. "That's against regulations, David."

"God *knows* I know that."

This is perhaps the riskiest thing he has ever done. They are out of sight of the cameras — the bedrooms of Regency's leaders, and their loved ones, are the one place that is not watched by the surveillance systems — but the fact remains that he is talking to, respectively, the sister of one of Regency's most powerful figures and its second-in-command, not to mention the girlfriend of its leader.

Were there any other way, he probably would not even have trusted Rayna and Ari with this request.

233

But there is no other way.

"The Darkroom leaves its mark," says Rayna. "They'll know if Michael hasn't passed it properly."

"No, they won't. I'll coach him."

They exchange a look. "David, can't you . . . ?"

He knows what the question is, and he cannot blame them for it: Can't you do something on your own to help this guy? Do you have to drag me into it? But all three of them know that is not how the system works. David may officially be Head of Security, but his job is to prevent people from destroying Regency from the outside. All security on the inside, and especially regulation of those who volunteer to join, is managed unofficially by Loren Arkwood.

He remembers the Darkroom from his own time there. It is the test that all who wish to join Regency must pass, and which Michael must now undergo: to be placed in an underground, pitch-black room for a period of several days, without food or water; to be drugged, in that darkness, and forced to see nightmares, to live out their worst fears. If, at the end of that, they are still sane, they are allowed to join.

David has no control over the Darkroom.

Except.

"They're going to give him the Insanity Gas," he says, suddenly remembering. "That's mine. I produce it. If the batch that gets pumped in that night is, say, mysteriously ineffective — if Michael isn't hallucinating — then will you help him?"

That is a first step, but still dangerous.

"I can try and bring him food," says Ari. She is the next most powerful person in the army after Felix, and one of the things she controls is the management of supplies in and out of the

234

complex. If anyone can get food to Michael in the Darkroom, it's her.

"I can try and do something about the cameras," says Rayna to David. "I'll distract Loren, but once the Darkroom isn't being watched, you're going to have to make sure the power fails. If Ari is seen —"

"She won't be."

Another uncertain glance. "David," says Ari, "is this guy worth it?"

"Absolutely. He has to get into Regency. He's prime materi —"

"No," says Ari firmly. "David. Is he *worth* it?"

He does not lie to her; he knows they have seen something in his eyes when he talks about Michael. It is not that important a secret to keep, anyway, not compared to all the others.

"Yes," he says. "He is worth . . ." He swallows. "More than my own life."

– Chapter 25 –

"We don't know where Greenlow is."

They had made a list of variables. Loren was crossing them off one by one. They sat around a table in the waiting area of Terminal 3, untouched cups of coffee growing cold in front of them. Outside the glass walls, it was very dark. The silence from ATC had sent the red word CANCELED unfolding slowly down the list of flights. The night was cloudy, and snow had been hovering in the air for at least a week now. The intercom announcements attributed the grounding to "weather," while Heathrow's security put all their considerable resources into repairing Air Traffic Control and allowing planes to take to the skies again. Everyone was now drawing perilously close to panic.

Loren went down the list with a pen. "We can't be sure that Greenlow knows we have his son, or whether he knows how many troops he's lost. We won't get intel out of the captured Gospel soldiers from the tunnel for a long while yet. We don't know what his plan was. We don't even know whether he's changed it." He sat back. "We don't know anything."

"Well, we appreciate that contribution," said Evelyn Wood coldly. She was still treating him, Tara, Robert, and Madeleine as if they were something particularly unpleasant she had found underneath a stone: their continued presence here seemed to have confirmed all her worst suspicions about the Department's lack of professionalism.

Loren glanced at her. "Thank you."

"We should tell them," said Maria. She and Nate sat together, looking shaken but determined. Neither of them, Rose knew, were willing to let themselves be beaten by Tristan Greenlow. "We can't let these people stay here while the Gospel are still lurking in the dark."

James shook his head. "We can't allow a panic."

"We can't *avoid* a panic."

"Believe me, when you see one, you will wish you'd tried."

"We should wait," said Madeleine quietly. Robert nodded. He had wrapped a scarf around his face again, now that there were passersby to stare at him. Evelyn Wood studiously ignored them both. "Let them play their hand. Then strike back."

Terrian looked aghast. "But if we wait, they could kill hundreds of people before we know anything about it."

"And if we act, we could send this airport into chaos before we know we'd be accomplishing anything."

"Personally," said Tara dryly, but very quietly, "I prefer chaos."

"Wait," said Rose. They looked at her. She still wasn't quite used to that. "Remember where you are. This is one of the most

237

watched places in the world. If the Gospel attack anywhere, the cameras will see it."

"But we don't have access to their cameras."

"James has a laptop," said Rose, flatly. "What is it they pay you for, again, James?"

James looked at her. "Yeah," he said, the realization slowly dawning on him, "I . . . I could do that."

Madeleine looked between them. "You're suggesting hacking Heathrow."

Loren laughed. It did not sound easy. "Welcome to life outside the law."

"Can't you just *ask* them for their security feeds?"

"Because we just decided we didn't want to cause a panic," said Loren, with a slight, bitter smile. "If we go up to Heathrow's management and ask to see their cameras, they'll know something's wrong as quickly as if we'd told them. When the Department start watching you, you know you're either going to be attacked or arrested."

There was a distinct note of bitterness in his voice, and no one met his eyes. Madeleine looked distinctly uncomfortable about the idea of hacking the CCTV feeds, but said nothing.

They all gathered around James to watch him attempt the hack, and, when no one was watching her anymore, Rose got up and walked away to one of the seats. It was very close to the window; she could reach out and touch the glass, if she wanted to. The planes sat, hulking and shiny, faintly gleaming in the dark. She took off her jacket and folded it under her head.

She must have slept, because when she opened her eyes again, an hour and a half had passed. The glowing digits of the clock reflected in the window read 23:56. She got up and went to stare at the departures board. All of the flights were canceled now.

James came to stand beside her.

"We did it," he said. "We're watching for them. Nothing yet."

She said nothing. 23:57.

"Do you want me to . . . ?"

She glanced at him.

"I could get a line through to the prison," he said, softly. "So you could talk to David."

Rose shook her head. It was as close as she would come to thanking him.

"Why not?" asked James.

"It's easier if I don't have to think about him. When I'm in danger. So I don't have to worry about . . ." She swallowed. "What would happen to him if . . . if I died."

She wondered briefly whether this made her sound heartless, then dispelled the thought: this was the Department, after all.

23:58.

"You're not going to die," said James quietly.

"Nobody knows that."

"It would take more than this to kill us. Any of us."

She looked at him, and said nothing. 23:59.

A long silence.

"We never really say good-bye," said Rose abruptly. "We never make our peace before we go into things like this. Is that not strange?"

A pause. James was still watching the clock.

"Sometimes I think that's the curse of the Department," she said, a crack in her voice. "Never being able to see your own death, even when it's right in front of you. Always thinking it's years away, even when you spend your life walking right up to it and daring it to take you."

The clock changed again, all four digits this time: 00:00.

"January nineteenth," said James, softly. "Happy birthday, Rose."

She looked at him, and smiled. He grinned back, relieved, and she looked away.

"How does it feel being sixteen?"

"Don't you remember?"

"I'll be eighteen in a few weeks. Sixteen was eons ago."

She nodded. "I'm an adult now."

"I know."

"I wasn't an adult thirty seconds ago, and now I am. It's a weird thing to get your head around."

"I know it is." He looked up at the clock, pushing his hair out of his eyes. "You've got the rest of your life to do it, though."

She nodded. "However long that is."

He smiled, but it looked pained. After a long time, he said, in a sudden, brave rush, but with an air of unconvincing nonchalance, "I used to love you, you know."

Rose stared at him. He looked back at her with that same broken smile.

"Make your peace, she says," he murmured.

"I don't . . ."

"You don't have to," he said. "It was a while ago."

He looked back at the departure board. It had turned to 00:02 without either of them noticing.

"But if it matters," he said, with grim hope, "you could . . . you could still have my heart, you know, if you ever felt like taking it."

Rose didn't speak for a long, long time. Then at last, when her voice had returned, she said:

"Long recovery period, is it?"

"The longest," he said. "And I've been ill for quite a while."

She rubbed her face with her hand. "James, I'm sorry, but . . . I can't. And it's not . . . I can't. I . . ."

She could see the color draining from his face.

"I did love you," she said, quietly astonished at her own pain, "a long time ago, I think, but . . . like a friend. Like a . . . a brother. Like I love Nate. And even if, if you hadn't done what you did, I don't think that ever would have changed. I don't think I could have loved you in *that* way. And I can't now."

She had tried to phrase it gently, but he still looked like she'd kicked him in the face. "Right," he said softly.

Silence. 00:05.

"You might have done," he said, as if unable to stop himself. "You might have loved me, if things had been different."

"If things had been different," said Rose wearily, "I might have done a lot of things."

<<< >>>

Nineteen years earlier (age 17)
March 30, 11:08 p.m.

The woman who runs the shelter looks very tired. He gives her the name and waits outside, half in shadow by the corner of the next building, in case he has to run. It is a darkened March evening, and pouring with rain.

He does not really know why he is here.

241

The man who stumbles out, staggering on the stairs, does not look like the one David is looking for. He is carrying something cylindrical and glimmering in his hand, and when he speaks — hostile, and to the empty dark — his voice sounds sluggish. From where he stands, he cannot see David's face.

"Who are you? What do you want?"

The voice makes David stop breathing and press his hand against the wall for support. The man turns immediately to where he stands beside the streetlamp, searching blindly for a face that he can recognize.

David goes for the easiest answer, struggling to adapt to his juddering heartbeat. He should go. He should really go.

"I'm from Regency."

"No, you're not," says the man disgustedly. His voice is not slurred at all now. "You're Gifted. She said." A vague wave with the bottle toward the door, behind which the woman who runs the shelter is doubtless standing, watching them. "She said you had green eyes."

The man's own eyes are gray. He is Ashkind, and therefore he will hate Gifted. The impact of this realization sharpens David's voice.

"So what does that tell you?"

It takes the man a second, and then he pales and steps back, staring around, trying to find David in the darkness. The bottle slips from his hand and shatters on the paving stone. "You're one of the Angels of Death."

David says nothing, letting him get there.

"Arkwood."

"Guess again."

"Elmsworth."

There *are* only two of them.

The man looks around for help, a way out, but all the doors on this street are closed. "Why've you come for me?"

"I haven't come to kill you, if that's what you're thinking."

The man does not stop looking for an escape, and David does not blame him. When the Angels of Death come for you in person, you are going to die. He would be able to bear that fact of life if it were just a baseless rumor.

It is not.

"What have I done to make you kill me?" asks the man wildly. His voice is hoarse, pained and painful. "I'm not a soldier."

"I know."

"I've never done anything —"

"I know," says David. And then he says it, almost without meaning to, unable to conceal the pain behind his words: "But you didn't come back."

"What?"

The man in front of him stares at where David stands, invisible in the darkness.

"Who are you?" he asks again, and now he sounds truly afraid.

"You never came back. You went on holiday with your parents and you didn't —"

"What? What the hell is this?"

He is terrified now.

"Caitlin told me where to find you."

"The f— What have you done to my sister?"

"Michael," he says, and the man looks up, eyes widening. Something about David's voice is finally sparking in his mind,

243

and then David steps into the path of the streetlight, lets it light his face.

There is a moment of utter, blackening silence.

Michael and David stare at each other.

Michael is older. They have not seen each other for almost a year; David does not want to think about whether he would have recognized this boy had they passed each other in the street. Michael's chin is dusty with stubble and razor scars. He is very thin and gaunt, his pale skin darkening to blue around his sunken eyes. The rain has plastered his hair to his head.

They look at each other and, for the first time in a year, David feels *seen*.

"So," says Michael, with a nonchalance that convinces neither of them, "you're calling yourself David Elmsworth now, are you?"

David says nothing.

"No," says Michael, and then, viciously, vehemently, furiously, "*No*."

David waits.

"You're not him."

And again.

"*You* are not *him*. You're not Elmsworth."

"I am," says David. He is astonished that he can still speak. "I am . . . David Elmsworth. That's my name."

"You. You're Regency's silent killer. You're the first Angel of Death. *You*."

A pause.

"*You*."

Michael looks like he is about to laugh. He does not laugh.

"I couldn't find you," he says, with hoarse fury. "I found

everyone we knew, everyone who was still alive. They said you'd disappeared, you'd died. I never guessed *that* was your name now."

They stare at each other. David feels like he should speak.

"I waited for you to come back," he says. "Waited for months. I couldn't . . . I had to pick a side, and my friends chose Regency . . . it ran away with me." This is not a good-enough excuse, but there is no good-enough excuse. "I didn't know what I would do."

"It went wrong, didn't it?" says Michael, emotionlessly. "Your little idea went wrong."

David says, "Yes." His voice catches in his throat.

They look at each other. Suddenly, Michael walks forward, and they are no more than three feet apart. He raises his fist and jerks it forward as if to punch David, who sees it coming, and does not move.

They look at each other.

"You know, don't you?" says Michael softly. No anger. "You know everything you've done. You know you've done terrible things."

"Yes."

Nothing anyone else can do to him can match the knowledge of his own actions. Nothing can match living with it, afterward. No physical violence can come close. Michael sees that in David's eyes.

"I was stuck in Spain," he says. "Over there, they tried to repair the boats and planes and the ATC stations before the civilian mains. I think they saw the War coming. I was on the first boat to London. Mum and Dad stayed there. They thought it was safer." His voice is very quiet. "Caitlin found me a few months ago. She tried to get me out of . . ." He gestures to the broken bottle. "This. I said no. As long as she and Eleanor were safe."

They look at each other, silently examining the space between them.

"I tried to find you," says David. There is nothing else.

"I know, I —"

Michael reaches up to push his hair out of his face, rainwater streaming like crystal from his hands. The realness of the gesture, the seeming unself-consciousness of it, is so startling that David reaches out to touch his hand almost involuntarily. Michael goes very still. David thinks it is surprise.

It occurs to David that they have never actually touched before.

Michael's skin feels smooth as water, warm and bright and real, shimmering with electricity. It holds David in place for a moment, standing there in the darkness, watching Michael's pearl-gray eyes.

They were sapphire blue, before — but that was long ago.

When they kiss, it is beautiful. Something deep inside David blossoms and surges through his blood, feeling more like magic than magic ever did, so hot and dark and acidic and sweet and gold-bright and trembling that it feels like the discovery of fire.

It feels like the sky is breaking again as he stands underneath its center; it feels like starlight in his veins.

When they break apart, allowing the rain between them again, they watch each other in stunned silence; each, for a moment, fearing the other will do something — run, perhaps, or disappear into the darkness, warm-eyed ghosts.

Michael's smile is breaking, and he slides his hand across David's neck, so that they both feel his pulse, snapping beats like rapid-fire lightning. He sucks in his breath in shock, and they both react to it, flinching in surprise. Then, hesitantly, David curls his grip on Michael's wrist so that his two fingers are on the vein, and Michael's pulse is thundering.

Their release of breath is like relieved half-laughter, the ending of a secret. They stand that way for the longest time — forehead to forehead, breathing each other in like smoke.

Chapter 26

"Got it."

They crowded around Loren at James's laptop. It was two in the morning and they were exhausted. Rose was coming to the slow and crushing realization that the world did not look immediately different to her as a sixteen-year-old adult than it had when she was a fifteen-year-old child.

Loren pointed to a man on the screen. "That's him. That's Greenlow."

"Which one?"

"Stephen. But . . ." Loren narrowed his eyes. "That's the boy. The younger boy. What's his name?"

"Tristan," said Nate darkly.

"Him. But they're going . . . they're going in different directions. What are they —?" Loren's eyes widened and he leaned back. "Oh," he whispered.

Terrian grabbed the laptop and turned it around. "What is it? What are they doing?"

"They're boarding a plane."

"They're *what*?"

"ATC should be back up in twenty minutes or so, so the planes have begun taking passengers again. Stephen and the boy are getting on a flight. No." Loren peered at the screen again. "Different flights."

Rose understood before the rest of them. "Are there others?"

Loren rewound the footage. "Yes," he said. "One more. They've all gone in different directions."

Terrian stared at the screen, frantic. "What do you mean?"

"They're boarding planes," said Rose. "The Gospel are going to get on planes and take the passengers hostage."

Terrian spluttered in astonishment. "What on —"

"Tell them," said Tara, quietly. "Tell the authorities. This is too serious now."

"That's one modus operandi," said Rose slowly, "or we could —"

Evelyn Wood skipped past objection and indignation and went straight to fury. "No. No, I will not allow it. You cannot handle this on your own. None of you can."

Rose ignored her. "Loren, when was that footage taken?"

"About ten minutes ago."

"So whatever has happened, they're almost certainly surrounded by passengers by now. If we tell Heathrow's security, providing they react quickly enough to be useful, what will they do?"

Wood was on her feet. "They'll be effective. They'll be thorough. They'll use —"

"Alarms," said Rose, "and guns and red lights on people's chests. Greenlow will see us coming clear as day. And they may not be able to take guns through airport security, but it only takes a flicker of magic to rupture an aorta or snap a spinal cord." She glanced at Terrian. "I suggest . . . subtler methods."

Terrian glared at her.

"All right," said Madeleine, watching Rose warily, "what do *you* think we should do?"

They were listening to her again. This was very odd.

"Pair off. Follow them onto their planes. Stop them if they try to act. If they don't, get them off the planes as quietly as possible."

Wood was icily skeptical. "And how do you know they won't just use their magic then?"

"Ah," said Rose, "but you forget, we have Greenlow's son."

"And how will we prove that to him?"

"Cameras," said Loren, getting to his feet. "All right then, pairs it is. Madeleine, you need to defend David tomorrow and I have the terrible feeling things are going to get dangerous, so if you're going to go home, now is the time."

Madeleine glanced at Robert. "I can stay."

Loren hesitated. "Madeleine, you're pregnant. You're not exactly in peak fighting condition. And if you can't fight, then you're just a liability."

Anger flashed across Madeleine's face, but she nodded.

"Robert," said Loren, "you're free to go with her, of course, but if you could stay we would appreciate your help."

Robert and Madeleine looked at each other. "Help them," she said, with a quiet strain of reluctance. He said something to her in a low voice, and she nodded. Then she turned and walked away, and did not look back.

"Nathaniel," said Terrian, "go with her."

Nate turned to his father, furious. "Dad. I'm an adult. I say I'm perfectly capable of—"

"And I am your father," said Terrian calmly, "and I say you are not. You're perfectly brave and clever enough, nobody doubts that, but you've already done this once and it got you injured. You need medical attention better than mine, and you need to rest and recover. You took a bad knock to the head back there. You're in no shape to fight again."

"I can rest after we've defeated them."

"And if you stop us from defeating them?" asked Terrian. His words were harsh, but they struck home well enough. Nate stared at him, hurt. "I will not have you become a liability."

"*I'm* asking you, Nathaniel," said Robert, with a glance at Terrian. "Please. Go with Madeleine. Protect the woman I love. I would consider it a matter of personal debt."

Nate looked hard at him, at the scarf around his face. Rose knew he could guess what lay beneath it.

"It's *Nate*," he muttered at last, and stomped off through the group toward Madeleine. They stayed quiet until he was out of earshot. Terrian watched his son out of sight, his expression terribly sad.

"Maria, are you staying?" Rose asked.

Maria glanced away from Nate's retreating back and looked around at them all. Rose saw her fingers twitch. She was a medical student. She had never wanted to harm, only to heal. And yet Rose saw the pull of all this affecting her, too: the draw of risk, and of fighting the good fight.

She glanced at Rose.

"If I can help," she said, shortly, "then I will."

251

"All right," said Loren, tensely. "That's dealt with. Let's get to work, then. Carlisle, Maria, you go after the boy. Tara, James, take the other one. Rose and I will go after Greenlow senior. Remember, whatever you do, do *not* attack them in full view of the whole airport. That would cause chaos and terror on a level Greenlow and the Gospel could only dream of. It would play directly into their hands."

"What about us?" asked Terrian.

"You and Wood stay here. Hook up some cameras so that we can show Greenlow that we have his kid. Put a gun to his head if you have to. I want no ambiguity."

"You must be joking," said Wood angrily. "I have twenty years of military experience, I should be fighting."

"You've got to stay here," said Loren tersely, "because you *look* like you would pull the trigger and Connor here actually would."

Terrian looked grim.

"Fine," said Loren, and for the first time in longer than Rose was willing to remember, he smiled. "This is going to be fun."

The triumphant announcement came over the intercom twenty minutes later, informing the airport that the "technical difficulties" that had grounded the planes for the past few hours had finally been fixed, and that flights would now resume as scheduled. This was met by a rough, incoherent cheer from the exhausted passengers in the waiting room.

Rose heard this from the airport security queue, just as the guard asked her to take off her shoes. She acquiesced, smiling, and heaved her bag onto the rolling scanner. She walked beside it, through the metal detector, and when it entered the black box she clicked her fingers and a spark landed on the leg of the guard watching the screen. He yelped, and ducked to clutch at his leg. By the time he surfaced again, Rose's bag had emerged from the other side. Rose smiled at him sweetly and pulled her shoes back on.

When she was out of sight of the guards, she sank to her knees, and closed her eyes, breathing hard.

Then she opened her bag and pulled a small white capsule from the inside pocket. She fitted the earpiece in and stood up, looking around.

"Are you clear?"

"I am," said Loren's voice in her ear. "I'm behind you, I can see you. Don't look around."

"Can you see Greenlow?"

"Not yet. You?"

"If I could, would I be asking you?"

A painful blast of static, which she assumed was him sighing. "Have you ever managed a conversation without being sarcastic?"

"Not to date, no."

"You should try it."

"It sounds remarkably boring."

"Boredom has its upsides," said Loren. "Walk toward duty-free. Scan the lounge. Keep your head down. Remember, if he recognizes you, that's stealth gone."

Rose went toward the bookshop, picked up a crime novel and ruffled through the pages, pretending to interest herself in the contents. "You know, you're not acting Head anymore."

"So?"

"So I'm your colleague now, not your subordinate."

He took a moment to reply. "Regardless, Private Elmsworth, I am twenty years your senior and I have more military experience than you will ever accumulate."

Rose bristled. "How do you know I won't accumulate it?"

"Well, the point of this is to prevent another war, is it not?"

"You gonna buy that?"

Rose whirled around, looking far guiltier than she should have, and saw the shop assistant looking suspiciously at her from the counter.

She hesitated. "No," she said. Instinctive answer. The shop assistant tutted, and slowly Rose put down the book and walked away.

"Trouble?" asked Loren in her ear.

"Nothing I couldn't handle."

"Words or violence?"

"How little you must think of me."

He didn't answer that. Rose walked slowly past the various shops, scanning the lounge for Greenlow.

"I notice you're not running," she said, after a while.

"What do you mean?"

"The whole point of locking you up was so that you wouldn't run away to rescue Tabitha."

"I keep my word," said Loren, testily. "I dislike being mistrusted, Rose, especially by those who have every reason to believe me."

"Welcome to the world of monsters," she said, very quietly.

She caught a glimpse of dark hair across the lounge, a familiar green eye. She ducked into a toy shop to watch. It had disappeared into the crowd. She waited.

"So," he asked, "since you bring it up, how long have you got?"

She flinched, closed her eyes. "You think that's appropriate for casual conversation? That's deathbed talk, Loren."

"Are you in danger of transforming here?"

She had lost the dark, wiry man. She scanned the crowd again for him. Her voice was terse. "In this *airport*? How stupid do you think I am, Loren?"

"It's not a matter of stupidity. It's a matter of time."

She sighed. "I have enough time."

"How long is enough?"

"You have no right to ask me that question, Loren."

"I have every right. I would be in danger if you —"

"Put it like this," she said, almost hissing now. Heads turned and she knelt down, pretending to look for something she had dropped, and lowered her voice. "You might very well die today, but it won't be my fault."

He took a while to reply to that. "All right," he said eventually.

She stood up, and had to almost throw herself backward into the shop as Stephen Greenlow walked right past her. For a moment they were separated by no more than three feet, and if he had turned his head just slightly to the left, he would have seen her, and it all would have been over. But he did not turn. He kept walking, toward the gate where the plane full of passengers sat waiting to be boarded. Rose stayed there, breathing hard, until he was gone. She kept her eyes on him.

"I've got him," she whispered.

Loren's voice was sharp, immediate. "Where?"

"Beside the café across from me. You see him?"

A pause. "Yes, I see him."

"What do we do? Do we jump him?"

"Do we jump him," said Loren, slowly, "in broad daylight in a crowded airport lounge with no reinforcements?"

Rose rolled her eyes. "Fine. Any better ideas?"

"Many and varied. Follow him. Don't get close enough to put yourself in danger. I'll be right behind you. If he stops and there aren't too many witnesses, let me know and *then* we can try jumping him, but don't do it alone, because he will beat you."

Rose began to follow Greenlow. He was heading toward the boarding gate. "You think so?"

"I know your chances are close to fifty-fifty, and we've only got one shot at him. It's not worth it."

Rose walked up the slow rise toward the gate entrances. "I have an idea."

"Hit me."

"That is very appealing, true, but I meant to deal with Greenlow."

He laughed, short and humorless. "Go on."

"You have your gun, still?"

"No."

"Why not?"

"I mean no, we are not going to take him out like that. The guns are self-defense, a last resort. And I'm talking *last*. We use magic before we use firearms. If we go close combat, hand to hand, then security might pull us off him if we fail. If we shoot him, then they will put bullets in our heads and that will be the end of it."

"But he'll be dead. So everyone on that plane will be safe."

"Yes."

"You truly value your own life more than three hundred other people's?"

"If I die here, Tabitha stays in Regency's clutches forever," said Loren. "What's your excuse?"

"I never said I had one."

"Go on, then," he said. "Take the shot."

She reached into her bag, put her hand around her gun. She felt how cold the handle was to touch.

"I was being rhetorical," she said quietly.

She could hear the smile in his voice. "Everyone is, until the end."

Greenlow ducked into gate twenty-nine and she followed him. The queue to get on the plane was already long.

"Dammit."

"No luck?" he asked.

"None."

"All right," he said grimly, "looks like we'll have to get on the plane."

James's target was stupid. Then again, James himself was stupid, to let the target see his face. In fairness, he hadn't thought the man would recognize him. It turned out that the Elmsworth trial had particularly good court artists.

The Gospel soldier ducked into the bathrooms to avoid him. James followed him easily.

"Got him," he said to the voice in his ear.

"Toilets?"

"Yeah."

"Classic," said Tara, knowledgeably.

The man went up to the urinal. James followed him, hands in his pockets.

"Hello," he said to the man, and hit him in the face.

The man stumbled and fell back, and James should have followed through there and then, but he was too slow, because the punch had landed right on the chin; he had expected his opponent to fall, and that would have been the end of the fight. But he did not fall. He hit the wall and pushed himself back to his feet, and there was James's opportunity gone.

He did not even have time to swear before the blows came. They rained down on him, head and neck and shoulders, but the man was shocked, so they were clumsy and haphazard. At any rate, James had been trained for this sort of thing. He stood strong, keeping his body locked against the blows, trying to get his thoughts in order. Then he concentrated, and the man's shirt caught fire.

The soldier shrieked and jumped backward, and James kicked him in the stomach and he dropped. He kicked him again for good measure, in the head: possible concussion but no broken neck. *Alive*, Terrian had said. Damn Terrian.

He raised his hand and the flames went out.

"That was messy."

The voice came from behind him as well as in his ear. He cursed, and pulled the earpiece out.

"I'm out of practice."

"You were a soldier once, weren't you?"

"For a few weeks."

"I take it things went wrong."

"Of course they did."

"Who saved you?"

He said nothing, and went to check the pulse of the soldier.

Tara folded her arms. "Did she mean to break your heart, or did you shove it underneath her foot to step on?"

258

He turned and glared at her. "Why are you even here?"

"My mother's last words were about David Elmsworth. I have to keep him alive so I can understand what she meant. I also have no particular desire to see the Gospel overrun London. Rose called me here, so I came." She indicated her own green eyes. "I might be Gifted, but I don't want to see Ashkind dead. If I can help defeat Greenlow, I will."

James pushed back the man's hair to check the depth of the cut on his forehead.

"Also," said Tara thoughtfully, "I want to keep Rose alive. Not just out of the goodness of my heart, of course. I'm not sure Elmsworth would outlive her by very long. I think he'd just . . . stop, if he lost her. Stop talking, stop fighting. Just . . . die, so he could join her."

The man was not seriously injured. James tried to think of places to hide the body; if a civilian were to come in here and find it, all their efforts to avoid a panic would be in vain. It would be chaos. Tara had crouched down beside him and was still talking.

"Does it ever occur to you that we're on two different teams here?"

He sighed. "In what sense?"

"Those of us trying to keep Elmsworth alive, and those who want him dead."

He pressed the heels of his hands to his eyes for a moment, and started to haul the man's body toward the storage cupboard. Tara continued.

"Me. Madeleine. Rose, obviously. Robert, if only because he'd rather be attacked by a Hybrid again than see Madeleine unhappy. I don't know if we can count the boy and the Rodriguez girl . . . I assume they'd rather see Elmsworth alive than Rose destroyed."

The door wouldn't open. He had to use the soldier's weight as leverage.

"Then there's you, and Terrian, and Wood," Tara continued, watching him struggle, "who would strap him to the electric chair as soon as you got the chance for keeping you in the dark about his condition."

James shoved the man into the cupboard and forced the door closed. "You make us sound more bloodthirsty than we are."

"Oh, right, sorry. What's a gentler word for someone who works toward the death of a broken man?"

He gave her a dark look. "He's a monster."

"Not by choice."

"He betrayed us."

"So he's dying for your hurt pride, then."

He turned, leaning against the door. He could feel the old bullet in his chest as he panted, hard and cold. "Why are you saying this?"

"For Rose's sake."

"How on earth would this help her?"

She got to her feet and didn't speak for a moment. "Do you have family, James?"

"Get to the point."

"This *is* the point. Tell me about your family."

He sighed. "Mother, father, stepmother, brothers."

"Older or younger?"

"Fifteen and twelve."

"How would you feel if they were the ones being destroyed in court?"

Heat came to his voice instantly. "They would never do something like this."

260

"That's what Rose thinks about David."

He stared at her. "You seriously believe he doesn't deserve what he's getting?"

"He is not a good man," said Tara, "but no, he doesn't deserve this."

James was quiet for a moment, turning this concept over in his mind. "What do you think he deserves?"

"Punishment," she said, "but not this. Imprisonment, but not alone. Anger, but not public destruction. Distrust, but not hatred. He deserves to be with Rose, and she does not deserve to have her relationship with him torn down."

"I'm not trying to tear it down."

"Well, then, tell me this," said Tara. "If there comes a day when he is dead and she hates you, will it be worth it?"

<<< >>>

Nineteen years earlier (age 17)
February 8, 4:09 p.m.

"What's this?"

Felix is ridiculously excited. He stares at the drawer with the semi-obsessive fascination usually displayed by creepy children in horror movies.

"I wouldn't know," says David, calmly.

He looks around at the clean white rooms. It used to be a scientific research facility. The sign on the door says AESCHELMANN LABORATORIES, but that was from a long time ago. The room is full of desks and computers and sinks and papers pinned up to the wall scrawled in what David feels should be crayon.

His thoughts are clean, and clear, and empty.

"These papers. They say this"— Felix waves the test tube in David's face —"is the Cure."

"Perhaps the people who worked here were just into gothic rock."

Regency found this facility three days ago. The soldiers who discovered it are now permanently demoted. Only Felix and David have set foot inside: Felix because he can, and David because he is Regency's resident scientist and Felix wants his expertise.

In this respect, he is very, very lucky.

"Do you have any idea what it does?"

Involuntarily, David's right hand goes to the injection scar on the inside of his left forearm. It is fading, now; in a few months it will be gone entirely. Felix doesn't notice the movement.

"No," he says.

"Well, you should," snaps Felix. He stands the test tube in a rack and moves around the desk, as if from a certain angle he might suddenly glimpse a label. "Use your brain."

This stings. "I'm permitted one gap in my knowledge, surely. I can't know everything."

"No," says Felix, absently; he is clearly not paying attention. "I meant to thank you for Maida Vale, by the way."

David flinches slightly, despite himself. They took the district on Wednesday, largely due to David's orchestration of a bomb attack on the Angels' military base there.

"You're welcome."

"Between you and Arkwood," Felix says, still staring at the serum but not seeing it anymore, "you're the two most useful people in my army."

He does not sound entirely pleased about this. Despite being the best military assets the army has, David's and Loren's involvement in Regency is a PR disaster. Regency, an Ashkind army, owes its success to two seventeen-year-old Gifteds, who should by definition be the enemy in this War. It is blatant hypocrisy, but Regency cannot afford to lose its strongest members now, no matter how damaging they are to the militia's image.

Felix straightens.

"They're starting to call you my Angels of Death," he says briskly.

David has never heard the moniker before, and it hurts more than it should—a juddering release of adrenaline, the useless compulsion to run. Angels of Death. What a name.

This is the point, he thinks, at which anyone else would have an epiphany. What am I doing? What have I become?

Not David.

He already knows.

All he can think to say is, "We're not Angels. Angels are far more powerfully magical, far greener-eyed—"

"It doesn't matter. You're closer to being Angels than anyone else in this army."

It is, without doubt, an insult.

Something sparks in David, something like anger, and he stalks over to the opposite sink. "Look, Commander!" he says. "I can see more of it here."

It is dried and solidified to a syringe, thrown carelessly into the sink. There is blood dried on the needle. Felix rushes over, sees it, and looks in astonishment at David. He says it before David has to prompt him.

"It's meant for injection."

"Clearly."

Felix stares back at the test tube on the desk. "Do you think . . ."

Wordlessly, David goes back, picks up the serum, and loads it into a clean syringe. Then he takes the cap off the needle and holds it out to Felix, who, in equal silence — as if compelled by some unearthly power — pulls down his sleeve.

David has never seen Felix's hands shake before.

It does not matter. This does not matter; this will, at least, be punishment, some form of justice for the man who has killed so many. At any rate, Felix has not been human by any compassionate definition of the word for a very long time.

He walks toward the door. As he opens it, he hears, "David."

He turns back. Felix is watching him, silently, and David can see the fear in his eyes. He holds the glass syringe like dynamite. Alarm bells are screaming in David's head, but it doesn't matter, because fury is shivering through his veins like nicotine and this is enough, enough, *enough.*

"Do you think I should?" asks Felix.

David looks at him.

"Absolutely," he says.

– Chapter 27 –

Rose had never loved safety-demonstration cards so much as she did at that moment. The wonderful thing about them, it turned out, was that they had tiny blueprints of the layout of the plane on the back, with the seat numbers marked.

Greenlow was behind her. Loren was two rows in front. She could see the back of his head. They were still wearing their earpieces, but these were somewhat redundant now that they were in an enclosed and relatively quiet metal tube, and didn't have the chatter of a crowd to cover their speech.

The captain came on the intercom. *"Good evening, ladies and gentlemen. My name is Captain Martin Davenport, and it is my pleasure to welcome you all tonight aboard this flight to Tokyo."*

Rose had not thought of what would happen if they failed and the plane took off. What if she ended up on the other side of the world for her father's verdict?

No point in worrying about that now.

She doubted Greenlow would let it get that far, anyway.

"We apologize for our earlier delays; the skies are clear now, and we have an estimated flight time of about eleven hours and thirty minutes, so if you would like to make sure all belongings are stowed away for taxi and takeoff . . ."

And there was her verification. Slowly, murmuring profuse, quiet apologies, Stephen Greenlow made his way up the aisle. He looked back every few steps, so it was not until he was out of sight that Rose could get up. Out of the corner of her eye, she saw Loren do the same.

". . . our pilots and cabin crew are delighted to wish you a pleasant flight . . ."

Rose glanced to her left at Loren in the opposite aisle. He walked slowly, calmly. She should do the same. She should be calm. She tried to seem casual as she ducked through the curtain into first class.

Greenlow wasn't there. Mentally, she swore.

". . . dinner will be served as soon as we are in flight . . ."

He could only have gone forward. Rose thought back to the map of the plane. The first-class cabin was at the very front, so, she thought, the only place he could possibly be heading for was the —

Oh, Angels and Ichor, no.

She sped up, all trace of calm falling away, and stopped at the end of the cabin, behind the curtain separating the two areas of the plane. He was just on the other side. She could hear his breathing.

She did not move.

A knock. "Excuse me?" Greenlow, his voice apologetic. His voice was hoarse. "Excuse me, I . . ."

The captain's voice. Davenport. "What's the matter?"

"I don't want to bother you, sorry, but, uh . . . I have some chest pains. Some quite severe ones, actually. I don't want to cause a fuss or anything, but, uh . . . They're quite painful."

The sound of a door sliding back. Where was Loren? She couldn't jump Greenlow alone.

"All right," said Davenport, his voice clearer now without the door to muffle it. "Sit down. Are you on any kind of medication, or . . . ?"

Stephen thanked him, the words juddering over each other like pebbles, and the door thudded closed again just as Loren emerged from their cabin. He looked between Rose and the curtain in dawning realization. She shook her head.

His eyes widened and he swore softly. She just caught it over the earpiece.

Slowly, they walked back toward the divide between the first- and second-class cabins. Rose met him beside the emergency exit. Through the translucent, scratched window beside them, there was only blackness.

She pressed her earpiece, muting it.

"What took you so long?" she muttered.

"Flight attendant blocked the aisle."

"Good timing."

He was indignant. "Oh, so it's my fault now?"

A flight attendant passed them. She stopped, raising her eyebrows in polite curiosity.

"Is there a problem?"

Loren drew her into the small compartment where the meals were kept. "Yes," he said. "Your pilots are dead."

The flight attendant's mouth fell open, and she looked at Loren in horror. "Sir, you can't . . . If you make one more threat like that, I will have to have you removed from the plane."

"It's not a threat. It's a fact."

From behind them, they heard faint, muffled screaming. It ended very quickly with two sharp snaps. Loren nodded.

"All right," he said, "*now* it's a fact."

He took the scarf from his face, and Maria said nothing. He lied his way past security with smiling ease, deflecting the questions and stares, and still she did not blink.

It was only when the child spoke that she started to become curious.

The girl was very small, three or four years old at most, hugging a blanket against her shoulders like a shield. Her exhausted-looking mother pushed a baby in a pram beside her, and did not at first react when the girl asked, "What's wrong with your face?"

Robert stopped. Maria knew that he did not for a moment consider that the question might be directed at anyone else. He looked down at the girl with cold eyes.

"My face?" he asked, very quietly.

The mother had noticed by now, and wheeled the pram backward hastily toward the girl. "Leila, no, I've told you —"

Robert turned to the woman, the movement of his head robotic. "I suggest you take precautions to control your child in future," he said, "lest she provoke aspects of the human condition beyond her limited understanding."

He walked off, condensing his anger into furious speed. Maria followed him warily.

"You're thinking I should be used to this by now," he said, without looking up.

She considered her response very carefully. "It might make things easier for you."

"It would, yes," he said. "I can take it when adults do it — that I can put down to malice, or deliberate idiocy. Children, though, and small children especially, mean nothing by it. They're just asking about the truth."

"They don't judge you."

He turned to her. "Of course they don't judge me. Why would they judge me?"

Maria said nothing, and they walked on.

The airport lounge of Terminal 2 was crowded. They split up, looking for Tristan. It took Maria a few seconds to figure out how to work the earpiece.

It was easier to talk to him now that she couldn't see his face.

"What will you tell the baby, when she asks?"

"The truth," said his voice in her ear. "Or whatever version of it she can take."

She nodded before belatedly realizing he couldn't see her.

"She won't look like me," he said. "I count that as a blessing. I'm hoping to stay out of her development as much as possible, to be honest. I want her to be clever and brave and strong and kind, like her mother. And if she has my face . . ." He sounded grim. "She will not *really* have my face."

A flash of blond hair. Maria started forward. The blond hair turned, and Maria saw Tristan's face behind it. She ducked behind a post.

269

"I see him," she whispered.

Robert sharpened immediately. "Where?"

"In the third row of seats: fifth, no, sixth to the left."

A pause. "Good," he said. "Now, Maria, I accept this is a very personal question, but are you any good at fighting?"

Her voice hardened. "I'm a doctor. Or I will be. I don't make a habit of hurting people."

He was quiet, and Maria sensed an unspoken comment about her choice of friends lurking in the silence. "Then I'm going to need you to do something very dangerous."

"Sell it to me, why don't you."

He did not laugh, perhaps because there was already a tremor in her voice. "Walk up to him."

"*What?*"

"Full view. Don't let him run. Call his name if you have to. Tell him you know what he's going to do. Try to talk him out of it."

"Robert, that's not going to work."

"I know it isn't, which is why I need you to walk him to somewhere quiet and isolated."

She hesitated. "Is there a Plan B?"

"To be honest, this is Plan B. I had hoped to catch him alone in the first place."

Maria swallowed.

"I'll be watching you. You'll be all right."

She nodded, hoping he could see her this time. "My life is in your hands."

"No it isn't," he said. "You don't trust yourself enough, Maria Rodriguez."

And in the end, Maria thought later, he was indeed right;

because it wasn't *her* fault everything went so badly wrong after that.

It took a good minute and a half to convince the flight attendant who the terrorists actually were. Rose counted every wasted second.

Loren tried first persuasion, then anger, letting the first threads of panic show briefly and starkly in his voice. Then he gave up and took out his passport so she could see it. She stared between the name and the photo and his face with wide-eyed horror. Loren rolled his eyes.

"You're . . ."

"Yes," he said, wearily.

"You're a murderer," she whispered.

He hesitated at that one.

"Not for quite a while," he replied.

This, unsurprisingly, did very little good. The stewardess appeared to lose the power of coherent speech for a good six seconds. Rose sighed and stepped forward.

"Do you know who I am?"

The woman started to say "no," and then froze mid-word. Clearly, she did.

Loren was furious. "*You* at least were supposed to be incognito, you idiot!"

"Yes, and no one was supposed to die. I assumed the plan only stretched to nothing going wrong."

The stewardess was quiet again. "You — you're the girl."

"Which still leaves you with about three and a half billion to choose from."

"You're — you're his. You're Elmsworth's."

Rose sighed. "There we go. I do have a name, you know."

Loren again. "We don't have *time* for this."

"We have plenty of time. Greenlow will play his hand, we'll see how fast we can react, and everything will proceed smoothly from there."

He stared at her. "You're mad."

Rose ignored him and spoke to the stewardess. "Please, try to make it seem as if nothing is wrong. Do what you normally do."

The stewardess opened and closed her mouth like an amnesiac goldfish. Rose sighed. "Hand out the newspapers."

Slowly, hands shaking, the woman walked to the cabinet and opened the drawer. She drew out the pile of newspapers and stumbled away.

Rose turned to Loren. "Any ideas?"

He opened his mouth, whether to answer her question or to swear at her she did not know, but was abruptly cut off by the sound of another, terribly familiar voice coming over the intercom.

"Hello," said Stephen Greenlow smoothly. "I'm afraid this is not your captain speaking, nor am I in any way qualified to fly a plane. I'm sure you will therefore be relieved to know that the scheduled flight to Tokyo tonight will not be taking place. Instead, you will be held here indefinitely, while I inform the authorities of your imminent deaths."

No one screamed. Not at first. There was a stunned, incredulous, slightly disturbed silence. Then someone shouted, loudly enough that Stephen would be able to hear him through the closed cockpit door, "Is this a bloody *joke*?"

"No," said Stephen, "it is not, and I have to say it would be frankly horrifying if you were to find this funny. My name is

Stephen Greenlow. You may have heard of me. I have devoted my life to making the world a safe space for those with magic, and an extremely dangerous one for those who grace themselves with the undeservingly clean name *Ashkind*. When the Parliament of Angels did not see fit to pass the laws I suggested, I reduced them to gibbering Leeched wrecks. Please will all the Ashkind on this aircraft get to their feet."

It was undoubtedly not a question, but no one moved at first.

"Some of my men are on their way onto this plane to help me," said Greenlow, "and they will be able to see your eyes. If you do not obey me, they will not hesitate to end you."

Slowly, and with much uncertain murmuring, the Ashkind got to their feet. There were, by Rose's quick head count and extrapolation, a hundred and seventy-two of them. If this went wrong, there would be a lot of blood spilled tonight.

Loren and Rose pressed themselves against the cabinets, out of view, as the Gospel soldiers strolled onto the plane. Their weapons hung almost casually at their waists. This was bad news. Anyone who had not yet fully absorbed the fact that guns were lethal weapons should never be trusted to use one.

Rose shook her head distractedly. That was her father's rule.

The Gospel soldiers asked all of the Ashkind to step out into the aisles. "Asked" was a kinder description than their rough, harsh words deserved, especially accompanied as they were with various obscene gestures with hands and guns, but Rose's heart-beat was too fast and her breathing too shallow to quibble over pedantries.

The Ashkind, wisely, obeyed. They knew what they were in for. They knew who these people were. Rose could see it in the wide set of their gray, gray eyes, and in the way they flinched away from the soldiers and their guns. Oh yeah, that's right. Show them your fear. That'll make them kind to you. They hate seeing Ashkind afraid. That's why they got into Greenlow's business of savagery. You morons.

Rose quieted herself.

Some of the Ashkind had Gifted family with them. They sat there in their seats, struggling with their fear and their anger and their protective instincts. None of the Ashkind were children, which was good. Any parental protectiveness would have gotten the whole family killed. The Gospel had no qualms about murdering their own kind, to further the cause.

Rose looked to Loren, because her own mind could offer nothing more constructive at that moment than sarcastic running commentary, and she hoped that by now he would at least have the rudiments of a plan. But so sluggish had her thoughts been rendered by the presence of so many hostile guns that it took her a good few seconds to realize that he wasn't there.

He wasn't —

How in the bloody *hell* had he managed to get away without her noticing?

She was losing her touch.

The Gospel had spent the last fifteen minutes rigging up some kind of mechanism in the seats where the Ashkind had been sitting. It consisted of several levers, a gun, and some string. As Rose watched, they pulled the Ashkind to them, tied the string around their wrists, then forced them back to their seats. The Ashkind did not sit down — not that they could have done so with their hands tied to the ceiling and their feet barely touching the ground. They looked bewildered.

Then, slowly, expressions of terror appeared on their faces.

"In case you need it explained to you," said Stephen Greenlow lazily. This, Rose thought, was what a malevolent god would sound like if he ever discovered public address systems. "You are currently standing on a weight-activated pedal. You have about ten seconds until that becomes active. When it does, it will be directly connected to the trigger of a gun which my men have placed in your seat. It is currently aimed at the back of your skull. Your hands are tied to the ceiling above you. If you place your feet for an instant on that pedal, this rather ingenious little mechanism will cause you to be shot in the head. If you try to stand on the floor, or on the seat, my men will take ingenuity out of the equation and shoot you themselves." He paused. There was a smile in his voice now; Rose could hear it.

"So, my little vermin," he said, "how long can you hang?"

Two died in the first few minutes. It was stupid, really: their foot on the pedal, the *snap-crack* of the shot, and then the slow slump of the bodies to the floor. Various people screamed. But no one said anything at all. No one even begged for their lives.

Pathetic.

It was after the second death that Greenlow came out of the cockpit. He strolled down the aisle, looking so elated that "Here Comes the Bride" intruded briefly into Rose's mind. She pressed herself further into the compartment and tried to be small.

She had never been small.

"So," he said, "any information you want to bargain with, for your worthless little existences? Any anecdotes about my enemies? Any gossip? I'm open to suggestions."

He was in his element. He could taste the fear around him like perfume, and he breathed it in, and kept talking. Rose could understand him, in that moment. The disgusting bastard.

"You may wonder why I'm doing this," he said, almost to himself. "People do wonder, you know. And I can understand, from a fool's perspective, how my methods might seem . . ."

He trailed off. He wasn't looking at any of them anymore; his eyes were unfocused, his expression thoughtful.

"You see," he said, "I am on the right side of history. When generations have passed, and no one can remember a world without magic, humankind will recognize non-magicals for the abominations they are. The world is far better off without such creatures. I have merely come to this realization early. I am an emissary from future historical consensus. I'll understand if you don't agree with me, though. You don't have to agree. You merely have to . . . step aside."

He smiled slightly, and then, suddenly, he froze. All the color drained from his face.

The passengers were in no state to notice anything, frozen to their seats in horror and staring at the hanging Ashkind, but Stephen Greenlow heard it, and so did Rose. The sounds were coming from the cockpit. They were sharp, muffled, and distinctly violent.

They were the best things Rose had heard in hours.

Stephen Greenlow turned. His voice was sharp. "What was that? What happened?"

In the ensuing silence, another Ashkind put his foot on the pedal. Idiot. The *crack* of the killing shot went almost unheard.

Loren ducked out of the cockpit, holding an unconscious Gospel soldier against him.

"Look, I'm sure you know the drill," he said. "You shoot at me, you kill him. You shoot again, you just make his corpse shinier. And maybe you get caught in the ricochets."

A woman screamed at the sight of his face. Loren looked around at her in mild exasperation. "Seriously?" he said. "After all of this, *I'm* what scares you?"

Greenlow looked furious. "Kill him," he told his soldiers.

Loren rolled his eyes.

"Kill him slowly. Kill him painfully."

Loren sighed, and pulled his comms tablet from his pocket. The screen was small, but Aaron's face and the gun pressed against his temple were still clearly visible.

Greenlow went very still.

Loren smiled.

"Put down your guns," said Greenlow in a hoarse, low voice. Slowly, bemusedly, the Gospel soldiers did so.

"Let the Ashkind go," said Loren, quietly.

Greenlow gritted his teeth. When the words came, they sounded pained. "Do what he says."

The soldiers, looking bewildered and furious, untied the Ashkind. They did not do it carefully, though, and two more shots rang out through the cramped plane. Rose wasn't sure if they found their marks.

"Now," said Loren, with a glance toward where Rose hid, "I'm going to ask you some questions and you are going to answer them."

Greenlow nodded slowly, his eyes still on Evelyn Wood with her gun to his son's head.

"My sister's daughter has been kidnapped. We know the Gospel have been taking Demon children. Where is she?"

277

"I don't know."

"You're lying to me."

"No," said Greenlow urgently, "I'm not. We had nothing to do with the girl. Regency must have taken her. She'll be in one of their bases."

Loren's eyes widened. "*One* of them?"

"Regency are taking Demon kids as well. I don't know where they keep theirs. Ashkind scum," he added, under his breath.

Loren struggled to process this. "Why are you taking children?"

"Demon children. They don't fight back. Easier to take than adults, and we need Demons."

"Why?"

Greenlow hesitated. "I don't know."

"What do you mean you don't know?"

"A source," said Stephen, struggling now for his words. "He talked to both of us. Regency as well. He told us about the Demons, to take them. For whichever one of us he chooses to ally himself with, in the end."

"Who?"

"Andrew Ichor."

Loren stared at him. The Gospel soldier he was holding slipped. Rose stared, too, because Greenlow had just provided incontrovertible proof that he was mad. Andrew Ichor was the teenager whose experiments had caused the rift in the veil between worlds, and brought magic to the human race, and, in doing so, had started the War. He could not be alive, let alone talking to Regency and the Gospel. It was not possible.

"Andrew Ichor's dead," said Loren.

"No, he's not."

"He died at the beginning of the War."

"He is alive."

"He disappeared."

"And now he has reappeared," said Greenlow, an edge to his voice. "He caused the Veilbreak. He created our world. He started the War. He's watching what happens now. He doesn't know who to choose. But when he does, he will need Demons."

Loren was speechless. "That," he said, and there was a heaviness to his words that already indicated resignation, "is impossible."

"Sir."

One of Greenlow's men, beside him, was trying to get his attention. Stephen glanced at him.

"Sir, there's a woman in the back who has information. She wants to exchange it for her life."

Stephen turned to him. "She doesn't need to. We can't kill her now."

Rose clenched her fists with rage at the bitterness in his voice.

The soldier shrugged. "She doesn't know that."

Greenlow looked at him blankly for a moment. Then, "What does she say?"

The soldier held up one of the newspapers the flight attendant had handed out. He flicked to page three. Rose glimpsed the byline. Oliver Keen.

The soldier pointed to one of the pictures. "That girl," he said. "The Elmsworth girl. She's on the plane."

Everyone moved very quickly after that. Loren swore violently. Rose could feel the countdown manifesting itself — she had very little time left — and grabbed a plastic knife from the store beside her. She snapped it in half. Now there was an edge

279

that could puncture an aorta. There was a sharpness that could end a life.

Her thoughts were racing too fast. Rose self-diagnosed panic.

There were people firing at Loren again. Soldiers strode past Rose's compartment. She didn't know whether the General had killed Aaron yet. She hoped so, but her luck had not held steady for a long time.

And then, oh miracle of miracles, Stephen Greenlow moved into her sight line.

She should have waited. She should have stopped to think and consolidate her aim. She should have done any number of things but what she did: she launched herself at him, trying to slice him open with her makeshift blade.

And she did break the skin. She got that one right. But though he hissed in pain, the damage was little more than a trickle of blood, and he moved away and watched as his soldiers wrestled her to the ground.

They were not gentle, but neither was she. She screamed at them, threats and obscenities, as they slid in the needle and the heaviness of forced sleep into her veins. She was screaming mostly to cover up the sound of her own thoughts, and of Loren's anguished cries of "Rose! Rose!" as he too was seized; and, as the darkness pressed in upon her eyes, she tried desperately to block out the sight of the color and the smile returning to Stephen Greenlow's face, his joyous realization that he had just snatched victory from the jaws, the very *jaws* of defeat.

"Oh, you stupid girl," he said softly. "You've just given me everything I need to take London."

* * *

Over the loudspeaker at Heathrow Airport three minutes later — blocking out the sound of Maria trying to call Tristan's name, cutting off James's and Tara's heated argument, and making Terrian and Evelyn Wood look up sharply from where they knelt beside Aaron — came Stephen Greenlow's voice.

"Hello," he said, silkily. "Anyone who places any value on Rose Elmsworth's or Loren Arkwood's lives lay down your arms."

A pause.

"Now."

And, slowly, they did.

– Chapter 28 –

Twenty years earlier (age 16)
October 18, 5:53 p.m.

"Three."

There are five people in the room: David, Felix Callaway, Loren, Rayna, and Ariadne. If this fails, Loren and David will die. Felix will not keep Gifted volunteers alive if they are not useful.

This is their chance to prove they are useful.

"Two."

Loren's and David's very existence within Regency has been a secret to all but Felix himself, Rayna — accepted into Regency without question, of course, due to her gray eyes — and Felix's second-in-command, Ariadne Stronach. Stronach is a quiet, dark-eyed young woman, possessing the kind of gravitas that would have made her a formidable politician in better days.

"One."

David steps forward and presses the button on the generator. With a glance at each other, he and Loren press their hands against the metal, and pour every spare joule of energy into the machine: magic flowing from their bodies like water, until David is exhausted and stumbles back.

He does not believe in God, not with everything that's happened, but he would not object to divine intervention at that moment. Silently, he starts reciting the Lord's Prayer. He gets no further than "hallowed be thy name," however, before the generator starts rumbling.

There is an astonished, overjoyed silence.

"No," says Loren, incredulous, and then: "No."

This is the first sign of electricity since the Veilbreak overload three months ago. Fifteen weeks. Fifteen long weeks. And nothing else, no flicker of light, in London in all that time. In the world, for all they know.

Rayna whoops, long and loud, and runs to hug her brother. They are saved, they are saved, they are *saved*.

Around them, the lights of the South London laboratory begin to flicker and then, unbelievably, to glow.

David starts to breathe. Felix and Ariadne are watching him.

"Impressive," murmurs Felix. "Lieutenant Arkwood?"

Rayna and Loren both turn. At the sound of their new ranks, a wide, identical smile begins to spread across both of their faces.

"I meant him," says Felix coldly, and David can see Rayna forcing herself not to glare back at him. "Arkwood. Elmsworth."

They watch him.

"I want your solemn word that you will never, so long as you live, use magic again. You are, from now on, no longer Gifted."

283

"You have my solemn word," says Loren, without hesitation.

"On whose life?" A stunned pause, before Felix adds, "Your own is a given. Who else's?"

There is only one obvious, and therefore correct, answer. Loren glances at Rayna, and says slowly, "On my sister's."

"And you, Elmsworth?"

David, Loren, and Rayna glance at one another.

"On both of theirs," says David.

"Consider it done," says Felix, and looks around the labs. David feels a stab of satisfaction at the knowledge that this bulky twenty-five-year-old, for all his jet-black eyes and his strategic intelligence and his army, has no idea how to use any of this equipment. Foolishly, he decides to risk rubbing it in.

"Nice labs," he says. Felix looks at him, unreadable, for a few seconds, and then goes toward the door. Ariadne pauses before following him.

"Good," says Felix. "They're yours."

<<< >>>

Rose woke at six in the morning. It was still dark, this being January, but she had a good view of the airport. They'd put her beside the window; they must have known how it would torture her.

Moving her head hurt for the first few minutes, so it was a while before she could look around. She was in a hard, white-painted room, blasted with thin light.

She did not bother trying the door.

She watched the window blearily as the lights went out in Heathrow Airport. It happened inexorably — one by one, terminal by terminal, darkness returning slowly to the skies.

"It was a condition of their release," said Loren in her ear. She gasped sharply, and berated herself almost before the breath had passed her lips. She had forgotten about the earpiece; it was still in her ear, still on. He was not here: she was still alone in this featureless, empty room. "He let the passengers go — the living ones — so long as the lights went out. Heathrow is blind now. It's easy to be taken when you can't see the enemy coming." She could hear his faint smile. "They learned from you and James."

Rose's voice cracked with pain. "That was your idea."

"We'll forget that for a moment."

"Where are you?"

"Close to you. Next room, I think." He was bitter. "Locked up again. Seems like I'm destined for this."

"No such thing as destiny."

"Arguable."

She was silent for a moment. "But we . . . I mean, Terrian and Wood, they still have Aaron."

"A factor negated by the fact that they have us. More than negated, in fact — there are two of us, and one of him. And, at any rate, Terrian and Wood are in Heathrow too, so unless they've escaped —"

"They will have."

"— then Greenlow might have his son back, and what's left of the Department as well, very quickly."

Rose burrowed her head into her hands. "Robert and Maria are in there."

"If you're worried about innocents, Rose, there are thousands of them there whose names you don't know."

She stared blankly at the darkened airport. "I am sorry," she said, quietly.

"We can debate the assignment of blame for days, Rose, and doubtless we will, but in the meantime there are greater arguments to be had."

She leaned back and looked at the wall, imagined she could hear his breathing through it. "Ichor."

"The boy who caused the Veilbreak," said Loren, reminiscently. "The teenager who broke the world. Possibly the most-hated child prodigy in the country. Or he would be, were he alive."

"He isn't alive."

"Of course he isn't alive. He disappeared off the face of the earth at the start of the War. No one could hide for so long. Not when the world knows who you are."

They were quiet for a long time.

"He's alive," said Rose.

"Well, obviously."

"And he's talking to the Gospel."

"And to Regency."

"If we believe Greenlow."

"He wasn't lying," said Loren, with conviction. "I saw it in his eyes. When we had Aaron, when he could see his kid was in danger, then he told the truth."

"But why would Ichor talk to him? Or Regency?"

He paused. "We don't know whether he ended up Gifted or Ashkind, so he could have been on either side."

"But *he* knows which side he's on. So he should have picked one side to talk to. He wouldn't be on the bloody *fence*. And why's he telling them to collect Demons? What could he possibly want with them?"

Loren sighed. "I don't pretend to understand this, Rose."

"Can you try?"

"Can I try to guess at the motivations of a warmongering teenager? No. I can't. And I won't waste time and effort attempting to."

There was a sharpness to his voice Rose was wary of. She let it drop into the silence. He had no answers.

The walls of Rose's cell were cold. Heathrow was entirely dark now, and silent. Not even the roars of engines tainted the still night air. Presumably, somewhere inside the airport, Ashkind were dying painfully.

"We failed, then," said Rose, quietly, almost to herself.

"What?"

She shook her head, disconcerted. "We failed. Us. The Department. We failed to protect them. We failed to . . . to save the world."

"No one can save everyone, Rose," said Loren wearily. "There are always sacrifices to be made, and bargains to be struck. Someone always gets the raw end of the deal. Someone always dies."

Rose stared out into the night. "I . . ."

She was too tired to speak, suddenly.

"Is that what they taught you?" asked Loren in her ear, sounding mildly amused. "When you were little, was this your mission in life? Is that what you thought your father did? Did you think you were supposed to save the world?"

"I always hoped to. Doesn't everyone?"

"In the abstract," he said. "But that would require courage and selflessness, and neither of those, I'm sure you've noticed, is in particularly abundant supply in the Department. I mean, they're certainly ruthless, but courage and ruthlessness aren't the same thing."

Rose's voice was cold. "Are you calling us cowards?"

"You say it like it's a bad thing."

"You certainly aren't saying it like it's a good one."

"Isn't it, though?" he asked, and she couldn't see his face but his voice was gentle. "Why is courage a good thing? Why do we prize those who put themselves in danger to save others?"

"Because it means they value others' lives above their own."

"But why does that make them better people than those who save the lives of others without themselves dying? Why are soldiers considered better people than, say, doctors?"

"I don't know," said Rose wearily, "but I'm going to guess you have a theory."

He ignored her. "I think it's that the more danger you put your own life in to save someone else's, the less likely you are to survive to regret your actions. If the other person survives and you don't, they'll think you dying to save them is a great thing, on balance, if they're alive and unharmed and you're not there to suffer the consequences. Morality is set by the living, not by the dead, Rose. Things would be very different if it weren't."

They sat in silence for a long time.

"Which suggests," said Loren eventually, "something rather unpalatable about the human conscience, doesn't it?"

"Which is?"

"A moral act is merely the one considered most useful by the person left alive."

"Why," asked Rose, irritably, "do you have to think out loud?"

Another long pause.

"Well," he said heavily, after a while, "I suppose this is it."

"Oh, Angels. We're not going to do dramatic good-byes, are we?"

"Of course not." Now he was annoyed. "I never say good-bye. If I die, I die. I'm not going to care afterward about the etiquette of the thing."

"So what is it, then?"

"There's something I should tell you."

"Come on. Not now."

"Oh, I may as well," said Loren tiredly. "It's highly unlikely I'll live to see the end of this, and I don't want the story to die with me."

Rose closed her eyes. "Loren, what is this?"

"I've told you about the first time I knew Felix Callaway was insane. Do you remember what it was?"

"His ex-girlfriend." Rose had to search for a few moments before she found the name. "Ariadne Stronach."

"Yes." Loren's voice was rough with old rage. "I think of her as his first victim, but he had probably killed hundreds by then. Indirectly, though. Ariadne was . . . different."

"He lay in wait," said Rose. The obscenity of it silenced her for a moment. "He lay in wait, and he transformed, and he . . ."

"She died."

The words meant nothing in comparison to the gruesome meanings that soured in Rose's mind.

"I was the one who found the body," said Loren quietly.

The horror of that took her voice for a moment.

"Doesn't it just break your heart, Rose?"

She said nothing. For some reason, this seemed to make him angry. His voice in her ear grew sharper. "No, of course it doesn't.

Of course. A woman died at Felix Callaway's hands, and she most likely died screaming, and you aren't . . . crying."

Bizarrely, she felt the need to defend herself. "It was years ago."

"More than a decade and a half," said Loren. "Does that make her pain any less?"

"Loren, they're dead."

This made him quiet. "Yes," he said, after a long time, and softly. "Yes. Felix and Ariadne are dead."

She needed to stop this. "Loren, please. Tell me what's going on."

"You should be crying," he said, with irrational pain. "You shouldn't be able to talk when I tell you this. You should be crying. Why aren't you crying?" His voice was rough. "Why don't you know? Why haven't you guessed?"

Rose was scared, now, and she didn't quite know why. "Angels, Loren, just —"

"It should break your heart, Rosalyn Elmsworth," said Loren with terrible weariness, as if the words were too much, as if he couldn't hold them back any longer, "because Ariadne Stronach was your mother."

Chapter 29

Tara sat beside him in the cell until he awoke.

He was pale, gaunt and emaciated, but alive, and that was enough. The guards — new ones, more highly trained and better armed, as the cell's security had been increased in recent days — had let her into the cell to see him because she had called herself Madeleine Ryan. When Madeleine came back, that would be a problem, but until then, she could sit here and watch David Elmsworth sleep.

It was time to ask him. She had run out of time and patience.

She heard his breathing change, but his eyes remained closed.

"Heathrow Airport has fallen," she said.

He said nothing.

"I risked my life to come here from there."

"You would have risked it more by staying."

His eyes were still closed. Footsteps from down the prison corridor, but they came no closer.

"You smug bastard."

"The Department cast me out," he said. "If they hadn't, Heathrow would still be in Government hands. I take what meager comfort I can."

"People are dying back there."

"Most likely, those people hate me."

"So their deaths are meaningless, then?"

The anger was showing in her voice. He opened his eyes.

"I will not cry for them," he said softly.

Tara stared down at him.

"I don't believe we've been introduced," said David Elmsworth, wryly.

"I'm Tara Priestley."

"Wonderful to meet you."

"My mother died two weeks ago," said Tara with careful steadiness. He said nothing to this; she was glad of it. "The last thing she asked me to do was to find your daughter. I think it was a warning. She died telling Rose, *I have found him, you cannot trust him, he is not free.*"

"Well," he said, gesturing weakly to the cell, "I'm not."

"Why did my mother use her last breaths to say that?"

"I have not the slightest idea."

"What did she know about you?"

"I don't know."

He closed his eyes again. Tara's hand had found the safety of the gun in her pocket.

"I will kill you," she said, trembling. "Believe me, I don't want you alive. I have been trying to save you only so I can get these answers."

"Well, I'm afraid I can't give them to you."

"Then you'll die. I can do it here. I can do it now."

He sighed, and opened his eyes.

"What was your mother's name?" he asked, dispassionately, for all the world as if she were a child asking a tiresome question about the nature of the sky.

"Clare Matheson."

His eyes widened. For a long time he sat there as though paralyzed, absolutely still. Tara's finger tightened on the trigger.

"What? What does that mean to you?"

He said nothing. What little color remained in his face had left it.

"Elmsworth, I am not patient."

He closed his eyes again.

"Are you willing to die rather than tell me?"

"I'm going to die," he whispered. "Trust me, my time is running out. I will tell you when I am about to die. Please. Give me these last days. I have things to do."

"I will kill you now, and leave them undone."

He was white with shock. Anguish crossed his face. "Tara . . ."

"Do not use my name." She drew the gun from her pocket and pointed it at him. "Tell me."

He sighed, and was so pale and still that for a moment Tara thought she had just seen him die — actually die — in front of her.

"By telling you," he said quietly, "I buy your utter silence, and your support, and your word not to kill me."

She nodded reluctantly.

Then, and only then, did he tell her.

"I think, Rose, you were born on All Hallows' Eve. I know it was raining that night, and the days after Halloween that year were bone dry and cold; our last respite. It was a murky, dark November. You cried throughout.

"Rayna had been staying with Ari for a week, in case the baby came, and I lurked on the street corners around the flat to hear her when she started screaming. The labor was short, from the little I know of these things. I heard the first of it at nine forty. You came into the world a few minutes before midnight.

"There was very little I could do. I ran, down the street and up the stairs, and my sister let me into the flat, but I had no medical training, I knew nothing of this process, I could not ease Ari's pain. I could only hold her hand. She was delirious; it was only to be expected. She thought I was Felix. She told me she loved me.

"I don't think she ever fully trusted me, you know. When she found out that she was pregnant, she came to Rayna, and she asked for answers. Rayna didn't have them. What Ari wanted to be told was that she could stay in Regency and have the baby there and she and Felix could raise it together and the child would be safe and warm and happy.

"None of this, of course, could happen. For one thing, Ari was a soldier. She went into battle on a regular basis. Her fighting capacity would be severely dented if she were pregnant, and without fighting, she could never command respect as a leader. Even if she could, the child of Felix Callaway and Ariadne Stronach would never be safe. Our enemies, and we had many and vicious ones then, would not hesitate to kill a newborn if they thought it would break Regency's leaders.

"And then, of course, there was the small matter of your father.

"Felix was not fit to raise a child. He was twenty-six then, I think, and absolutely obsessed with defeating the Gifted, which was a lost cause if ever there were one, though we didn't see that at the time. Rayna and I knew that if it came to a choice between Regency and Ari, he would choose Regency in a heartbeat, no matter how much he loved her. She never had the courage to tell him she was carrying his child. That, we all knew, was a bad sign.

"So she left. She ran away under cover of David and Michael's escape attempt. By the time we had captured them, she was already gone. She broke Felix's heart that night, and I don't think it was ever whole again; he believed she no longer loved him, and in a way he was right.

"Rayna and I brought supplies to her tiny flat in Islington, while the pregnancy developed. At around four months her fetus shifted from being an *it* into a *he*. You were to be called Christopher, for her father, and you were to have all of Felix's courage and intelligence and handsomeness, and none of his . . . I don't know what you would call it. We didn't call it 'insanity,' not then. Ariadne's son was to be Felix angelic.

"I heard her make her plans and I said nothing.

"We didn't think of what else Felix might have made you.

"That night, when Ari's screams were louder than the rain, I held her hand and I tried to tell her stories. She asked me for my name, my real name, and because it felt like base cruelty to keep anything from her then, I told her.

"If it makes any difference to anyone now, Rose, I was once called Matthew Langley. Our father was an American business-man with a wife and two children of his own, and our mother was a medical student, whom he abandoned. She died of eclampsia between our births; we were twins, seventeen minutes apart. Our parents' names were Matthew McCauley and Ruby Langley, and so those were the names we were given in childhood. I hated being Matthew Langley. At sixteen, the man I envisioned Loren Arkwood being was a better person, a good person, a hero. It was never going to turn out that way, of course, but I kept the name.

"I only said all this because I didn't think she would be listening. I talked to myself to drown out her screams. I was nineteen, and selfish.

"Rayna delivered you. I thought there was too much blood, but what did I know about it? I counted sixteen seconds before you started crying. It was the most terrible silence I had ever heard. Then, of course, you cried, and Rayna cut the umbilical cord, and took you to the sink to wash you and to swaddle you. Ari was asking for Christopher, what had happened to Christopher, where Christopher was, and Rayna was trying to say there was no Christopher, you were a girl, there had never been a Christopher. I held Ari's hand and tried to tell her she had a daughter. She didn't understand me for a long time.

"Then Rayna put you in your mother's arms. Ari just stared at you, for so long I thought there must be something wrong with her. And then she smiled, and her smile was beautiful, and triumphant. She named you Aisling, for her mother, and said you looked like Felix. In the days afterward, she told me it was a shame, that if you had been a boy she would have called you Christopher Matthew.

"So that was your time as Aisling Stronach. And it — well, the good bit of it — lasted exactly six weeks.

"Can you guess what happened after those six weeks?

"You didn't hurt anyone. You were weak in your first transformation, and Ari could protect herself. Afterward, she was shaken, but she said she could manage it. She had loved Felix as a Hybrid; she could love her daughter, as one. It took us a few days to come up with the obvious reason. Becoming a Hybrid had changed Felix's DNA, and you were half-Felix. You had inherited his monsterhood.

"Yes, Rose, I lied to you. Does that still surprise you now?

"When you were three months old, Ariadne came to me when I was on patrol. She was ragged and gaunt and frightened, and you were in her arms. 'Felix has found me,' she said. 'I think he's going to hurt me,' she said. 'He can't know about Aisling. Please, protect Aisling, for me.'

"I told her yes, of course I would. But Felix wouldn't hurt her. He would never hurt her.

"I took you back to the flat I shared with Rayna. You missed your mother, I think. You cried on waking, every dawn, without her.

"Then, four days after that, I found her dead.

"I committed my first acts of mutiny that day. I carried her back to Regency and lay her there on the stage of the Command hall, so everyone could see what Felix had done. I cried hot tears and swore vicious curses on whoever had killed her.

"I loved her, you see, if it means anything.

"And David, David whose own love I had killed, came up and swore them with me. He walked up onto the podium and promised vengeance against Felix, for killing Ari. He had trusted Ari, I

297

think, and liked her; she had been his last ally in Regency's High Command, even when Felix and I had both turned against him. *I claim your death as my own,* he said; and the look in his eyes made us all believe him.

"And I knew then that there was only one way you could ever grow up safe.

"That night I went back to the flat and I sat there and looked at you. I couldn't find either of your parents in your face. For some reason that made me hate you slightly less.

"I put you in a shoe box and walked to the street where David lived, and I left you there in the dark until he came. The rain never touched you."

– Chapter 30 –

Loren took out the earpiece and gave it to Stephen Greenlow. When he spoke, his voice was shaking with hatred.

"Is that enough for you, then?"

"More than," said Stephen. "That was . . . most amusing."

Loren stood up, keeping himself tight and restrained and cold. "I'll kill you one day for that."

"A lot of people have promised to kill me," said Greenlow. "You'll notice none of them has managed it yet."

"You will release me. You will release her."

"Oh, yes. I'm a man of my word. That story, and the Department returning my son to me . . . more than worth your release."

"I hate your *words*."

"Words are effective weapons," said Stephen Greenlow. "You have just wielded them with admirable expertise. Even my son could not have lodged the knife in the girl's back with such precision. The scale of your betrayal, and your lies — giving *me*, of all people, the secret of the girl's parentage and condition, to ensure your own release —"

Loren punched him in the face. Greenlow rocked backward, rubbing his cheek, and kept talking calmly, as if there had been no interruption, watching him.

"At any rate, once we take Broadcasting House, we'll tell the world that the girl is a monster, and she'll be hunted down without us having to raise a finger. I thank you for so helpfully ensuring her death, Arkwood."

Loren pushed back the reflex to punch again, to inflict the pain on himself this time, to claw and break his own skin. The anguish and the guilt were clear in his voice. "You will never get that far."

"Oh, give us a few days. London is falling to us already, now that we have Heathrow. It would fall more quickly, but I want to take the legal system first. I want David Elmsworth executed by a jury. I don't want him a martyr."

Loren laughed harshly. It felt like choking. "He's certainly not that."

"So where are you going? Back to your Department, to try to defeat us?"

Loren said nothing. Greenlow raised his eyebrows.

"You're abandoning them?"

"Not . . . abandoning them."

"But where would you go? To Regency, to rescue your niece? But they would kill you. Unless . . ." Greenlow's eyes brightened. "Unless you've already been negotiating with them for her. Unless you've already offered them a deal. Unless you began preparing to betray the Department the moment they turned their backs." Greenlow laughed. "Oh, this is better than I could ever have hoped. You are a despicable man, Matthew Langley."

Loren tried to punch him again. Greenlow caught his fist mid-strike, and sent a bolt of magic through his hand. Loren felt his finger snap. He hissed, pulling his hand to himself, cradling the pain.

"Don't you dare tell yourself you didn't deserve that," said Stephen Greenlow calmly.

"Don't use that name."

"Why not?" He stood calmly and surveyed Loren as a doctor might look over the corpse of a failed patient. "You have given me your name, as you have given me the words and the histories of the woman you loved; as you have given me the secrets and the life of her daughter, to do with as I wish. You have no right to your name anymore."

Loren's hand was agony. He lowered himself to his knees and closed his eyes, imagining he could hear Rose's breathing through the walls.

"You are a coward, Loren Arkwood," said Greenlow.

"Yes, I am."

"You have betrayed her, and now you will betray what loyalty to the Department you still retain, for one of their worst enemies. For what you have done, you have relinquished your courage."

"Yes."

"Get up."

Loren did, hating Greenlow.

"I'm not going to kill you," said Greenlow, softly. "The moment the Department see that you have left them for Regency, no matter why, they will suffer more pain than your death could ever cause them. Especially the Elmsworth girl."

The door behind him swung open.

"I will find you," said Loren.

"I don't doubt it. Matthew?"

Loren turned back to him, letting his blistering rage and hatred show in his face this time. Greenlow held up the earpiece. The red light on its side was still shining. It had relayed their entire conversation to its counterpart in Rose's ear.

Loren stared at it.

"You promise you'll let her go?" he asked Greenlow.

Greenlow smiled slightly. "Of course. It won't do her any good, of course, but I keep my word."

Loren swallowed. "I'm sorry, Rose," he said, and then he left.

"Do you believe yourself a monster?"

"What kind of a question is that?" David asked irritably.

Madeleine, who looked exhausted from the events of the night before, had asked him all the standard questions; the jury had remained stone-faced throughout. Now it was Teller's turn. David was pale and gaunt, and gripped the side of the dock with one hand to stay standing; faced with such easy prey, the attorney was smiling.

"May I remind the defendant that he is under oath," said Justice Malvern, tiredly. David closed his eyes. "The truth, the whole truth, and *nothing* but the truth, Mr. Elmsworth. Please confine your remarks to admissible evidence."

There was a pause.

"No," he said wearily, "I do not consider myself a monster."

"Do you consider yourself human?"

This was met with tense silence, not least from the gallery. David scanned their faces.

"A variant thereof," he said, slowly.

Madeleine put her face in her hands. Teller, understandably, leaped at this.

"You consider yourself not quite human. Because your kind has evolved to kill humans."

"Firstly," said David loudly, over the end of Teller's question, "my *kind*, as you call us, have not evolved to do anything. We have existed for not quite twenty years, which is nowhere near long enough for an organism to undergo any kind of evolution. Secondly"—as Teller tried to interrupt—"I do not have a *kind*. I have a condition. Mr. Teller, in all your efforts to kill me, have you thought to speak to one expert on Hybrids? One academic, one student, one family member of the kind you call monsters?"

Teller shuffled his notes, apparently too contemptuous to answer.

"Of course you haven't. Well, given that their professed expertise would be nothing to mine, let me enlighten you as to a key aspect of my condition. I am not a monster. What resides inside me"—he tapped a fist against his chest—"is unquestionably monstrous, but it is not *me*. What is done to me, what you have seen done to me, every six weeks is nothing more than a dramatic hijacking. My body is changed and my mind is silenced. I am merely the walking vessel of this monster, with the added benefit that it only has the strength to take me over every six weeks. For the rest of the time, I am human. Do you understand?"

There was a pause.

"Oh, yes," said Teller softly. "I understand perfectly."

303

Quiet, through which they could hear the muttering of the jury. Malvern called sharply for silence again.

"So, Mr. Elmsworth, have you ever killed anyone?"

David looked up. "I'm sorry?"

"Have you killed?"

David blinked at Teller. They had seen him kill, on video, in this very courtroom. "Yes," he said. "But my actions were protected either by the amnesty enshrined in the Great Truce or by the fact that I was acting under Department jurisdiction."

"And would you have killed those people if you had not been a Hybrid?"

David, hot with anger, answered before he saw the genius of the question.

"*Yes*," he said emphatically, and then it seemed to hit him. He looked around in the stunned silence of the courtroom. He had just branded himself a murderer, regardless of his condition. There would be no question now, in the mind of the jury, that he deserved no clemency.

Madeleine's nails pressed into her palm so hard they drew blood.

"No further questions," said Teller, and David sank to his knees in the dock.

The court adjourned for no more than an hour. Madeleine and Tara stood outside the bars of his cell. Tara was not looking at him. After a while, he seemed to realize something and blinked, staring at the wall.

"What?" asked Tara impatiently.

"It's Rose's sixteenth birthday today," he said softly. "She's an adult, now. Where is she?"

They were silent.

"Is she in danger?" he asked, levelly.

Madeleine and Tara glanced at each other. Tara had fled Heathrow as it fell; the last thing she had heard was news that Rose and Loren had been captured, and that the Department — including, thought Madeleine with a now-familiar horrible, sickening jolt, Robert — was scattered and in chaos. But telling David that his daughter was in Stephen Greenlow's hands would not do anyone any good.

Nonetheless, he seemed to understand their meaning: that she was indeed in serious danger. He turned to them and looked them both hard in the eye.

"To hell with my acquittal then," he said. "There's no chance of it now. Bring out our Hybrid expert. Let her tell the court what she knows. If I'm going to die anyway, I want to see them afraid."

Madeleine had only just asked Cassandra Mayhew to state her name when the soldier burst into the courtroom. People screamed. Malvern stood up.

"You will put your weapon down, Lieutenant, or you will not be heard."

The soldier dropped his gun; it clattered loudly to the floor. "The Gospel," he said, when he could breathe again. "The Gospel are coming here."

"Do they intend to harm us?" asked Malvern, calmly.

"They intend to ensure the death of the defendant. They're going for Broadcasting House, as well. It's made of glass, so . . ." The soldier shrugged. "Won't be long."

A shocked silence. Madeleine glanced at Oliver Keen in the gallery. He had gone white.

"So what of it, Justice Malvern?" asked a voice from higher up the benches. David's head snapped up. Rose Elmsworth had her feet up on the bench in front of her; she looked perfectly at ease. A gasp ran around the courtroom. Madeleine's eyes widened. "Will you be pushed from the path of righteousness by the threat of violence? Will you be dissuaded from due legal process by Stephen Greenlow?"

"How in the hell did she get here?" whispered Tara, beside Madeleine. "How did she escape Greenlow?"

Malvern glared at Rose. "I will have silence in the courtroom," she said shortly. Then she addressed the soldier. "If Greenlow comes here, tell him I will do my duty while there is still breath in my body, and that if he wishes to silence me, he will have to do so permanently."

Rose Elmsworth gave a long wolf whistle from the gallery in mock celebration. David was smiling.

"What is she doing?" muttered Tara angrily.

Malvern sat down. "Ms. Ryan, please continue to examine the witness."

The tension was now palpable. Madeleine nodded to Cassandra, who began to speak, steady-voiced, steady-eyed, her gaze on Teller. "Ms. Mayhew. Do you know anything about the defendant's condition that might be of interest to the court?"

"I know everything about his condition," said Cassandra calmly. "I have it myself."

A shrinking, fearful silence. Any sympathy that Cassandra might have had with the gallery dissipated instantly into the cold January air. Madeleine glanced up at Rose. Her eyes were clear and sharp. She looked at the witness with a narrow, tense sort of curiosity.

306

"I became what you would call a monster several days before the Great Truce was signed. I was attacked at random, or so I believe, at night, when I was alone. Of the attack itself, I have almost no memory. I remember that I was in pain, of course, but I cannot remember what the creature looked like. I do not know who it was who attacked me, and if I did, I would not blame them. I know now that monsters pay no heed to the common humanity of those they corrupt."

She looked at Teller, cold-eyed, as she spoke.

"I was healed by my son. He found me bleeding in the street. He was only twelve — powerfully Gifted, but unskilled. I bear many scars, of course, but that's not his fault. Hybrid wounds don't heal. The venom keeps the marks on the skin."

"Were you ever any danger to your son?" asked Madeleine.

Cassandra glanced at David. "Never. I knew what I had become, or what I was becoming, and for the whole sixth week after I was attacked, I stayed well away from him, in an uninhabited part of the city. The first time I transformed, it was . . . terrible. The pain is enough. It feels as if you are being torn apart, from your heart outward. But almost worse is the insanity. You do go insane, but very quickly. It's as if a gap, an abyss, opens up in your mind, and your thoughts slip into it — like forgetting, but all of you vanishes, until only the monster is left. There are parts of you left, enough to feel as if you are doing what you're doing, but not enough to stop yourself. When you come back, when you turn human again, you don't know where you are, and then . . . you do. It's like resurrection. You die, and then you return with blood on your hands."

There was total silence in the courtroom. David and Rose were watching Cassandra with sharp alertness. It did not look quite like trust.

"I tried to keep it hidden," said Cassandra, to the stricken jury. "I lasted six years. Not quite as impressive as the defendant, but still considerably better than I had expected. Then I handed myself in."

"Why?" asked Madeleine, quietly.

"My son fell in love," said Cassandra, "and I killed someone."

Quiet. Fear, palpable, lurked in the spectators' breathing.

"I didn't mean to. I just miscounted the days. I didn't get as far out into the fields in the countryside as I hoped to. The monster could smell blood and headed for the nearest town. It never got there. The man who died was a hiker. I don't know who he was. I woke up miles away. There was no blood on my hands, but I knew something was wrong. I had to go deep into the memories to find the death. I didn't like that. I don't usually touch the memories."

Cassandra swallowed. David held her gaze until the silence ended.

"The woman my son loved was a good person, kind, and clever, and brave — and, best of all, they adored each other. I knew he was happy with her. So I left, in the middle of the night. I saw no need for good-byes."

"Tell the court what happened when you gave yourself in," said Madeleine.

Cassandra swallowed. Her voice was rough. "I didn't go to the Department. I went to the police, and told them what I was, and asked them to protect me from what I would do. Then they knocked me out. I woke up in a cell. I still don't know where that was. I was kept there for weeks. Then, two days before I transformed, an Angel came to me. She would come every month after that, for the five years I was in captivity. It was a year before she told me her name."

"And what was that name?"

"Eleanor Redmond. I believe her twin sister testified to this court very recently, about their brother Michael's involvement with the defendant."

David had gone very pale again.

"She was a Parliamentarian," said Cassandra. "She still is, now, but she was Leeched with the rest of them by Greenlow last year. She has been hospitalized for six months. I went to see her." A faint grin drifted across her face. "She is not well."

"How were you freed from your captivity?"

"By killing. They kept me in that cell, experimented on me. But . . ." A slight smile twisted Cassandra's lips again. "A year ago, my son tracked me down. They didn't expect that — Hybrids don't usually have families, you see. He slipped into the compound in disguise, saw the conditions in which I was kept. He threatened to expose the horrors of that place to the world unless I was freed. They couldn't take the risk. They put me on a sort of parole. I have to hand myself in every few weeks, to transform, but otherwise . . . I am free. They couldn't take the risk of a public backlash, you understand. I wasn't worth that."

A pause. Malvern looked stunned.

"And during those visits," said Madeleine quietly, "what did Eleanor Redmond tell you?"

"She told me what Demons are," said Cassandra, calmly, "and why some of them can do magic."

Immediate uproar. Teller leaped to his feet. "Objection," he shouted furiously, over the deafening noise of scribbling from the gallery. "This is patently ridiculous. Demons do not have magic. They are Ashkind. It's impossible."

Malvern never looked at him. She kept her eyes on Cassandra, who gazed back with unmoved serenity. "Objection denied," she said, and her voice carried over the courtroom, and brought astonished silence crashing down on the court. Teller's mouth had fallen open. David was smiling.

Cassandra waited until she was sure she had the attention of the courtroom. It did not take long. She had them rapt now.

"Angels have memories of the time their souls were separate," she said. "Because they are so powerful, they can remember being disembodied, on the other side of the Veil. The memories are faint, but they are there. And they remember a war. A long war, longer than ours. Thousands upon thousands of years. So long that all the beings that walked the earth died, and filled the heavens, and came back down to fight their war as disembodied souls. It was a war of nations, one half, one *geographical* half of their world, against the other. And as soon as they died, as soon as they left their bodies, they became souls, and all of the souls — every single one, on both sides — had magic."

Absolute silence. No one said anything. Clearly, they were trying to work out whether Cassandra was a prophet or a madwoman. The low surety of her words carried the faint echoes of scripture, but she herself — a ragged, gaunt woman with a monster in her gray eyes — had as little of the otherworldly about her as any of them.

"Then, after millennia of that war, one side surrounded the other, and trapped them, and drained the magic from them. And when Andrew Ichor opened up the break between our worlds, those souls without magic became one with humans, and we call them Ashkind. And the ones whose magic had not been taken from them became Gifted. And some of the Gifted, who had the strongest magic, became Angels."

"And Demons?" prompted Madeleine.

Cassandra drew a deep breath. "When the trap was laid, when half of that world lost their magic, some of the souls escaped unscathed. There were only a few hundred of them among billions, but they kept their magic hidden, and when they came and joined with humans, they became magical Demons. All Demons were as powerful as Angels in another life, but the vast majority of them had that power taken from them in that world, with the rest of the Ashkind, and so they have no magic now. But some of them retained their magic secretly, even when they joined with humans. Magical Demons are very, very rare, but they do exist."

The court remained silent with astonishment. Cassandra seemed to know this was only a matter of time, and sped up.

"The Parliament of Angels — the Government, in other words — have always known about this. They know that if Ashkind find out that they once had magic, that their magic was taken from them by the Gifted long ago, there might be a rebellion, or another War. So they find the magical Demons, the proof of their crimes in another world, and just to make sure, they tell the rest of the world that Demons are evil and dissentious and violent, so nobody will want to stay close to them long enough to realize that some of them are magical."

A wave of angry shouts drowned out the last of her words. Most of the gallery were on their feet, yelling in protest and shaking their fists. Malvern tried to make herself heard, to ask for silence, but to no avail. Tara stood up, and nodded to two burly-looking Ashkind farther up in the gallery. They descended, pushing past the guards by the witness stand, and flanked Cassandra, glaring menacingly at anyone who came close. She walked with them through the crowd of journalists and out of the courtroom.

Madeleine followed her under the wall of noise. Malvern's eyebrows were furrowed, and Teller, for once, was not protesting at being denied the chance to cross-examine the witness. His gray eyes were wide, and David Elmsworth's defense team noted with grim satisfaction that his powers of speech seemed, for once, to have deserted him.

– Chapter 31 –

"They're getting close."

Rose sat down beside Cassandra. The bars of the prison cell once again separated her from her father. Madeleine and Tara had been pacing restlessly for the last hour, but at Rose's reentry, they looked up sharply.

"Any news about Rob?" said Madeleine immediately. She had been asking after her fiancé every five minutes since they had left the courtroom, apparently unaware of the frequency of her questions; she became increasingly tense and distracted with each unhelpful answer.

Rose shook her head. "He hasn't been seen since Heathrow fell. Neither have Terrian or Wood — or Maria." Her voice broke, and then immediately sealed again. "Nate must be sick."

Her tone made it clear he was not the only one. Madeleine's face closed.

Tara glanced at her. "Any resistance?"

"Some, by all accounts, but quickly ended. The people are either too sympathetic or too terrified. They are not soldiers."

"They were," murmured David. Rose's gaze switched instantly to him.

Something flickered between them, and hung there, on the air.

"I have questions to ask you," said Rose.

"Not now."

"Oh, yes, now. The Gospel are coming for us. They'll take Broadcasting House eventually, and when they do, things will get interesting. Stephen Greenlow found out what I am."

David's face went a dead, bleached white. Rose's expression was flat, unsympathetic, her gaze on him cold.

It became suddenly apparent to everyone else present that she was very, very angry.

"Now I have your attention," she said, grimly.

David could not speak. Cassandra appeared to be trying to sleep; Tara and Madeleine were staring at each other.

"I've just spoken to the guards," said Rose. "The jury have begun their deliberations." At Madeleine's cry of shock, she said, "I know, it's ahead of schedule. Apparently Malvern has decided to discard due legal process after all. She wants this over as quickly as possible."

"You'll be found guilty," said Tara to David. "You don't stand a chance." She did not sound upset about this at all. David did not glance at her. Neither did Rose.

"How did Greenlow find out?" he asked, hoarsely.

314

"Loren told him," said Rose. David's eyes widened.

"I should have killed him," he said viciously. "I should have killed him years ago. Where is he now?"

"Gone. He exchanged information about me for our release. He's gone to Regency, I think, for Tabitha. They have him in their power now. I suppose you could call it a defection."

Cassandra's eyes snapped open. Tara stared at Rose. Madeleine actually took a faltering step backward in shock. The Elmsworths ignored them all.

"That's what Regency were waiting for," said Rose, calmly. "All those months they spent in hiding, and the Department couldn't find them, and we all wondered what they were planning. He was what they were waiting for all along. Loren. They were waiting to kidnap Tabitha, so they could force him to work for them again. He'll do anything they want as long as they have a gun to Tabitha's head. And with him on their side, I'd say they have a decent chance of defeating even the Department, now that it's just Terrian running it. And then it'll be Regency versus the Gospel. Gifted versus Ashkind. A Second Angelic War."

David's voice was hollow, empty. "I will find him, and I will skin him."

"You will do no such thing," said Rose sharply. "I will not have you harm him. He's gone, now, he's not coming back, and I doubt you could find him anyway."

"He's betrayed us," said Madeleine, in quiet astonishment. Rose did not look at her.

She examined her father for a moment, the edge of a smile playing on her lips. "I lied," she said, eventually. "I have only one question for you."

"Rose, now is not the time."

315

"How dare you," she said, with sudden, cold fury. "How dare you try to decide when I get answers? I have every right to ask you anything. You are behind bars. You are on your knees. You have no power, not anymore."

David looked as if she had slapped him. Rose watched him, her green eyes cold.

"What do you know?" he asked, in a whisper.

"Wrong question."

He swallowed, and glanced at Tara. "All right, what's the correct one?"

"The correct question is, what did *you* know?"

He looked at her, uncomprehending. Rose knelt down beside the bars of his cell, so that they were at eye level. She wrapped her hands around the bars.

"I don't want your explanations," she said. "I don't want your excuses, or your apologies, not that you would make them. I just want to know this. When you arranged to have me cause Felix Callaway's death, did you know he was my father?"

David stared at her. The color began to return slowly to his face. Rose stood up and leaned against the wall, looking down at him with the air of a tired experimenter watching a rat run into the wall of the maze for the fifth or sixth time. "I thought so," she said.

Tara's eyes were wide; Madeleine seemed oblivious with worry. "He was *what*?"

Rose glanced at her. "It was a fairly self-explanatory statement."

David's voice was steadier now, but it came slowly, like a disused reflex. "Would it have changed what you did?"

"Not at all. If anything, knowing what he did to my mother, I

316

would have asked to fire the gun myself. But that is not the point, and you know it."

"No, I don't."

Rose scrutinized him as if trying to read his mind.

"No," she murmured to herself after a few moments, "you don't."

She began to pace, speaking to the walls instead of to him.

"You didn't trust me," she said. "You didn't trust me to do the right thing — to kill him — if I had known who he really was to me. That, I suppose, is forgivable. I was a child, after all, and I had never killed, so asking me to help engineer a death was risky. You would have been within your rights to worry about my resolve. But you took that information and you decided the best thing to do was not to tell me what he was. You used me," she said, turning suddenly to him as he tried to interrupt, her eyes blazing, "you *used* me as a weapon, nothing more than a walking revolver. You took my love and my trust, and you used it to your advantage, as if I weren't human. As if I were some kind of unthinking *monster*."

Her eyes were bright, and she almost spat the words at him, knowing how they would land. David flinched. Madeleine looked sharply at her.

David rose slowly to his feet. "And if I had told you, for all I knew, you might *not* have killed him."

Rose kept pacing. "True."

"So what good was there in telling you? Was the soundness of your information worth the lives he would have taken if he'd lived?"

She went still and quiet. Then she turned to him, her eyes clear. "Yes," she said. "To you, it should have been. It should

317

have tormented you to know that you had persuaded me to kill my own father without knowing what I was doing. To you, the soundness of my information should have been worth anything."

They looked at each other for a long time, through the bars.

"I don't understand," he said.

Rose sighed. The sound of footsteps and shouting seeped slowly in from under the door to the corridor. Cassandra's eyes flicked open instantly. David rubbed his eyes, and leaned against the wall; clearly these noises were routine to him.

"They're coming to take me away, ha-ha," he said, dryly.

The door burst open and two irritable-looking Ashkind guards came into the corridor. They made immediately for the cell, where David stood with his wrists held out, but Madeleine blocked their way.

"Where do you intend to take my client?"

One of them brandished the cuffs threateningly, but the other one said, tiredly, "Back to the court. The verdict is in."

"I don't believe you. It's only been an hour."

"Well, thanks to Greenlow's lot, that's as long as we have."

Madeleine hesitated, then stood aside. David stood with patient weariness as they cuffed him and pulled him roughly out of the cell. He moved with them, the routine worn to instinct.

Halfway down the corridor, he wrenched from their grip and turned back to Rose, his eyes wide.

"Wait," he said, "what do you mean you *had* never killed?" but she said nothing, and they pulled him onward.

They were counting their way up the Piccadilly line from the east.

"Northfields."

"Here."

"Boston Manor."

"Present and correct."

"Osterley."

"Absolutely, sir, yes sir."

Tyler sighed. He had been awake since three in the morning, and he really didn't have the energy to deal with piss-taking grunts. "Osterley, I'm going to ask you again . . ."

A sullen hiss of static. Then: "Tube station under guard, all occupants taken hostage, no casualties as yet, *sir.*"

"Thank you, Osterley."

No reply. Tyler moved on. "Hounslows, all in order?"

East and Central chorused back immediately; West was more sluggish, but Tyler couldn't blame her. No one had opened a coffee shop in that hellhole since the War.

"Hatton Cross."

"Yes, sir."

"And, finally . . . Heathrow."

"Damn right yes, sir."

Tyler allowed himself a smile. Heathrow Airport in the hands of the Gospel. He'd been dreaming of this day for years. He took off the headset and stood up. "Sir?" he called back. "We've got it, sir. We've got the whole bloody city."

Silence.

"Sir!"

Tyler moved out of the control room. The vast supply warehouse they were in was empty, apart from a few guards. Until a few hours ago, it had held Loren Arkwood and the Elmsworth girl. But apparently the boss had made some kind of a deal with them and let them go. Tyler would have kept hold of them himself, but his was not to reason why.

"Sir?"

When no answer came, he followed his hunch to the small white-painted room where Rose Elmsworth had been held, and found Stephen Greenlow's dead body curled in the fetal position on the cold floor, his jacket pulled over him like a blanket.

A tiny drop of blood was drying into the paint from the bullet hole in his head. There was no sign of a struggle, but of course there would have had to have been one. Stephen Greenlow, of the mighty Gospel, ruler of London for all of two minutes, would never have gone down without a fight. Whatever had happened, Rose Elmsworth had won it very quickly, and, Tyler prayed, painlessly.

She must have outwitted him.

There was a note, pressed gently into Greenlow's cold, clenched, hardening fist. Elmsworth must have put it there. On the paper were two words, in flowing script. Her hands had not even shaken.

My condolences, she had written.

Chapter 32

The foreman of the jury was a tense, morose-looking man. He looked terrified as he got to his feet.

Madeleine didn't look at David as the foreman readied himself. She watched Rose, and her low, half-hidden grimace of a smile.

The journalists too were smiling. They wanted to hear David Elmsworth convicted, wanted to see him fall, after all this time waiting for it.

No one seemed to be moving. Madeleine closed her eyes and waited for the ax to fall. She had, at least, done everything she could.

She deserved something for that. She deserved Rob's safety.

Please, please let him be safe.

The foreman drew a deep breath.

*   *   *

David seemed oblivious to the atmosphere in the courtroom. He was looking around for Rose, but she had vanished as soon as the final verdict had been read out. She had not been the only one: the jury had sprinted from the room as though they too had been released, in such a hurry that some of them had even left their bags behind.

"Where is she?" he asked Madeleine, in lieu of saying "thank you." They walked together in silence, unaccompanied for once by armed guards, out of the courtroom, where Rose stood by the windows. David rushed over to her.

"How the hell did you manage that?"

Rose did not even try to maintain her innocence. "It doesn't matter."

"Of course it matters. You just intervened in due legal process. There is no way on earth they would have acquitted me under normal circumstances."

Rose pointed out of the window. Gospel soldiers stood arrayed around the building, guns pointed at the outside walls. It would be a hell of a job getting out of here. "These aren't normal circumstances."

David ignored them. "Rose, what have you done?"

She snapped, and turned on him. "I just saved your life. Is that not enough for you?"

He was silenced briefly. "I would not retain my life to see you stain your soul."

"Then you need to check your priorities."

He looked at her for a long moment.

"All right," he said quietly. "What do you suggest we do now?"

"You need to get out of the city. Out of the country, if you can."

David stared at her. "Are . . . would you not come with me?"

"Do you not have calendars in those cells?"

He looked at her, hurt and uncomprehending, and Rose sighed. "It's the nineteenth. I officially became an adult at midnight. I can stay here, if I want to."

"It's not safe here for you."

"It's not safe here for anyone."

He looked at her. Out of the corner of her eye, Madeleine saw Tara beckoning her silently to the courtroom door. Slowly, Madeleine retreated, and left David and Rose to argue. Tara was holding a handbag.

"They all left their bags," she whispered, watching Rose. "The whole jury. They left their bags on the benches."

Madeleine blinked. "Why?"

Wordlessly, Tara handed her a crumpled, coffee-stained note from inside the handbag. The words had been typed.

I have hidden a small explosive device inside your bag, it read. *If you vote to convict the defendant, it will explode.*

That was it.

Madeleine stared at it. "You're joking."

"There's no explosive device," Tara said, in tones of hushed awe, "and she had no way of knowing how each one of them would vote. She was *bluffing*."

Madeleine put a hand to her mouth, and began to laugh, for the first time since Robert had disappeared. It sounded slightly mad. "You know what, Tara? I think our Rose may just have snapped."

A pause.

"It worked, though," said Tara, still staring at the note. "You can't deny that."

*   *   *

The Gospel soldiers stood outside and waited for the Elmsworths to come out.

After a few minutes, they heard a loudspeaker announcement inside the courthouse, telling everyone inside to stay where they were, and not to go outside under any circumstances.

They waited patiently, and after a few minutes Rose Elmsworth walked out of the building, holding a gun. The soldiers stayed motionless and wary. The girl smiled.

"I assume you have been sent here to kill me," she said. "In this brave new world of yours, I must be public enemy number two."

No one said anything.

"Look," she said, "it's very simple. You can shoot me, fine. I'll bleed out on the courtroom steps. It'll be a dramatic death. A hero's death. You'll be commended for doing it. Except, of course, there's one tiny catch. You see, my reflexes are very, very good, and in order to shoot me, you're going to have to move your hand a little. Just a tiny bit. But I will see it, and I'll see it fast enough to shoot you. It won't be enough to save my life, of course. Your bullet will hit me, and I'll die anyway. But not before I've killed whichever of you does it."

The girl smiled. Her green eyes seemed to glow.

"So," she said, "which one of you wants a martyr's death with me?"

No one moved.

Elmsworth walked forward, down the steps of the courtroom.

They were motionless. She walked forward, passing between them like trees in a forest. Not one of them moved an inch. When she reached the other end, and emerged from the crowd of soldiers, she turned to look at them.

324

"I'm just playing for time, you know," she said. "I'm been trying to draw your attention while my father escapes through the other entrance. It's all right, there's no point guarding it now. He'll be gone already."

She paused.

"And there's something else I feel I should tell you," she said. "I'm afraid I killed Stephen Greenlow."

She walked away out of sight, leaving them shaken, incredulous and silent. When she was gone, one of the soldiers picked up his walkie-talkie with shaking hands.

"Sir?" he said into it, hesitantly. "General Greenlow, sir?"

The base was twenty feet underground. It was protected by the tightest security measures money and magic could buy, and staffed by ten heavily armed Gospel soldiers. It was also watched from street level by dozens of hidden cameras, the feeds of which were closely monitored by guards in a state-of-the-art control room.

None of this did Natalie Greenlow any good, in the end.

She was trying to sleep when her walkie-talkie awoke, like a sad alarm clock. "Mrs. Greenlow," said Lynch's voice. She stirred, and stared at the blinking blue light in the dark. "Mrs. Greenlow, you're needed."

She slept fully clothed these days, and Lynch knew that, so she had no excuse for being late to wherever he wanted her to be. She picked up the walkie-talkie, held it above her mouth like a small child with a toy plane. "I'm coming," she said loudly.

"Good," said Lynch, and disconnected.

She dragged herself out of bed and pulled on her shoes, disoriented. Outside the door, her guards waited. They knew where she had to go; they had already been informed, as they always were. Natalie had no idea why Lynch considered it so imperative that *she* be kept in the dark. He was Stephen's right-hand man, insofar as Stephen allowed anyone power and influence over the Gospel to rival his own. He had strong magic, but he had been part of the swell of recruits to come in only after the Parliament of Angels had been Leeched, and as such Stephen never completely trusted him. It showed no true loyalty, as he always said, to join Caesar when the Rubicon had already been crossed.

Natalie waited until it became clear she was being taken to the meeting room, and then asked to be allowed to get her coat from the cloakroom. It was January, after all, and she was cold. Grudgingly, they let her slip out of the corridor and pull her leather coat from the racks, and then they walked on. Natalie's fingers closed around the penknife in her coat pocket. She didn't trust Lynch any more than Stephen did.

The guards left her outside the door and walked away. Natalie watched them go with narrow eyes. When she was sure she was alone, she tightened her grip on the knife, and opened the door as silently as she could.

It didn't matter.

Lynch sat at the table. His hands and feet had been duct-taped to his chair, and his head drooped forward onto his chest, which rose and fell slowly with his breathing. On either side of him were Aaron and Tristan. They weren't moving. Natalie cried out, and ran to her sons, terror thumping impossibilities through her blood.

"As you can see," said a voice from the head of the table, "we have returned your eldest son to you."

Natalie's head snapped up. As she took in the sight of Loren Arkwood leaning back lazily into Stephen's chair, her fingers found a beat in Aaron's wrist.

"If you've hurt them . . ."

"Of course I've hurt them," said Arkwood mildly. "I knocked them out and dragged them here. I can't imagine that was painless. But, you see, I haven't *killed* them, and that's what counts."

Natalie went to Tristan, found his pulse. It was steady. "I'm going to kill you."

"A rather unimaginative revenge."

"I'll call the guards."

Arkwood took out his gun and put it on the table. "No you won't."

Natalie turned to him, steeled herself, and took a step forward, her hand clenched tightly in her pocket.

"Take your coat off," said Arkwood, sounding bored. Natalie hesitated, and did so, cursing silently. The blade of the penknife met the table with an audible *clunk.* Arkwood raised his eyebrows.

"What do you want?" she asked him, her voice shaking with fury.

"I don't want anything. Well, nothing *you* can give me, at least. I was sent in here looking for control of your army, and I have that now, so unless you have a coffee machine cunningly hidden away here somewhere that I could use . . ."

"You're talking out of your arse."

"I feel your grasp of anatomy is somewhat lacking."

"You're a Pretender. You're an Ashkind-lover. You could never take us."

"On the contrary, I can and I have. You see, what you trumped-up collection of politically illiterate weapons enthusiasts consistently fail to realize is that, for all your Leechings, for all your slurs and your oratory and your numbers, you are amateurs. I was in the revolution business for nearly a decade, and a dozen of your clumsy thugs wouldn't have a hope of taking me down in direct combat — as, indeed, they proved ten minutes ago."

Natalie moved toward him, snarling. "You couldn't take us down with a thousand men."

"Perhaps not," said Arkwood, "but I did very well on my own."

"And how exactly do you think you've managed that?"

He sighed, and slammed a fist into the desk. A slat of wood dipped with the blow, and rose on silent hinges to reveal a computer screen attached to its underside. Natalie stared at it.

"Your husband's," said Arkwood. "Do you not think, with all his hunger for power, he would not have protected himself against defections? Under *interrogation,* I suppose we can phrase it, your son Aaron told me that his father kept a database of every single one of your thousands of recruits — combatant and non-combatant, open and covert, violent and peaceful. On this computer before me is a list of the loved ones and the weaknesses of every soldier in this army, and now that list is mine. Stephen Greenlow's paranoia is this army's greatest liability, you see. I know where to find each and every pressure point of every soldier in your army. I own your soldiers; I own the Gospel."

"You do not."

"There is a line between courage and stupidity, Ms. Greenlow, and I fear you may have crossed it."

"Who are you working for? Who has told you to say this?"

Arkwood closed his eyes again, and twirled his fingers as if conducting. "Isabel, Anthony, make yourselves known."

A stirring from behind Natalie. She turned as two figures stepped from the shadows. The woman was holding a revolver, and was grinning broadly. The man was not smiling. His face was worn, his eyes sunken with grief. Nevertheless, there was something of savage satisfaction in his gray eyes.

Their gray eyes.

A wave of terrible realization loomed over Natalie Greenlow, threatening to crash on top of her.

"Ms. Greenlow, let me introduce you to my *colleagues*," said Arkwood, and suddenly there was a bitter edge to his voice. "Anthony here lost his son to the Department last year, and has since been hell-bent on destroying them, so you have at the very least something in common. As for Isabel, well, this was her idea. They are the current representatives of the army known as Regency."

"He owns the Gospel," said Isabel quietly, "and we own him."

"You do not *own me*," said Arkwood with sudden fury, rounding on her. Isabel did not flinch.

"We have your child," she said calmly, "and thus we have you. You are in no position to argue, Arkwood."

"Get on with it," whispered Anthony hoarsely, his eyes on Natalie.

Arkwood glanced at him, and turned back to Natalie. "They have my niece, Tabitha," he said, with some difficulty, "and so, as Isabel says, they . . . *own* . . . me. Their plan, for the past few months, such as it was, was to wait until they had me in their power and you had conquered London, and to then simply send

329

me in to defeat you. Having your sons as a source of information was admittedly a help — it made things go much more smoothly. You capture London; Regency defeats you and claims the city as its own. Maximum results with minimal effort." He rubbed his face. "I should have realized. I was an idiot."

Natalie stepped back, trying to keep all three of them and her sons in her field of view. "I don't understand."

Arkwood sighed again, and got to his feet. Natalie stumbled backward, and he stopped dead as if she had struck him. He looked down at her from across the room, and it was a moment before he spoke.

"They have my child," he said, with some anguish, "so I have to do whatever they want. You do understand that, don't you?"

"I'm sure she does," said Isabel, with a glance at Natalie's unconscious sons.

Arkwood's lip curled in disgust. "I was their pet coward, their Angel of Death, in the days when they protected my sister; and I am so again now that they have my sister's daughter."

"How times change."

Arkwood shot Isabel a dirty look.

"This database," he tapped the console, "gives Regency the power to blackmail every single Gospel soldier into doing whatever they are told. It tells . . . *us* . . ." A flash of pain crossed his face, quickly gone. "It tells us where to find their husbands and wives, their sons and daughters, their parents and their siblings. As long as we have that control over them, they will not care who they fight for, just as long as we don't kill their loved ones. If we tell them to fight for Regency — for us — then they will. We therefore own them. We own the Gospel. And we thus own London."

Desperation, and the possibility of the truth, shot through

330

Natalie's brain like spiked adrenaline; she pushed the feelings down. "You will never defeat us," she said furiously. "So long as there is breath in my husband's body, you will never make us *submit*."

There was a silence. The three Regency leaders glanced at one another.

"Oh," said Arkwood sadly, "I really wish you hadn't phrased it like that."

– Chapter 33 –

The lock had not yet been broken, so Rose had to use her keys to get into their old house, where they had agreed to meet.

She stood in the hallway, looking around.

The last time she had been here, it had also been to wait for her father. It had been two days before she let herself accept that he wasn't coming. For three weeks after that she had had to fight the terrible suspicion that he was dying somewhere, alone, or already dead.

Then, of course, he had returned, and given himself up to the police, and this whole hellish nightmare of a trial had begun.

She still didn't know where he had been for those three weeks.

Yet another thing to ask him about.

She stood there for another few moments. There was silence. She did not call out to him; her own voice echoing through the empty house would have done nothing to calm her. Instead, she went up to his room, and stood quietly outside the door.

There was no sound of footsteps from inside, or breathing, and the shadows stretching from under the door did not move. She closed her eyes. Perhaps he was late. Please, dear God, say he was just late.

She could not take anything else.

She went into the bedroom and saw the broken things and the blood. The first thing she looked for was a body, but there was none. Instead, someone had carved the words *Behold the Interregnum*—Regency's slogan—into the wall with a bloody knife.

She stared at the words for a long time. Then she lowered herself steadily onto her knees, and screamed, and cried with frustration.

No, please, not again.

Not him. Please. Not again.

Downstairs, her thoughts churning, acting on autopilot, she paced the floor furiously. Then she turned on the television for something to do with her hands. BBC News came up first. That was odd, that they were still able to broadcast; had the Gospel not taken Oxford Circus yet?

The sound was turned down. She turned it up with a shaking hand.

"The rebellion by the armed activist group calling itself the Gospel seems to have been hijacked by Regency, a War militia intent on destroying Gifted rule. Regency units appear to have

333

coerced Gospel soldiers into working for them, and are currently moving toward Department headquarters. If anyone is in there, please, run. It is believed they intend to kill you all."

Rose stared at the television for a long, long time.

Regency. Of course. Of course, they would have taken David just when they were strongest. Only then could they be sure they could hold him.

He would have been safer in his prison cell.

She put her face in her hands.

She had killed Stephen Greenlow and now the Gospel had fallen, and Regency were overrunning London.

All right. All right. She had nothing. No allies that she would not have to win back, no resources that she would not have to find herself, no weapons that —

Wait.

She went back up to her father's bedroom, her footsteps creaking on the stairs. Even in his absence, ignorant of whether he was even still alive, she felt on the edge of reproach by going in there without his permission. Her heart was already breaking for him.

No, please, not him, not again. Just when she had won him back . . .

The prosecutors had confiscated his guns for evidence, for all the good that had done them, but they hadn't known all of his hiding places. Rose unlocked the compartment of the windowsill, then paused and turned to look at the note Regency had carved into the wall.

The guns hadn't done David much good, either.

She did a quick inventory: two SA80s, an M16, a revolver, and a submachine. They had laid untouched for six months at least,

334

but were still in decent condition. Rose left the submachine — too bulky and inaccurate, for all its power — and took the rest. David's green bomber jacket was on the back of his bedroom door, and she put that on, and hid the guns under it. The jacket made her want to cry again — he hadn't even had a chance to wear it after he'd been released, during his so brief, so brief taste of freedom — but she pinched the inside of her wrist until she was cold and still and calm again, and then she moved on.

Outside, the wind was cold and sharp. It was nearing three o'clock now. Rose's birthday had barely ninety minutes of daylight left in it. Rose hated being a winter baby. But, of course, she reflected, she hadn't been one after all. All Hallows' Eve. The dying days of autumn.

Close enough.

There was no question about what she was going to do. It felt like the decision had been made a long time ago — before she had saved her father from the jaws of justice, even before she had killed Stephen Greenlow. Something had fallen away from her when Loren had told her what she was, *who* she was, and then abandoned her; it was apparent, suddenly, that the world cared a lot less about right and wrong than she had always done, and that no one would ever care enough to punish her if she stopped caring too.

And then her path had become glowingly clear. She would save the people she loved, by whatever means necessary, and to hell with anyone who tried to stand in judgment over her. She knew what the important things were in the world.

And with that realization came power: the power to kill, to walk through a hostile army unharmed, and to sway a jury. The freedom to do anything.

And with that power, she would save her father.

The walk took twenty minutes. The building that served as the entrance to the Department's temporary underground base was surrounded by gray-uniformed troops. Regency uniforms. Some of the soldiers were green-eyed; they held their weapons unwillingly, fear carved into their faces. They had been Gospel — now they had been coerced into fighting for Regency, who hated them and all their kind. Rose grinned. Served them bloody well right.

A fire had been lit at the entrance to the building — an attempt to smoke out the inhabitants, she assumed, although she doubted it would have any effect. The Department were cleverer than that.

She went to the corner and found a manhole cover. She stood above it and looked down, scrutinizing it. It did nothing.

She kept looking at it. It remained stubbornly where it was.

When she was sure no one was beneath it, waiting to ambush her, she knelt and pulled at it. It moved as silently as a heavy iron weight could be expected to move, but none of the soldiers looked around.

She stared down into the darkness beneath the manhole, and took out her house keys. She looked at them for a few moments. Whatever happened after this, whether or not she and David were both still alive by the time this was over, they were never going back to that house again. If there was such a thing as a curse, then it was on that broken-windowed, dark-basemented, scarred hulk of a place.

She pulled her key off the chain and dropped it into the darkness. The wet *clink* came back very quickly. No sewage, then, and no death drop. All right.

She lowered herself quickly into the gap, breathed, and jumped. The hole was only about six feet deep, but the ground was hard, and set a snap of pain through her ankles. She bent double, teeth gritted. When she was all right again, she pulled the manhole back over herself so she was in complete darkness.

It was good that she had slept earlier. She opened her hand, and a light drifted up to hover tentatively, like a firefly below the roof of the passage. She walked toward a T-junction — if road metaphors could apply in whatever the hell this was — directly ahead, her hand on her gun.

She stopped at the junction. Left or right?

Did it matter?

To her right, the shadows shifted. She should just have taken that as a cue to go left, but of course she did not; she pulled the M16 out and pointed it down the right-hand passageway.

"Who's there?"

Stupid question. No one with the element of surprise would ever answer it, and no one without it would be a threat. There was a silence. Then, just as she thought she was going to have to kill again, a low voice said, "If you fire that, there'll be ricochets."

Rose lowered the gun warily. "James."

He stepped out from around the corner, his arms folded. He didn't look as if he had been hurt in the Heathrow attack, and she was almost surprised at the strength of her relief at this. He looked exhausted, but not . . . damaged. There was no love in his expression now, not even heartbreak, just mistrust.

"You're alive," he said.

"Yes."

"Your father was acquitted today," he said, in a coldly level voice. "And Stephen Greenlow was murdered in the early hours of this morning."

"I know."

"And you don't have *anything* to do with either of those things?"

There was no point in lying to him. They looked at each other across the darkness for a long moment. James put his face in his hands. After a while he said, "Why have you come back?"

"To defeat Regency. Or at least take out a few of its soldiers."

"And how exactly do you plan to do that, Rose?"

Rose started walking forward, the light drifting in her wake. James stayed where he was.

"Put that out."

"Why?"

"Even if you disregard the ban, and I'm sure you do, the peacetime law forbids magic in public places or in a private place you don't own without permission from the owner. Whichever way you cut it, you're breaking the law."

Rose stared at him through the ghostly illumination. "That law is dead. All the laws are dead. Regency own the law now that they have the Gospel's soldiers."

"I don't care. You're not Regency, are you?"

Rose gave him a dark look, but extinguished her light. They stood in darkness.

"How did you get out of Heathrow?" she asked.

His voice was disconnected, almost eerie. "We got to the van before the Gospel soldiers overran the airport. We couldn't fight, because . . ." His voice darkened. "They would have killed you and Loren."

She had nothing to say to that. It seemed to her that that act of weakness — letting Heathrow fall, for her and Loren's sake — was a relic of the old Department days, when they had all

338

had one another's backs, and fought for one another's lives. She had thought that was gone.

There was a silence. They began to walk.

"So you got him acquitted, then," said James, the would-be casualness of his voice unable to disguise its bitter edge.

She focused hard on the location of his voice. If she knew where he was, she was fine. "I didn't do anything. The jury acquitted him."

"Oh, don't give me that. You're Department just like I am. We're not in the habit of letting anyone else pass judgment."

Rose was quiet.

There was a long silence. They walked for a few minutes through the crushing darkness.

After a while, she said, with great effort, "I said once that I would . . . forgive you . . . the day he was exonerated."

He didn't turn around; she couldn't see his face. "It doesn't matter. I didn't believe you."

Another long pause. Rose tried to identify the cause of the hard feeling in her stomach, as if she had been hit; she realized that it was hurt, and examined it with astonishment.

"Where is he now?" he asked, with an air of wary resignation.

"It doesn't matter."

"The hell it doesn't. Tell me where he is."

She said nothing. James's voice was suddenly white-hot with fury. "Don't tell me he's disappeared again."

"Not for the reasons you think."

He turned, or walked. Rose couldn't tell, could only hear the echoes of his steps and the moving water. The noises sharpened against the walls. "Rose, when will you learn not to trust this man?"

"He hasn't run away!" Now she was shouting; and there she had thought her days of defending David had been over. "*Regency* have him!"

James stopped, very suddenly.

"Are you sure?"

"I have rarely been surer of anything."

"You know that means he's dead."

She was silent.

He sighed. "Follow my footsteps," he said heavily, "and don't walk into a wall if you can help it."

She followed him tentatively through the echoing darkness, hands out to skim the slimy walls. It took her three turns to trust him, and after that a faint light set the damp walls gleaming. Rose could make out James's silhouette a few yards ahead, and she walked now with more confidence; she had never been able to see in the dark very well.

They came to the gray metal door at the end of the passage — the entrance to the Department's underground base. Light drifted bleakly toward them from under it. James knocked on it.

Nate's voice. "Who is it?"

"Oh, for God's sake," said James irritably, next to Rose. "Who do you bloody think?"

A scraping, heaving sound, and the door opened. James pushed past Nate wordlessly, but Nate stood there, staring at Rose. She looked back at him, bemused.

"Yes," she said, "it's me."

Abruptly, he moved forward and hugged her. She stiffened unthinkingly in his grip. "Thank the Angels," he whispered.

"Have Regency made some kind of announcement? That

Greenlow's dead and the Gospel's soldiers answer to Regency now?"

Nate released her, and stepped back. "*He* has," he said, his voice tight with anger.

"Ah. Loren."

"He betrayed us. For *Regency*." Nate sounded furious, whether at himself or at Loren she wasn't sure. "Why would he do that, Rose?"

"Tabitha. He won't be doing any of this of his own accord, trust me. He'll just be obeying whoever has her, whether he wants to or not."

"How did he get the Gospel soldiers to work for Regency?"

"I'd imagine Regency found some kind of hold over the Gospel soldiers," said Rose calmly, checking the cuffs of her sleeves. "The same kind of hold Regency have over him. Blackmailing them with their loved ones."

Nate glanced at her. A shutter seemed to have fallen over his eyes. "You guessed that quickly."

She stared at him.

"Your minds must work along the same lines," he said quietly. "Curious, isn't it?"

Rose tried to retort hotly, but she had not got out two syllables before Terrian confronted her. His hands were bloody.

So he had made it out of Heathrow alive too, then.

"*You*," he said furiously. "You've got some nerve coming here. You've ruined us. If it weren't for you helping him, Arkwood would be dead, and none of this would have happened."

"If it weren't for me helping him," said Rose evenly, "Arkwood, as you call him, would have revealed my father as a Hybrid last year; he would have been put on trial that much earlier; Felix

Callaway wouldn't have died, and with him at Regency's helm, the Gospel would have been defeated and the city would have fallen in June. My actions bought London six months of time. If not for you, though, the War Rooms fiasco would never have happened, and the Gospel would not have had the citywide panic to give them the courage they needed to Leech the Angels. We make our own beds, Connor."

His face darkened with rage. "Don't you dare use my name, you treacherous bitch."

"Wash your mouth out," said Rose calmly, "and your hands. Who have you been trying to heal?"

He started to answer, but she was already moving. A mattress and a makeshift curtain had been set up near the back of the office. She didn't need to be any closer to know who it was. Maria knelt beside him; at the sound of Rose's footsteps she leaped to her feet. There was blood on her hands, as well.

"Rose! I got him back. He was shot, I tried to heal him, it didn't work, I'm sorry, I couldn't . . ."

Rose murmured to her briefly — she wasn't entirely sure what she said — and knelt down beside Robert. The wound was in his stomach; his hand lay gently on his bloodstained shirt as if in self-defense. The pallor of his skin made the purple, clotted, contorted line of his scar all the more visible. Monstrosity, thought Rose bitterly, showed in the wrong people.

His breathing was mottled, rotting. He stared up at the ceiling, his eyes unfocused.

Rose knelt beside him. "What do you need?"

His voice was hoarse, but steady. "Madeleine."

"She's trapped in the courthouse, but she's well guarded. Regency won't harm her."

342

He did not smile. "Good."

They sat there for a few minutes, Rose watching him as if trying to guard him, Robert trying to keep his breathing even.

"I suppose," he whispered, "that I'm supposed to give you some useful deathbed advice."

"You're not dying."

"Don't," he whispered. Blood trickled out of his mouth. "Don't you *dare*."

Rose was silent.

"Keep Madeleine alive," said Robert in a low, twisting voice. "Value her life above all things, including your own. Tell . . . my daughter . . . tell her the truth about me when she is born; tell her what I was like, what I looked like, what I have done. Tell her the truth. Keep them safe, and keep them happy."

"I will."

"Swear it on everything that matters."

Rose gripped his hand briefly. "I swear on my blood and on my souls, on my life and my magic, on my love and my memory and my own happiness, that Madeleine and the baby will be safe and happy as long as it is in my power to do anything about it."

"Exceed that power," said Robert, shortly.

He lay on that filthy mattress in rattling silence for fifteen minutes before he stopped breathing.

Rose released his hand and got to her feet. She realized that she was shaking. She forced herself to stop. Shaking was not going to bloody help anyone at all.

Maria rushed over to her. "Is he —?"

Rose left Maria trailing in her wake and approached James and Terrian, who were arguing in low voices in the corner.

That sense of purpose shone brighter inside her with Robert's death: that clarity of vision, that absence of feeling. She knew what she had to do.

It was time. At last, it was time they knew.

They watched her apprehensively as she came toward them. Nate, who was guarding the door, slipped warily over, perhaps sensing bad news. Good, she had the attention of all four of them. Rose rubbed her hands together.

"What do you want?" asked Terrian, low resentment simmering in his tone.

"Robert Carlisle is dead," said Rose, "and, to avenge him, I am about to do something suicidally heroic. You are going to plead with me that it's not worth it; I will stoically resist. I believe that's how these things go."

They stared at her.

"What?" asked Nate, blankly.

Rose sighed. "Robert is dead. Tara and Madeleine are as safe as it's possible for them to be while Regency still holds London. Loren is with Regency, and Tabitha and my father are in the hands of his manipulators. By process of elimination, then, I have exactly four people left to lose, and by a happy coincidence they are all under attack from the same forces at the same time. So I'm going to save your lives, now, very dramatically, and at great cost to myself. Please feel free to try and reason with me."

They continued to stare. Rose looked around at them all, and rubbed her face. Despite her easy resolve, something inside her was falling away.

They would never look at her like this again.

"I'm going to assume you'll process this when it's all over," she said. "Please remember me like this, then, when I knew what I was doing. And whatever you find out over the next few minutes, please keep quiet about this until you've actually checked my vital readings and you know I'm dead. I would appreciate that."

They were trying to see the joke. She could read it in their faces.

Rose smiled, rather sadly, and fixed the memory of them firmly to the wall of her mind. She knelt down and pulled a head guard from the drawer beneath the desk, and strapped it on. It would not protect from lethal concussion, but it would at least serve to dissuade her attackers from going for her head.

Her nerves were buzzing.

She stood up. Maria caught her shoulder.

"Rose," she said, eyebrows furrowed, "you're not going to do anything stupid, are you?"

Rose smiled grimly again, and walked away.

She was heading for the barred metal door at the end of the office, and as she approached she heard Maria's and Nate's voices rise, concerned, and then James's joining them in tumbling chorus, and then, as Rose was six feet away, the words forming from incoherence: "Stop her!"

They were too late, of course. Rose threw herself toward the door, wrenched it open, and slammed it closed again before any of them could reach her. She held it closed with her weight as she pressed her hand to the scanner and initiated the locking mechanism.

"Locked," said the computer, almost nonchalantly, and Rose took out her gun and smashed the glass of the scanner with the handle as James's weight slammed against the door from the other side. It was unexpectedly painful.

She could not take any chances with her losing her nerve. She could not allow herself a way back.

"Rose!" Damn the builders for not soundproofing this door. "Rose, don't do this!"

"You don't know what I'm going to do yet."

"You can't. Don't put yourself in danger! Please, Rose!"

Rose pressed the forehead of the guard against the door. "James," she said, "I am truly sorry that you care about me. Now would be the ideal time to stop doing that."

"Rose, don't you dare . . ."

"We have long since established that you have no right to control what I *dare*, Lieutenant Andreas."

"Rose, I . . ."

Rose looked down at the small, smashed pane of glass.

"I'm not coming back," she said quietly. "Good-bye, James."

"Rose, please, you have to listen to me, you can't . . ."

She allowed herself to listen to his pleas for a few seconds, then, when this proved too distracting, blocked them out and walked away from the door toward the staircase at the other end of the dank, dark corridor, stepping hesitantly through the shifting silence until his muffled cries faded away to nothing. Every stair upward made the air warmer, drier, thicker. It almost convinced her that she was moving toward safety.

She wasn't. Not at all.

And then suddenly the clarity of purpose faded to nothing more than a delusional memory and she was left alone, the cowardly remnants of a more courageous version of herself, facing at best the absence of all her allies, and at worst —

Death was not the worst that could happen to her. There were a hundred different forms of pain that were worse than death; like James's, beating out his anguish and desperation against that metal door for her. Nevertheless, the probability of the end of existence held a special kind of fear within the human heart.

But that wouldn't change her. That wouldn't change what she was going to do.

She was too strong for that now.

She ascended, shaking. The light in the lobby of the building was white and cold and flickering. She had a few feet left of shadow before she made herself seen, and she knew this was an office block, and that Regency stood guard over the entrances, trying to starve them out. Eventually they would get impatient, and storm the small, dark, easily defended entrance; but there were far too many of them to fight off. When they grew bored, the Department would fall, and James, Nate, Maria, and Terrian would die with it, fighting to their last breaths, with no means of escape.

She would not let that happen.

It almost made her smile. Redemption at last.

She almost didn't notice that she had crossed into the light and off the carpet, giving her shadow substance and her footsteps sound. She walked out into the lobby, and stood there in front of Regency's soldiers at the door. They were facing the other way. For a moment Rose, in her dreamlike state, thought they wouldn't hear her, that she would be able to stand there silently for minutes and hours while she worked out what to do; but of course they did hear her, and they turned, guns out, to see with astonishment the solitary dark-haired girl with a head guard strapped to her face, in front of their assembled might.

She took her hands out of her pockets, trembling violently, and raised them either side of her body, to make herself look big, like she thought she was flying.

347

"I'm Rose Elmsworth," she said to them. "Do your worst."

And it was a bluff, obviously it was a bluff—that was what they would think, anyway; she had bluffed them so many times this way, standing there daring her enemies to shoot her with a wry smile that told of some ace up her sleeve. But she could not smile this time, and so her reputation and her past escapes bought her only a few seconds.

They were good soldiers. They assessed the situation, and analyzed the threat.

The only logical course of action was to open fire.

Rose did not see the bullets come toward her in slow motion, of course, and for that she could only be grateful; there was only the momentary indecision, the sudden burst of impossible hope that they would leave her alive, followed by the first impact. She focused all her magic on blocking the pain, but she could not stop the feeling of the bullet breaking her skin and lodging inside her body.

The first, and then the second, and then all that came after.

She fell quickly under the barrage of metal and noise.

When she was riddled with bullets, broken irrevocably, she lay there, trying to keep still, losing magic as she bled, trying to concentrate on not feeling. It was so difficult.

She had never felt more alone in her life.

Regency were whispering.

"Is she dead?"

"I think she's dead."

Rose did not see her life flash before her eyes, which was disappointing, but for a moment at that conjecture she was eight years old and sitting with her father in his study listening to Monty Python: a vinyl record that had belonged to his parents.

I think she's dead.

No, I'm not . . .

She wanted him to be here. More than anything, a deep ache in her heart, she wanted him to be here, when this happened. If she died, now . . . If this didn't work . . .

She had always imagined he would be there at her deathbed.

She had never, ever envisioned herself outliving him.

"You want to check?"

"You do it."

"Dear God, no. What if she's like Elmsworth? What if she's one of them?"

The pool of her blood was growing. So someone had guessed, after all.

Someone came over. An old man, wolf-grizzled. He held his machine gun as if it might just as easily shoot him as it would her. He stared down into Rose's staring eyes and spreading blood. The pain blossomed underneath the edge of Rose's feeling. She seemed to have lost the ability to blink.

"She's dead," he said.

The pain grew sharper. It took all Rose's concentration to hold it back. The man walked away. The underside of his shoe was red.

She stared up at the ceiling blankly. The glossy white of the tiles showed her the pallor of her face, the light fading from her eyes.

Panic spiked, jagged, through her thoughts.

She blinked, and stared up at the ceiling, and saw that the eyes of her reflection were white.

She became very calm very quickly.

"NO!"

An anguished yell from behind her, and running footsteps. A

burst of gunfire. The soldiers cried out, scattered, reloaded again, and James knelt down beside her, uncaring. The pain carved his face into terrible age.

"Rose, Rose, no, no, dear God no —"

Her blood was on his hands, now. It dripped onto her face as he removed her head guard, cradled her dying body in his arms.

"No, no —"

He hadn't looked at her eyes yet, not for any decent space of time, anyway. Rose wished she could explain to him exactly why it was so imperative that he run, now, but she could not speak, and her will to was fading fast.

It started on her fingertips, with her arm draped over his knee. The pain coalesced and smoothed, the skin fading to a corpselike gray, and then darker, to blue-black, splitting and smoking. He didn't see it. He wasn't looking. He was crying. Rose wanted him to stop. His tears were for someone who would, in a few seconds, no longer exist.

"Rose, Rose . . ."

The transformation spread up her arm, the skin sealing and the blood re-forming and the bullets melting away before monstrosity laid claim to it. She was being given back her life, but the price she was paying was her humanity. That was all well and good.

Perhaps, if she had remembered to bring the cuff from the basement that triggered her transformation from Loren's house, on the night Tabitha had been kidnapped.

Perhaps, if she had been closer than six hours away from turning naturally.

Perhaps she wouldn't have had to walk into gunfire to force her body to transform.

Ah, well.

The Regency soldiers were readying themselves to fire on James. His tears were drying now, the flow ebbing, as he stroked her hair. He thought she was dead. He wasn't looking at her eyes.

The transformation took her shoulder in a hard, splitting seizure, and Rose's body convulsed in James's arms. He stopped, rendered immobile by astonishment and fear and hope.

His vocabulary had been carved down to one word.

"Rose?"

His bloodshot green eyes brightened, and then the skin of her neck began to change.

James looked at it for a long time as it spread up her throat and touched the edge of her jaw. He watched her blankly as the skin hardened and split and smoked. He touched her skin and cried out as it burned him. And yet he still didn't understand.

Rose's thoughts began to split and fracture. The bones of her face began to stretch and shift, and dreadful understanding kindled in his eyes.

"No," he said, and then he said it again, the word, and there was feeling in there that he didn't understand.

And he touched her face. And the muscles in his face twitched and stretched. And he knelt over her, his neck over her face, and her torso began to scream with changes, and she trembled with the pain. And then the words he was saying became louder, and the smell of him became stronger, and her body broke its fabric constraints in a savage rush, and movement returned with old instincts, and it opened its mouth and went for his vein.

The boy with the red hair scrambled out of the way, pulling his scent out of reach, but it had already forgotten about him. Its muscles stretched and pulled and settled, and it leaped across the room with new strength and power, enjoying how this body destroyed the distance beneath its feet. Its skin was hot; its claws scratched black marks into the gleaming tiles. It shivered, sending sparks tumbling like rain from the ceiling, and then it turned to them.

The red-haired boy was holding a metal tube —*gun*, said a quiet voice in its head. He was crying. Behind him, they were fleeing, or firing, or both.

It jumped again, the glass of the building entrance disappearing into dust against its skin, and reached for them as they fled, and some of them made high-pitched noises, and burst red against its claws.

Bleeding, said the voice in its head, with a terrible quiet.

The bleeding ones did not get up again. The others, the ones still unscathed, were running for a big metal box on the side of the road.

Warehouse.

The voice sounded surprised. The monster didn't like that.

It flicked its mind like a claw tip and the road broke open, earth exposing itself like blood and sinew to the sunlit air. The humans screamed and ran faster, and went into the warehouse and shut the metal door against it.

As if thin metal could stop a monster.

The last of them to go into the warehouse was the red-haired boy. He looked back at the monster, and there was something terrible in his eyes.

It gathered its wits about it, and the metal twisted and dented.

And then, abruptly, its mind stopped working.

A hellish screaming noise forced its way into the monster's thoughts and spiked them with pain. It fell to the ground, roaring against the agony. The sunset sparkled with the sound of exploding glass.

The noise stopped suddenly. A human knelt in front of it, his small green eyes level with its own. He opened his mouth and made noises. The monster went into the girl's crushed mind briefly, and took her powers of understanding, and listened until the human's noises gained meaning.

". . . don't expect you to know who I am," he was saying to it. "But I know you have Rose somewhere in there. I just want to thank you, for leading me here. I didn't know they'd moved the Demon children to this warehouse. You've just given me my niece, and my freedom. Most likely, that means nothing to you, but it means a lot to me."

The human stood. He was grass-eyed, yellow-haired, and his face yielded no age. The lines on his face were deeper than the girl's memories showed. The monster looked through the memories, tried to find a name and a history, but the ideas were blurred, buried. The girl was hiding something.

"I'm standing here in front of you," said the man to it. "You could kill me effortlessly, and yet here I am. I'm well within range. If you were brave and in control, and you knew what I'd just done to you with that speaker system, I would be little more than blood and bone on the pavement by now."

The monster bristled. The ground melted beneath it into roiling stone.

"But I am here," said the blond man. "Standing in front of you, with my niece in that building, putting us both in lethal danger. Why do you think I'm doing that? What do you believe I have that would be a match for you? Whence my sudden courage?"

It tried to find *whence* in the girl's memory of words, but the

353

girl hid that, as well. The voice in its head was smiling. It could hear the girl's hope. It watched the moving vein in the blond man's neck and waited, wary, the ground cracking around it, the power tensing and rolling in its muscles.

"Rose would know," said the blond man. "Rose would know exactly what I'm doing. She was the one who told me to do it, days ago. She told me how to slow down Hybrids, and I did some more research, just in case. You have a wider range of hearing than humans, don't you? So if I make a high-pitched enough noise, I can confuse you. Not for long enough to stop you, of course, not long enough to save my life, but I have words for that. No one's ever tried to talk down a Hybrid before, you know that? Rose wouldn't have thought it possible."

He smiled. The monster growled.

"But that, of course, might not be all I have. I might have more than a high-pitched noise and words up my sleeve. I might have more imaginative ways to hurt you. If you try to kill me, you'd find out. Or we could do it the easy way. You could give me Rose back."

The blond man walked slowly around the monster. The warehouse was silent. In the blond man's hand was a small black plastic rectangle, and on the side of the warehouse were larger black boxes —*speaker system*, he had said. It plumbed the depths of the girl's memories furiously for an answer, but the girl was stronger now, and she told it nothing.

"These are the weak points, yes?" asked the blond man from behind it, and stabbed into its leg. It screamed as smoke billowed from the wound, and the knife melted into the muscle. The pain was hideous.

"I don't know how this works," said the blond man. "I don't

354

know if you can transform back at will, or if you just have to run out of energy. I'm hoping that just stabbing you at random satisfies both criteria. I'm going to continue doing this until you give Rose back to me. It's a simple ultimatum, really."

Another stab, this time in its side. It screamed louder. It could see the knife this time. The blond man came around into its line of view.

"Ask her," he said. "Ask her, if you can, why you can't kill me."

Another stab, and it began to weaken. Its breaths came shorter. Its skin-smoke began to thin and spread out. The sun was going down.

The blond man smiled.

"That's right," he said softly. "That's what we want to see."

And it broke.

Slowly, still screaming, the gaps in its skin began to close up and seal. It railed and screamed against what was happening, but the girl was calmer and fought back. The blond man started laughing as the monster's limbs began to shrink.

"Yes!" they heard him say, delighted. "I just defeated a Hybrid!"

The monster roared, but the roar became a scream, and the gray of the skin began to pale, and the bones melded and straightened, and the structure of the face became less jagged, and the teeth blunted and smoothed, and as the girl's body was returned to her, the monster asked plaintively what the blond man would have done: and the girl went with it into unconsciousness, smiling, and said, *He was bluffing, you idiot. He wasn't prepared. He just improvised. That's what he does.*

- Chapter 34 -

Twenty years earlier (age 16)
September 1, 10:03 p.m.

The window breaks in the middle of the night. He wakes silently, his breathing stopped without conscious deliberation; he lives these days in a state of more or less constant fear of attack, and is almost pleased to find it finally justified.

He is lying on the sofa in the living room. There is a cold breeze on his face and broken glass on the carpet. It is very late, and his mind is heavy with sleep, but he manages to put two and two together and realize what is happening.

He rolls over the edge of the sofa and lands on the other side, pressing himself against the warm fabric and sending heat coursing along the skin of his hands in preparation. He has just stilled himself when the footsteps land hard on the floor. Their proximity is unnerving; he can hear the intruder's breathing. He makes a few appraisals, foremost among which are: male, full-grown, magical enough to levitate and get through a broken window without screaming.

"Ugh," says the intruder. There is a slight northern undertone to his voice. Most likely his disgust is because he has just seen the dark brown, crusted blood dried into the carpet of the doorway; a danger sign if ever there was one, but the intruder stands his ground.

"Come out, come out, wherever you are," he calls, low and melodic and menacing. "I know you're here."

Yes, of course you know I'm here; you can see the imprint in the sofa, can't you?

"I won't hurt you."

Of course you won't.

"I've heard a lot about you," says the intruder. "They say you don't eat, don't sleep, that you're immortal. They say you can't be killed. That you can fight off any enemy."

But you don't believe that, clearly, or you wouldn't be here.

"Come out," says the intruder, and he steps forward, and suddenly a line of spiked blond hair is visible over the edge of the sofa. A twitch of focus, and it catches fire. The intruder doubles over, but he has magic too, and in a moment the fire is out.

"All right," says the intruder, but the smoothness is gone now from his voice. "Get the hell out or I will hurt you, ghostboy."

A twist of indecision. Then the heat in his hands explodes outward, and the sofa shoots across the room, slamming into the intruder's chest. The impact knocks a cry of pain from the stranger's mouth.

He gets to his feet, looking around to see where the intruder has gone, if he's still alive, but there's another shadow in the doorway and suddenly something wooden hits him in the shoulder and he is knocked backward into the wall and slumps down to the ground.

The pain is excruciating. All he can think is *How the hell did he get over there?* before realizing that he didn't, of course; there must be two of them, and he curses his own idiocy and plows what remaining concentration he has into trying to work out if anything in him is broken. Nothing seems to be, but he cannot move.

He watches the second figure rush from the doorway and kneel down beside the intruder. They mutter to each other.

"Loren? Loren, are you all right?"

The second intruder is a woman.

A low, pained grunting. "Kill him for me."

"I will."

The woman helps the man to his feet. The man is limping. As they get closer, he sees from his fetal position on the ground that they are younger than he thought; no more than sixteen or seventeen. The way they move together, reading each other's intent, suggests closeness, and he notices that the shape of their faces and the fall of their hair are identical; brother and sister, then. The boy has magic, and looks extremely aggrieved. The girl is gray-eyed and coldly furious.

"Who are you?"

He curls into himself and doesn't answer. He's going to die anyway; he may as well do so anonymously.

The girl kicks him in the arm. "Give me your name."

"I don't have one."

358

"What do you mean?"

"I don't have a name."

The girl sighs, and at a sign from her the boy leans down, gritting his teeth with the pain, and pulls him out of the fetal position. The girl crouches down, pulls a gun from her jacket, presses it to his foot.

"You'll live if I do this," she says to him. He is tense with sudden fear. "Do you believe I will?"

He nods.

"I don't want to kill you," she says. "I want you to teach my brother how to use magic."

"Why do you think I can?"

"They say you can't die."

He grits his teeth. Her finger tightens on the trigger.

"What's your name?"

"I abandoned my name."

"What do you want to call yourself? We need to call you something if you're staying with us."

"Am I?"

"We did come here to get you, and I'm the one with the gun, so . . ." She shrugs.

"Can I sit up?"

The girl keeps the gun to his foot as he pulls himself carefully up on one elbow, keeping his hands out to the side so she can see them. It is raining outside, but he can still read the street sign. He lowers himself again. "Elmsworth," he says aloud. The girl narrows her eyes.

"First name or surname?"

"Surname."

"What's your first name?"

A brief consideration. "David."

"Good," says the girl, relieved. Her brother, above her, grunts in annoyance and limps away to stand by the broken window. The rain lashes his face like seawater. "We're making progress."

<<< >>>

She woke up with the shadows of the bullets trembling in her body, the spaces where they had been suddenly hollow. Slowly, the sensation faded, and she lay there on a mattress in the darkness, her eyes closed, trying to stop the convulsions of her body.

She settled and lay still.

Her left hand was shaking, and she could not stop it.

She was alive and she was not hurt. Even the ghost of her pain was fading.

She was alive.

She allowed herself to consider that for a moment, the staggering evil that had led to her still-beating heart. She kept her eyes closed and brought the memories of the deaths to the surface of her mind, like pebbles rising through clear water. The monster had seen it with something less than innocence, but Rose saw every detail full of meaning: the blood, and the fear on their faces, and the light as it left their eyes.

The light as she took it from their eyes.

She should be dead. By rights she should have died with the hail of bullets, bled out quickly on the floor of the lobby, reduced to that unknown ethereality in which at least one and possibly both of her fathers now lingered. But no, mundane as it felt, she was alive, with a tremor in her hand, lying . . . where?

She opened her eyes.

Loren's house: his dead sister's bedroom. Tabitha sat beside her, stroking her hair. Rose surveyed them for damage, and found none.

"Did I . . . ?"

"I expect you're hungover," Loren said, from the corner, "or whatever it is your equivalent of a hangover is."

"I don't drink."

He nodded. "Wise."

Rose looked up apprehensively at Tabitha. "How are you?"

"I'm okay," said the little girl. "They didn't hurt me."

There was something in her eyes that suggested a hurt deeper than physical wounds — new fear scarred into her, nightmares waiting to surface. But perhaps Loren couldn't see this, and she was alive, so . . .

"I'm glad you're all right," said Rose, quietly, and Tabitha hugged her.

Loren looked at her. "Eight dead. All Regency soldiers. No one else harmed."

"How was I stopped?"

"My relentless brilliance and your inherent stupidity."

"Don't listen to him," murmured Tabitha, glowering at her uncle. "Are you hurt?"

"I don't think so. I take it you no longer ally yourself with Regency, Loren."

He leaned back and spoke to the ceiling. "I never did. The moment I had Tabitha back, I was gone." He shrugged. "Still, you know . . . All those years working for them, and then I spend a decade out of the business and they welcome me back without even a training course."

"For all of six hours."

"True."

"And while holding your niece hostage."

"Yes. So, all right, there have been better job offers."

Rose sat up in bed, holding her hands out in front of her face, weak, warm, fragile-boned, human. Another six weeks until the next one. She felt like hell. She looked past Tabitha to Loren.

"You have apologies to make," she said. "You did a lot of things in those six hours. You gave the Gospel to Regency. You gave *London* to Regency. And helping me doesn't change that."

He studied her, and crossed his arms. "You killed Stephen Greenlow."

"It was an accident."

Loren looked away.

Rose folded her hands around the back of her neck, tensing herself. "He let me out half an hour after you. He was pleased with himself, off-guard. He wasn't protecting his gun. I went for it. I managed to get it from his holster. I got out of the way. He was angry. I could feel the heat of him, the magic he was about to do. He was going to kill me. I fired at his head. I didn't expect it to hit. I didn't expect that to be the end. But it was. It killed him. *I* killed him."

Loren watched her and said nothing for a while. When he did speak, his voice was low, closed.

"Never easy, is it?"

She stared at him. He smiled grimly. Tabitha looked between them. She looked thinner and paler now. Her days in captivity seemed to have shrunken her.

"Welcome back, Rose," said Loren, quietly.

She had nothing to say to that. Her coat had been hung up

on the door. She got up, walked past them, pulled it on with their eyes on her back.

"So what do you do now?"

"Follow your old advice," said Loren from behind her. She stayed where she was, her hand on the door handle, staring down at the chipped wood of the door. "Leave. Once Regency notices I'm gone, which no doubt they already have, they'll be watching the Thames, but the suburbs are too chaotic to monitor. We'll hot-wire a car and go to Dover."

Rose's throat was dry. "And from there?"

"Wherever the ferries are going."

She opened the door of the bedroom and walked out into the corridor. Tabitha followed her silently.

"You do realize," said Loren, from his chair, "that was an invitation."

"I know."

He considered this for a moment. "How rude."

"I need to rescue my father."

"Who has him?"

Rose stopped, turned back to Loren. "You don't know?"

He shook his head.

"Regency took him this morning."

He nodded slowly. "Then it was Isabel Vinyara who gave the order. They didn't tell me."

She scanned his face briefly and gave a quick nod.

He got to his feet. As she reached the top of the stairs, he said wearily, "I'm afraid I'm going to have to stop you."

Rose paused, hand on the banister. Tabitha looked fearfully between the two of them.

Rose said, still looking at the stairs: "Are we going to do this again?"

"I tried to go after Regency when they had Tabitha, and you went to admirably despicable lengths to stop me. I feel it only my duty to pay back the favor. They'll kill you if you attack them."

"There's a difference."

"And what is that?"

Rose glanced at Tabitha. "She was taken so that Regency could negotiate with you. That's not why they have Dad. Regency don't care about me."

"That's not going to stop you playing into their hands."

"I'm not. I won't be going to them as Rose Elmsworth. I'll use the name I had when I infiltrated them for the Department. Lily Daniels has nothing to do with David Elmsworth. They won't suspect."

"Ah," he said, and was silent. Rose took a step onto the staircase. Then, from the bedroom, he said: "It's still too dangerous."

"I disagree."

"I made a promise to your mother that I would protect you from harm."

Rose turned to see him standing in the corridor, watching her with sadness in his eyes.

"That was sixteen years ago."

"The promise still holds."

"You have walked me into danger for your own ends. You never cared about my well-being then."

He was quiet. "But you were never harmed."

"No, I was never *killed*."

He looked as if she had hit him. She gritted her teeth, and kept walking down the stairs.

"Rose," he called after her, as she reached the bottom and moved aside the coat stand to reveal the safe. "Please."

"Leave. Get out of the country. You'll be fine."

There was genuine pain in his voice. "But you won't be."

"I can look after myself."

"No, you can't."

She twisted the dial. 1-9-0-1-2-0-2-3. The safe opened, and the small pile of silver-and-green hologram controllers rolled out onto the floor. Her father had programmed these for her before his arrest; she had removed them from the Department before her banishment all those eons ago. Rose picked one up and examined it.

"That promise applied when I was a child," she called back. "I'm not a child anymore."

"Perhaps you don't think of yourself as one, no."

"Your argument is getting less persuasive by the syllable."

She went into the kitchen and found a roll of duct tape in the drawer under the oven. She broke a piece off with her teeth, pulled up her sleeve, and taped the green and silver ball onto the skin of her forearm. She felt the sharp shiver of energy as the hologram kicked in, and knelt to examine the black-haired, gray-eyed girl in the reflection in the oven door. This was the girl Regency had called Lily Daniels. The girl Felix Callaway, her father, had called Lily Daniels, without recognizing her.

When she stood up, Loren was watching her from the doorway.

"I can't let you do this."

"There is one key, debilitating flaw in that logic. Would you like me to point it out to you?"

"Rose —"

"It's that you *can* let me do this. And, even if you couldn't, it wouldn't make a shred of a difference."

"You underestimate me."

"You're exhausted, you're weak, and your magic is far less powerful than mine even on a good day. No, I really don't under-estimate you, Loren."

These should have been deadly insults to him; he merely looked at her. "Come with us."

"I can't leave him."

"He's most likely dead, Rose."

"Then I will bury him."

"It won't have been kind."

"Then I will burn him."

"Even if he is alive, he might be terribly injured."

"Then I will heal him."

Anger crossed his face for the first time. "Will you listen to reason?"

"I appreciate your concern for my well-being, Loren, but I have to do this and, believe me, no one values my life more than I do."

"You walked into gunfire two hours ago."

"That was to rescue the others."

"You have other means of rescuing him."

"No, I don't," she said calmly. "I have no resources. I have no allies anymore. I'm on my own now." The image of James's bloodshot, widening eyes darted across her consciousness; she dismissed the accompanying stab of pain with adaptive coldness. "They will hate me now. I can't go back to them."

"You think too little of them."

"No. I've just learned too much."

"Yes," he said, sadly, "yes you have, Aisling."

Rose walked up to him. He did not move.

"We will part allies," she said softly, "and I will remember that to the last you tried to protect me from harm."

For a moment she thought he would not react. Then slowly, he raised his shaking hand and held it out, the tremors barely controlled on the cold January air. She grasped it, and they shook.

"Good-bye, Matthew Langley," she said.

His expression did not change; he stayed perfectly still, in front of his niece, his arms folded. "Good-bye, Aisling Stronach."

After a moment, they walked together to the door, and she took her gun out of her holster, and he opened the door for her on to the night air. The night of her sixteenth birthday. She stepped out of Loren's house and looked up at Tabitha on the stairs, and smiled.

"The first time we met," she said, "in that classroom, you said that my life would be easier for not meeting you."

"Yes, I did."

"I think you were wrong," she said, quietly. "Whatever happens to me now, don't forget that."

Loren gave her a brief smile, and Rose walked away from her last ally, into the darkness, alone, her gun swinging in her grip.

– Chapter 35 –

James woke slowly, nudged from sleep by the hard press of cobblestones against his torn shirt. He lay there for a long time, eyes open, breathing hard into the smoke-edged wind. It was night, and the streetlights had vanished, quick-dying as fireflies. He lay there and played a spot-the-difference game in his head with this and traditional church images of hell.

It was much colder, here.

He tested his weight on his elbow and found he could push himself up. He did a quick body scan: head, yes, torso, yes, legs, yes, and the pain seemed to be coming from his arm. Blood and pain, but no broken bones, so far as he could tell: a blossoming bruise, and a skin-deep cut.

He put his hand to his chest, found the press of the old bullet in the passage of his breaths. He had endured much worse.

He closed his eyes, and looked up at the flickering traces of the starlight through the lids. The image of her snapped violently into his fragile peace of mind. He destroyed it.

The black veins in her face; the ash-strewn crumbling of her skin.

He groaned in anguish, and pulled himself to his feet.

Dizziness claimed him for a moment, and he gritted his teeth until it was over. The night was even colder standing up. He looked around, found the glowing remains of the Department's entrance building.

Long recovery period, is it?

He cleared his head with effort.

You've come here to try and convince me that he's a killer.

He forced his way over the debris toward the shattered hulk of the building. There was a silhouette in the doorway, stark against the strip lighting of the destroyed lobby.

And that's not going to happen.

Terrian. The silhouette was Terrian. James forced his way toward him. There was dried blood on Terrian's face. He was shaking with anger, and his eyes were bloodshot with things that surely could not be tears.

"No," he whispered. "I do not, I refuse to —"

"Yeah," said James, hoarsely. "So do I."

"We try to do some bloody good in the world, and there they come, cuckoos in the nest, lying insidious pieces of —"

"I know."

"I trusted them," said Terrian, and his voice broke. "That girl was near my son. He thought of her as his *sister*, you know that?"

Disgust flecked his voice. James closed his eyes.

"She never hurt him," he said, heavily and without meaning.

369

"You loved her, didn't you?" asked Terrian, but not without pity.

James moved past him roughly, down the stairs toward the underground room where Nate and Maria lurked. The office was near empty; everyone had fled when the coast was clear. They knelt beside the dead body of Robert Carlisle. James sat down to join them in their silent vigil.

"I don't understand," said Maria, quietly.

"I do," said James, his voice breaking, now that Terrian could not hear him. "I understand."

"No, you don't."

They looked up at Nate. His voice was grave, and he kept his gaze on Robert's open, staring eyes. After a while, and with what looked like a tremendous effort, he said, "We don't understand what she did, or why she did it. We can't know anything about what she's done. We cannot say she is evil. David, fine. But not Rose."

"What's the difference?" asked James savagely. "They're exactly the same. They always were. They lied to us together; they were always in it together. They never trusted us."

"Well, why should she?" said Nate fiercely. "Look at us. Look at what we did to David. If she mistrusted us, we more than bore her out on that. Think about it." Nate looked up at James, his eyes fierce. "She feared us. Just imagine that. She was afraid of *us*, of what we would do to her."

"We wouldn't," whispered Maria. "We wouldn't have harmed her."

"What reason did she have to believe that? We captured Hybrids. She saw us. She even helped us. She saw the experiments, what we did to them. Even if she didn't think that would

370

be done to her, it would at least have been enough to persuade her not to take the risk. She must have thought it was easier to stay hidden."

"How can you possibly defend her?" asked James viciously. "After what she's done —"

"I have known her for far longer than you have," said Nate, quietly, gripping Maria's hand, "and I believe she would never hurt me. I believe she sacrificed our love to save our lives. I believe I know Rose Elmsworth."

They knelt there for a long time, staring down at Robert's corpse. Nate's knuckles were white, and Maria looked deep in thought.

"I wish I could believe that," said James, hollowly.

There was a long silence.

"So what do we do?" asked Maria.

"We do the only thing we have left," said James, savagely. "If she's alive, she will have gone to Regency to get David back. I don't care if they have the Gospel's soldiers. We've got nothing left to lose now, have we? We'll ask the army to help us. We'll kill Regency. I'll kill them all."

And then, finally, he wept, and to his great relief, Nate and Maria did not try to comfort him.

– Chapter 36 –

The news of the monster's attack on Regency came back to them slowly.

It was a blow, certainly, but not a fatal one, and it did little to dent their morale. They had London at their feet, after all, and the hated Gospel under their command. The Gospel soldiers themselves were less than happy about this, of course, and there had been whispers of mutiny, but they were far too afraid of what would happen to their loved ones to mount any serious resistance. Without Greenlow, they were nothing.

Regency had defeated them, and they were even close to breaking the Department. One soft-spoken monster girl could not seriously disrupt them.

Arkwood's disappearance, however, was another matter. The Department's leadership might have been destroyed, but their soldiers, not to mention the national army, were still fighting

Regency for every street and every building. The brief surge of strength that Arkwood's presence had granted Regency had vanished with him, and left them drained: outnumbered and outgunned, they could not sustain the fight against the army indefinitely. They had retreated back to the Cabinet War Rooms, their old base, and huddled there recuperating, licking their wounds like wolves.

The junior soldiers, the cannon fodder, were sent up into the darkened streets to patrol, in case the Government troops decided to fight dirty. In this lawless, honorless war, as Vinyara said, you could not be too careful.

Amelia Rodriguez, Maria's older sister, was a private, one of Regency's remaining disposable soldiers, and so just before midnight she was sent up with Jordan Daley to scan the area for enemy snipers. They had come to know each other well over the past six months: Jordan's girlfriend Katya had disappeared six months ago on the night of the rebellion, the night Felix Callaway had died, and as for Amelia's ex-boyfriend, Aaron Greenlow . . . well. Little enough to be said.

Amelia and Jordan had met in the weeks afterward, when Vinyara had seized control of the organization and taken Regency out of the rebellion to recuperate, to wait and see what progress the Gospel made toward destroying the Department. Amelia and Jordan were friends now, or a little more; they were kept together in battle and in the barracks by a shared fear of dying.

Wordlessly, they walked out into the dark together, holding their guns close to their chests. They met with silence on every street corner and moved on; no matter how much evidence of safety they found, they would never feel truly safe until they were back with their comrades.

Something shifted in the passageway behind Amelia, and they both turned, pointing their guns into the darkness.

They waited, hearts juddering, nerves singing.

Nothing.

Slowly, they moved toward the last alleyway, a dark place where the few drunks still reckless enough to venture outside were usually to be found semi-comatose against a wall. Tonight, as usual, breathing stained the quiet. Jordan nodded to Amelia and cocked his revolver, and they moved as silently as possible into the shadows.

"Hello," said a warm voice.

They would never admit it afterward, but they screamed as they turned with fingers on the triggers of their guns. The girl stood calmly in the dark, piss-streaked alleyway, watching them. She eyed their weapons with something less than fear.

"Don't you remember me?" she asked.

Amelia did. She lowered her gun in astonishment, and gestured for Jordan to do the same.

"Lily? Lily Daniels?"

The girl spread her arms wide in welcome. "Amelia Rodriguez. You put me in the Darkroom."

It did not, perhaps, come across as warmly as the girl intended.

"Where have you been?" asked Jordan suspiciously.

"The Department captured me on the night of the attack last year. I only escaped a few days ago. I've been trying to find you."

"How did you survive?"

The girl's eyes went cold. "They don't kill. They do much worse."

"Prove it," said Jordan, and Lily regarded him for a moment, blank-eyed. Then she pulled up her sleeve, showed them an ugly purple scar in the crook of her elbow. It looked like a gunshot wound.

Lily and Jordan watched each other.

"Do you believe me now?" she asked, and Jordan nodded, eyes on her scar. Lily pulled her sleeve down again and turned back to Amelia.

"Are you all right? How have you been?"

Amelia nodded silently, to say that she wasn't injured or dead, which meant she was okay by Regency standards, and Lily smiled sadly.

"I heard about what happened. The night of the attack."

"Yeah," said Jordan shortly, "bet you did."

"Can I help? I mean, can I come back? I just . . . I want to fight with you." She looked earnest. "I've been dreaming about this for months. And I passed the Darkroom test last year, didn't I? I'm loyal."

Jordan beckoned to Amelia, and they came close, whispered to each other, tried to read each other's faces. Then Jordan muttered something to her, and she nodded, and they turned back to Lily Daniels.

"You can come with us," said Amelia, and Lily's face lit up.

They walked together through the darkness back to the entrance to the War Rooms, Amelia and Jordan on either side of Lily Daniels, trying to be as quiet as possible in case any more unknowns lurked in the unsearched alleys. They reached the blown-wide hole in the pavement and hopped down into it, Jordan wincing as the impact with the wet earth twisted an old injury in his ankle. Lily looked around at the tunnels that led off under the roads into the damp rocky ground. Amelia watched her, trying to gauge her thoughts.

"The lights are off," was all Lily said.

"Yeah. They found a couple of old Blitz posters, and it gave them ideas."

At the end of the leftward tunnel was a lift. The back wall was scarred with gunshot marks. Lily examined it with her fingertips, like a doctor with a corpse, before they descended to the privates' floor.

This was the dankest, coldest part of the complex. Lily stepped out of the lift and peered down the corridor, smiling.

"I remember this," she said.

Amelia and Jordan led her in silence to an empty bedroom. Jordan opened the door for Lily, and she sat down on the bed.

"We're going to go and get you some kit," he said. "You stay here, okay?"

Lily nodded, and they left, walking quickly down the corridor. Jordan looked at Amelia as soon as Lily Daniels was out of earshot.

"Her story —"

"I know," said Amelia, quietly. "I don't know what the hell she's playing at, or what the truth is, but she's not here to fight for us. She wants something else. I don't care what it is, so long as she doesn't get it."

Jordan nodded. He looked relieved. "So which way's the lieutenant's office?"

"Oh, I don't think we should go to the lieutenant," said Amelia, grimly. "I think Slythe and Vinyara would want to know about this. This way."

They closed the door, and she listened as their footsteps retreated into silence, as the grinding of the lift gears lifted away. Then she

376

stood and opened the door again. In their hurry to get away from her, the idiots had forgotten to lock it.

She walked back to the lift and waited until it returned to her. Amelia and Jordan had vanished. She stepped inside. The buttons told her that they were on the bottom floor, which couldn't possibly be true, because David would be kept in the deepest and most secure part of the complex, assuming he was still alive, and David wasn't . . .

. . . here.

Rose looked up at the ceiling of the lift, and then walked out of it, and regarded the steel door at the other end of the corridor with detached apprehension.

She walked closer. There was a half-asleep guard standing beside the door. She called to him: "Hello?"

The guard jerked awake, and squinted at her in bleary anger.

"Who're you?"

"Lily Daniels," said Rose, clear-voiced. "I'm here to see the prisoner."

The guard's eyes narrowed. "No, you're not."

Rose abandoned the pretense; it was late, and she was tired. "No, I'm not. I'm his daughter."

The guard shook his head, still half-asleep. "Doesn't have a daughter."

Rose stopped, and watched him as he awakened, blinking at her.

"You have David Elmsworth in there."

The guard shook his head. "Don't."

"You have a prisoner in there, don't you?"

"Yep."

"Thirty-five, Gifted, brown hair, pale, six foot two . . ."

377

"'Bout that, yep."

"But not David Elmsworth."

"Nope."

Rose walked forward, very close to the guard, so that she could smell the alcohol on his breath. "Are you going to let me in, or not?"

"You gonna hurt me?"

"Only if you don't cooperate."

He hesitated.

She pulled out her gun and pressed it to his stomach.

The guard looked at her for a moment, turned, and opened the door with shaking hands. Deeper, thicker darkness lay behind it, and faint breathing carried on the silence like smoke. Rose looked into the space for a moment, then turned back to the guard, an idea sparking and flowering in her mind.

"The people who brought him here, did *they* give him a name?"

The guard nodded. There was a silence. Beyond it, she thought — perhaps imagined — she heard the distant breaths stop.

"Another name?"

He didn't answer. A terrible feeling — not quite realization, not yet, but close — was building slowly in Rose's mind. She did not want to ask the question. She knew that she shouldn't — *couldn't*— ask the question.

But she did.

"And what exactly," Rose asked the Regency guard apprehensively, "did they call him?"

– Chapter 37 –

Twenty years earlier (age 16)
August 3, 10:40 p.m.

The man is found bleeding in the street, surrounded by some terrified-looking teenagers playing paramedic. They're trying to bandage his wounds, or tourniquet them at the very least — not that they would know what *tourniquet* meant if forced to read out a dictionary definition, but he supposes it's the thought that counts. They're muttering among themselves in low, anxious voices when Andrew approaches them. He doesn't want to make himself known at first, just wants to watch and see how it plays out, but then he sees the injured man's face and steps forward into the dim starlight.

"He's mine," he says aloud. The incompetents turn and look at him, and his tone is of such authority that a vein of hostility darkens their expressions, even though he does not threaten them. They whisper among themselves again, then scatter into the shadows. They do not want the injured man. They do not want to be blamed when he dies.

Andrew drags the man up the nearest flight of stairs and through the door. He is vaguely aware that they are in some kind of living space, a flat; there is a sofa in the corner, yes, with flowery cushions, and he considers getting the injured man's blood on it just out of spite, but his breaths are low and hoarse and he is pale and any more movement might just drag the life out of him, leave it drying there on the beige carpet.

Andrew curls up, knees pulled to his chin. He considers using magic to save the man, but he knows his magic is not strong enough to save him; there is no magic strong enough to save him. The invalid is as close to death as it is possible to be while still breathing. His lifeblood is soaking into the welcome mat.

After a few minutes, the injured man opens his eyes. Andrew flinches. The irises are bright green, deep green; the incompetents would call him an Angel. He would have had the *capability* to fight off whoever inflicted these wounds, but he had not had the instinct, or the ruthlessness, or the common sense to do so. This . . . this death, this man's death was not inevitable. Andrew burrows his face into his knees.

"You're the boy," says the injured man, hoarsely.

Andrew goes still.

"The mind . . . in this body . . . had a memory of a boy."

It takes him a moment to reply to that. "And what happened to that mind?"

"Gone," says the injured man, with no malevolence, but simple honesty, and Andrew wants to stab him again. "I . . . I don't remember."

"You're not of this world."

"I don't understand."

"Neither do I."

"What is happening to me?"

Andrew swallows, summons the coldness to respond. "This body . . . it's been hurt. You're dying."

"What is dying?"

He has no answer for a moment. When he speaks, his voice is suddenly sharp, crisp, as if he has no feeling, as if the words have no meaning to them.

"The mind that was in this body. There is still enough left of it to give you this language. You know what *dying* means."

The injured man is silent. "Oh," he says, in a very small voice.

Andrew nods.

"Why am I here? Why am I in this body?"

Andrew grows marginally stronger with this question. "Your soul and the old soul that was in this body, they fused together. Usually, the old soul would be more or less intact, and yours would be wiped out. Only your magic would remain. But this time it went the other way, because you were too strong. You are alive, and he is . . . gone."

"But I am dead."

"No. You are *dying*."

"What's the difference?"

"'Dead' is a past participle occasionally used as an adjective. 'Dying' is a gerund."

The injured man is silent again, presumably not having

understood a word Andrew has just said, and for a little while Andrew thinks he really is dead. Then he asks: "Who were you . . . to him?"

Andrew's voice leaves him for a moment. "His son."

"Who is the woman in the memory?"

"Which woman?"

"The dead woman. She has been dead a long time."

Andrew is silent again, longer this time; the words seem not to want to be spoken. "His wife," he says. "My mother."

"Why did she die?"

"I don't know," says Andrew, with unreasonable anger; after all, the creature in his father's dying body knows nothing, is no more deserving of rebuke than a puppy. Andrew closes his eyes. "I don't know," he says again, wearily, and after a few seconds he realizes that the silence is untainted by breathing now.

He looks up, and his father's body is dead.

He stares at it for a long time, because he can think of little else to do. The pain of the sight increases with time, so he gets up, almost surprised at how the energy has drained from his limbs. He goes to the window, and focuses on not breathing and not crying, and for a while it almost works.

The darkness gave him to her slowly. She had to walk what felt like miles, the wet ground crushing the sound of her footsteps, before she could make out the faint illumination that guarded him. The single strip light above his cage kept them both from blindness: it glinted off the bars, the rusted, gnarled metal roots that twisted around him as if protecting him. Water dripped from the rocky ceiling above, seeping like heavy thunder through the dense mass of earth that kept him from the starlight.

She came to the other side of the bars, but did not touch them. Instead she sat down, dirt-streaked and patient in front of his cage, head bent low. He watched her. His face was pale; dried blood crested the curve of his forehead. They had not allowed him to shave.

He broke first; he spoke first.

"Elmsworth Avenue," he said. "That's where I got the name. It's in Ealing, a quiet, cowardly little place, full of big empty houses. I hid there for a few months after the Veilbreak. It was where the Arkwood twins found me."

She did not look up, but he did not need that to know that she was listening.

"As for the first name, well, that was easy, if slightly misguided. The provisional name for the Veilbreak Project was Goliath."

She spoke softly, reluctantly. "Is it true?"

His voice was hoarse, sharp. "Use your intuition."

"My intuition . . ." She trailed off, the words drifting out of her reach. "My intuition fails."

"Then examine the evidence before you and come to the appropriate conclusion. Honestly, one would think I had taught you nothing."

Her head jerked up, and she looked at him, the muscles working in her face, her eyes glassed over by the light. "Is this the last of it?"

"Yes," he said. "Yes, this is it. My last secret."

She repeated it as if that would allow her to understand. "You're Andrew Ichor."

He ran a hand over his face. "Oh, please. Can we skip the slow

383

realization? Can we move past the piecing together, the adding up of the numbers? You know who I am, and you know what I have done. I made this world. I brought magic here. I started the War."

She bent her head again, and said nothing.

His voice was rough with anger. "What is this? Is this mercy? Or is this some twisted, righteous punishment? Are you to leave me here unjudged, to rot in my own guilt? Is this what you have decided for me?"

She kept her silence, allowing him to run himself into the ground as they had in court. Her heart seemed to be beating more slowly than normal.

"I never expected to live so long, but I knew I could not live forever. Some punishment, however paltry, must eventually be meted out to me. But I never foresaw some great tribunal, some inventive execution. The charge they eventually brought against me was a mere insult compared to the true extent of what I'd done. The truly evil don't die in the noose or the electric chair, Rose; they die alone in the dark, with a snap of the neck or a bullet to the head, unburied. And I'm truly evil, I suppose."

He gave a slightly bitter laugh.

"So you, Rose, you're my judge, my jury, and my executioner. I'll die at the judgment of my own daughter, and that will be my punishment. So do with my life as you see fit. I kneel . . . at your feet."

His voice broke, and after a long, long moment, she raised her head slowly and their gazes met through the bars. He looked emaciated, and terribly old.

"If I'm going to be your judge," she said, "then tell me everything."

<<< >>>

Twenty years earlier (age 16)
July 18, 6:43 p.m.

When he loses his mind, the first time he transforms, it feels like alabaster.

He finds this out at night, and it takes him by surprise: later, over the months and the years, he will learn to recognize the signs with hawk-like accuracy, and the idea of not noticing the changes and not being ready will be as unthinkable as it is terrifying. But this is the very beginning of it all, and he is young and inexperienced and does not realize what is happening to him until almost the very end, the moment he loses his mind.

It slips away very quickly, through the pain of his body changing, and he almost does not notice. It leaves a void within his consciousness, a crushing emptiness, before the shadows slip in to fill it. The slipping away of sanity from his mind is hard and white and irretrievable, like alabaster peeling from a wall. He appreciates that, in a sense. It means there is no point in fighting it, and he has never been one to fight.

Not that he has time to think through any of this coherently. It is too quick for that: pain, and alabaster, and emptiness, and shadows. And then, of course, nothing.

Well, not nothing. A lot more than nothing. But he tries to forget about that.

Later, when he wakes, gasping and human on the cold earth, he will stumble blindly through the streets in darkness and try to understand what has happened, and when that fails, he will abandon his name and leave it there, wandering off without it into the night.

But none of that now. That will come later. Now just darkness and alabaster, and the end of being human.

July 18, 11:14 a.m.

Everyone's gone now, and that leaves him free to conduct his own experiments. Not the obvious ones, of course. He knows the limits of his new gifts, his new green eyes, and that's clearly a dead end — a helpful dead end, of course, but dead nevertheless, because it cannot be worked with or developed. No. He's thinking of something else.

The citywide power is gone, but there are still such things as batteries, and they are not unsalvageable. The machine he has put together is rigged up to a power pack. He hopes that will be enough.

The creatures are everywhere, packed into the air around them like dense clouds —invisible, but there. The one inside him, fading by the day, showed them to him that first night for a brief moment, when they came together. They flood in even now from the crack in the sky, but that is slowly healing, and they're not going back. Which means one of two things. Firstly, that they do not know they will be trapped here — which is unlikely, given their proximity to humans. Or secondly, that this dimension is preferable to whatever is on the other side of the break in the Veil.

He turns on the power pack and steps back. The machine is silent for a moment, and then murmurs in response. Lights begin to flash. The glass container on the top opens slowly as the lights grow brighter. He watches eagerly.

The container snaps shut like a Venus flytrap.

The lights shut off. The power is operating at a deeper level now. A terrible keening sound comes from within the container; something is beginning to form there, a slice of translucence that whitens to opacity, emitting a high-pitched, anguished noise that sounds remarkably like screaming. It is shapeless, formless, but gaining physical mass with every second it spends inside the container. Which, of course, is the objective.

It screams and screams, terrible and endless. And then everything stops.

The machine dies quietly, spark-less and without explosions, but he knows that his chances of being able to use it again are very slim. It doesn't matter. He steps forward tentatively, opening the container with the care of a parent for their child. Inside is a thick, white, viscous substance that clings to the glass like goo.

"A soul given physical form," he says to the empty lab. "Not hugely appealing, is it?"

Now for phase two. He takes the razor blade from the desk beside him and slides it across the palm of his left hand. The blood comes quickly and plentifully, overflowing the skin. He holds it over the contents of the jar, and when the blood makes contact it sizzles, instantly boiling. Sparks fly off it like smoke. While he watches, fascinated, he places his right hand over the cut on his left; he concentrates, drawing on his new magic, and the skin closes and knits together.

"Beautiful," he says, watching it. He goes to the sink while the reaction finishes, washing the rest of the blood off of his hands, not taking his eyes off the jar. The substance within it is now a smooth, silver-white serum.

"Beautiful," he says again.

Then he goes to the medical bay, taking the jar with him. The syringe is ten cubic centimeters large, so there will still be a little liquid left over in the jar, but he can leave that as a sample, for future experiments; perhaps he will find someone else worthy of being elevated above pure humanity. The needle is easily three inches long, but his veins show blue underneath the skin. This will be a simple operation.

He picks up the syringe, and rolls up the sleeve of his right arm.

July 5, 9:45 p.m.

The sky splits open above him, and he jumps up into the air with bright, savage joy, gripping the balcony railing as if it were a weapon.

"I told you!" he screams. "I *told* them I could do it!"

<<< >>>

That was how they were found, just where Daley and Rodriguez had told High Command they would be: kneeling together in the dark, on opposite sides of the bars. The soldiers burst through the door, screaming, firing off shots at the ceiling. Stone chipped and fell to the ground, echoing wetly. Ichor himself was powerless in his cage, but they knew too much about the girl to leave her unguarded, and surrounded her with the barrels of their weapons. They cuffed her hands behind her back. She took it all silently, and Ichor did not protest as they dragged her away. All of that was over now.

Chapter 38

"*Aha.*"

Amelia ripped off the tape on the girl's arm, and the hologram with it. She winced, but the quick flash of green light was enough to cover the brief admission of pain. Her hair, it was revealed, was lighter, mahogany instead of black; she kept her eyes closed so they could not see the green within them. As if that would do her any good.

"*Lily Daniels,*" snarled Jordan. He kept his gun very close now. "Did you think that would fool us?"

Rose Elmsworth's voice was soft; she leaned into the pole she was tied to with weary effort, head upturned as if searching for the sky through her eyelids. "Yes."

Amelia unsheathed her knife, pressed the edge of the blade to the blue vein that ran trembling through Rose's forearm. "What do you know about our enemies? Tell us."

Rose sighed, the sound shattered like choking, and licked her lips. Her words were almost inaudible. "Your sister is worried about you."

Amelia stilled.

"Your parents, too," said Rose softly. "I hear they've been searching for you. Up and down the city . . ." She rolled the back of her head against the pole, pulling her cuffed hands up as if stretching. "Your sister has a boyfriend now. Nate Terrian. He works for the Department."

Amelia pressed the knife deeper into Rose's arm, and all movement stopped. She hated the look Jordan was giving her.

"Enough," said a voice from behind them. Vinyara pushed aside the door of the cell impatiently, flanked by two guards. Rose's eyes snapped open; Amelia saw, not that she had needed to, that they were olive-green. Gifted scum.

"Ah," Rose said quietly. "The cavalry."

Vinyara ignored her and folded her arms, examining her prisoner dispassionately.

"And what makes you think," she said at last, "that you can walk in here, into the very center of our operations, and expect to live?"

Rose closed her eyes again, her voice lowered to a hoarse whisper. "It worked before."

"Why did you come that time?"

"For information. For sabotage. I killed your leader. I killed Felix Callaway."

"No one killed him. It was a trick."

"Of my father's design," said Rose, "and my implementation."

Vinyara's knife flicked out faster than Amelia could follow, and drew a line of blood across Rose's arm. She hissed and bent

390

slowly, absorbing the pain. As Amelia watched, the cut sealed up. Rose's green eyes flickered open again, a gleam of triumph within them.

"You see," she murmured. "I am invulnerable."

"No one is invulnerable."

"No one is invulnerable to *everything*. I am invulnerable to you."

Another slash, another hiss and a running of blood. The cut healed itself more slowly this time, but the skin was still smooth before the first drop hit the ground.

Vinyara put the knife away now, and ran a hand through her hair. She considered before speaking again, eyes on the monster's face.

"Why have you come this time?"

"To find my father."

Vinyara watched her. "And have you found him?"

Rose took a moment to answer. "No," she said, "and I never will again."

"Did you know who he was?"

"No."

"What does he intend to do now? Why did he want us and the Gospel to kidnap Demon children?"

"I don't know."

Vinyara rubbed her face. "What does he *want*?"

"Redemption," said Rose, "but he knows he will never find it."

"Tell us what he planned."

"Will it buy my life?"

"No, but it might save your pain."

Rose bowed her head, and spoke in a low voice, as if through a confessional grate.

"He wanted to kill Felix Callaway," she said. "That plan relied on Regency shooting a man who they thought was him. That meant that if the Department fighters got there before Regency had a chance to kill Felix, when the hologram had already kicked in and he looked like my father, that would allow him to live and escape. That would be disastrous. So, just in case, he had to give the Department fighters a reason to shoot a man who looked like David Elmsworth. So he revealed himself as a monster."

Rose licked her lips, forcing the words through a dry mouth.

"Then he disappeared. He went away for weeks, and destroyed everyone and everything who might know that he had been Andrew Ichor, so that he and only he knew. But revealing himself to the Department had meant giving up the resources he had held when he was their leader, and whatever his eventual plan was then, whatever he wants to do now, he needed resources. He needed allies. He contacted you during those three weeks, didn't he?"

Vinyara nodded slowly, wariness overcoming the low, weary hypnosis of the monster's voice. "We rejected him."

"What exactly did you say to him?"

"He told us he was Andrew Ichor. He told us that he was ready to come back to us, that he could win us this new war. He showed us proof — pictures of his old laboratories, destroyed in the fifth year of the War, I think, but he had pictures of himself as a boy, working there. You say he destroyed all other photographs?"

Rose nodded.

"I wanted to simply reject him out of hand," said Vinyara, "but Slythe had another idea. He said to tell him to go back, go back to his Department, go and stand trial, obey his precious law and order, and if he was still alive at the end of it, then yes, he could come back to us. Slythe was counting on the trial to break him."

"He went to the Gospel, as well," said Rose. "Sent them messages as Andrew Ichor, presumably with the same proof, and told them to start kidnapping Demons. The children would be the easiest to capture. Greenlow obeyed. But they would never accept him if he actually physically approached them, because they would see that he was David Elmsworth, who had always hated them. So he had no choice but to do as you said, and give himself up."

"We saw the Gospel taking the Demon children," said Vinyara. "We didn't know why, but we thought at least we could take something they needed, stop them from getting too strong. So we started taking them as well."

"As he knew you would."

"As he . . ." Anger was hardening in Vinyara's face as she saw how she had been played. She swallowed. "What else?"

"He stood trial, as you asked him to, and I saved him from conviction. But when he had gone on his destruction spree, wiping out all evidence of who he was, he had forgotten the Redmond sisters. Or perhaps he hadn't. Perhaps he just cared too much for Michael's memory to kill them. Either way, that came back to haunt him. Caitlin returned to testify."

"And then, when he got out of court . . ."

"You came and took him back, because he had passed your test and stood trial as you had asked him. You put him in a cage, because you didn't trust him. And I . . ." It struck Amelia how bitter Rose Elmsworth's voice had suddenly become. "I came running into your clutches trying to save him from a fate he himself had engineered."

Vinyara scrutinized her, and seemed to decide that she was not lying: after all, Amelia thought, what reason would she have now to defend Ichor?

"All right, then," Vinyara said, and rubbed her face again. "All right."

She turned away. As she walked out of the cell, she gave one last order to the guards.

"Kill the Elmsworth girl."

There was a silence.

"No," Rose said, quietly.

Vinyara stopped for a moment in the corridor, and looked back at her with something like pity. "I would say I am sorry," she said, "but you killed Felix Callaway, and so, really, I'm not."

"No," said Rose Elmsworth again, an edge to her low voice now. "I meant, that is not my name."

Vinyara narrowed her eyes. "Well," she said, after a while, "I suppose that was never anyone's name. Ichor invented it."

"I know," said Rose. "But don't you want to know what my real name is?"

Amelia wanted to stop her. She knew now not to answer any questions a monster asked. And she didn't think she would have to; she thought Isabel Vinyara, with all her fighting experience and her shrewd intellect, would know better. But apparently there really was something hypnotic about the monster, because Vinyara asked, slowly, as if fearing the answer: "What is your real name?"

And the girl leaned forward, hanging from the chain of her cuffs off the pole, and opened her gleaming eyes, and said, "My name is Rose Stronach. You knew my mother when she was alive, didn't you, Isabel?"

Vinyara's eyes widened. She looked over at the monster with realization blossoming sharply in her gray eyes, and whispered, "Oh, dear God . . ."

Amelia didn't understand what they were talking about, and wouldn't, for a long time. And so she didn't imagine what *could* have happened, then: how close Vinyara was to taking her gun out and killing the last scion of Felix Callaway's line there and then.

What actually happened, however, was that the arm of one of the guards flashed out and slammed into Vinyara's neck. She dropped instantly.

Amelia and Jordan cried out and whirled their guns out as the traitor drove the butt of the submachine gun into the chin of the other guard, who stumbled back into the wall and slid slowly to the floor. Jordan fired a warning shot into the ceiling.

"Don't move!" he yelled.

The traitor ignored him, pulled off her helmet, and stared directly at Amelia with piercing grass-green eyes.

"Go on then," said Maria. "Shoot me."

Slythe did not come quietly when the Department attacked.

"How dare you — scion of magic, preternatural scum — get back, get away from here, put down your guns!"

Goading, thought James dully, as he raised his semiautomatic.

"You don't need them, do you, arrogant dead-eyes — you have your magic, don't you. What cowardly weakling must you be to need bullets when you have —"

The old man was trying to back away even as he shouted, but he could only go so far, and James backed him into the wall of the tunnel and pressed the barrel of the gun right up against the skin of the Ashkind man's forehead as the Department soldiers sprinted down the corridors behind them. The old man's words spluttered and failed very quickly against the cold metal.

"One thing," said James. "I need one piece of information from you, and then I will deal with you. Where is the girl who called herself Lily Daniels?"

The old man said nothing, his silence burning with defiance. James hit him across the face as motivation, but Slythe went willingly into unconsciousness with the blow. James sighed, and knelt to handcuff him. They would be taken and tried, every single one of them. Justice must work once in a blue moon, just by sheer weight of probability.

"James?"

Nate crouched down beside him. He seemed alive with this battle, despite himself; his gun seemed to weigh almost nothing in his hands.

"Did he say anything? Where are they?"

"I don't know," said James, tightening the cuffs hard on Slythe's wrists. "Go deep. If they've captured her, that's where she'll be."

Nate didn't say that there was another, more obvious reason why Rose hadn't come running to find what was left of the Department as soon as the shooting started in the upper floors of the War Rooms; another, more obvious thing Regency would have done to her, and to Maria, if they had been captured. Both of them knew; the possibility hung heavy and rejected in their hearts. But they said nothing. The women they loved were too clever and too brave to be struck down by mere possibility.

Nate rose, and joined the stream of soldiers running into the darkened earth. James spotted Terrian among them, running

396

furiously into the depths of Regency's lair, holding his gun tightly. James hauled the old man's body to the hole in the earth, where the early morning sunlight scarred the edges of this godforsaken place. He turned his face up to the sky.

"I've got another one," he called up wearily.

Jordan nearly fired, but *nearly* wasn't anywhere close enough to kill Maria. Nevertheless, the twitch of his finger on the trigger was enough to draw an anguished scream from Amelia, and to pull her toward him to wrench his gun away. Maria watched her with as close to detachment as she could manage.

"Put your weapons down," she said. She kept hers raised, her hands shaking, pointed into her sister's face. Amelia looked at it uncomprehendingly. She put her gun on the floor only when Jordan did.

"Please, Maria," whispered Rose Elmsworth, exhaustion and pain threading through her voice. Maria kept her gun trained on Amelia and Jordan, and walked warily up to Rose. The girl slumped forward, held to the post by the chain links of the handcuffs straining around her tense arms. Maria stared at her impassively.

Rose moaned softly again.

"Look at me," said Maria.

She raised her head. Her face was growing whiter by the second.

Maria held up her machine gun. "Look at me," she repeated, anger surging low and strong in her voice. "I was a medical student. I was going to swear the Hippocratic oath: *It may be within my power to take a life; this awesome responsibility must be faced with great humbleness and awareness of my own frailty.* Yes? And I just hurt two people. I could have killed them. I am holding a *gun*, Rose. This is what loyalty to you has done to me."

Rose's chin had sunk onto her chest. Maria grabbed her, forced her to look up so they were eye to eye.

"And how do you repay me? You lie to me. Again, and again, and again."

Rose murmured something inaudible.

"You did not *have to*. Maybe the ACC would have hurt you, maybe Malvern, maybe even Nate's father, but *I* would never have raised a finger against you. I would have listened, and I would have understood."

"It wasn't worth the risk," murmured Rose hoarsely.

"Says who? What is *this* worth, then? Did you think you could hide this forever?"

Rose muttered an incoherent negative.

Maria strode around the pole and started sawing at Rose's chains with a serrated knife. They snapped within a few seconds under the cresting blade. Rose Elmsworth staggered forward, stumbled, fell to her knees.

"I don't know who you are," said Maria, standing over her, "but I know that I used to trust you, to love you."

Amelia's heart cracked.

"I am saving your life for the girl I knew, not for you. Do you understand?"

Rose Elmsworth was rubbing the blooming red, raw skin of her wrists, and did not respond. Maria turned to Amelia.

"It's good to see you," she said.

Amelia nodded mutely, dry-throated.

"The Department are attacking," said Maria. "Run. I don't

think they'll hurt you. If you get to see daylight again, tell Mum I was the one who found you. And then explain to them why you did what you've done."

"They'll never take me back."

"You can persuade them," said Maria, flatly. "Don't bring *him* with you, though." She gestured with her gun to Jordan. Amelia nodded again, breathing slowly. Maria smiled tightly, and turned back to the monster.

Amelia and Jordan edged along the wall, breaking into a run as soon as they were out of the room. As they left, they heard Maria say, "Rose, this is your last chance. Is there anything else you need to tell me?"

Rose Elmsworth's response was too quiet to carry.

<<< >>>

Twenty years earlier (age 16)
April 11, 3:16 p.m.

He stays in the shed while Michael and his father have a blazing row inside the house. He can hear their voices through the wall, so he huddles in the back, out of the way of the raindrops leaking through the roof. They drip dangerously close to the computer, so he pulls the desk slightly out of the way. The notebook is on the shelf on the back wall: *Guide to the Spotting of Monsters*, a comic he and Michael have been writing together. In it they've put descriptions of every kind of evil they know of — murderers, extortionists, rapists, torturers. He pulls it out and starts annotating Michael's drawing of a serial killer.

It is ten minutes before any footsteps come near the shed. It

399

sounds like the walker has something against the gravel, so he lurks uncertainly in the shadows until the door is slammed open.

"Andrew?"

He steps, relieved, into the light. Michael's hair is dark and damp from the rain, and he looks furious.

"Everything all right?" Andrew asks, as innocently as he can.

"No," says Michael, collapsing grumpily into the chair. "He and Mum want to go on holiday to Spain with me."

"You should go."

Michael glares at him. "You want me gone?"

"Of course not. You need a break."

"The *hell* I need a break. I'm just getting to the end of this section of code."

"The code can wait."

"No, it bloody can't. I need to finish it."

Andrew sits down on the floor underneath the hole in the roof. "Take your laptop."

"No. I need peace. I need concentration."

"You seem happy enough with me around."

Michael glares at him. "Don't pull that card."

"Sorry."

A moment of silence. Andrew can feel the raindrops drip through the cracks in the roof into his hair, and waits until Michael bursts into angry speech again before moving out of the way.

"They *know* I need to work on this! Why do they want to mess it up?"

"Maybe they think there are more important things," Andrew suggests. Michael gives him the finger without looking. The computer murmurs to itself as it fires up.

"Do you have any idea why they've suggested this now?" asks Andrew, in his best approximation of a reasonable voice. Michael shrugs. It is a very violent shrug, devoid of indifference.

"Well, Eleanor and Caitlin are gone now, so I suppose I'm the *last remaining child*."

He spits it.

"I thought they said you could have their bedroom when they went to uni."

He shrugs again. "They're coming back for Christmas."

"That'll be nice," Andrew ventures tentatively. Michael shoots him a savage glare.

"Yeah, that can be my break. Christmas with the twins. Not this moronic . . . *Spain*."

He stabs the keyboard, and chooses a new line of attack.

"What about you? When was the last time *you* took a holiday?"

"Not since Mum died," says Andrew tersely, and Michael doesn't say anything for a while after that but "Cigarette?"

Andrew considers. "Thanks."

They light up with swift, practiced movements. It was Michael who taught Andrew to smoke; he has never had the courage to do it anywhere else, even in the office. They both watch each other, trying very hard to appear casual.

"What are you working on, then?" asks Michael, in a would-be nonchalant sort of voice.

Andrew briefly weighs up the idea of the truth, and ends up wordless.

"Does your dad even know about it?"

"Of course he knows. I update him whenever I visit him, but there's only so much I can say in front of the whole psych ward."

401

Michael snorts. "*Update.* Andrew, he has a PhD, and you're —"

"If you say *a child*, I will actually —"

They are both on their feet, and they realize it at the same time.

Michael walks toward the door. "So when the mandarins do their accounting for all the different parts of the Government, they'll find that the Department for Extra-Dimensional Exploration is run by a sixteen-year-old."

"No, they won't."

"Why not?"

"It's not on the record."

Michael watches him for a little while, in a way that makes Andrew want to cringe. "Nothing I say is going to change your mind, is it?"

"Change my mind over what? We're just running a routine test; you shouldn't even —"

"I shouldn't even *what*?" says Michael, angrily. "I shouldn't know? Because I'm a civilian in your war against the rest of the world?"

"Michael, for the love of *God*!"

"Look at me. Just look at me."

Something about his voice snaps the quiet into place, and Andrew looks. Michael's eyes are a dark, cold blue.

"Andrew Richard Ichor," says Michael softly, his hand on the doorknob, "swear to me, on the beating hearts of everyone you love, that you know what you're doing."

"Of course I do."

This doesn't seem enough for Michael.

"Listen," he says, hoarsely. "If I go to Barcelona with my

402

parents for two weeks, can you promise me — promise me — that when I come back you're going to be fine?"

"Yes," says Andrew, without hesitation.

Michael closes his eyes. "Andrew?"

"Yes?"

He pauses. Then he walks out of the shed.

– Chapter 39 –

The following is an accurate transcription of the discussions that took place on the second of March, in the Nineteenth Year of Angels, concerning the terms of the Second Great Truce.

The content of this transcript has been declared highly classified.

Delegations:

Natalie Agatha Greenlow and Peter Damon Lynch, of the organization known as "The Gospel"

Isabel Soraya Vinyara and Anthony Oscar Slythe, of the organization known as "Regency"

Connor Nathan Terrian and Rosalyn Aisling Stronach, of the Department for the Maintenance of Public Order and the Protection of Justice

Chair: Judge Louise Malvern, QC

CHAIR: I call to attention the delegates from the various parties. Are the delegates all present and correct?

R. STRONACH: We are, madam.

I. VINYARA: As are we.

P. LYNCH: And we. If I could raise the first point . . . ?

CHAIR: Please do.

P. LYNCH: Would the delegate from the Government Department aforementioned be able to enlighten us as to the whereabouts of the war criminal Andrew Ichor?

C. TERRIAN: I certainly would not be able to.

P. LYNCH: I was not referring to you.

R. STRONACH: I am afraid I cannot help you, either.

P. LYNCH: And I am afraid I do not believe you.

R. STRONACH: You assume that I knew all of his secrets, just because I knew and shared in one. I do not. I knew *what* he was, but I did not know *who*. If I had, I assure you he would not be alive now.

P. LYNCH: How do you know that he is alive?

R. STRONACH: You forced him in front of a jury, and he survived. You forced him into battle, and he survived. You let him be captured by his oldest enemies, and he survived. A mere disappearance won't kill him. He's alive.

CHAIR: Is your query answered, Mr. Lynch?

P. LYNCH: No, it is not. Would the delegate from the Department tell us what punishment she would suggest for Ichor, if he were caught?

R. STRONACH: [silence]

CHAIR: Will you answer the question, Ms. Stronach?

R. STRONACH: I assure you I would, if I felt it to be relevant.

P. LYNCH: It is entirely relevant.

R. STRONACH: Ask me again when he is captured alive. Do you have any further questions regarding Ichor?

P. LYNCH: [pause] I do not.

CHAIR: Then we arrive at our next point of negotiation: division of troops.

N. GREENLOW: The Gospel wish to have all of their troops returned to them, safe and well.

I. VINYARA: Then the Gospel is delusional.

CHAIR: The delegate from Regency will keep her language diplomatic.

I. VINYARA: Regency won control of the Gospel's troops, and it did so in the theater of war. The Gospel has no right to attempt to take back what is not theirs.

N. GREENLOW: But this isn't about money, or strategic locations; this has nothing to do with — with military advantage. These are *people*. Can't you understand that? People with hearts and minds and blood and fear, and you are — [pause] The delegate from Regency is effectively holding these people hostage. Surely the chair and the delegates from the Department agree that this is against every kind of law.

C. TERRIAN: Yes, we agree.

R. STRONACH: Is the delegate from Regency determined that there will be no release of the captured Gospel troops?

I. VINYARA: Not without sufficient incentive.

R. STRONACH: And how exactly would you define that?

I. VINYARA: A guarantee of amnesty for every single Regency-allied soldier.

C. TERRIAN: Never going to happen.

I. VINYARA: May I formally request that the delegate from the Department keep his language diplomatic.

C. TERRIAN: So long as I live, I will never allow a single one of you to escape trial.

R. STRONACH: Connor, please.

C. TERRIAN: I speak for the Department; my word is our position.

R. STRONACH: Then reconsider your words.

C. TERRIAN: [inaudible]

R. STRONACH: We are prepared to offer you a universal amnesty.

C. TERRIAN: Oh, are we now?

R. STRONACH: But under certain conditions.

A. SLYTHE: What do you want?

R. STRONACH: Firstly, that you accept that this amnesty would apply only to crimes committed in war, and that should any member of Regency commit a crime *after* the treaty is signed, they will be arrested and prosecuted exactly as would any other member of the public.

I. VINYARA: We accept that.

R. STRONACH: [pause] Secondly, that you return to the Gospel control of the underground base that you took from them.

A. SLYTHE: [to I. VINYARA] We can't do that. They're trying to trick us.

I. VINYARA: Do you believe her cleverer than me?

A. SLYTHE: That base is strategically important.

I. VINYARA: Not anymore. We have all their soldiers — we don't need the base. What is your third condition?

R. STRONACH: You.

A. SLYTHE: What?

R. STRONACH: The delegates from Regency will give themselves up to the police, and stand trial, charged with all the crimes that Regency has committed during this war.

A. SLYTHE: They will bloody well not.

CHAIR: The delegate from Regency will acknowledge that profanity is not conducive to debate and cooperation.

407

A. SLYTHE: It's a ridiculous condition. The delegate from the Department shows an utter lack of respect for the l —

R. STRONACH: In return for which, if and when you are released, you will return to find your army ready and waiting. And if you do not return, if you are executed, someone else will take up your position. Regency will live to fight again. Is that not worth your freedoms?

A. SLYTHE: You ask for our lives.

R. STRONACH: Don't you give them?

I. VINYARA: [pause] Do you promise we will be treated well? That our trials will be free and fair and unbiased?

R. STRONACH: I only catch the criminals; I do not convict them, and so help me God I have no intention of setting foot in a courtroom ever again.

I. VINYARA: So you can't guarantee our safety.

R. STRONACH: I have never been in the habit of making promises I am not able to keep.

C. TERRIAN: [inaudible]

R. STRONACH: And I certainly don't promise people that which they do not deserve.

I. VINYARA: The delegate from the Department will refrain from claiming a moral high ground she does not possess.

R. STRONACH: You wanted to be a monster; I didn't. You agree, then?

I. VINYARA: No one wants to be a monster.

CHAIR: Will the delegate from Regency please answer the question.

I. VINYARA: We do.

A. SLYTHE: [pause] We do.

N. GREENLOW: And what about us, then? Do you have a prison cell ready for us?

R. STRONACH: On the contrary, I offer you precisely the opposite. The delegates from Regency have just agreed to hand over the base they captured from you five weeks ago. In that base is the computer containing the names and close family members of every Gospel soldier. You will hand over the data concerning every officer higher than a private, and in return you have our word that neither you nor your sons will ever be harmed by us.

P. LYNCH: You would take our army from us?

R. STRONACH: I have just given you back your army. I am even allowing you to keep the grunts. What more do you want?

A. SLYTHE: *What?*

R. STRONACH: If the delegate from Regency cannot hear me, he is encouraged to raise a point of personal privilege.

I. VINYARA: You promised there would be no handover of the Gospel troops.

R. STRONACH: No, *you* said that; and since it was your agreement to this deal that broke that assurance, it is your sincerity, I feel, that is in question here.

A. SLYTHE: This is outrageous.

R. STRONACH: No, just ingenious.

N. GREENLOW: So this is it? We are to be disarmed?

R. STRONACH: You entered these peace talks a broken organization, little more than a group of angry leaders, armed only with bitterness. I have returned to you the untrained thugs, the inexperienced revolutionaries you started with. You took London because the Department were weakened, and because Parliament were caught off-guard. But there are new Angels, new Parliamentarians, being brought in from all over the country, and I promise you, the Department will never be weak again.

N. GREENLOW: This is your version of justice, is it?

R. STRONACH: Oh, yes. You came from powerlessness, and unto powerlessness you shall all return.

I. VINYARA: The Department were not known for taking vengeance, as I remember it.

R. STRONACH: The man who called himself my father considered vengeance an amateur pursuit. I intend to make it a profession.

<<< >>>

Twenty-one years earlier (age 15)
May 24, 1:22 p.m.

He knows what's happening when his father starts breaking things. He knows what it means when he locks himself in his room for days without food or sleep. He knows what it signifies when Richard talks to himself, shouts to himself, for hours, without noticing that his son is trying to talk to him. It is called, in the jargon, a *nervous breakdown,* and it is frankly astonishing that it has not kicked in before now; Richard Ichor's sanity has been on borrowed time since the death of his wife, and it shows phenomenal mental stamina that he has not succumbed to this in the four years since.

Andrew is not afraid, of course not, and yet even he notices the depth of the breath he takes outside his father's room. He attributes that to nerves. He is not entirely sure what to make of his father in this state of mind. But that does not mean he is *afraid.*

He steps into the room, and nothing is thrown at him. This is, he deduces, a good sign.

Richard is curled up on his bed, rocking back and forth and muttering. These phases are usually interesting, if not mildly humorous, and since his eyes show no sign of focusing, Andrew sits down in the chair in the corner of the room and listens.

"I don't, I'm sorry, I can't, I wish too, I'm sorry, I'm doing everything I . . ."

This is immediately too painful, so Andrew says loudly, "Dad," and unusually for these phases Richard snaps back into near-lucidity almost immediately. His eyes focus sharply on his son.

"You look like her," he says.

"I know. I remember."

"You remember her?"

"Of course I do."

"She wants a baby," says Richard anxiously, and Andrew realizes wearily that Richard doesn't know to whom he is speaking. "Six years married and no baby. We both want one. Rosalyn wants a little girl. I don't mind. But there should be a baby. We think there might be something wrong with one of us. No baby."

Rosalyn Matheson had no brothers; which male relative would look like her? Her father, perhaps? Andrew rubs his face. Richard's condition is deteriorating severely if he can't distinguish his son from his long-dead father-in-law.

"I don't know," mutters Richard, and Andrew realizes he is waiting for an answer. He swallows.

"There will be a baby, don't worry."

Richard's eyes brighten. "You think?"

"Oh, yes." He feels, oddly, like a time-traveler, bequeathed some unearthly power of prophecy. "Another two years, and then a baby. A boy, though, I'm afraid."

"Yes? What's his name?"

He can't take this. He stands up, leaves the room; Richard does not call after him. Presumably he has already forgotten. Andrew stands, gripping the landing rail, eyes squeezed shut. He feels out of his depth.

No, that doesn't quite capture it.

He realizes that the word he is looking for is *orphan*, and his head snaps up to stare at the opposite wall for a moment.

He is gripped by a sudden strength. He holds it within himself for a moment, examining it, and asks what he is supposed to do.

Then he goes down the stairs, takes the phone off the hook, and keys in the three-digit emergency number. On the second 9 his hands shake so badly that he nearly drops the phone, but he stills himself; this is what must be done.

– Chapter 40 –

Two weeks after they left London, they found each other. He saw the two women sitting together calmly by the side of the A2, holding up a sign asking for a lift to Dover. As he got closer, he saw who they were and sped up, but Tabitha gasped in recognition before he could roar past them.

"Dad, look! It's Madeleine! And Tara's with her!"

After that, he had no choice but to pull over. The two women filed silently into the backseat of the battered Peugeot. Ryan's belly was growing too swollen for her jeans. This Peugeot was the fifth car they had hijacked, switching every few days and doubling back on themselves so neither they nor their intended destination could be identified; blood was dried into the boot. If they noticed, they said nothing about it. Tabitha had long since learned not to ask these kinds of questions.

After a mile and a half, Madeleine spoke.

"Robert's dead."

Loren checked in the rearview mirror. The engagement ring was still there. Ryan's voice was hard and tearless.

"I'm sorry," he said. Tabitha was silent.

"They shot him at Heathrow. He died in the Department."

"And now you're here."

"We're leaving," said Tara. "Whatever happens to London now, we've got no place there. We were too heavily involved."

That was all they said for a long time.

Loren paid for a room at the next motel with the contents of the Peugeot driver's wallet, and it was only in the hotel room, as he and Tara rummaged in the closet for sheets to sleep on — there were only two single beds, and of course they had to go to the child and the pregnant woman — that he heard Madeleine Ryan speak again.

"Show me your magic."

Loren turned to see Tabitha looking taken aback. She glanced at him for approval. He nodded. Tabitha stretched her small, trembling hand out toward Madeleine, and a light sparked and grew to glow above her skin. Madeleine's gray eyes widened.

"You're a magical Demon."

Tabitha nodded. "Dad told me it's because my other soul escaped something, a long time ago."

"Apparently so."

"Where's Cassandra?" asked Loren — stupidly, it seemed to him in retrospect. Tara shook her head, and he closed his eyes, cursing his own lack of foresight.

"How?"

"The Gospel found her," said Tara, simply.

Over the next few days, as the miles between them and Dover shortened, the silences cracked and broke. Madeleine spoke quietly about Robert, about their unborn daughter, about her cases. She told them about the murderers and activists she had defended and convicted. Loren knew what she was asking for, and after two days he relented, and turned on the radio.

That was how they found out.

"Peace talks have been set for a week from today . . ."

He could not hear them breathing.

". . . between delegates from the Department, Regency and the Gospel."

Neither Regency nor the Gospel would ever engage in negotiation unless they were already defeated. He knew that much. They listened hard for their own names, but Loren Arkwood and his niece were not mentioned, and neither was the lawyer who had defended David Elmsworth from certain and overwhelmingly popular death.

David Elmsworth.

The BBC understands that the criminal known as David Elmsworth has been revealed to be merely an alias for the war criminal Andrew Ichor, who was only sixteen years old when he triggered the Veilbreak that brought magic to the human race nearly twenty years ago.

The Peugeot swerved across the open motorway before Loren regained control of himself.

"Did you know?" whispered Madeleine. Tabitha was silent; she, of course, would barely recognize Ichor's name. She was too young to know the fear and awe that it inspired in anyone old enough to remember the Veilbreak.

"No," said Loren.

"Yes," said Tara.

He stared at her in the rearview mirror, and saw his own shock mirrored in Madeleine's gaunt face.

"How?"

Tara was quiet before admitting it: "He told me."

In the silence after that, the newsreader informed them: *"Ichor's whereabouts are currently unknown."*

Of course they were.

Three days after that, in the next hotel room, listening to the live broadcast of the swearing in of the new Head of the Department, Tabitha pulled herself gently to her feet and held out a piece of paper to Madeleine.

"Here," she said.

Madeleine took it, and looked blankly at her fiancé etched in ash on the paper. The scar swept with a sort of elegance through the deep-black, smoky-gray shades of his face; it did not mar him, as it had in life.

They stood in hesitant silence as the voice of Rose Stronach swore eternal loyalty to the Angels in smooth static on the radio.

Madeleine looked up at the little Demon girl.

"You draw very well," was all she said.

<<< >>>

Twenty-one years earlier (age 14)
December 4, 8:17 p.m.

They light up outside the kebab shop. Caitlin and her boyfriend Jackson are drinking cheap coffee inside. It's dark. Andrew has switched his mobile phone off.

"It's freezing out here," says Michael. He slumps down in the plastic chair, his face lit only by streetlamp residue and the concentrated gold of his cigarette end. "You'd think with these temperatures they could at least give us a white Christmas."

"Once you get down below a certain temperature it's too cold to snow. There's not enough moisture in the air. Not in London, anyway." He ignores the way Michael looks at him. "You asked."

"I didn't, actually." Michael regards him with mild amusement as he takes a drag. "You smoke like a man now."

"I smoke like a nicotine addict, Michael."

"And whose fault is that?"

Andrew glares at him, keeping the cigarette away from his gloves so they don't catch fire. "Yours."

"Nope. Marshall Keaton's." Andrew doesn't ask, so he carries on. "Eleanor's old boyfriend. Eleanor taught Caitlin, Caitlin taught me . . ."

"And you pressured me into it."

"Don't give me that. No one forced you. When you die an early death from lung cancer, you'll only have yourself to blame."

He says it cheerfully, and as he does it begins to sleet. Andrew steps under the canopy of the kebab shop and doesn't answer.

"What?" asks Michael. Silence as he begins to cotton on. "What did I say?"

"Nothing." The word brings up smoke, and he descends into a coughing fit. When he surfaces, Michael is beside him.

"You all right, mate?"

"Yeah."

"Did I say something to piss you off?"

"No."

"Andrew, please. The truth."

417

Andrew takes a drag on his cigarette, trying to find an excuse for quiet. The sleet is heavier now. Michael waits.

"Is there something you haven't told me?"

He's not going to let up, so Andrew searches for a way to say it. "You know how you've never met my mother?"

"I've never met your dad, either. What —?"

Andrew can hear him cycling back through the conversation, finding the piece that fits. Then he says, "Oh," in a very small voice, and after that they are both quiet.

Then Michael says, "I'm sorry."

"I thought you might be."

"When . . . ?"

"Before we met. I was eleven."

"Lung?"

"Ovarian. It was inoperable when they found it. She hung on for a year. I guessed about three months before, and by then it was just . . ." He tries to indicate a downhill slope with his hand. "Yeah."

"Oh." Michael glances back into the kebab shop, where Caitlin sits with her boyfriend, and Andrew knows what he is thinking. He is counting the number of times he has complained to Andrew about his family — his own mother, and his father, and his twin sisters. All five of them, gathered together like harvest. And then Andrew, alone with his father and his mother's ghost.

Andrew drops the cigarette and stubs it out on the pavement.

"You quitting, then?"

There is no joke in Michael's voice, and Andrew looks at him. He considers his answer.

"I knew when I started I was in for the long haul."

"Yeah." The sleet is white-hard, almost hail, coming as thickly as wind. "Me too."

They sit for a while underneath the canopy. Through the glass of the kebab shop, Caitlin is sitting on Jackson's lap and they are kissing. The boys glance back at them.

"You ever thought about getting a girlfriend?" Michael asks Andrew, who takes another cigarette and lights up again.

Andrew shrugs. "What are you supposed to say to that?"

"Most people say 'yes.' "

"Yeah," says Andrew. "I guess they do."

<<< >>>

CHAIR: A question has been raised about the legitimacy of the amnesty declared in the Great Truce in this situation.

P. LYNCH: Who raised it?

C. TERRIAN: My colleague.

R. STRONACH: The Great Truce was drawn up thirteen years ago; it is now redundant, given that it entirely failed to prevent another war.

I. VINYARA: What do you want?

R. STRONACH: I'm not suggesting prosecuting every single soldier involved in the First War. I merely suggest drawing up a Wanted list of those who committed the greatest crimes, so we can have some form of justice and closure, and prevent the circumstances for a Third War ever arising.

I. VINYARA: You will never be able to do that.

R. STRONACH: We can never do that for certain, but we can try.

P. LYNCH: Who would be on this Wanted list?

R. STRONACH: Firstly, all those whom we have already agreed to prosecute at this conference. The delegates from Regency, of course,

419

and the officers of the Gospel: Ms. Greenlow, if you would be so kind as to provide their names . . .

A. SLYTHE: What's the point of this? What does this achieve?

R. STRONACH: To be frank with you, Mr. Slythe, all it really does is frame a tenuous *fait accompli* as a decisive action on the part of the Department. We have a public to answer to, after all, and we must be seen to clamp down on the criminals. We don't have to tell them how easy the criminals made it for us.

I. VINYARA: In which case, let me suggest another name for this Wanted list.

R. STRONACH: By all means.

I. VINYARA: Andrew Ichor.

R. STRONACH: Oh, but of course. His name will be right at the top.

I. VINYARA: [inaudible]

A. SLYTHE: All right then, let *me* suggest one: Loren Arkwood.

R. STRONACH: [silence]

CHAIR: Does the delegate from the Department agree with this suggestion?

R. STRONACH: What crimes would the delegate from Regency charge him with?

A. SLYTHE: With war crimes. With crimes against humanity. He was one of us in the very darkest days; if you want to put one of the Angels of Death on that list, you may as well have the other. He killed hundreds in the name of war without blinking an eye. He was Felix's right-hand man. What law would excuse him from punishment for that?

R. STRONACH: [silence]

CHAIR: Would the delegate from the Department please answer the question.

R. STRONACH: No; no law.

C. TERRIAN: Well, then, on the list he goes.

CHAIR: If none of the delegates has any other matters to raise, then that will conclude proceedings for today.

I. VINYARA: If there is nothing else, then the delegate from Regency would like to congratulate the delegate from the Department on having the courage of her convictions.

R. STRONACH: I start as I mean to go on.

<<< >>>

Twenty-five years earlier (age 11)
April 3, 11:09 a.m.

He locks himself in his room afterward. His father thinks it is the grief, but it is not, not really; it is not the grief itself that puts him in here, but rather the self-control. He knows that if he allows himself to go free, he will go to her room and try to convince himself she is still here; and he does not want the memory of her, the smell of her, to be tainted with the memory of *this* — this hard incomprehension, this blank illogical insistence that she cannot be dead, she is not dead. She *is* dead, of course, and he wants to protect the memories of her from the grief.

That, he thinks, makes sense.

He knows about funerals, knows how terrible they can be, so when his father knocks hesitantly on his door and says that they are going to a *celebration* of his mother's life and all of their *family* will be there and it won't be *easy* but it might *help*, he knows what he is in for. He puts on his best clothes, the ones that make him look like he is trying to be a man and in doing so make him feel even more like a boy, and he goes with his father in the car to the funeral.

He leans into his father's chest, and listens attentively to the eulogies, hoping to find something more of his mother than he knew of her in life; but all they give is meaningless praise, heart-felt endorsements of Rosalyn Matheson's work, and her brilliance and her ingenuity and how much she did for her parents and sister and husband and son. His father goes up to the lectern and talks about how much he loved her, his voice tight and level, as if he can feel the inadequacy of his words. Andrew, he says, looks more like her every day.

They bring the coffin past the mourners, and Andrew wants to disappear.

After the funeral he locks himself in his room, and this time it really is the grief keeping him there.

Four days afterward, there comes a knock on his door. He waits, curious to know what will happen without his intervention, and the door opens anyway, as he expected. It is, of course, his father. Richard walks in silence and sits down on the bed. Grief has set to work on him, too; it has drawn the color from his face and a little of the light from his eyes. He is thinner than he used to be, and colder, somehow. Andrew briefly considers the implications of the weaponization of grief. Whole populations could be reduced to emaciated wrecks in days. He wonders if anyone has tried that yet.

"Do you think you can work?" asks Richard.

Andrew looks at him hard. "I don't want to go back to school yet. I can do the homework, but I don't want to see the others."

Richard rubs his eyes. "I wasn't suggesting that."

In the car on the way over, Andrew sits in the backseat and watches the back of his father's head. Richard looks straight ahead these days. They drive in silence. Andrew knows where they are going. He is irrationally afraid, but he should not be — his mother never walked these floors, never talked to the people there; there is no danger of Rosalyn's memory taking him unawares, like a malevolent ghost.

He takes a little strength from having seen that coming. He remembers knowing, when his mother lay white and thin and cold and barely voiced in her bed with the IV stands crowding her like trees, that it would hurt to remember her when she was gone, more than it would have hurt if she had never been there. The memories had lost their element of surprise. The idea gives him the illusion of control over them. Of course, it is nothing more than illusion; he will never have control over this.

Never. Not even if he lives to be eighty.

But surely, even if the memories of his mother never leave him, they must weaken with time; people do recover from grief, after all, and go on to live normal lives. The thought is frightening. What length of time could wreak that kind of change?

Who would he become?

They pull up alongside the building, and sit there in the car for a while. Andrew watches his father deliberate. Richard gets out of the car after a few moments; the way he slams the door is savagely determined. Andrew is nervous. He takes his father's hand as they look up at the office block. Andrew has been here before, when he was smaller; he knows it is not really an office block, and the name on the sliding glass doors — AESCHELMANN

423

LABORATORIES — means nothing, as the ring on his father's left hand means nothing. These offices are called the Ichor labs, for his father. Andrew is proud of his father.

They walk into the building and up the stairs to the fourth floor. This is where Richard works. When they open the door, the office falls very quiet. No one comes up to give their consolations, but Andrew knows that is not insensitivity; some of the people here have lost loved ones, too, and they know how little their attempts at consolation would mean.

"Hello, Richard," says one of them. "Is he yours?"

"Yes," says his father. "His name is Andrew. He's eleven. He's going to be coming in with me for a little while, just until I get things . . . sorted."

No reply. They take it as understanding. Everyone goes back to what they were doing. The woman who greeted them comes over and crouches down beside Andrew. She seems friendly. "You all right?" she asks, and he knows it is not the same question that his friends ask, but rather a statement: *You are still alive, you're still functional, and it will get better*, and he nods and tries to look grateful. She stands up, and goes away, and he is more grateful still.

His father, too, checks that he is all right, and goes away. Andrew wanders slowly over to one of the computer banks, at the running strings of numbers. He watches how the office workers type them with love.

He sits down on the floor and watches them, knees pulled up to his chin, trying to discern their meaning.

After two hours, when he is almost certain they have forgotten he is there, his father comes over and sits down beside him. They say nothing for a few moments. Andrew is still watching the numbers.

"You like this, don't you?" says his father.

Andrew nods slowly.

"How did you know?"

"Your mother said you would," says Richard, and Andrew looks at him sharply, sees that he is twisting the meaningless ring around his finger. Then, more quietly, he says: "She said to keep you away from here."

Andrew is silent.

"Tell me, Andrew," says his father, "am I doing the right thing?"

"What are you trying to do?"

Richard runs a hand through his hair, and doesn't reply.

"I'm trying to change the world," he says at last.

– Chapter 41 –

They had made their arrangements knowing that they would be hunted, but not by whom. They had too many enemies now to rule any out. Loren knew that some element of Regency, some rogue angry soldiers, would still be alive; and as long as they were, he would be in danger.

But that, of course, was why they were leaving in the first place.

After two weeks, the Peugeot had died quietly in a rest station parking lot. Loren had been unable to restart it, and it wasn't like they could call the bloody AAA or anything, so he had hot-wired the blue Mini sitting next to it and they had driven away before anyone noticed.

It only occurred to him a few miles after that that he had become a criminal again.

He smiled grimly, despite himself.

There was a wallet stuffed into the glove compartment, and he used it to pay for the next few nights' accommodation. After that, he had to save money for the ferry tickets, so they slept in the car. He had to force himself to slide into unconsciousness, fighting the instinct to keep awake just so he could make sure that Tabitha's breaths did not vanish from beside him. She had been taken from him twice; the paranoia would never leave him now.

Nearly five weeks after they had left the city, they finally reached the ferry terminal. They abandoned the car and walked the last few miles on foot. Loren and Tara stood a few steps behind Madeleine and Tabitha; they were close enough to hear the guard ask for Madeleine's passport, check it briefly, hand it back. Loren breathed.

"What are your reasons for leaving?"

Madeleine smiled and wrapped an arm around Tabitha, holding her stomach with the other. "To find a better school for my daughter once her sister is born."

The guard nodded, clearly bored, and waved them through. Tara was muttering gritted obscenities through her teeth, in what seemed to be her version of relief. Loren and Tara came to the front of the queue. The guard asked for their passports: this had been introduced a few weeks before, as an extra security measure, by the Department. Loren handed them over, ears ringing, pleading silently for the guard not to recognize the face, not to know the name.

"All right," said the guard, and handed the passports back. Loren forced himself to walk on, silencing his heartbeat, silencing his thundering blood. Relief crashed through him. Oh, thank God. Thank bloody, bloody God.

They caught up to Madeleine and Tabitha, who were still pale with fading fear. They didn't say a word until they got to the ticket desk; they had learned by now how dangerous words were. When they came to stand underneath the departures board, Loren crouched down beside Tabitha, at her eye level.

"So where do you want to go?"

So many cities on the board. Amsterdam, Calais, Reykjavík, Bergen, Lisbon, Cádiz, Rabat. Loren doubted she knew half of the names. She stared up at them fearfully and then buried her head in his shoulder. She said nothing.

He went to the counter and asked for four tickets to Amsterdam. He paid for them and went to sit down with the others in the ticket area. Tabitha crawled into his lap and curled up, catlike, blind to the world. After a while he thought she might be sleeping. The ferry left in ninety minutes.

Ninety minutes left of this.

He closed his eyes.

What could he have done differently?

He started to count the minutes. Eighty-seven. Eighty-two. Seventy-six. Seventy-one, seventy-one minutes left . . . if he could make it seventy-one minutes, if his luck could just, for once, hold out that long . . .

With fifty-four minutes to go, Tara came over and crouched down beside Tabitha. The girl's black eyes opened instantly. Tara whispered something to her, pushing her hair out of her eyes, and then went back to her seat.

Tabitha sat up. The fear was back in her eyes again.

Loren looked away as he spoke to her. "What is it?"

She recited it low and urgently. She had already learned the art of quiet. "Two, one on the balcony up and ahead of us, and one behind us, on our floor. Armed."

"Who are they?"

Tabitha looked frightened. "I don't know."

"Mr. Arkwood?"

A tap on his shoulder. He turned around, and saw an elderly woman holding her hand out toward him. "The young lady asked me to give this to you," she said. "I'm not sure . . ."

She was an innocent; the confusion on her face was genuine. He thanked her warily, and took the small, white earpiece. The red activation light was glowing. Tabitha was watching him, unsure. He put the earpiece in, leaning back his head to stare up at the ceiling.

"Rose, I —"

"There are guns pointing at all four of you right now," Rose said, her voice steady. "I have absolutely no intention of giving the order. Whatever you do, I will never tell them to shoot you. But if you try to walk away now, or try to fight back, the matter will pass out of my hands, and into those of people with significantly fewer qualms."

He closed his eyes and spoke softly. He could hear Tabitha's breaths shortening beside him.

"What do you want?"

"Send them away. I want them out of range. Then, come to the waiting room. You need to talk to us."

"I'm coming."

She said nothing.

He pulled out the earpiece, sat up, and wrapped his arms around Tabitha beside him. She leaned closer. "Stay with them," he whispered. "If anyone tries to hurt you, use your magic."

She pulled back, her eyes wide. "You're not —"

"I'm not leaving. I'm just coming a bit behind you."

She nodded. Madeleine and Tara had come to stand beside them.

"The Department?" asked Madeleine, low-voiced.

"Yes. They only want me, and I don't think it's . . . I don't think it's permanent."

"We'll leave without you," said Tara, more as a realization than a threat. He nodded, and pushed Tabitha toward them.

"Look after her. Protect her with your lives."

"Please don't go," whispered Tabitha.

Loren stood up, straightening his jacket, and bent to kiss her on the forehead. Madeleine and Tara pulled Tabitha gently away, and Loren looked around, found the sign. He walked away from the lounge, toward the cold, quiet sterility of the waiting room. He passed through the doorway, and the chattering of the crowd disappeared.

Rose sat on a single wooden chair, head in her hands.

"Commander," he said.

She winced. "Major, actually."

"Comes with the job, does it?"

"It would seem to."

He stood before her. In that chair, she looked to be alone; but he knew there would be people watching them, and that she was thus armed just as surely as if she held the gun in her own hand. Loren understood, in that moment, that even if the whole world had been set against her, even if all the monsters on earth conspired to stand before her, fate would have engineered a way

430

to place the Department at her feet; because what other human purpose would befit this young woman with Felix's ruthless clarity of vision, and Ariadne's easy authority, and David Elmsworth's unearthly calm?

"How did you get this gig, then?" he asked her.

"I was the most palatable of all their monsters."

"By which you mean there was no one else."

"Precisely. Terrian was against it, but look at him; London fell to the enemy under his watch. He knows that I'm a monster, but I am at least prepared to do monstrous things for the Department, and that is all they really ask of anyone."

"Are they all getting used to it?"

"Nate and Maria can speak to me, but not touch me. James . . ." She breathed through her fingers. "James at least understands monsters. He knows how I work."

"You must be hiring new people now."

"Yes. They're all older than me, of course, and I worried about that, but they have enough respect to listen to me. *They* don't understand monsters, and therein lies my one great advantage."

"To be unknowable. Mysterious."

"To them, yes." She stood up. "How are the others?"

"Tara is okay. Tabitha is . . . recovering."

"And Madeleine?"

"No."

Rose closed her eyes. "I am sorry about Robert. I was with him when he died. He used his last breaths to say he loved her."

"I think she already knows that."

"Good."

431

"Why am I here, Rose?"

She stood there, green eyes closed, soft breeze in her hair, and said nothing.

"You're not telling me, because you think if I know, I'll fight back," said Loren. "Perhaps I won't win, but I want the chance to decide whether or not to fight; I want that choice. Do you not owe me that, Rose?"

She was silent for a while, and there was one, shivering second where he expected a hail of silver bullets to come raining down on him without her word. Then she said, "I've come to arrest you."

He stared at her.

"You're a war criminal. We want you for what you did during the First War. You were an Angel of Death, Loren."

"But the amnesty —"

"No," said Rose. "No more amnesties; no more absolution. Justice is blind again, and for the people who died at your hands, Loren, you must feel the weight of your guilt."

They looked at each other, shuddering, and for a moment he knew what they were both seeing: the shadow of a classroom around them. Rose raised her hand.

"Go on," she said softly. "Fight me."

He stared at her, found Felix's ruthlessness again in her green eyes. Then, with shaking hands, he lowered himself to his knees, and held out his hands. She came forward and clicked the handcuffs into place around his wrists.

"And what about you, Rose?" he asked, his eyes on the waiting room floor. "Are you absolved?"

She locked the cuffs, considering her answer.

"Someone has to be," she said, at last.

<<< >>>

Thirty-one years earlier (age 5)
July 22, 8:32 p.m.

Today they are cleaning the house because they will be seeing Clare and the baby. Clare looks young but when Andrew says that she laughs and he doesn't know why but he knows his mother's expressions for *You should understand that, you're being stupid* and *You're not meant to understand* and this is one of the things he's not meant to understand. He sits in his room very quietly and tries to pretend it is clean and that he is doing something when his parents come upstairs. He thinks they might notice but they don't say anything.

There is a knock at the door and his father opens it and it is Clare. Clare is holding a carrier with the baby in it and his parents say how beautiful the baby is and how she looks just like Clare and like Mark, who is the father of the baby, who is also here. Rosalyn and Clare hug and make each other laugh because they are sisters and this is what sisters do when they are grown. Andrew comes downstairs trying to be invisible but they see him anyway. Clare bends down and kisses him on the forehead and Mark says how big he's getting and Richard says yes he's quite tall for a five-year-old and then they all go into the kitchen.

His mother pours out wine and they drink it and Andrew sits in the corner and listens. Richard and Clare both work with computers so they talk about that. Mark is a lawyer and he says it's not very interesting anyway, and Mark and Clare keep trying to talk about the baby and Andrew's parents smile and pretend it's not boring. After a little while they go into the garden. It is light even though it is late because it is July, which is summer. Andrew is left in the kitchen and the baby is making small gurgling noises, which is interesting. He goes over to see it and climbs up on the chair so he can look down at it.

The baby is a small red thing with a scrunched-up face which makes it look ill, but he knows this is normal because it is only a few weeks old and all babies who are a few weeks old are small and red. It will not look normal until it is much older like him. He knows it cannot speak yet because it doesn't understand but he wonders if it can hear him, because he can see it has ears but they are small and red too and he doesn't know if they work yet. He leans over the baby and it stares up at him but he doesn't know if its eyes work either. "Hello, baby Tara," he says loudly, but the baby does nothing.

– Chapter 42 –

The woman who lived at 48, across the road, was called Siobhan
Abshire. She was a War veteran of about fifty, and Rose had seen
her coming and going a few times when she was growing up;
enough to know her name, but not to know her. This was London,
after all. Clearly, however, Mrs. Abshire knew more about the
Elmsworths than they had realized, because when he showed up
outside the house at seven in the morning, a few minutes before
dawn, she did not call the police.

Instead, she called Rose.

Rose had gone back to sleeping fully clothed a few weeks ago,
so she was at the front door armed and ready in all of thirty seconds. She let herself out, putting the keys back into her pocket
with one hand, pointing the gun into his face with the other.

He spoke first. "Those are my keys."

"It was here or Loren's place, and this is technically mine. Why have you come?"

"A dignified death."

She didn't lower the gun. Briefly she ran through the images in her head — fire, the snap of his neck backward, blood flying as he fell, the corpse on the floor with a smashed face — and did not flinch. "Don't think I won't do it."

"Ah, Rose, but the problem there is that I *don't* think you'll do it, I'm afraid. Not for a moment."

She moved her hand slightly to the right and fired. The shot cracked past his head and into the trunk of the tree behind him. He turned slowly to look at it.

"One tremor," she said, quietly.

"Your hands don't shake."

She lowered the gun slightly. "They do now."

He turned back to her, and they faced each other across the dark. The light threw a streak of gray across his chestnut hair. It was not, she knew, what had deepened the lines on his face. "What do you want?"

"I want to come in."

"The hell you do."

"I want to go to the basement."

"I will quite happily kill you."

"There were days when you would kill *for* me."

She put the gun down, walked over to him, and hit him across the face. Anyone without his training would have walked away from that with a broken jaw. He did not react; he did not hit back. She wanted him to. She wanted to know where they stood.

"How dare you," she said, her voice trembling with fury. "How dare you use the promises I made to you against me. I thought you loved me when I said that."

"I do love you."

"You are a coward and a liar."

It was too dark to read his face. "I am David Elmsworth," he said. "I am no more Andrew Ichor than you are Aisling Callaway, scion of Regency. Those people are dead. They died a long time ago."

"You said you wished Ichor had died alone and in pain."

"He did."

"Don't give me that. Don't wave all of this away as *metaphor*. Everything you are is a lie."

"Is it? Andrew Ichor was sixteen. I am older; I grew up. I cast off his name. I cast off what he did."

"You can't forgive yourself for what you've done."

He was implacable. "Sleepless nights have a cutoff point."

She hit him again. This time he stepped back, hand to his face, glaring at her through his fingers, and she saw such rage in his eyes that she nearly flinched. She kept steady. "You destroyed a whole world. You destroyed whole civilizations."

"No, I didn't. I *changed* the world."

Her fury set her nerves on edge; a new instinct was emerging, telling her calmly *pick it up, pick up the gun; kill him, he deserves to die.*

"Say it," she said.

"What?"

"Say it. Say your name."

"My name is David Elmsworth."

"Liar."

437

Now he was breaking. "The truth is subjective."

"Say your name."

"No."

"Say it," she said. "Tell me the truth, just this once. Didn't you see this coming? Did you not foresee a day when you would have to look me in the eye and admit what you'd done? Or did you think I would be too good a person to make you do it? Did you expect me to be your redemption?"

"Yes," he said. "You are my . . . redemption."

"No, I'm not. I'm the Head of the Department. I've already betrayed as many people as you ever did. You took a baby and made her into a monster, a soldier. All you do is repeat. Don't you see that? You tried to run from what you did as Andrew Ichor, and you became an Angel of Death. You tried to run from Regency, and you became the most brutal intelligence officer the Government had ever seen. You cannot escape; you never escaped your name. Say it."

He was silent for a very long time. When he spoke, his voice was hoarse. "My name was Andrew Ichor."

"Present tense."

A longer silence. "My name . . . is . . . Andrew Ichor."

She picked the gun back up, pointed it into his face again.

"Two choices. You go away now and never come back, or you come in and I call the police."

He shrugged. He was shaking now. "Call them."

Rose backed slowly away. She kept the gun raised while she unlocked the door. She couldn't see his face now.

"Go and sit down in the kitchen while I call them."

A flash of anger in his voice: "This is my house."

"No. It is David Elmsworth's house, and when his will was

438

read out, it said that in the event of his death, this house was to pass to me."

He was tightly furious. "I am alive."

"Yes. David Elmsworth is dead; only you remain."

"Rose, please, I am the same m —"

She raised her hand, fired into the wall beside him, and he was silent.

"Go and sit in the kitchen," she said, calmly.

He was still, and then he pushed past her, trembling with rage. She kept the gun trained on him as he passed into the kitchen. She closed the door, locked it from the outside. Then she went into the living room.

"Call James Andreas," she said, and the TV awoke. The voice-activation software answered only to her now. James was in work early today. His face appeared grainy and exhausted-looking on-screen.

"Major," he said, gravely. His face was implacable. He hadn't used her name since January.

Rose rubbed her face. "Don't, James, please. He's here."

His eyes widened. "Ichor?"

"Call a squad team. Quickly. I'm trying to stall him."

He nodded, then disconnected. He still cared about whether she lived or died, at least; how reassuring. She tightened her grip on the gun and went back into the hall. When she unlocked the door, he was pacing the kitchen. He moved past her wordlessly toward the closet under the stairs. She followed him, aiming at his back.

He opened the closet, pushed aside the coat to find the scanner. He placed his hand on the red-lit glass; the beam of light swept across his hand. A pause.

Nothing happened.

Rose stepped forward, and pressed her hand to the scanner. The sections of wall separated immediately to reveal the dark, ghost-lit passage to the basement. He was staring at her.

"You locked me out?"

"You are responsible for the deaths you cause now."

"What? Since when is *that* a rule? How long has it been for you, a week? Is that how long it has taken you to forget what it's like? It is a total abdication of responsibility. You cannot hold me to acc —"

"You created Hybrids," she said, cutting him off, anger burning through her voice. "You are responsible for all of this. Everything I have gone through, everything I am, is *your fault.*"

He was quiet, searching her face. Then he ducked into the passage and began to walk. She still had her gun trained on his neck. Spine, veins and arteries, airway. You couldn't live without a neck.

"What do you want?" she asked, ignoring the ricochets of her voice off the metal walls.

He didn't answer, not directly; instead he held up a small vial of a clear, whitely opaque liquid. "I set the Gospel's Demon children free. I only needed two of the magical ones. I Leeched them and kept their magic." He shook the vial. "They were very powerful."

She knew his reply, but she said it anyway: "It's impossible to store energy from Leechings. You don't extract their magic; you just destroy it."

"No," he said. "It is *impossible* to commit the greatest crime in human history and then take on a new name and live undiscovered for twenty years. It is *impossible* to break the Veil between

440

worlds at sixteen. It is *impossible* to hide your monsterhood from your coworkers in the highest-security government Department in the country for a decade and a half. It is *impossib —*"

She couldn't fire in here, because the passage curved downward at all sorts of beautiful angles and who knew where the bullet would end up. So all she did was slam the butt of the gun into the metal wall beside her, but the noise was deafening and he whirled around with no color in his face and his teeth bared, clearly expecting to die. They stared at each other.

"I don't care," she said, softly.

He was angry, and shaken, and, with any luck, frightened, so she desperately, desperately hoped that when he said, "You look like your father," it was out of spite more than objective observation, and that he didn't mean it. But she knew that he had meant for her to believe it, had meant for her to be hurt, and so she abandoned love and logic and grabbed his shirt and shoved the barrel of the gun under his chin.

They stood very close, unbreathing. When she clicked off the safety, they both heard it like the snap of bone. She let the monster show clearly in her eyes, and sent white-hot magic coursing along the skin of her hands, and bared her teeth, and showed him without mercy what looking like her father would truly mean.

"Don't," was all she said.

His eyes widened, and he shoved her backward roughly away from him and turned to walk away. Rose straightened her jacket and raised her gun again. The reminder of the difference in their physical strength was unsettling, but not enough to negate the fact that he had resorted to using it at all; he had had no words or arguments to defeat her. She had silenced David El —

She had silenced him.

She followed him down to the end of the passage, gun still trained on the back of his head. He came to the door of his cell, and suddenly Rose realized — she had not been in there since Ichor had been discovered, and she had only moved back in here a month ago, so in that three-week-long gap when the house had been empty, he could have come back, he could have . . .

He opened the door and she saw it. It was a great, hulking mass of iron and light and wires, held together by rust and gravity and darkness; and she saw him, saw how his movements eased as he slid into the room, how he stepped around it without hesitation, sure-footed, safe in the knowledge that it was his.

She stepped into the room, gun still trained on his head.

"What is this? Why have you come?"

He did not answer; he flicked a switch on the console and the beast began to light up, slowly awaking with a blinking, humming roar. The metal walls behind him were soot-black and scarred with claw marks from not-his hands, and Rose pressed the gun to the console itself and he stopped dead like a stilled marionette.

"I will not ask again," she said, softly.

He looked her up and down, eyes flickering as if failing to process her. "Shoot first, ask questions later, yes?"

She moved the gun to one of the glass panels. Beneath it, wires glowed.

"It's a machine," he said.

"I can see that."

"It — " He rubbed his face. "You wouldn't understand."

She flipped the gun around with unblinking ease and smashed the glass with the handle of it. He cried out, jumped toward it. The wires beneath it were unharmed; the beast-machine roared on. He stared at her.

"Have you really," she asked, voice low and steady, "forgotten who I am?"

He closed his eyes, leaned forward onto the console as if fighting a headache. "See the white gas in the glass vial on the top?"

She did not look. "Yes."

"That's Leeching Gas."

He had invented that, as well. So much he was responsible for. "Yes."

He glanced at her. "This," he said, "is my redemption."

The pieces came together in her head. "You're going to Leech everyone."

"Not quite," he said. "I'm not just going to *Leech* them. I'm going to destroy their second souls. Gifted and Angels and Pretenders, Ashkind and Demons and almost-humans, they'll all be gone. No more of that. No more magic. The world will be as it was."

"The world . . ." The concept seemed so inhumanly repulsive that she almost fired there and then, put an end to his ambitions with a twitch of her finger. "I don't . . ."

"Unfortunately," he said, "it requires the precise amount of energy provided by three souls to work. Three souls, to be burned up to nothing. I have the magic of one soul in this vial," he held it up, "and given that everyone living currently has two, if someone were willing to *volunteer* . . ."

"No," she said immediately, backing away from the console. "No, I will not."

He stared at her, appalled. "Of course not. I wasn't asking you to."

"Then who?" she said, and then the realization snapped into place, with his words, outside in the darkness: *I have come for a dignified death . . .*

443

She couldn't say anything; there were no words for her sudden, screaming reaction.

"Think of it, Rose." His eyes were bright again, his green eyes, gleaming with an inspiration that was not quite sanity. "No more of it. No more Gospel, no more Regency. None of it, not anymore."

"You're mad," she said quietly. "You really have gone mad."

"Madness is just the label assigned to the ingenious but mistrusted."

"You're not ingenious," she said. "You've just been too lucky for too long."

That anger flashed again through his eyes, and she waited for a moment until he turned back to the console before she lunged, gripping a clutch of wires from the machine, and before he could flinch away, she twisted them roughly around his wrists, cuffing him. The machine sparked nervously as the wires were bent, and he growled at her — actually *growled* — so that she could see his bared white teeth, and the shadow of the monster in the lines of his face.

"How dare you," he said, softly.

"I'm not going to let you do this."

"You don't have any choice."

She looked at him. In a very low, level voice, she said, "Are you threatening me?"

He said nothing.

Then, finally, she heard it. The distant, muffled rise and fall like the murmuring of a river, the overlapping shouts: the distinctive voice of a mob.

They stared at each other for a long moment.

"You never were above endangering me for the sake of what

you thought was good," she said, quietly. "What did you do, tell the remnants of Regency and the Gospel where you were going? To the house where I live? So they could follow you here?"

"There are a lot of people who want me dead," he said, in a carefully flat voice that sounded no less pained for it. "Almost as many as want your life, Major Stronach."

She very, very nearly flinched at the bitterness with which he spoke her name.

"So you can go out and fight them off, and let me do what I need to," he said, "or you can stay down here and let them storm the house and kill us both. The Department won't come in time."

"This is blackmail, Ichor."

"Call me by whatever name you want," he said, with sudden savagery. The skin of his wrists was white against the wires that bound him. "I know you, Rose, and I always will. You would never sacrifice yourself for a principle, or a moral goal. You're too selfish."

"You can't goad me," said Rose. "Not anymore."

Above them, there came a sudden, shuddering crash: the mob had broken down the front door. They had minutes, if that, before they found the small metal room underground, and killed those within it.

"You know," she said, quietly, "this plan of yours, it relies on me letting you kill yourself to save the world. It relies on me prizing my life above yours. It relies on me having disowned you."

His eyes were cold.

"Haven't you?"

Voices rose above them: the mob hadn't found the passage that led to the basement yet, but they would.

"This doesn't redeem you," she said. "This doesn't make you good."

"No," he said, "but it does make me brave, doesn't it?"

"Bravery isn't everything."

"It is when you die for it. Those who die bravely are always remembered well."

I don't want you to die, she almost said; she could feel the words in her throat, a solid presence. But the idea that she had any claim on how someone chose to die was a childish one, and she was not a child.

Hearts could not be controlled, but thoughts could always be, and in that moment she knew that they had moved past love as a rationale: now she had only reason, and logic.

The old version of him — the one she had loved — would have been proud.

They looked at each other for a long time.

Then, slowly, she walked forward and slid the wires off his wrists. He rubbed them, but did not break her gaze.

"It wasn't a lie, was it?" he asked, and try as she might, she could not ignore the plaintive note in his voice. "I didn't imagine it. You did love me once. You were happy."

"Of course I was. Of course I did."

He nodded, and after a moment he swallowed. "I love you."

There was a pause: she had no reply, no words, for a long instant.

"I didn't change," she said, at last, and the words felt awkward, oddly weighted in the silence. "You changed. I never did. That's why . . . why I can't . . ."

His eyes were dark. "Oh, you have changed, Rosalyn. But it will never make any difference to me."

There was nothing left to say: they looked at each other again, and then Rose nodded, and he made an odd sort of movement with his head, and then she turned, and walked out of the room and upward toward the mob, to fight for both of their lives for the very last time.

Chapter 43

Now the room was silent and empty, and it was only him. He walked slowly around the console. His footsteps echoed; they were the only things that broke the silence, apart from the murmur of angry voices upstairs, muffled by distance and the metal walls. He thought that odd. When he had envisioned this, this noble self-sacrifice and dignified death, there had always been people imploring him, begging him not to do it. But she had never said it. She had never said, *No, I don't want you to do this, I don't want you to die.*

Perhaps he had lost her more conclusively than he had imagined.

But she was not there, her voice was not there, and he had only the silence; no one was trying to stop him. Only his own fears remained to play devil's advocate, and he could not listen to them, because he knew how much stronger fear could be than reason.

Was this reason?

Gunshots echoed down the corridor.

Rose . . .

He looked up, and was confronted again by the machine. Goliath, he had called it, for its namesake. Building it, from scraps and memories, had been a disturbing experience; he had not liked how easily the old skills came back to him, after twenty years. Andrew had been harder to erase from his soul than he had imagined.

His hands were steady. He pressed the vial of impossible magic into its receptor, and it blinked and beeped, and after a moment a green light glowed from the glass bulb at the summit.

Ready, it meant.

He closed his eyes. That bloody silence. Nothing to stop him; nothing in his way. Was this some kind of twisted punishment? To be forced to do this without objection, without obstacle or enemy, to be confronted only by his own doubts?

Final doubts, he reminded himself. Final thoughts. And the idea felt like a lie, because whatever this was, it did not feel like dying.

He looked around the empty room, and wondered why.

Dear Rose,

He placed his hands on the console.

I want you to be human,

He found the first switch, and flicked it.

and this will make you human

He adjusted the dials on the panel to his right.

because monsters cannot survive without magic.

He walked around to the other side of the console, and opened the vial, let the white powder seep slowly into the machine.

So this will cure you of my faults

The last of the powder slipped away, and the vial was empty. Goliath's beeping sped up.

and I wonder if you'll like it, being human, I wonder if

He keyed the frequency into the keypad with shaking fingers.

you'll understand why I'm doing this

Goliath hummed in recognition.

but how could you not understand?

He reached under the console, pressed his hand to the scanner.

This isn't just my redemption.

He felt the red light sweep over his palm.

I'm trying to save the world.

The machine roared, deep inside itself, a hulk of wires and twisted metal.

And you never asked me, you never

The glass gleamed with the speeding lights.

asked me my name, not even when you knew, you never

Now all it needed was for him to press the button.

thought it worth asking, or wanted the answer, you never

An easy action. He should have made it harder.

asked me what I thought my name was, which is probably a good thing, because

The button was small and blue and unremarkable. He didn't know what he'd been thinking when he designed that.

I think I know now. I think I know.

The house collapsed slowly, with dignity.

It folded in on itself as if taking a bow, crumbling from the inside, reducing itself to rubble with a weary elegance. The grinding, shifting screams of its destruction brought the residents of Armitage Crescent out in the receding dusk to watch in astonishment and fear; they saw first the shivering ball of green light that rose slowly from the remains of the house to hover, tentative as if close to dissipation, above the clouds of dust.

They saw it shoot, faster than the human eye could follow, into the graying sky; saw it strengthen to an emerald star in the air above the house, and then explode, a flash of light, smashing apart the sky in a rippling, rushing wave.

As it passed over them — and then the next street, and then every street in every city in the world — they cried out. They felt themselves torn and emptied; with a firm finality, the laws of the world reasserted themselves, and they knew without trying that the air and the light would not obey them anymore.

Under a piece of rubble within the collapsed house, the body of a woman who had once been a monster lay silent, her face pale, her eyes closed, as if she had fallen asleep willingly.

The pool of blood from her crushed right hand spread slowly out from underneath the fallen bricks.

Sirens wailed in the distance.

Acknowledgments

I owe this book, and all my happiness, to these people:

Kate Howard, the best editor I could have wished for, for her patience and genius — I hope all is well with Mist; Emily Kitchin, for her kindness as well as her incredible multitasking; Zelda Turner, she of the quick eye and the wise copyediting, to whom I am forever grateful; Fleur Clarke, the most sympathetic and knowledgeable Internet native I have ever had the good fortune to meet; and Becca Mundy, for her endless enthusiasm, compassion, generosity and endurance (mostly of me). I have no idea how any of you do any of it, but I am so, *so* happy you do.

My thanks of course to everyone at school: to my teachers, for their patience with me (I made the first-draft deadline of this book in large part because I was let off PE lessons to write. I think my sports teachers were as grateful for that as I was). To Francesca, Tika, Lara, Frannie, Hannah, Carlotta, Eloïse, Tash, Grace, and Elizabeth — as always, for everything — and to everyone else whom I would like to thank here but can't, because apparently these things have a word limit.

Thanks and apologies to India Stronach, Serena Bhandari, Chris Wilkinson and Tabitha Georghiou — I very much hope you don't know why. Chris, I'm still practicing, I swear.

Thanks to Cat, Kate and Claire for all their brilliance, wit and cake, and for their wise, reassuring calm in the face of my panic. I can never repay you guys. Any of you.

Thanks as always to my family — especially to my grandparents. Please stay safe and well. I love you.

And finally, and most importantly — to Dad, of course; to Mom, obviously; and to Catherine, always.